HARBINGER

www.mascotbooks.com

Harbinger

For more information, please contact:
Mascot Books, an imprint of Amplify Publishing Group
620 Herndon Parkway, Suite 320
Herndon, VA 20170
info@mascotbooks.com

Library of Congress Control Number: 2022951267

CPSIA Code: PRV0123A
ISBN-13: 978-1-63755-600-9

Printed in the United States

To my wife and daughters, the three beautiful women in my life.

"In the universe there are things that are known and things that are unknown, and in between, there are doors."

WILLIAM BLAKE

"The great dragon was hurled down . . . he was hurled to the earth, and his angels with him."

REVELATION 12:9

P.A. VASEY

HARBINGER

MASCOT
BOOKS

PROLOGUE

The ship cut its star drive when it was ten billion kilometers from the G-class star and entered the system from north of the plane of the ecliptic. Red and elongated like a cigar, and a kilometer in length, the ship corkscrewed like a bullet until it slowed to four hundred thousand kilometers per hour and started to intentionally tumble to avoid detection by resembling an asteroid.

Stealth was vital in case the *others* were watching.

As it passed through a zone of space consisting of icy bodies and a dwarf planet approximately two thousand kilometers in diameter, it started scanning, using radar and laser ranging systems. Image accelerators amplified the available photons and scanned for objects on collision trajectories, and gravitational-proximity warning systems came online. The ship started looking for particle types that could have been concerning for unwanted company—neutrinos, muons, and the like—and began mass spectrometry on any trace atoms and ions that it encountered.

It then turned its attention to the system's planets. It counted eight: four gas giants and four rocky planets in various orbits. It logged the moons orbiting the planets as well: 214. Most of them were around the gas giants, and the two hot, rocky inner planets had none.

As it passed the two largest gas giants, it decelerated slightly and intensi-fied its scans of their moons. Most were dead, cold worlds. But then the ship's hydroscanner detected a water plume erupting on the warmest part of the surface of a moon orbiting the largest behemoth. It scanned deeper, using thermal imaging, and detected a salty liquid ocean below the surface. Mass spectrometry confirmed that the necessary ingredients for life were there: liquid water, energy sources, and the right mix of chemicals.

The ship noted all this, then moved deeper into the system, falling toward the star.

The same features were found on the largest moon of the next gas giant, a slightly smaller planet adorned with thousands of ringlets made of chunks of ice and rock. Again, it detected an abundance of hydrogen molecules in water plumes rising from striped fractures on the moon's icy surface. Deeper scru-tiny confirmed an ocean beneath the surface; the hydrogen originated from a hydrothermal reaction between the moon's ocean and its rocky core. It knew that life found a way in the harshest of environments, like vents in the deepest parts of the ocean floor.

It logged these things and moved on, accelerating inward as the star's gravity took hold.

The third planet from the star was very promising; it was a blue world with large bodies of liquid water covering much of its surface.

The ship detected an atmosphere with reduced temperature extremes between day and night. It consisted of mainly nitrogen, but there was also oxygen, argon, carbon dioxide, and small amounts of other gases, in addition to a variable amount of water vapor. The planet was also in the star's habit-able zone and had an average surface temperature compatible with the genesis and sustainability of life.

The ship altered its trajectory with a nongravitational acceleration, so gentle as to be consistent with a push from solar radiation, and which should not raise suspicions. It reasoned that the cause of this acceleration would resemble comet-like outgassing, a frequent occurrence as volatile substances inside a comet evaporated as the approaching sun heated their surface. It considered for a microsecond whether to eject a tail of gases to complete the deception but decided that the outgassing should have increased its speed without the gases being detectable. It took another millisecond to calculate that any significant outgassing would have theoretically caused a comet or asteroid to spin rapidly due to its elongated shape, resulting in the asteroid tearing apart. If the *others* were watching and saw this, they would see through the deception.

But the ship also understood that its prime directive allowed it to weigh up all possibilities and act autonomously, and that if there was enough reason to do so, certain risks could be taken.

And that applied here.

The ship allowed its velocity to be dictated by the gravitational pull of the approaching star and calculated that the achieved perihelion would be sufficient. It used the star's gravity to accelerate to over three hundred thousand kilometers per hour and bent its orbit in a sharp turn northward at its closest approach. It passed the blue planet at twenty-four million kilometers and released the probe. It directed tight-beam laser targeting sensors to follow the probe's journey to the planet, carefully observing its arc and trajectory. The intelligent operating system of the probe was fully capable of landing itself autonomously, but the ship was compelled to oversee it, just in case of malfunction.

An error diagnostic shimmered into existence through its cortical modules, and so it scheduled a systems diagnostic that took five long milliseconds. There was a discrepant reading. The probe was off course, and the information suggested that it was oscillating, as if it had been in a collision. The ship detected hundreds of metallic objects orbiting the planet, but it was unable to determine further what they represented. It knew they could be artificial satellites, and therefore an indicator of intelligence, but its current speed and distance were now too extreme for more detailed analysis. In any case, the probe would be able to confirm for itself in due course.

The ship sent a pulse query to the probe, demanding a systems update. The return message was banal, merely declaring no technical problems.

The ship pondered what to do and reviewed its directive and operating algorithms. Up until now, it had never had cause to doubt its faculties and systems, and every probe it had dispatched had operated flawlessly. It had visited hundreds of solar systems over many millennia, with a perfect operating record. It ran simulations and reanalyzed the simulations before streamlining the process some more. It considered ignoring the data, but too much was at stake to dismiss the possibility of error. It ran another functional check, which took a further, incredibly long, ten milliseconds. Seven milliseconds later, it decided that the probe was operating perfectly, and it transferred its attention back to transorbital calculations. It reasoned that the probe would make planetfall in a few hours, and that any positive data would instantly be streamed back.

Time passed, and nothing happened.

The ship allocated a millionth of its sensor capacity to reverse-mirror passive scanning and headed back out of the system. It analyzed and reanalyzed the data it had received from the blue planet, searching for conclusive evidence of life. There were pollutants present in the atmosphere, but the ship was unable to determine whether these were natural or produced by an intelligent industrial society.

Also, the probe remained silent.

The ship continued its journey out of the system, taking care not to appear like anything other than a piece of space rock or an asteroid. When it passed the larger of the gas giants, it allowed itself to transiently slow down just sufficiently to release two other probes into the candidate oceanic moons. It followed their trajectory diligently until they made landfall, then waited patiently for any data.

None was forthcoming.

The ship prepared to shut down its systems and catalog its findings while in abeyance. It programmed the navigational system to calculate the route to the next star with exoplanets: a red dwarf that was part of a triple-star system 4.2 light-years distant. However, as the ship passed beyond the orbit of the dwarf planet and was about to engage its star drive, it received a message. The probe on the blue planet had sent a qualified but positive signal.

The ship hesitated, pondering what to do, for three milliseconds. But this was what it had been built for. Its reason for existing.

It triangulated the signals, boosted the gain, and opened the transmitter. The return package was sent at the speed of light. A data stream containing thousands of terabytes of information, tightly beamed and focused.

Then the ship turned its star drive on and disappeared forever.

CHAPTER ONE

The beat was vibrating the walls as I entered the club. The Saturday-night crowd was out in force and ready to party. A subwoofer reverberated through my feet and caused my head to pulsate in time to the rhythm. I couldn't see the dance floor, just wall-to-wall people. The strobe turned every clap of their hands into a freeze-frame. Faces frozen in time; eyes closed; drunk, high, or both. Some were still wearing masks, but most weren't. Life was going on, post-pandemic. As I squeezed myself in between revelers, I had a flash of anxiety. I'd never been claustrophobic before, but in this swell of humanity, I felt mild panic rising in my chest. I could smell them, too, an unholy mixture of body odor, perfumes, and colognes. A fan blew ineffectually from somewhere above. A girl gyrated against me, her eyes closed, a beatific smile on her face. I rested my hands on her hips and moved her sideways.

The bar was through a small archway adjacent to the dance floor. There, hundreds of conversations were happening in loud voices, all competing with the music dominating the atmosphere. Most were young, students and wannabe models, with a smattering of guys my age in groups or as lone wolves. I wound my way through the warm bodies and found a gap. Drinks were flowing just as fast as the bartenders could make them. Sweat was already starting to drip down my neck and back, plastering my T-shirt to my skin. I leaned in and managed to attract the attention of one of the bartenders and ordered a Bud.

As one track segued into another identical-sounding number, I made my way back out to the dance floor where there were tall tables dotted around the edges. One was free, so I leaned against it and poured my Bud into a glass half filled with ice. Taking a long drink, I felt the chill run down my gullet, and my head made an involuntary shake. Numbness crept into my brain the way it did when I was a kid drinking too much Slurpee too fast. When the glass was drained, I took the ice between my molars and bit hard, feeling it melt into cold pools on my palate.

Someone nudged my elbow. A tall blonde had backed into me; her hair was platinum and cut short and spiky. She was slim yet athletic, wearing fitted black Lycra pants and a sparkly tee. She had a cocktail in her hand with a paper umbrella adornment.

"Hello?" I said.

She turned. She had high, angular cheekbones and, unusual for Southern California, skin the color of alabaster.

"I'm sorry," she replied. "Did I spill your drink?"

"No, but—"

She'd already returned her attention back to the guy with her. A big fellow dressed all in black. He shot me a brief look but then lost interest.

I checked my phone and the app. The girl I was meeting was a brunette. I let my eyes drift over the dance floor and to the other side railing and grimaced. Nico was leaning on the guardrail opposite, a beer dangling from his fingertips. He had a grin plastered on his face and looked pretty wasted; his sandy hair was combed back and gelled. He waved at me, and I reluctantly acknowledged him with a nod. He ducked behind a balustrade and made his way round to where I was standing. When he arrived, he clapped an arm around my shoulders and leaned close, breathing stale-cigarette halitosis into my face.

Nico was my best friend and business partner. We'd met and bonded over beach volleyball and, of course, girls. He'd come from an Italian American family, with a bunch of overprotective and older sisters. I'd come from Irish stock and was an only child. I'd thought he was a jerk at first, but he was so damn funny. He could find anyone's weak spot, even the teachers', and shine a spotlight on it. I started out trying to take the higher ground, but soon I'd been too busy doubling up with the rest of the class. We'd lost touch after Afghanistan but then reconnected when our tours finished. He'd been in the navy; I'd been in the army. Obviously no competitiveness there.

"Is this her?" he yelled in my ear, looking the blonde up and down.

"No," I said, trying to move him away so she wouldn't hear him.

"Nice ass. Dude, there isn't much I wouldn't do for that." He winked, grinning wider, and took another swig from his beer. Then he lowered his head to my ear. "Dump the date and check her out. Reckon she might put out after a couple of drinks, know what I mean?"

I did know what he meant. I forced a smile. "Yeah, man. Maybe, maybe."

He pulled a face and shook his head. "Don't bail on me. You'll never get back in the saddle unless you take some risks."

I tried to think of a snappy rejoinder, but the noise was deadening my brain.

"Gotta go to the john," I managed. "Back soon."

Nico just looked disappointed. "Come on, you can be my wingman any time."

"Quoting *Top Gun* just shows your age," I said.

He gave me the finger. "Shows my past life, dude."

Nico was an ex–navy pilot. Something he never forgot to remind me of. My army days weren't something I dwelled on, as they hadn't been that exciting. A single tour in Afghanistan, and then I mustered out. It wasn't for me.

The bathrooms were past the bar and cloakroom—almost at the exit. A couple of security goons bookended the doorways, checking people going in and out, presumably looking for cokeheads and dealers. This was LA after all. I nodded to one of them, getting nothing in return apart from an undercurrent of Neanderthal genetics and a predatory stare. The exit beckoned, and I took a breath. I could see a couple of cabs lined up out front, and the pull to leave intensified. I checked my watch: 10:30 p.m.

"What was I thinking?" I said under my breath.

"Are you leaving already?"

I turned, and the blonde was standing there, still holding her cocktail.

I tried to be cool. "Do I know you?"

She smiled and sipped her drink. Dark eye shadow enhanced ice-blue eyes that never left mine. "I felt a connection," she said.

My eyebrows furrowed. "Right . . ."

"Clearly, neither of us like the sun," she said with a head tilt.

"We should live in a different part of the US," I said. "Paleness is an adaptation to cooler weather. Less melanin, more vitamin D." She smiled, so I continued. "Everyone should feel comfortable in their own skin, don't you think? I'm good with my paleness. I think of it as my Irish heritage coming through, those Celtic genes passed down the generations."

She looked impressed. "Interesting."

I shrugged. "I'm full of interesting shit like that."

She gestured to the exit doors. "Want to share a cab? I've had enough for one night."

You've seen those photographs where the background is all blurry, where the only part in focus is the person in the frame? That was her at this moment. Every other detail of the club was just background noise.

"Are you . . . Emma?" I said.

"Who's Emma?"

My heartbeat increased a little, and I swallowed. This kind of thing happened to other people or in the movies; it didn't happen to me. It wasn't that I was bad looking, just that I was kind of average. Over six feet tall and with a full head of hair, but not the kind of guy women hit on—certainly not women like this. Surely, she got hit on all the time, looking the way she did. She was alone now as well. What happened to the guy in black?

"The girl I was supposed to meet here," I said. "Sort of a blind date."

Actually, it was a Bumble date, but I wasn't going to tell her that. Nico had pushed me toward Tinder, but I'd told him I considered it free prostitution, that all the guys wanted was free sex and had little or no interest in getting to know the girl. I told him that the culture needs fixing. That we all need soul mates and partners who stand by us no matter what. He told me I'd been off the scene for too long—"use it or lose it" was his motto.

Well, it *had* been two years since—

"She stood you up, then?"

I blinked out of my reverie and looked around. "I guess."

She put out a hand. "I'm Caroline."

I hesitated briefly before reaching out for the shake. Her grip was firm, her skin smooth and warm.

"William. Will to my friends."

"Where do you live, Will?"

"Santa Monica," I said.

"Cool." She nodded.

"It is indeed," I said. "You?"

"We're practically neighbors. The Palisades."

My eyes widened. Only one of the richest areas of LA. Maybe she had rich parents. Or a rich boyfriend. Or just . . . what?

"Wow. What do you do?" I blurted out, sans filter.

The corner of her mouth twitched. "I'm in marketing, actually. Very boring."

There was an awkward silence as I deliberated what to say next. Then she indicated the exit once more. "Shall we go? My place is on the way. It does have a great view."

I was about to reply when Nico swaggered over, sipping his beer, Hawaiian shirt now fully open, deliberately (I was sure) to show off his six pack.

"Dude, it *is* her then! Aren't you going to introduce us?"

Caroline's face had frozen over like Lake Louise in winter. She glanced up at one of the security guys at the door, and he wordlessly stepped between Nico and us. He was the size of a house, with arms as thick as my legs and hands the size of dinner plates.

Nico pulled up short, and his face creased in puzzlement. "What the fuck, man?"

The goon folded his arms. "Back inside."

Nico laughed, looking at me. "First time for everything. I usually get thrown out of clubs, not into them."

Caroline took hold of my elbow and gave it a gentle tug. "Let's go, Will."

I stood my ground. Suddenly, nothing about this felt right.

"Think I might just stay with my friend," I said.

She shook her head. "I don't think you want to do that."

The other goon stepped in and took my arm. He was nowhere near the size of Goon Number One, but his shaved head and thick brows made him look just as scary. His head dipped so that our eyes were six inches apart, and we started a no-blinking contest.

"Don't make me do something you'll regret," he growled.

I twisted to look at Caroline, only to see her talking animatedly on her cell phone. Then I was being frog-marched toward the club exit. Goon Number One pushed the door open, and we walked out into a drizzle of rain, which added to the heat and humidity. A black Lincoln Navigator pulled up, tires screeching. A different goon (was there an endless supply of them?) jumped out of the passenger side and opened the rear door. The interior was all black leather and blacked out windows and very unwelcoming.

"I'm not getting in there—" I began, angrily.

He shoved me in without that usual head-dipping thing you see the police do on the news as criminals are shoehorned into the black and whites. My cell phone tumbled out of my jeans pocket, and he scooped it up before I could grab it. Caroline slid in next to me, and the door was slammed shut. I could see Nico face down on the boardwalk, his arms pinned backward, Goon Number One kneeling on his neck and laughing.

I turned to Caroline, and as I did, her hand whipped up to my neck. A sharp prick caused my head to jerk sideways with the pain.

"What the hell—"

"I'm sorry, Will," she said, pulling the syringe away.

Before I could protest further, my vision blurred, and the world vanished.

CHAPTER TWO

My eyelids flickered open. I closed them again, and the last few images and sensations from my dreams lingered. I was in a rain forest, all soft light and humidity, jungle noises falling into place like an auditory jigsaw puzzle. The patter of rain on wet leaves, the intense aroma of intoxicating and rich vegetation. Then the fear of being watched by an unseen predator. Something at the top of the food chain, something prehistoric and primeval. Unchanged by thousands of years of evolution.

My eyes snapped open, and I went from asleep to wide-awake in one heartbeat. Every thought was suddenly in high resolution; my heart was thudding in my chest, and every nerve ending was sparking like I'd been jump-started. I sat up, my eyes struggling to adjust in the semidarkness. The gentle hum of an air-conditioning unit was the only sound, and dim, diffused light was coming from somewhere underneath me. I was in a big, square room with featureless dark-gray walls and no windows. I was lying on a king-sized bed, fully dressed, wearing the same clothes from the club. My shoes and socks were tidily placed on a low stool by the facing wall along with my cell phone and watch. I swung my legs over the side, and they bumped into a bedside table that had a jug of water and a glass perched precariously near its edge. A small en suite bathroom was visible through a smoked glass sliding door.

A desk and chair were against another wall, and sitting on top was a device I recognized but had never been able to afford: a HoloWeb transmitter. It was comprised of a thick black base supporting a scaffolding of carbon nanofiber, which in turn supported an array of lasers energizing a holographic bubble. The whole thing resembled a basketball-sized globe of blown glass, scarlet-tinged as if stained. There was a conventional curved keyboard and a sphere of black onyx, which I presumed was a wireless mouse.

A dim red light blinked slowly from the base of transmitter.

I stood up and quickly regretted it as the room whirled and what felt like a jagged spike lanced through my temple. The headache was the kind that stopped the other synapses from firing, as if they'd met with stop signs. I shuffled into to the ensuite, and a light activated automatically, revealing a toilet, a washbasin, and a shower cubicle. Fluffy towels were draped over a rail.

I relieved my full bladder and washed my hands, then splashed cold water over my face. I looked in the mirror. I looked like shit. Bags under my eyes the size of coal sacks. My hair stuck down one side of my face. I put a hand up to my neck and felt a lump where she'd jammed the syringe. I twisted, feeling it tighten and pull on my trap muscles.

I walked back out into the room. More lights had activated, subtle downlights in the corners. There was a door with a thin handle, some kind of touch pad, and a small LCD screen. A pinhole camera poked out above the door, its green light flashing dimly. I tried the handle.

Locked.

I leaned against it and listened. I moved nothing but my eyes, my mind racing but every muscle stock-still.

Nothing, just the air conditioner's hum. "Hello? Anyone out there?"

Still nothing.

I'd never been kidnapped before, and I was starting to feel a little uneasy. I convinced myself this was a natural and normal emotion produced by my brain to keep me safe. I wasn't sure how it would help me here. I picked up my phone and watch. Both were dead. Powered down. I tried to turn them on, but nothing happened. Out of habit, I put the watch on, then sat down in front of the transmitter. The red light continued to pulse, rhythmically and hypnotically. I reached out and touched the sphere.

The bubble expanded, and I sat back in surprise. Big green letters appeared, floating and in 3D.

GOOD MORNING, WILLIAM.

I blinked and sat back. I stared at the words. Then I pulled the keyboard toward me and typed: *What the fuck is going on?*

My reply appeared in smaller red letters, scrolling along the bottom of the bubble. I sat back and waited. I didn't have to wait long.

BREAKFAST IS HERE. YOU HAVE ONE HOUR.

There was a whirring noise by the water jug, and a rectangular slot in the wall opened and a tray appeared. I smelled fresh coffee. There were croissants, bagels and cream cheese, and orange juice. Breakfast of champions.

I typed: *Wait, what . . . ?*

But the bubble collapsed and went dark.

I ate like it was my last meal. "Be prepared" was the Scouts' motto, I recalled. I wasn't sure what was going to happen in an hour, but it seemed like food might be important to have on board. I then went back to the ensuite and stripped my clothes off. I caught a glimpse of myself in the mirror and saw needle marks in the crook of both elbows. Someone had taken blood . . . or given me something last night.

The shower was piping hot and felt good. I stayed in there for at least ten minutes, sitting on the floor for the last five and trying to process what was happening.

I'd been kidnapped, that much was obvious. But why? And by whom? I wasn't rich. I didn't know any national-security secrets. I didn't have any enemies—that I knew of. Could this all have been a mistake? Maybe they'd gotten the wrong guy . . . yes, that could be it.

Just need to stay frosty, and it'll work itself out.

I toweled dry and gave my T-shirt a sniff. Not too bad, all things considered. I pulled it on and squeezed into my jeans, then sat on the bed. I was lacing my Converse when I noticed the red light blinking again.

I went over and nudged the mouse. The bubble lit up again. FOLLOW THE DRONE. DO NOT DEVIATE.

The door clicked and swung open.

An egg-shaped thing the size of a football hovered there. It was like nothing I'd ever seen before. There were no rotor blades or obvious method of propulsion. A single red eye stared balefully at me. I hesitantly reached out, but it spun on its axis and floated off down the corridor. I briefly considered just staying put but realized I wanted answers, so I set off in pursuit.

The corridor gently curved left, lit by green phosphorescent strips at regular intervals. A gentle breeze wafted in from fans along the ceiling.

The drone suddenly stopped and turned to face a blank wall.

"Now what?" I said.

The wall unzipped noiselessly from the top to bottom, and a doorway appeared. I stared at the drone. It just hovered there, watching me.

"After you?" I said.

The drone didn't reply, so I walked through the strange door into another square gray room. This one had a table with four chairs: three on one side and one on the other. A large mirror-like wall faced the single chair.

Your typical interrogation room. I'd watched a lot of cop shows.

The door closed behind me, and I was alone. I walked up to the mirror and cupped my hands, trying to see behind it. I saw a vague impression of shadows but no movement. I sighed and moved around to the single chair and sat down. And waited.

Lights came on behind the mirror. Two people sat facing me.

The platinum-blonde woman and a large, middle-aged black man wearing an expensive looking suit and a shiny red-and-black-striped tie. His hair was cut short to the scalp and graying. He had a goatee and sported fashionable

Ray-Ban tortoiseshell glasses. He was staring at me.

I decided to start the ball rolling.

"Hi, Caroline, if that's your real name. I'm here. What's going on?"

She didn't look up, just started tapping on a touchscreen on the desk in front of her. The guy continued to peer at me, his eyebrows furrowed. Then he flicked a glance at Caroline, who nodded and sat forward, steepling her fingers. Her voice boomed out of speakers set in the ceiling.

"Your name is William Logan. You are thirty-two years old. You own The Bean Machine, a coffee and juice bar on Ocean Avenue, Santa Monica. You live alone, above your shop, in a two-bedroom apartment. You left the US Army after a single tour in Afghanistan with a purple star. You received a bullet wound to your shoulder, which required several surgeries and ultimately a reconstruction—"

"So what?" I interrupted, folding my arms.

"You own 50 percent of a gym called Monica's Muscles with your best friend whom you met during your military service, Nico—"

I leaned forward and slapped my palms on the table. "Big deal. What's all this about?"

Caroline blinked slowly, reptilelike. Then she continued, "You drive a blue 2015 Ford Raptor. You play beach volleyball three times a week. You run ten miles up and down the strip each morning before you open the shop. You have $15,700 in savings—"

"So, this can't be about the money, right?" I smirked, sitting back in the chair and adopting a look of studied nonchalance.

She stopped and pursed her lips. "Is that what you think, Will?"

I shrugged again. I was getting good at it. "I don't really know what to think, so why don't you tell me why I'm here?"

The guy removed his glasses and started wiping them on a handkerchief that matched his tie. He hadn't stopped looking at me during Caroline's speech. "That's the billion-dollar question, Mr. Logan," he said in a deep baritone voice.

I sat back and returned the stares. "I'll tell you what I've figured out. You're not cops, 'cause this place is too plush, and cops tend not to tranquilize suspects. Plus, I've seen no ID and there were no Miranda speeches. So what? Are you some kind of secret governmental agency? Is this a 'black site'?" I made bunny ears with my fingers.

"Tell us about Alex Park," said Caroline.

My brain stuttered for a second, and I guess they saw the shock register on my face before I could hide it. A minuscule smile played on her lips, and now she sat back and waited.

"None of your fucking business," I growled, feeling the chill in my blood.

"Your cool is slipping, Will," she replied.

The man folded his arms and pursed his lips. "We know she disappeared. We're not asking about that. We want to know more about her. Who she was? What kind of person was she?"

"Why?"

"Indulge us."

I threw my head back and laughed. "You drugged me and brought me here to ask about my dead wife? You coulda done that back at the club without going through all this drama."

Caroline gave a half smile and turned to the man in what I thought was a knowing, "told you so" kind of way. Or maybe I was reading too much into the look.

"Look, fuck you all," I said, pushing the chair back and standing up. I strode toward the window and pressed my face up against it. The man recoiled slightly, but Caroline just continued to stare directly at me. Then she shook her head slowly.

"We'll do this again, soon."

She stood up, and the lights in their room went off, leaving me gaping into the blackness. The door behind me unzipped silently, and the drone was there, floating, defying gravity.

"I'm not leaving without some answers," I shouted at the mirror.

The drone turned and headed down the corridor again. I took a deep breath and sat on the table. And waited.

A minute later, the drone returned.

"I'm going nowhere," I said.

A little flap opened underneath it, and there was a puff of smoke. A sound like a mosquito whined past my ear, and then I felt a prick on the side of my neck. I felt instantly light-headed, and the room spun.

"Ah, shit not again . . ."

I thought I was going to vomit, but before I could, darkness fell.

CHAPTER THREE

This time I woke up facedown on the bed.

I turned over slowly—aware of a dull throbbing behind my eyes—groaned, and sat up. My stomach grumbled, and my bladder was full. I wished I were Jack Reacher with that clock in his head that always told the exact time. I made my way to the en suite to pee and caught my reflection again in the mirror. I had an evolving five-o'clock shadow, so it was definitely the same day.

After splashing water on my face, I wandered back to the desk and sat down at the HoloWeb. I wiggled the mouse, but nothing happened this time. The bubble remained inert.

A whirring noise announced the opening of the food-delivery slot. A tray appeared, this time containing two bowls and a can of Coke. I lifted the lids: spaghetti bolognese and a green salad.

The bubble then flashed: YOU HAVE FIFTEEN MINUTES. Then it went dead again.

I rubbed my eyes. I wanted to throw the tray against the wall, make some kind of protest. But I was hungry, so I didn't. The food tasted good. Normal, even.

I wasn't being mistreated, if you could ignore the fact that I'd been tranquil-ized twice and brought here against my will. I figured that they weren't going to kill me, although the fact that I'd seen their faces worried me somewhat. Didn't that mean they weren't worried about the consequences of what they'd done?

After finishing the meal, I walked over to the door and waited, listening for the drone. I tapped into my inner Zen, trying to stay cool. A minute later, the door soundlessly slid open, and the drone was there. I peered at it, again looking for some kind of mechanism for how it was staying aloft. I even looked to the ceiling for wires. Nothing.

It led me down the corridor to the interview room again. This time the door was already open, and to my surprise, Caroline was sitting at the table in the room itself. She had her touch pad in front of her and a glass of water. On the other side of the table was another glass, presumably for me. I hung back in the doorway and folded my arms.

"You're taking a chance in here with me on your own, aren't you? Or have we got company behind there again?" I said, nodding at the mirror.

She looked up. "Naturally. Please take a seat."

I walked around the desk and sat down facing her. The drone entered the room and drifted soundlessly up into the corner of the ceiling where it hovered, red eye blinking.

"Bodyguard?" I said.

"Backup," she replied with a straight face. "But I can handle myself."

I checked her out. She was wearing a dark pencil skirt and a crystal-white short-sleeved shirt that matched her hair. For the first time, I noticed her arms: toned, ropy muscles. There was a hint of a tattoo on her wrist. Some Latin writing I couldn't quite make out.

She tapped her fingers over the pad and then put her elbows on the table and interlinked her fingers. Her gaze trapped me. Her eyes were stunning and so blue I thought they must be contacts.

"Starting over," she began. "My name is Dr. Caroline Heidrich. I work for a company called Singularity."

"So, you're not in marketing, then?" I deadpanned.

"Not exactly."

"What sort of doctor are you?"

She shrugged. "I have a PhD."

"In what?"

"Astrobiology."

I raised my eyebrows. "What does an astrobiologist do?"

"We research the origins, early evolution, distribution, and future of life in the universe. According to Wikipedia, that is."

"But really you—"

"—consider the question of whether extraterrestrial life exists, and if it does, how we can detect it."

There was an uncomfortable silence for a few seconds as I processed this. I leaned forward and put my elbows on the table, mirroring her.

"So, Singularity is concerned with finding little green men?"

She gave a short laugh. "You're thinking of SETI. Singularity is a private company with many subdivisions, none of which are involved directly in the search for aliens."

I pulled a face. "Right, so why do they need an astrobiologist?"

"Maybe I switched careers. Secretly."

"Ooo," I said, giving a theatrical shiver.

She sat back and looked bored. "I've given you some of my background, Will. Let's consider this a quid-pro-quo situation."

I folded my arms and said nothing. We stared at each other again for a few seconds before she blinked and looked down at her pad. She spun it around so that I could see what was on it. Now it was my turn to blink.

The headshot was of a young Asian woman dressed in scrubs with a stethoscope around her neck and blowing a kiss at the camera.

"Tell me about her," Caroline said softly. I closed my eyes, saying nothing. The silence dragged on until Caroline broke it. "I know what the media reported," she said. "Alex Park was an emergency-room physician and adventure junkie. She'd been on a solo trip down the Amazon, starting from Iquitos in Peru, when communications abruptly ceased. She'd left waypoints and map pins describing her whereabouts, but no trace was found at her last documented location. Nothing. Her boat and possessions had all vanished."

I opened my eyes and felt moisture there. Alex is—was—my wife.

I nodded slowly. "Alright, I'll bite. The local police had searched for weeks and ultimately found her upturned boat. It was discovered by another tour guide under the roots of a tree by the riverbank. Another couple of weeks searching turned up nothing. The police report concluded she'd been taken by a crocodile, one of the large black caimans that are common in the area."

"This was two years ago," Caroline said.

I looked away and rubbed my eyes. I'd been in complete denial for weeks afterward. I would walk the seafront and gaze out at the waves as they lapped on the shore. I wasn't aware of traffic or other walkers. They were like photographic images: two dimensional and static. Bereavement became my companion, a shadow that in time had just barely diminished. Where the darkness once was always holding my hand, I was only now starting to find happy memories and some closure. Where there was previously pain—so much pain—there was now a form of joy and pride in who we'd been and what we'd meant to each other.

"I've never really accepted she died, despite everything. As far as I'm concerned, she is just *missing*."

"What was she like?" Caroline said softly.

"She was . . . beautiful," I said, a catch in my voice. "But it wasn't just that. She had a beautiful soul. Nothing was ever a problem to her. She lived in the moment. 'Money will come,' she'd say and, 'Today is more important than a hundred tomorrows.' Those were her mantras, her philosophies. Today was given, tomorrows were only a concept, you know what I mean? Everyone was her friend, and judgment wasn't her thing. She slid effortlessly between social groups and avoided competition in any form, be it exams, sports, or political opinions. She flowed through life like water—" I stopped short, realizing I was babbling and actually quoting lines I'd written for her wake.

Caroline tapped on her pad for a few seconds and then looked up. I thought her eyes were glistening. "How did you first meet her?" she asked.

"She used to get a to-go coffee from my shop every day. Her SUV would pull up out front, and she'd jump out, wearing her scrubs, and I'd have her almond latte ready for her. Same time every day. We exchanged pleasantries, then later, some mild flirting. Then one day, she stayed. I could tell she'd been crying. She'd pulled up a stool by the window and just watched the traffic without touching her coffee, so I joined her. She told me there'd been a drive-by shooting. I'd heard about it on the news that morning, but hey, this was LA, so that sort of shit happened every other day. Two kids had been killed. Alex said that they'd been brought into her ER, and she hadn't been able to save them. They were twins. Four years old."

"You were her shoulder to cry on," Caroline said.

"I guess so. We talked for ages. An hour at least. As she was leaving, I asked if I could take her to dinner that night. She said yes. We hit it off. That evening, we properly talked, just the two of us. I can still recall the conversation and how she made me feel. At the end of her worst day at work, she cared about my life and me. We started seeing each other regularly after that. Within a month, we'd become inseparable."

"She sounds too good to be true."

"She was too good for me," I replied. "She was clever. Whip smart. Could've had anyone she wanted."

"But she chose you."

I sniffed and rubbed my eyes absentmindedly. "When I met Alex, my life was—to be cliché—like a stagnant pond. Going nowhere, just existing day to day." I fixed Caroline with a stare. "Why are you interested in Alex and me?"

She blinked and looked away. "I can't tell you that right now."

I gave a scornful laugh. "So much for quid pro quo, then. What can you tell me?"

"That I'm sorry we had to kidnap you. That—" Something on her pad screen flashed, and her head twitched sideways a fraction. She frowned and stared, soundlessly mouthing whatever was on it. Then she looked up and said, "We'll do this again tomorrow. There's someone you need to meet."

CHAPTER FOUR

The next morning (Caroline had been kind enough to tell me the time before sending me back to my cell the previous night), I woke to the usual sound of the food slot opening and breakfast arriving. The HoloWeb transmitter was already blinking red, but I ignored it and decided to wake up with a cold shower. Mysteriously, a toothbrush, toothpaste, and a comb had appeared in the bathroom.

Luxuries.

Finishing up, I dressed and then sat down with breakfast at the transmitter and nudged the mouse. The bubble burst into life.

GOOD MORNING, WILL.

Will. So, we're friends now?

I pulled the keyboard over and typed: *What's on the agenda for today? Do I get to stretch my legs in the yard with the other inmates?*

There was no immediate reply, so I typed: *I have friends who will be looking for me. How long are you keeping me here?*

I sat back and stared at the bubble, willing it to respond. I'd just finished my coffee when the reply scrolled across it: BE READY IN FIFTEEN MINUTES.

Well, I was ready now.

I lay back on the bed, closed my eyes, and thought of Alex.

I couldn't for the life of me figure out what their interest in her, or me, was. She'd been dead for over two years, and I wasn't anyone special. We had no criminal records, and I wasn't rich. Her family was back in South Korea, still grieving. Her father had died many years back, but her mother and sister still lived there. Her sister was a clothes designer and ran a small business. Her mother was in her early seventies.

The door hissed open, and Caroline stood there, dressed in a simple but elegant white one-piece dress and matching stilettos. To my surprise, the black guy was with her. He was still wearing the same suit but with a different matching tie and pocket square. The ubiquitous drone floated silently behind them.

The guy walked over and, to my surprise, reached out for a handshake. I contemplated being pissy and folding my arms, but I reciprocated. Being angry hadn't gotten me very far at this stage.

"Will, my name is Jeremiah Wade. You can call me Jerry." He glanced at Caroline. "We thought it's time to, shall we say, give you some clarity as to what we do here. Maybe move things along a little."

"I thought it was all hush-hush, *Jerry*," I countered.

"Oh, it is. Kind of. You'll see." He waved his hand at the door. "Shall we go?"

I shrugged and followed them out, the drone bringing up the rear. Caroline glanced back over her shoulder at me and smiled. "Sleep okay?"

I resisted the urge to say, "I know you bastards are watching me," and instead said, "Sure, you?"

She gave a little head wobble. "Meh."

We walked in silence for a few minutes along the corridor until it ended at an elevator.

We got in, then Jerry inclined his face toward a wall screen, and a red light played over his eyes. The doors swished closed behind us, and my ears popped as we hurtled upward. Ten seconds later, we arrived at another corridor, this one lined with windows. We seemed to be in a glass tube suspended above a rain forest. Leaves wrapped around the glass, and sunlight streamed through, stripy golden streams igniting every gap. The air was warm, and every few yards along the tube there was an open section letting in the sounds of the forest.

"This doesn't seem like California," I said to no one in particular.

"Well, you're not in Kansas anymore, Dorothy," Jerry wisecracked.

I shot him a sarcastic smile, and we continued through to another doorway. Jerry did the eyeball-scanner thing again, and the door swished open into yet another corridor, this time indoors. A loud buzz of conversation broke through; we were on a kind of mezzanine, and I stretched my neck over the balcony to see below. A large square space with seats and benches and tables spilled onto a grassy knoll that ended right at the edge of the forest. People were milling around, just walking, talking, standing, and drinking coffee. Every- one was wearing either white dentist-like smocks or identical blue overalls.

Caroline came up to my shoulder and leaned in. "Not what you were expecting?"

"Didn't know what to expect, actually." That much was true.

So, this was not a prison, then.

She tugged on my sleeve and walked us toward where Jerry and the drone had stopped in front of a set of double doors with Lecture Hall written above them. Jerry opened the doors and gestured for me to walk through. Lights came on as I entered, causing me to blink as my eyes adjusted. We were on the top level of an auditorium. It was huge, maybe a couple of hundred seats and desks arranged in a big oval with stairwells at regular intervals leading down to a circular stage. Impressive bay windows wrapped around the upper levels, and a glass cupola topped off the ceiling.

"Let's go down to the stage," Jerry said.

We made our way slowly down the steep stairs, while all the while I checked out exits and looked for other people. I thought I saw another one of the drones hidden in an alcove, its red light pulsing like a heartbeat.

There were four chairs on the stage surrounding a low circular stone table that looked expensive, like it was made of onyx or marble. On it was a faintly glowing object that resembled a white Christmas tree. But the nearer we got, the more it became apparent that it wasn't solid; it resembled a snowflake with perfect geometric shards expanding in all directions. It was rotating slowly, and the words *Singularity, Inc.* came and went in sharp 3D, lit up with a cobalt iridescence. I recognized the logo, which had become almost as famous as Apple's or Microsoft's in the tech industry.

"Take a seat," said Jerry, pulling out one of the chairs.

I complied, and Caroline sat down next to me. She put a hand on my arm. She had long shapely fingers, and her nails were immaculately done in different sparkly colors.

"What?" I said brusquely.

"Try and keep an open mind about what you're about to hear," she said.

"Okay," I replied, unwilling to give an inch.

She inclined her head to the hologram. "Good, then watch."

The display spun and reformed into a rotating 3D head: Caucasian but tanned, early middle-aged, slightly too-long dark hair, sunken cheekbones, and deep curves from the sides of the nose to the mouth. It was a familiar face.

The picture became live, and the man's gaze focused on me. "Mr. Logan," he said, his voice deep and eerily magnetic. "I'm Christian Becker."

I knew who he was. Everyone did. One of the most famous men on the planet, Christian Becker was both a legend and an antihero in equal measure. He'd been headhunted by Google to lead their Innovations Team and was then very publicly sacked for insider trading and selling technology to the Chinese and North Koreans. His trial had been livestreamed for two months.

Zuckerberg, Musk, and other Silicon Valley luminaries gave evidence either in person or via video link, and mostly not supportive of him. It sounded like he hadn't made many friends during his time there. Anyway, he was found not guilty, and everyone expected him to countersue Google, but he didn't. He appeared on talk shows and wrote a tell-all about the infighting and shenanigans in Silicon Valley's IT sector. By his own account, he was a brilliant man, but I remember thinking that he just came across as an arrogant jerk. Then he dropped off the scene, and nothing further was heard from him. It was as if he'd just vanished from the face of the earth.

"They are taking good care of you, Will?" he said.

"I'm a prisoner," I said evenly. "Are you going to tell me why?"

His eyebrows furrowed, and he inclined his head to look at me. It gave the impression of being looked down upon by a god, and I reckoned that was intentional. Intimidating. It was working.

"We'll get to that. First, do you know what we do here at Singularity?"

I shook my head. "I've no idea. Never heard of Singularity."

"Right. You've been under a rock for the last few years. But you know me, right?"

"Everyone knows Christian Becker. You were famous for a while. I watched Oprah."

He gave a smirk. "Wrong. No one knows Christian Becker."

I said nothing, wondering whether he was going to start referring to himself in the third person from now on. Trump used to do that. It'd sounded arrogant and self-delusional then as well.

"So, what is it you think we do here?" he said.

I folded my arms. "I have no idea, and frankly, I don't give two fucks."

"Will . . . ," warned Caroline.

"No, I'm getting a little tired of this. Just tell me why you've kidnapped me, and we can get this all straightened out."

On the hologram, Becker's eyes narrowed, and his face became haughty. "All in good time, William. And please don't speak to me like that again or you might never get out of here."

I angrily looked over at Caroline and Jerry. Caroline looked uncomfortable, and Jerry just avoided my stare and tapped a couple of times on his tablet.

"All right, William," the voice boomed again. "Let me tell you about Singularity."

The hologram changed to a diagram with *Singularity, Inc.* at the top and multiple branches spreading out below.

"Singularity is a diverse company with multiple subdivisions. We started out making novel computer games. These were immersive, 3D, first-person adventure games. Stunningly realistic visuals. Think *Avatar* on steroids. Have you heard of *Alien Annihilation*? That's ours. Became the number one game on all platforms. Within a month of its release, it was making us $250 million a week. And that was only the beginning. We were soon releasing a new game every two months. All under a bunch of proxy electronic gaming companies and visual art houses."

I frowned. From what I remembered of Becker he wasn't a programmer. I was about to say so when he continued.

"I reinvested all this in our technology division. Recruited the best people from around the planet to work here on this purpose-built campus. Paid them a fortune for their talent and their nondisclosures, right, Caroline? Jerry? These people have done revolutionary work."

I glanced up at the drone hovering in the corner. Becker noticed me looking and smiled.

"That drone's nothing compared to what we're developing." The hologram now flicked rapidly between different images. "A battery that will revolutionize every application it powers—twice the energy stored, a quarter of the mass, and chargeable in seconds. An amalgam wire that is a superconductor at room temperature and will completely transform the energy sector. A new solar panel that is so efficient that we could meet all our current global energy needs by harvesting the sunlight striking an area smaller than 0.01 percent of the Sahara Desert."

The hologram now pixelated into a human body, rotating, and alternating between X-ray imaging of internal structures and naked skin. "Medical advances in artificial limb replacement that can be linked directly to the nervous system and controlled seamlessly by the user. Nanofiber skin replacement for burns, indistinguishable from normal skin but ten times as tough and self-healing. 3D printed organs to replace a patient's own failing ones and make them better and stronger as a result. Computer designed drugs—specifically anticancer therapies—using the body's own immune systems. Wearable tech that can monitor you for the early detection of hundreds of diseases. Caroline, show him yours."

Caroline stretched out her arm. On her wrist was a thin black bracelet with multiple interconnected silvery spheres.

"We call this the ISIS bracelet," Becker intoned. "Named after the Egyptian goddess of healing and magic."

"Not the terrorist group." Caroline smiled.

"Good luck trying to sell that in the USA," I said dryly. "Anyway, what's the difference between this and a Fitbit or a smart watch?"

"That's like asking what's the difference between a Boeing 787 and the Wright brothers' Flyer," said Jerry with a sour expression.

Caroline pressed one of the spheres, and the air above it shimmered and condensed into numbers and graphs and figures. They revolved slowly, displaying multiple parameters and data. Caroline flicked one of the graphs with a finger, and it expanded to form a brightly colored representation of her lungs with data describing her current oxygen intake, CO_2 conversion rates, percentage efficiency of the transfer of oxygen across the membranes to the blood stream. All in real time and changing with each breath.

Becker's voice continued, now tinged with awe. "Extraordinary, isn't it? This is her life, right there, in full holographic 3D. Her metabolic rate, cardiovascular and respiratory status, multi-organ functions—in fact a complete real-time assessment of her health and wellbeing. It can be downloaded instantly to cloud storage or to any physician or surgeon with the appropriate software and skills to interpret it. Or ultimately, a sophisticated AI will interpret the data instantly and diagnose any condition."

He paused for a second as the picture changed to an overhead view of a massive gray aircraft carrier plowing through rough seas and performing a tight turn.

"It's not all healthcare, of course. We are very diversified. We have a contract with the US military that is going to be worth over $200 billion in the next two years. Autonomous weapon systems. Autonomous drones. New kinds of selective munitions. We'll be bigger than Amazon and Apple combined in five years. We will dominate all areas of technology. I have flooded the world's patent offices with inventions via various proxies and intermediaries—"

"So how come I've never heard of any of this stuff?" I cut in.

"We're not ready for prime time yet," Becker replied in a frosty tone. "Furthermore, if the US government—any government actually—found out about these technologies, then they would shut us down or try to steal them. I mean, do *you* trust your government to do the right thing, William?"

I folded my arms. "Well, this is all very fascinating. But you still haven't told me where I fit in here."

His gaze became predatory again. "We have a big problem, you and I."

I looked at Caroline and Jerry who were now staring at me. I opened my hands. "Again, I have no idea what you're talking about."

Becker's face darkened. "All my systems, my machines . . . everything has shut down. Factory production is at a standstill." The hologram head turned to Caroline. "Show him, Dr. Heidrich."

Caroline pushed her tablet toward me. On it were two photographs, side by side. One was me, and the other one was Alex. She was wearing her scrubs, a stethoscope around her neck, and sunglasses pushed back on her forehead. She was blowing a kiss at the camera. I remembered the photo well. I'd taken it.

"When Singularity's systems crashed and became inoperative, these images appeared on all monitors and screens," Caroline said. "No words, no explanations. Nothing."

Becker's face expanded so that only his eyes peered down at me. "I don't like mysteries, William. My business is suffering. What have you done to my company?"

The force of his voice made me sit back in the chair; the anger coming from the hologram was so palpable. I gripped the armrests, hackles rising, and met his stare.

"Read my lips. I've no idea. What part of that don't you understand?"

The anger radiating from the hologram intensified, and the drone detached from its ceiling anchor. It slowly drifted down toward me, humming like a nest of wasps. As it approached, a little hatch slid open on its lower half.

"Wait just a minute," I said, inhaling sharply.

"I have waited long enough, Mr. Logan," Becker said, his teeth bared. "Time for answers."

This time there were no whining sounds or invisible stings. A small, mirrored sphere flew out of the hatch and stopped a few inches from my head. I scrabbled out of the chair, pushing it away with my feet, trying to get some distance between me and the sphere. The sphere followed me, silent, focused.

"Remember that military contract?" Becker growled. "This is one such innovation. An intelligent missile the size of a pea that can target individuals at will, virtually invisible and undetectable. It contains a small explosive charge that, when pushed through the eye of the target, will detonate and kill—bloodlessly and instantly. It will make possible the assassination of the leaders of rogue nations, terrorist groups, and dictators . . . no one will be able to hide. Not from any country or military that possesses such technology. Wars could become obsolete. A million of these drones could be dispatched from a single AI-controlled aircraft, weapons of such mass destruction and yet able to selectively execute only a certain type or category of individual, leaving all other innocents unscathed."

I looked sideways at Caroline who had moved her chair back as well and was trying not to look as scared as I was. Jerry appeared unmoved, playing absently with his ISIS bracelet.

"Listen to me," I said. "I can't help you. I don't know why our pictures are there. Surely you don't think I could do this?"

The sphere now flicked left and right, as if it was deciding which of my eyeballs to fly through. I wondered if I could get my hands up quick enough or whether the thing would just fly through them like a bullet.

Caroline leaned forward. "Christian, if you kill him, you'll never get the answers you need."

The giant holographic eyes continued to peer down at me, and I realized I was holding my breath. Time stood still. I stared at the sphere, seeing my reflection fish-eyed on its mirrored surface. Then, abruptly, it returned noiselessly to its docking hatch. The drone powered down and came to rest on the table. I stopped holding my breath and slumped back down in my chair, feeling the sweat on the back of my neck evaporate.

"Fix him with an ISIS bracelet," Becker said, "and lock him back up."

"Wait—" I began.

But Jerry had moved catlike and snapped one of the bracelets around my wrist like it was a handcuff. It squeezed automatically, becoming snug to my skin. I tried to get a finger under it to push it off, but it actually squeezed tighter, and my hand started to hurt.

"Don't try and take it off," said Jerry. "You don't want to lose your hand, do you?"

CHAPTER FIVE

Caroline and the drone took me back to my cell. I tried to engage with her, but she seemed distracted and provided me with one-word answers or grunts, so after a minute or so, I gave up. The room was exactly as I'd left it: dark and featureless. I flopped on the bed and closed my eyes. My mind was racing, but I was tired. The air conditioner sent cool drafts across my face, and in no time, I was asleep.

I awoke to a vibration coming from my wrist. The ISIS bracelet was glowing with a pearl luminescence and pulsing in time with my heartbeat. I was about to tug at it when I remembered Jerry's warning about losing my hand. I twisted my wrist so my palm faced down, and the glow suddenly stopped and the interconnected spheres went back to their dark silvery hue. I shook it, but nothing happened.

My brain stubbornly replayed the last few scenes of my dream. It was one I'd often had since Alex's disappearance. I'd been in a race, running as if my legs were moving through molasses. I never won the race, no matter how hard I tried. Everyone was ahead of me and getting farther away with every step. Occasionally someone would run past me, and it was always a girl with

Alex's face. But it wasn't her. I'd almost always woken up feeling miserable and dejected after this dream, and this was no different.

I swung my legs off the bed and yawned. A bout of dizziness came over me, and I was about to lie back down when out of the corner of my eye, I saw that the transmitter was flashing its usual insistent red. I made my way over to the desk, moving like a sloth. I touched the mouse, and the bubble exploded to life, this time expanding to a milky-white, smoky, ovoid shape three feet in diameter. As it became translucent, a human figure emerged. It started out blurry, then slowly came into focus. Female, dark hair . . .

I pushed my chair away from the desk as far as it would go. My heart pounded in my chest, and I felt the blood draining from my face.

Alex stared at me from the bubble. Not a photograph. Moving. Real.

"Will, is that you?"

I grabbed the sides of the chair and tried to slow my breathing to ward off a full-blown panic attack. I looked around the room, but there was just the usual darkness in the corners and monochrome shadows.

"Alex, how—"

She shook her head and pointed at the bottom of the bubble. "Will, I can't hear you because your transmitter is muted. Please use the pad. Tell me it's you?"

I stared, dumbstruck, my mouth hanging open. Her image was crystal clear, but the background was blurred like a camera on portrait mode. There were fuzzy shapes behind her but nothing recognizable. She was wearing a simple blue patterned shirt that I recognized; it was one I'd given her just before that last, fateful trip. Her chestnut hair was cut short in a bob; her eyes were the color of wet earth. God, I missed those eyes. She looked and sounded like Alex always did. More beautiful, in fact.

"Please, Will. Is it you?" she pleaded.

I concentrated on my breathing, ensuring full inhalation and following it all the way to full exhalation just like in my meditation exercises. One breath at a time, I sensed my heart rate slowing and my anxiety level plateauing. I tried to turn off my emotions, temporarily, at least.

I knew it couldn't last.

With shaking hands, I pulled the keyboard over and typed: *Yes, it's me.*

She reached out and touched the edge of the bubble, her eyes filling with tears. "Oh my god, I can't believe it. You're here."

I caressed the bubble, my hands passing through the ephemeral image. My fingertips tingled and aligned with hers. Then I typed: *How can this be you? I thought you'd died. Everyone did.*

She lowered her hand to her waist, and her face fell. "I'm scared, Will."

What happened to you back in the Amazon?

She spread her hands in front of her face and started weeping. "I don't know," she said in between deep breaths. "I can't remember."

What's the last thing you do remember?

She wrinkled her eyes shut, and her mouth tightened. "Rain forest images. Soft light coming through a canopy of leaves. Humid, intoxicating rich smells. Noises of small creatures hidden in plain sight."

She went quiet, her eyes closed, her mouth moving silently. I waited a few seconds and then typed: *We found your boat, but nothing else, Alex. Do you—*

Her eyes opened wide, and she started to shake her head uncontrollably. "I'm a prisoner here, like you! They're drugging me. You've got to help me!"

Wait, why are we both—

She suddenly leaned forward, and her face loomed larger than life. "Please, you need to get me out of here! Will, help me!"

I stood up from the desk and ran my hands through my hair. For a moment I wondered if this was still a dream. A vivid hallucinogenic experience. Maybe I'd been drugged again. How would I know? A dream within a dream or something?

I sat down again and typed: *Alex, calm down. Where are you? Can you describe your surroundings?*

She lifted her head and furtively looked around. "I'm in a bland square room. Like a hotel, but with no decorations or windows. There's a bed, a small bathroom, and this HoloWeb terminal."

I'm in a similar room, I typed.

Her face became animated again. "They allow me access to the HoloWeb for a few hours each night. Only on selected sites, of course, and I can only browse, not send. Are you able to send any messages out?"

I've not got access to anything. Then I had a thought. *Alex, how is it we can talk to each other through these transmitters? Surely we are being watched.*

She stared blankly at me. "Will, why are we here? Why are we prisoners of these people?"

I frowned and wondered what to type. She'd avoided my question. I went with: *I don't know.* Then I thought about the pictures of us. Clearly they were relevant. *Did they show you the photographs? The ones that apparently came up when their systems crashed?*

She frowned deeply. "No, they've not shown me anything like that. Why would they do that? What kind of photographs?"

You'd know them if you saw them. Headshots of you and me. The one of you was taken the day we got engaged. Remember when I took that? On the beach, we'd hired those bicycles—

"Will, I can't stay here much longer. I'm going insane."

I nodded. *Alex, they think we're somehow responsible for their systems going down.*

She put her hand up again and wiped her nose with the other one. I noticed that she wasn't wearing an ISIS bracelet.

Alex, did they give you one of these? I waved my bracelet at the screen.

Her eyes widened, and she smiled. "Yes, but I managed to get it off earlier today. They don't know yet."

How did you do that? I typed. I remembered Jerry's warning about losing my hand if I tried.

She leaned forward so that her face filled most of the screen. "Hold it up in front of me." I lifted my wrist so that the ISIS was in front of my face.

"See the three silvery spheres in between the two black ones? They have a hidden ratchet mechanism in them. Can you feel it?"

I ran my fingers over the spheres and felt little bumps like braille, and a groove. I nodded.

"Turn the middle one ninety degrees to the left. It should pop off."

I did what she said. There was a click and the sphere changed color to an iridescent blue and started pulsing. The ISIS tightened slightly, and then, just as I was starting to panic, it slackened off and the sphere's color changed back to its previous silver hue.

However, the ISIS was still firmly attached to my wrist.

It's still there, I typed.

Her mouth turned down. "That should have worked. Try it again?"

I did, but this time nothing happened at all. No color change or anything. The groove was almost impossible to locate, and the little bumps had vanished. I looked up at her and shrugged.

"Maybe yours is different than mine," she said with a shake of her head. She sat back in her chair, and her eyes were wet. "I've missed you, Will."

I melted a little inside and had to stop myself from tearing up as well. I typed: *I couldn't bring myself to believe you'd died. I never let you go.*

"I knew somehow you would find your way to me." I didn't know how to reply, so I smiled and nodded. "Get me out of here, Will," she said.

I nodded again but typed: *I don't know where you are. Are you here at Singularity?*

She looked sideways, as if she was afraid someone was listening. "Yes, I'm here."

Then how—

"Will, they have a computer on this campus. It's very special. They call it Pandora. It's the one designing all the tech. The one that's making all their money. Ask them to show it to you."

Now it was my turn to look puzzled. *Why?*

She leaned forward; her face was now very earnest. "Tell them you'll cooperate but that first you need to see Pandora. Tell them you know what's going on, and they'll have to agree."

Why is it so important that I see this computer?

"Tell them, Will!" she insisted.

Okay, but—

She looked sideways again. "I have to go; someone's coming. I love you."

I typed: *I love you, Alex,* but the bubble imploded before I could finish.

CHAPTER SIX

When the next message came through a few hours later, I was up and ready, pacing the floor. I'd not slept, because my mind had been in overdrive. A million and one thoughts were crowding in and crawling over each other. Images of Alex were exploding in high-resolution technicolor, and the emotional rollercoaster was bringing back all the stages of grief that I'd been through, culminating now in a nagging doubt and an underlying feeling that something wasn't right.

But at least she was alive. For two years she'd been missing, presumed dead, and I'd only just started to try and get my life back on track. To actually reclaim a life, that is. The blind date with Emma was just the first toe in the water. Nico had encouraged it, and after months of coercion, I'd given in and we'd sat there on my laptop flipping through pictures and bios, waiting for women to acknowledge me and set up a rendezvous. I was suddenly grateful that it hadn't gotten anywhere and that Emma had stood me up. It then occurred to me—was Caroline actually Emma? Was this all part of the setup? I filed that question away for later.

BE READY IN TEN MINUTES.

I'd already had breakfast. I'd planned to ignore it, but when the flap opened and the tray slid into the room, it'd smelled too good. Bacon and french toast with maple syrup, whipped cream, blueberries, and bananas. Coffee fresh from a bubbling percolator. Orange juice.

I wondered if this was a last meal for the condemned.

When the door hissed open, Caroline was there, drone at her side. As usual, she looked stunning. Platinum-blonde hair gelled back, sharp cheekbones, and this time a black one-piece jumpsuit. She said nothing and gestured that I follow her. I stood my ground.

"Same again?" I said. "Another interrogation with Darth Sidious? I mean, really, the big holographic head? What's with that?"

She put her hands on her hips. "The sooner you cooperate, the better. Christian is losing patience. As are we all."

I nodded. Time to take the plunge. "I'll tell him what he wants to know, but first I want something."

Her eyebrows shot up. "You *want* something?"

"Yes. Remember the quid-pro-quo arrangement you and I set up? Well, this is a continuation of that."

She inclined her head in thought and walked slowly out of the room. I followed, the drone humming gently as it took up the rear. Caroline threw a cursory glance back over her shoulder. "What did you have in mind?"

"Take me to see Pandora."

She stopped and whirled round. "What did you say?"

I folded my arms and put on my best nonchalant face. I hoped she wouldn't figure out that I was bullshitting. I wondered if the biological data being collected in real time from the ISIS on my wrist was being reviewed at this moment, and if my deception would be uncovered. I imagined scientists in white coats evaluating my data—my rapid heart rate, my increased sweating, and the rest—and know the truth. However, instead of siccing the drone on me, she put her hand to her ear and looked skyward, listening. I feigned disinterest and waited.

"So, you're admitting that you know about Pandora, then?" she said to me in a low voice.

I'd rehearsed my answer as, "I know everything about it," but I figured she'd instantly know I was full of shit. Instead, I shrugged and said, "I just want to see it, and then I'll help you."

She snorted. "I don't think that's going to be—" She put her hand to her ear, listening again. I watched her almost imperceptibly shake her head and then nod.

"We're good?" I said.

She sighed. "Apparently we are, Will."

I folded my arms. In for a penny. "Then I'd like a drink first."

This time she gave a chuckle. "Don't push your luck."

We took the elevator again, but this time got out on a different level. The doors opened onto a long, thin platform that led to a hemispherical dome some forty yards or so across. It was opaque and made up of triangular elements, and it seemed to have one entrance: a big circular door. On either side of it were a couple of security guards dressed in black military-style uniforms and carrying nasty-looking submachine guns.

We stepped onto the platform, and I reluctantly looked down. There was a sheer drop to a watery moat twenty yards or so below, and there were no guardrails.

"What is this place?" I said to keep my mind off the abyss on either side of the platform.

"This is a geodesic dome and a Faraday cage," she said. "Do you know what they are?"

"I've no idea," I said truthfully.

"Didn't you learn anything at school, Will?" she said with a twinkle in her eye. "It's an enclosure used to block electromagnetic fields and radiation. Often made of metal or wire mesh, but in this case, it's a weave of superconductive material. Nothing can get in or out."

"Why is that important?" I said.

"You'll see."

At our approach, the guards nodded at Caroline and moved aside. There was some sort of high-tech interface sprouting from the platform like a green shoot, and another hologram-generating laser sparkled above it. Caroline wafted her hand with the ISIS through it, and the sparkles transformed into a sphere of pulsing white light. Another beam flicked out from the interface and shone into her eyes. Then there was a hiss and a clunk, and the door spun open from its center like a camera aperture. A blast of cold air hit us, as if we had opened a freezer door.

"Temperature regulated," she said, noting my discomfort with a slight smile. "Kept just above freezing."

I peered through the aperture. There appeared to be some sort of ante-chamber leading to an air lock. The drone drifted through first, and Caroline waited until I entered before following. The door snicked shut behind us, and for a second, we were in perfect darkness. Then a dim red light slowly came on and provided a kind of darkroom illumination. As my eyes adjusted, Caroline handed me a pair of what looked like sunglasses from a shelf on the wall.

"You'll need these once we're inside."

I took them; they were surprisingly heavy and styled like black wraparound ski glasses. A row of green lights ran along the earpiece, one of which was pulsating slowly.

I put them on and couldn't see anything.

"No . . . once we're *inside*," she said exasperatedly.

"Oh, this isn't inside then," I said.

"Seriously? Okay, are you ready now?"

I wasn't sure. Was I? "Okay," I said.

She walked toward the far wall, which automatically involuted, opening another antechamber, this one smaller and with an arched ceiling. I stepped through after her, ducking around the drone that this time remained behind. I straightened up and knocked my head on something solid. I could just make out metallic, colander-like objects hanging down, resembling showerheads. I counted six of them, with many similar objects protruding horizontally from both walls.

"Stand with your arms out by your sides," Caroline instructed. "This is for decontamination."

"I've seen *Schindler's List*," I said, trying to make a joke.

"It's harmless radiation and UV light. Takes ten seconds. Plus, I'm here with you as well, you idiot. Think about that?"

I did as she said, and the lights went out as a timer on the wall counted down from ten to one. When the lights came back on, I looked myself up and down. I was somewhat surprised that I was still wearing the same clothes and they weren't shredded by some experimental invisible radiation.

Caroline waved the glasses at me. "Now is good."

She turned to the other end of the chamber and waved a hand through another hologram that had shimmered into existence. This time the entire wall spun open in that very camera-aperture way, revealing the last room. It was a spherical chamber, about ten or twelve yards in diameter, ringed by a platform that went completely around its circumference. Suspended in the middle and seemingly defying gravity was a pulsating black sphere that looked to be about six feet wide. Dozens of smaller spheres orbited it at various distances like planets around a sun, each sending out sparks of plasma. The whole thing resembled an enormous orrery, with a rotating black hole at the center. Sparks ricocheted between the spheres and occasionally jumped to the ceiling, producing a pond-like ripple effect in the atmosphere before dissipating. There was a smell of ozone every time the plasma hit the roof, and the hair on my arms and neck stood up. Every couple of seconds, the black sphere blurred and became indistinct, as if a TV signal was being tuned in and out.

"What is this?" I said to Caroline.

She turned to me, and her mouth was crooked. "You said you wanted to see Pandora. Well, here you are."

I gazed, open-mouthed. "That's not a computer—"

She laughed. "You're looking at the most powerful quantum computer on planet Earth. Isn't it extraordinary?"

I walked slowly around the platform, dazed, taking in the scene. My eyes couldn't seem to focus on the sphere because of the blurring. It was like when people's faces are deliberately pixelated on TV to keep them from being identified.

"Why, 'Pandora'?"

"Christian thought it was an appropriate name for it. From Greek mythology."

I pulled a face. "Indulge me."

The corner of her mouth crinkled at my ignorance. "In Greek mythology, Pandora was the first human woman created by Hephaestus on the instructions of Zeus. Each god cooperated with Zeus and gave Pandora many unique gifts. So her name actually means 'she who produces gifts.'"

I nodded, trying to appear smart. Then I frowned again. "What's a quantum computer?" I said, rewinding my thoughts.

"The ultimate parallel processor," she replied. "It seems to work by sharing information with huge numbers of versions of itself throughout the multiverse. It gets answers faster here in our universe by getting help from the other versions."

I shook my head. "The multiverse. Okay. So . . . how fast is it?"

"Almost incomprehensibly fast. Computing speed is limited by energy, right? We've calculated that a one-kilogram computer could perform at most 5×10^{50} operations per second—which is about thirty-six orders of magnitude more than my laptop—and store at most 10^{31} bits. We've extrapolated that we would expect to get to that limit in a couple of centuries from now, with normal technology progression."

"But this—" I began.

"This"—she pointed to the sphere—"weighs about two hundred kilograms and is storing about 10^{50} bits per kilogram, which works out to be about a trillion, trillion times better. It uses electromagnetic radiation to communicate between the atoms. This permits, we think, 5×10^{50} operations per second.

Truly mind-boggling."

"So compared with today's best supercomputers," I said, trying to get my head around the numbers, "it's in a league of its own?"

She shook her head at my naivety. "There's no comparison, Will. Today's supercomputers are as far removed from this computer as they are from the windshield wiper switch on your Ford. That's a device that stores merely one bit of information, flipping it between on and off about once a second."

I stood in silence, hypnotized by the little spheres orbiting the big sphere and the lancing plasma strikes connecting them.

"You guys built this?" I said.

She laughed. "Not me, Will. I'm an astrobiologist, remember? No, this was built by Christian and his team."

I didn't know what to say. I wasn't a geek, though I certainly wasn't unaware of how fast progress could be, but this seemed to have jumped light-years forward rather than taking the usual baby steps of technological progress. Caroline seemed to agree.

"It's truly incredible, isn't it? When I first saw it, the word *groundbreaking* didn't even begin to cover it. This will change the world."

"Then why the secrecy?" I said, turning to her. "You need to share it with everyone."

She nodded. "Eventually, of course, that's the plan. But for now, we're getting all our ducks in a row—"

At that moment, one of the spheres' orbit changed, and its trajectory brought it close to where we were standing. A finger of plasma lanced out and hit me squarely in the chest, fragmenting into thinner tendrils that wrapped around my body before terminating at the ISIS bracelet like it was a lightning conductor. It felt like a punch from Mike Tyson, and I was slammed against the wall, winded and gasping for breath. I rolled over the platform and was teetering on the edge of the abyss when Caroline pulled me back toward the wall. I clutched my ribs, every breath sharp and intense. I coughed and nearly vomited with the pain.

"I've never seen that happen before," she said, kneeling next to me. "Are you okay?"

"What do you think?" I groaned. "Ever been hit by lightning?"

She looked puzzled. "It's not electricity, so isn't lightning. There shouldn't have been any pain like that. It should have gone straight through you. It's happened to me dozens of times."

"Well, clearly I'm special." I winced, trying to stand and failing miserably.

Caroline helped me up, and I leaned against the wall, wheezing.

"Let's get you to the medical bay for a checkup," she said, concern in her eyes. "Nothing works at the moment, of course, but there are still real doctors there."

CHAPTER SEVEN

The medical facility was like nothing I'd ever seen. Stainless-steel sinks, ice-white ceramic floors, and a transparent, high-arched ceiling that made it seem like I was standing in the open air. The space had a pure, disinfected fragrance, clean and sterile. Four beds organically extruded from one wall, seemingly floating without any supporting legs. Behind each bed, widescreen monitors as big as headboards flashed images of Alex and me. Glass-like IV drip stands and their tubing hung in repose, waiting for their patients. One of the drones floated by the doorway, its single red eye swinging to follow my movements. At the end of the room was another oval-shaped door with a camera-aperture-style opening. A sign hung over it: "Do not enter unless authorized nanofiber laboratory genomics researcher."

A young doctor was waiting for us. He had tired-looking eyes, lank hair, and a face cratered with acne scars. He was wearing a creased, short white coat with a stethoscope around his neck, and underneath, a Hawaiian shirt and board shorts. Caroline guided me over to the nearest bed and helped me lie down. The doctor came over and, without a word, took my pulse and blood pressure and lifted my shirt to listen to my heart and lungs. He prodded at the reddened area that had appeared on my breastbone, and I winced. Not once did he acknowledge me, which pissed me off.

"You've got a shit bedside manner, doc," I said, pushing his fingers away.

Caroline looked mildly amused but just folded her arms and waited. I glanced up at the monitor and lifted my hand, the one with the bracelet. I shook it. Nothing happened. All the spheres had lost their opalescence, now appearing dull and gray.

"So much for this technology downloading my medical data," I said.

"Nothing here works anymore, Will," she said frostily. "You were going to tell us why, if I recall. Quid pro quo."

There was a clattering noise and a side door opened. Jerry stormed in, sweaty and angry but still buttoned up in his suit and matching accessories. He got straight in Caroline's face, ignoring me. "What were you doing in there with him?"

Caroline put a hand on his chest and pushed him back, a look of thunder on her face. "Back off, Jerry, right fucking now. Christian gave the okay. I spoke with him before we went in."

The muscles in the side of Jerry's face bunched. "There's a chain of command, if you recall."

"Christian called me directly, Jerry."

I watched this exchange, my own suspicions confirmed. Clearly, nothing I did or said was private. In that case, I wondered if they knew about Alex's communication with me. Surely that would have been the first thing Caroline would have mentioned this morning—but it'd seemed like she had no idea. Hmmm.

Jerry turned to the doctor who was now prodding my stomach. "Jin, what've you found?"

Jin shrugged and looked frustrated. "Well, I can't find anything significant, but without the equipment working, I'm limited with respect to what I can diagnose."

"Well, what *can* you tell us, *doctor*?" said Caroline, an edge to her voice.

Jin shrugged. "His heart and lungs sound okay. He's afebrile. Blood pressure is one sixty over ninety-five."

"That's a bit on the high side, isn't it?" said Jerry.

Jin nodded. "Pulse rate is fast as well, one hundred, but in sinus rhythm."

Caroline turned to me. "How do you feel?"

I took a deep breath and coughed. "Like I've been kicked in the chest. Pain's settling down, but it still feels raw."

Jin squinted up at the screens and then at me. "Hey, you're that guy, aren't you? *The* guy."

Jerry gave him flat eyes. "Do your job, doctor. Why don't you take some more blood?"

"What for?"

Caroline gave a snort. "Jesus, Jin, why do we pay you?"

Jin muttered something unintelligible and wandered off to a nearby console and started rummaging around in a drawer. I looked at the displays again, at the images of Alex and me, side by side. She was wearing the same clothes in the photo as when she'd appeared to me last night. A nagging feeling of something being not quite right persisted. Something off-kilter. I couldn't put my finger on it. An itch I couldn't quite scratch.

Then the ISIS on my wrist started to flash. The interlinked spheres were alternating white and red, the pulses becoming faster and faster. I could feel my wrist heating up like someone was twisting my skin in a friction burn.

I looked at Caroline and Jerry. "Is it supposed to do this?"

Caroline frowned and took my hand. She turned it over and over, caressing the spheres. "No, I've never seen this before."

"Take it off," I said. "It's hurting me."

She looked up at Jerry, who nodded with a look of annoyance. She produced a silver pen-shaped object from a pocket and waved it over the ISIS, which unclasped and dropped to the side. I rubbed my wrist, massaging the circulation back into my fingers. The ISIS powered down with a soft whining noise, its spheres once again becoming lifeless and gray.

Abruptly, all the systems in the room came back to life. There was a crescendo of humming as all the monitors and scanners powered up. Lights flickered and screens flashed as pieces of equipment rebooted and uttered beeps and pings. The images of Alex and me disappeared from the monitors and were replaced by the Singularity logo spinning in blue, phosphorescent 3D.

"What did you do?" said Jerry menacingly.

I had no idea what had just happened, but I wasn't going to give him the satisfaction of knowing that. "You wanted your stuff back up, there you are," I said, folding my arms.

He leaned down, and I got a waft of his cologne. "What. Did. You. Do?"

"Tell me what you've done with Alex," I said.

Now it was Jerry's turn to frown. "What the fuck are you talking about. We'd never heard of Alex Park until her picture came up."

"I don't believe you," I said.

Caroline had turned away and was on her cell phone. People were arriving; technicians and scientists all huddled around the now-active stations. The door to the restricted area swished open as one of the techs swiped a card on a panel, and I got a glimpse of a cavernous white-on-white room before the doors slammed shut again.

Caroline hung up her phone and turned back to me. "Christian's flying in. He wants to see you in person."

I shrugged and said nothing.

Jerry snapped his fingers and the drone activated and descended to my bedside. "Take him back to his room."

I lay on the bed and stared at the featureless ceiling while listening to the gentle hum of the air-conditioning unit. They'd told me Christian Becker was arriving by private jet in about six hours.

I had asked whether they were planning to let me go now that they'd gotten everything back up and running, but I got no answer. Caroline had given me a strange look and whispered, "Think about what you're going to say when he gets here."

What *was* I going to say?

I was still no closer to finding out why I was here. I'd almost blown it by mentioning Alex, but they still didn't acknowledge they had her—or why. They had to be keeping her prisoner on this campus, but what the hell for? Alex was a doctor and . . . well . . . was supposed to be dead. I'd tried to get a sense about what Caroline knew about Alex—I assumed she knew everything, of course, as I didn't trust her—but either she was a good liar, or she was in the dark as well.

I looked down at my wrist where the ISIS bracelet had left reddish-purple welts. I absently massaged the bruises, tracing them with my fingers. Caroline hadn't enlightened me on what had happened in the Faraday cage with Pandora when the plasma bolt had struck me. Maybe she was being truthful when she said she didn't know.

I swung my legs off the bed and rubbed my face. I'd lost track of time once more. My stomach rumbled.

The light on the transmitter started flashing again. I rushed over and pulled up the chair. I flicked the mouse with my finger, and the bubble exploded into a six-foot-high holographic movie in high definition, indistinguishable from reality. Alex was there again, wearing the same outfit. Her eyes widened with joy, and she put her hand up again, reaching out toward me.

"Will! Are you okay? I was worried. I've been trying to reach you."

I put my hand up again and our fingertips overlapped. I started to say something and then remembered I had to type.

I went to see Pandora, like you said.

Her face became animated. "That's fantastic. What happened?"

I rubbed my wrist, wondering what to tell her.

It's nothing like I expected. Incredible, actually. But why did you want me to go and see it?

She came right up to the edge of the bubble and knelt down. "I was hoping . . . I don't know . . . maybe—" She stopped, and her eyes filled with tears. "Will, I love you so much. I've missed you every day. I can't stop thinking about you."

I felt a lump in my throat and took a few shaky breaths. As the time had passed, I'd learned to deal with the pain of missing her and had learned to be happy again. I'd still missed the warmth of her embrace, the whisperings in my ear, the timbre of her voice. The sense that her soul, her presence in my life, was eternal.

I typed: *Alex, what happened to you? I need to know.*

She looked around again, almost furtively. Her brows creased and she gave a little twitch, like a nervous tic. The picture blurred for a split second before reforming. She looked up. "I wish I could tell you, I really do. But there's just a void. An emptiness. Like I was given an anesthetic and have just woken up from a long, dreamless sleep."

I typed: *What have those people done to you?*

"Which people, Will?"

Becker, Caroline, and Jerry.

She just shook her head again and looked puzzled. "I don't know those names. Who are they?"

I started typing but she interrupted. "You're still running the café, I hope? And the gym with Nico?"

I shook my head and felt my face starting to crumple. We'd gone from an existential crisis to like we'd just lost touch and were catching up over a coffee.

"How was my memorial service? I saw it on the HoloNet. Did you post it?"

I sat back in the chair and said nothing; my mind was all over the place. Now she was asking about her funeral. I stared into the bubble, searching her face.

"I listened to the eulogy," she went on. "It really touched me. The things you said. Nobody understood me like you did, Will."

I made my face straighter than a poker player's and typed: *Alex, you need to stop there. We need to figure out what's going on. Why we've been brought here.*

Her face was lifeless. "I've told you. I don't know."

But you knew about Pandora. Why was that imp—

She glanced over her shoulder and leaned in. Her brown eyes sparkled, and it felt like I was being sucked into a whirlpool. "I'll tell you more later," she whispered. "Someone's coming. I love you. I'm certain that—"

The bubble re-opacified again and shrunk back to the stained-red glass bowl and disappeared. However, her words lingered in the air for a few seconds afterward.

"—we'll be together soon."

CHAPTER EIGHT

Some hours later, the door swished open, waking me. I jerked upright, heart pounding, expecting to see Caroline and a drone at least. But to my surprise, there was no one there. My anxiety increased a notch. It was like touching a cattle fence—not enough voltage to kill you but enough to make things uncomfortable. I sat on the bed and pulled my shoes on, expecting someone to appear at any second. The HoloWeb transmitter seemed to be inactive, and the air-conditioning unit was silent.

"Hello?" I said, looking around the room for the hidden cameras. "What's going on now?"

There was no response, so I walked over to the door and peered outside. The corridor was dimly lit, and a blue light was flashing somewhere around the curve, almost like a police roadblock. There was a strange odor I'd not noticed before, weakly pungent and sticking to the back of my throat.

"Do you want me to go somewhere?" I said, looking back at the HoloWeb machine.

As no reply was forthcoming, I decided to treat it as an invitation and set off down the corridor. The blue flashing was coming from lights along the floor, leading the way like emergency lights on an aircraft pointing toward the exits. Around the first bend was the familiar elevator with the access pad on the wall. The doors opened automatically as I drew near, which made me hesitate. I took another look over my shoulder and flattened against the wall. I peeked tentatively into the elevator, expecting to see, well, anything or anybody. But the elevator was empty.

I swallowed; lots of conflicting emotions were wrestling in my head. It felt like I was being shepherded somewhere. Like a lamb to the slaughter. I shook my head to stop the metaphors coming, which really weren't helping.

"Come on, Will, keep it together," I muttered under my breath.

I got in the elevator. The doors shut instantly, and with a sudden lurch, the car hurtled skyward. I braced my legs and held on tight to the railings as my ears popped and my stomach hit the floor. A few seconds later, it shuddered to a halt, and the doors opened. I'd arrived at the floor with the glass walkway tube thing suspended above the rain forest. Night had fallen, and the nocturnal sounds of the forest could be heard through the open windows.

I set off slowly, all senses on full alert. The strange, pungent smell was less evident here, and there was moisture in the air as if it had been raining. It was as black as pitch outside, but I could just see the doorway at the end of the tube. I remembered that this led to the mezzanine. As I drew near, a ring of glowing ruby lights activated and lit it up like a bull's-eye. It then opened automatically, just like the others. Beyond, the space was just as dark, as silent, and as foreboding as where I'd come from. I took another step, and a cool breeze tickled my brow. I walked through the door to the balcony and stopped at the handrail to look below. The outdoor dining area was deserted. All the seats and benches were scattered, as if a tornado had ripped through. Remnants of food and drink littered the space; dark liquid patches splattered the floors in a crazy abstract sort of way. The grassy knoll leading to the edge of the forest was partially illuminated by moonbeams, but beyond that was just more inky blackness.

A ping sounded behind me as another elevator door opened. I flinched, but again there was no one inside. I looked around, uncertain and on edge. It definitely felt like I was being herded somewhere. For a moment, I wondered what would happen if I declined to go in, but I knew I would be fooling no one. I also decided I wasn't feeling that brave. Someone had told me once that being brave was on the spectrum between foolhardiness and cowardice. I wondered where this particular situation would sit.

I got in the elevator.

Another stomach-turning descent later, and the car stopped. As the doors opened, a blinding strobe light made me squint and put my hand up to my eyes. It was coming from the medical facility directly opposite. Its doors were wide open, and from what I could see in between strobes, it was a mess. All the screens above the beds were showing snowstorm static, and the banks of expensive, state-of-the-art equipment were tipped over. Sparks of electricity and little burping puffs of smoke made the strobes into a dry-ice disco effect. Bags of colored fluid and drip stands were lying on their sides, entwined together like skinny silver lovers embracing.

The doors to the nanofiber laboratory were also open.

I willed my legs forward, passing the banks of diagnostic equipment, upturned chairs, beeping lights, and discarded lab coats. As I passed the bed I'd been in, I noticed a dark smear on the sheets. I dragged my finger along it and brought it to my nose. I recognized the odor. It had the coppery smell of blood.

Out of the corner of my eye, I caught a blur of movement past the lab entrance, like a shadow passing in front of a light. Fast. Small.

"Hey?" I whispered, my mouth parched. "Who's there?"

My breathing was now coming in quick, short gasps. I tentatively stepped through the doorway, my whole body tense, my eyes tracking left and right. Butterflies rippled in my stomach, and I shivered, goose bumps covering my skin. I reached around the side of the door and found a bank of light switches. I flicked them on and off, but nothing happened.

A white beam speared through the darkness like a laser pointer. It moved erratically but then found me and shone into my eyes. I raised my hand to block it, and the light moved away from my face and tracked along the wall to the switches. There was an audible click of circuits connecting, and the main room's lights slowly came up.

The laboratory was a huge circular space, with walls twenty feet high covered in enormous flat-screen monitors showing nothing but gray-black static. Curvy desks and chairs lined one wall linked to futuristic-looking workstations. In the very center of the room was a raised dais with a single hospital-type bed, with fixed armrests on either side like a crucifix. Above it were four robotic arms connected to power couplings and wires that hung from the ceiling. I looked closer at the arms and at the claws and knife-like implements that hung off them. There was blood dripping from the claws. A mesh-like web was draped over the bed, glistening crimson and silver in the half light.

A drone silently appeared. It slowly floated closer, its light blinking and focused on me. I took a step backward, not taking my eyes off it. I waited for the little hatch to open and one of those marble-sized missiles to be launched into my eyeball and blow my brains out. Cold sweat layered my forehead, and I backed away farther, only to be stopped by the wall behind me. I thought about trying to grab hold of the drone and smash it against the wall, but before I could attempt anything, it turned and headed toward the dais. Its thin searchlight appeared again, apparently scanning the room, flicking over all the surfaces and workstations.

I took a step forward, and my foot hit something soft and squishy. On the floor was a shape, only vaguely human. It was the doctor, Jin. Or what was left of him.

I caught a pungent smell and gagged, putting out a hand to steady myself. My stomach twisted, and I vomited, my abdominal muscles spasming. Nothing but gastric juices and acid came up. I wiped my mouth on my sleeve and closed my eyes until my stomach had stopped cramping.

His white coat and Hawaiian shirt were ripped open and smeared with black-and-red goo.

There was nothing recognizable. No head, no body . . . nothing. Just a grue-some, unformed pile of gore. Thin web-like strands of the mesh stuff were strung along the floor and attached to a machine the size of a vacuum cleaner with a solitary arm that finished in a jagged set of metallic pincers.

I took a step backward, and I heard the drone approaching me again. This time, its light had changed to a blue beam, which it pointed at the floor at my feet.

Words appeared: WILL, FOLLOW THE DRONE.

I swallowed, thinking of *Alice in Wonderland*. I was supposed to follow the white rabbit now.

The drone tumbled on its axis and flew through the door to the medical facility. I pushed myself unsteadily off the wall and followed at a distance. The drone and I took another elevator; it floated to one corner and I the other, squeezing as far away from it as I could. Its single red eye continued to look dispassionately down at me. The blue laser flickered on again, this time point-ing at the wall, painting letters: WE'LL BE TOGETHER SOON.

I blinked. "Alex?"

The doors opened onto the platform that led out to the geodesic dome of the Faraday cage where the Pandora computer was kept. At the end of the platform, the two security guards were lying face down, one of them hanging over the edge of the sheer drop. The terminal still had the hologram twin-kling above it, but the doors to the dome were open, and I could see right through to the air lock. The drone entered first and shone its laser on a panel that opened the inner air lock to the antechamber with the row of protective glasses. In the room beyond, lit by the flashes from the strobe, the quantum computer looked dead. The sphere was crumpled and dull black with furrows all over like a raisin. Scattered around the platform were the smaller black spheres, similarly crumpled and inert and no longer emitting plasma energy.

Sitting against the far wall was a naked female figure. Unmoving, head down, chestnut hair tumbling over her face.

The drone crossed the chamber and hovered over her, its light playing over her body. I inched closer, moving around the platform step by apprehensive step, not wanting to think about what was happening, only knowing that I had to know. My foot scraped on the side of the railing, and she looked up.

It was Alex.

"Will?" she croaked.

I broke into a run, caution thrown to the wind, tears blinding me. She tried to get to her feet, but then I was there. She reached up with both arms, and I hugged her, pulling her close.

"Ohmygodohmygod . . . ," I blabbed over and over again.

Her eyes were dull, but she tried to smile. "I knew you'd come," she murmured.

I squeezed her as tight as I could, my eyes brimming over with tears. I could feel her shaking as she wrapped her arms around my back, and we lay there, rocking back and forth, for what seemed like an eternity. Eventually I relaxed my grip and leaned back to look at her face. It was smeared in a colorless liquid, very jelly-like in its consistency. I wiped it off her eyelids, and her lashes fluttered as she tried to focus on me.

"Do you think you can stand?" I said.

She nodded, so I helped her to her feet. She leaned against me, her weight sagging in my arms. In the light of the strobe, her skin looked ashen and gray.

"I'm okay," she said softly into my ear. "Now that you're here."

She was shivering badly, her whole body convulsing like she was having a seizure. I sat her back down and huddled into her again. Her eyes had rolled back into her sockets so that only the whites were showing. I gently shook her head, and she came to, blinking, her neck jerking with little muscular spasms, her teeth chattering uncontrollably.

"Wait here," I said. "I'm going to get you something to wear."

I ran back outside to where the security guards were laid out. I checked the nearest one for a pulse. Nothing. There was no indication of injury or cause of death, and I couldn't see any obvious wounds. But he was definitely dead, that much was certain.

"Sorry, buddy," I said as I stripped his black overalls from his body. I also took his boots, as he had surprisingly small feet.

I helped Alex put on the overalls and then the boots. The shaking was still there but seemed to be settling. She got up and leaned against the wall, taking deep breaths.

"Do you know what happened here?" I said, indicating outside. "To all these people?"

I thought at first that she wasn't listening, but then her head snapped round, and she stared at me.

"We need to get out of here," she whispered. "It's not safe."

CHAPTER NINE

We hurriedly made our way through the air locks to the thin walkway that separated the Faraday cage from the rest of the facility. At first, Alex had been content to be guided and almost carried by me, but as we passed the stalk-like computer terminal and the prone figures of the security guards, she detached herself from my grip and knelt by the guard whose clothes she was wearing. She placed a hand on his forehead and then seemed to be feeling for a pulse in his neck.

"They're both dead; I checked," I said, nervously looking around.

She got up and went over to the other guy and did the same thing.

"There're no signs of injury to either of them," I said, squatting down next to her. "What do you think happened here?" I wasn't prepared to tell her about Jin's gruesome remains in the medical lab.

"A mistake," she said.

I frowned and was about to ask what she meant by that when she got to her feet and crossed to the computer terminal. It flickered to life as she approached, bringing up a slowly turning holographic representation of the Singularity facility. It was a huge donut-shaped compound with the geodesic dome of the

Faraday cage right in the center. The mezzanine and outdoor area were at the top end, and there were laboratories labeled Medical, Military, Biological, and so on around the circumference. At the southernmost end was a generator room and power plant, and along the western curve of the donut were computer servers, lecture theaters, staff accommodation, a kitchen, and another dining area. On the eastern side there was garage or hangar-sized area containing multiple vehicles, leading to a road labeled "To the airstrip."

Alex pointed to it. "They have heli-planes; that's our way out."

"When did you learn how to fly?" I said, raising my eyebrows. She gave a half smile but said nothing.

As we waited at the elevator, I looked her over surreptitiously. She was just as I'd remembered her: high cheekbones, chestnut hair, a little mole by the side of her lip. She caught me looking and stretched out a hand, which I took.

"Do you remember what you said at my wake?" she said softly.

I pulled her to me again, nuzzling against her hair and neck. "Of course," I said, the little white lie slipping out easily. I'd gotten so drunk that Nico had put me to bed while the wake was only half over.

Alex leaned back and peered into my face, her eyes as open and honest as any child's.

"You said, 'I would've followed you to hell if that's what it would've taken to keep you safe. I was supposed to be your protector as you were mine, one to shield the other. Not a single soul came before you. I would've stayed with you as you would've stayed with me, trusted in you as you trusted in me, and together we would've ridden through every storm, waiting to see what the new dawn would bring.'"

My eyes glistened as my own words speared through me. I'd written that as part of the eulogy I couldn't remember saying. Nico had filmed it, of course, and now I realized how much I'd failed in those lofty aspirations.

"I need you to protect me now," she said.

I nodded. If this were a second chance, I would take it with both hands.

The elevator pinged, and the doors swished open. We got in, and Alex accessed the panel. A floor schematic appeared. She ran a finger over it, drawing a red line starting from where we were and taking it out to the airstrip.

"We get off at subdivision level zero, where the research labs are. The passageway to the ground-vehicle storage area is close by."

Immediately, the elevator started moving. My ears popped, and I swallowed to relieve the pressure. I had a thought. "There must be more security than we've seen so far," I said. "Do you think they're all dead as well?"

"I don't know," she replied after a moment's hesitation.

The elevator halted, and the doors opened into a large glass-covered dome resembling an inverted fishbowl. Here, the air was cool and unmoving, and there was no sound. The full moon shone through the branches of the trees reaching over the glass, casting monochrome, spidery shadows.

Lumpy, misshapen silhouettes lay still on the floor and along the curves of the wall. Dozens of them.

I grabbed Alex's hand and pulled her to the side, hugging the wall. "More bodies," I whispered, my voice tight.

"We need to go that way," she replied and pointed down the corridor.

I frowned. "Did you hear what I said?"

She looked up at me. "Yes. It looks like everyone's dead."

She said it so matter-of-factly, I was momentarily taken aback. I was about to say so when she disengaged from my grip and started walking. I closed my eyes and took a deep breath and hurried to catch up.

The bodies, dappled in the moonlight, were horribly pallid and twisted in uncomfortable ways. Many still had their eyes open, their mouths contorted in agony. We passed a woman in a crumpled laboratory coat, lips a shade of blue, eyes black with exploded pupils.

One shoe was missing, and her arms were outstretched like she was crucified.

"Alex, you're a doctor. Should we . . .?" I started, my heart thudding in my chest.

"There's nothing we can do for them," Alex said, not looking up.

I gritted my teeth and reluctantly stepped over the body. I could tell she'd been a beautiful woman, but there was no such thing as a beautiful body when death had claimed it. Death was death. The flesh rotted, the bones decayed, the hair matted and dropped out. I'd seen enough of it in Afghanistan to last me a lifetime.

I glanced back to Alex, but she wasn't with me anymore. She'd stopped and was facing one of the doorways, staring at the nameplate.

It read: Astrobiology, Dr. Caroline Heidrich, PhD.

The door was closed, but it had a smoked-glass window halfway up. I cupped my hands and peered inside but couldn't see anything. Alex pushed on the door, which was locked, and rattled the handle loudly.

I grabbed her wrist. "Hey, what're you doing? We can't hang around here." I pointed to the end of the corridor where there was a sizable rectangular doorway set into the wall. "I think that's the way to the garage."

She ignored me, and her fingers flew over the security panel. The lock unclicked, and without hesitating, she walked through. I uttered a curse under my breath and followed.

Compared with the high-tech labs I'd seen already, this one was more conventional. Benches were strewn with gas cylinders and trays containing bottles of odd-colored liquids. Ancient analog-looking equipment with tubes and wires snaking in and out occupied one side of the room next to some biohazard stations that resembled miniature greenhouses. Each station had access holes in their glass frontages covered by plastic bags where the operators would have put their hands through to manipulate their experiments.

I peered inside the nearest one. There were rock samples, test tubes, blue-and-red topped bottles of clear liquid, and little boxes with dials and illuminated screens.

"Hey, look at these . . . ," I began, turning to Alex.

She was standing next to another door at the back of the lab. She waved me over, an air of impatience in the gesture.

"What? Why do you want to go in there?" I whispered loudly.

She looked up and waved me over again.

I gritted my teeth and walked over. "What's in there?" I said.

The door was completely made of semitransparent glass, and there was another office behind it. I squinted in the half light. There was an old wooden desk paired with an ultramodern black leather chair, and an Apple Mac computer-printer set up. Piles of papers and journals were scattered untidily on the desk and the floor. The office was on an external wall with a big picture window.

We went in. Alex walked up to the desk and started moving papers around. I picked up a photo frame from the desk that showed a younger-looking Caroline, her arms around an older man. He had similar sharp features, gray-white hair, and a goatee, and I guessed that was her father.

"Look at this," Alex said, pointing to a large painting of a shadowy cigar-shaped rock floating through a dark background of stars and interstellar dust.

"I remember this picture," I said, taking a closer look. "A couple of years ago, it was a big thing in the news for a few days. I could never get my tongue around its name."

"They called it 'Oumuamua," said Alex, pronouncing it *oh-MOO-uh-MOO-uh*. "In Hawaiian it means 'a messenger from afar arriving first.'"

I wrinkled my forehead, thinking. "The talk was all about aliens until scientists concluded it was just a big asteroid." I glanced back into the lab at the biohazard stations. "Do you think the rocks in there are pieces of it?"

Alex shook her head. "'Oumuamua never came close to Earth."

"Then what . . .?" I froze. There was a noise outside. Running footsteps. Lots of them.

I grabbed Alex's hand, and we ran back into the main lab and ducked behind one of the larger benches with a biohazard station on top. I could just see the lab's open door. Booted figures ran past; they wore black combat pants, masks, and guns.

"We need to get out of here. Did you see a back door?" I whispered urgently.

"Wait a minute," she said, looking at me sternly.

The sound of the running feet receded. After a minute, everything was quiet again. Alex stood up and tiptoed over to the door. She looked outside, left and right, then slowly closed it. She put a finger to her lips and waved me over to the biggest biohazard station. This particular station had robotic manipulators, as if the protection of the plastic shield was not enough and only mechanical limbs could be trusted to touch the rocks. Inside were half a dozen reddish-black rocks. They were smooth, like pebbles from the bottom of a fast-running stream.

Alex put her hand through the covered portal and ripped the plastic screen in half. There was a hiss of escaping gases, and the hood deflated. She picked up a rock approximately six inches in size and turned it over and over in her hands, brow furrowed in concentration. Then her lips compressed, and she dropped the rock on the floor.

"It's not here," she said.

I opened my hands. "What isn't here?"

She closed her eyes, seemingly concentrating on something. I grabbed her by the shoulders and shook her. "Alex, what the hell are you doing? We need to get out of here."

She pushed my arms away and took a step backward. I raised my arms again, but this time, she put a hand out, signaling me to stop. She cocked a head toward the door, and I turned as the sound of running feet came again. We dove back behind the station, but now the footsteps had stopped outside the door. We hunkered down as far as we could go as the door clicked and swished open. I held my breath as people entered the room. I could make out many black combat boots, but there was also someone wearing track pants and white Nike trainers, and a woman wearing heels. There was a gentle rhythmic sound like Darth Vader breathing, and then the clicking of the safety coming off multiple firearms. I glanced at Alex who had her eyes closed and had curled up into a ball.

The footsteps moved through the laboratory and into to Caroline's office. After a couple of minutes, they returned and left, closing the door to the corridor behind them. Stillness fell, as if a storm had suddenly quelled. I nudged

Alex, who slowly opened her eyes. I flicked my chin upward indicating that we should try and make a getaway. She nodded and took my hand, and I pulled her up.

"Ah, there you are," came a raspy voice. "Thought you might be in here."

Caroline Heidrich. She was wearing a respirator and carrying a firearm. Her business attire had been replaced by jeans and a cream sweater, but still with heels. She was alone. I glanced behind her at the closed corridor door.

"They'll be back," she said, noticing my look. "I reckon you've got less than five minutes."

She peeled off the respirator and took a deep breath. Her face was tight and angry, her eyes cold. She tapped the gun against her leg. "It looks like the gas, or whatever it was you used, has dispersed. Or I suppose you'd both be dead as well."

I held out my hands, palms upward, and took a step forward. "You think we had something to do with—"

She brought up the gun and pointed it unwaveringly at me. "Didn't you?"

"Of course not. How could I, being stuck in your prison cell?"

Caroline's lip twitched. "Well let's ask Dr. Park, then, shall we?" She swung the gun round and pointed it at Alex. "Where did you come from, by the way? I mean, how did you get in here?"

I laughed. "You're kidding me. You've been keeping her here as a prisoner all this time. It's you who owe us answers—"

But Caroline was staring at Alex like she'd never met her before. Her eyes were narrowing. "Dr. Park. I need to know how you got in here."

Before Alex could reply, the main door was flung open, and a man burst through. He was wearing a Nike track suit and a respirator, and also carrying a firearm. He looked at Caroline and then at us before ripping his respirator off and throwing it to the ground.

Christian Becker.

His face was thunder, and he raised the gun and pointed it at Alex. "You. Give me back my fucking facility now or I'll kill you."

I took a step forward, palms out. "Hey, whoa, as I've been trying to tell you, we aren't responsible for this."

Becker didn't take his eyes off Alex, who grabbed my hand and squeezed tightly. He snorted. "Then how do you explain the photographs? Coincidence? What do you take me for?"

"It's bullshit," I spat. "We've nothing to do with anything that's happened here." I pushed Alex behind me, out of the line of fire.

"You and her are working together," he said, spittle dripping out of the side of his mouth. "What do you want? Money? No problem. How much?"

Caroline had lowered her pistol and was frowning at Christian. His gun was shaking, and there were beads of sweat on his forehead, which had a red line etched in it from the respirator's mask.

"Put the gun down and we'll talk," I said, as calmly as I was able.

Alex pulled on my hand, and I gave her a quick look. She almost imperceptibly shook her head and silently mouthed, "He's going to kill me."

All right, time to man up.

I took a step toward Becker. He wasn't particularly tall nor was he athletic-looking, despite the tracksuit and running shoes. But he did have a gun. And so did Caroline, for that matter. She'd moved off to the side slightly and was still watching Christian, an unfathomable look on her face. I wondered when the security detail would be back, and knew I had to act fast. But it was suicide, wasn't it? I was trained in hand-to-hand combat and had gotten into a few scraps over the years, but again, he had a gun and wasn't within arm's length of me. But I wondered whether he'd ever shot anyone. I suspected not. Someone with his money would've gotten other people to do any dirty work—of that I was certain. But Caroline . . . ? She looked cool and collected. Would she shoot me?

Fuck.

I was mulling over my next move when Alex charged Becker, wrapping her arms around his torso and knocking him backward over a bench, scattering glassware and equipment. They fell to the ground in a tumble of arms and legs, the gun spinning out of his hand and under one of the other benches. I looked at it and made to grab it but heard a click from behind my ear. I turned to see the barrel of Caroline's gun an inch from my face.

"Uh-uh," she said.

I froze and watched helplessly as Becker and Alex grappled. She had her legs wrapped around his torso and was pulling at his hair, but he was already twisting and turning. He shifted so that he was now on top. She swung a couple of punches at the back of his head, but they just bounced off ineffectively as he continued to wriggle on top of her, using his weight to pin her down. His hands went around her neck, and he bared his teeth and started to squeeze.

"No!" I shouted, turning to Caroline. "You've got to stop this!"

She gave a brief nod and took a step backward. "Christian, let her go."

There was no sign he'd heard her, or if he had, he'd no interest in stopping. Alex's face was looking paler, and her eyes had turned upward. Her arms were now flailing uselessly against his head and back, the movements becoming weaker.

"Do something!" I screamed at Caroline, who seemed frozen with indecision.

I pushed past her, jumped on Becker, and ripped his arms from Alex's neck. With a heave, I threw him off, and he tumbled away, crashing into the wall. I knelt behind Alex and lifted her head up, relieved to see that she was still breathing and conscious. Her eyes fluttered and opened, and then they widened like a deer's in headlights as she looked over my shoulder. I twisted around to see Becker scrabbling to his knees, gun in his hand, and his face ablaze with fury.

He raised the gun and fired.

I flinched and ducked. The report was deafening in the confined space. Alex's shoulder jerked backward as the bullet went straight through and gouged a hot channel in the floor. Blood splattered over my face, and she screamed in unholy agony.

I threw myself on top of her, attempting to shield her with my body. I figured that if he shot me, the bullet would likely pass through to her, but some of the sting might be taken out of it. I waited, eyes tightly closed, but nothing happened. I peeked and saw that Caroline was on him and had twisted his wrist, so he'd dropped the gun. She'd grabbed him in some kind of jujitsu head-lock: her arm around his neck, the crook of her elbow under his chin, and her forearm and bicep coming together like a pincer, blocking off his carotid arteries. His eyes bulged, and he flailed, trying to reach her, but after a few seconds, his arms and body went flaccid. She hung on for a few more seconds and then gently lowered him to the ground.

I eased myself off Alex and tried to assess her gunshot wound. There was a lot of blood, and the tip of her shoulder felt soft and mushy. I gathered the material of her shirt together and pressed it hard against the wound. Her eyes fluttered, and she screwed up her face in pain.

"You tried to protect me," she whispered.

"Of course I did, stupid," I said.

Caroline appeared by my side. "Here, let me help."

She'd grabbed a first-aid box from somewhere. Inside were scissors, gauze swabs, bandages, and some iodine liquid. She cut the arm off Alex's shirt to expose the entry wound. It was an inch-wide circle oozing blackish blood. She reached around Alex's back to where the bullet had emerged, and her mouth tightened. "There's a big exit hole. We'll need to plug both sides."

She poured the iodine over the injury, pressed the gauze swabs into the exit wound, and wrapped the whole shoulder in a spiral bandage. She then used the cut-off shirtsleeve as a makeshift sling to support her arm.

"Can you get up?" Caroline said, putting a hand on Alex's other shoulder.

Alex nodded, and so we gingerly helped her to her feet. She looked terribly pale but wasn't too unsteady. She leaned against the wall, taking a few deep breaths.

"Why are you helping us?" I said to Caroline.

The muscles in her cheek bunched together, and she shook her head. "Kidnapping wasn't in the job description."

"Thank you," I said, meaning it.

She acknowledged with a nod, and I noticed that she had the gun back in her hand. "It won't be long before the security detail comes back," she said. "Do you have a plan on how to get out of here?"

"We were going to take one of the heli-planes," I replied, still not quite believing that.

Caroline's face gave nothing away, but I could see the cogs turning over in her head. She'd just rendered her boss unconscious and was probably thinking about how she would explain that to him when he came to.

She tucked the gun into her waistband and unlocked the ISIS bracelet from her wrist with the silver pen. She tossed both into a nearby trash can and gave me a mirthless smile. "Guess I'm coming with you."

CHAPTER TEN

With Alex between us, we limped out of the lab and across the corridor to the rectangular doorway that was now framed by flashing orange lights. The pathway beyond was a gradual slope that curved left and was lit up by neon strips.

"I think that goes directly to the landing site," I panted.

Alex sagged, and her legs started to slide rather than hold her weight. Caroline shifted so that Alex's good arm was around her shoulder. She'd kicked her heels off and was holding them in her other hand.

"There should be some jeeps around that bend," she said, nodding toward the doorway. "We'll grab one and drive the rest of the way."

"How far is it?" I asked.

"About a mile, give or take."

We hobbled toward the doorway as fast as we could, which wasn't very fast. I kept looking behind, expecting to see the shadows of approaching security guards. Or a very angry and vengeful Christian Becker.

"By the way," said Caroline, looking over Alex's head at me. "What was the gas you used on everyone?"

I sighed. "How many times do I have to tell you, I had nothing to do with any of this."

Her eyes narrowed. "Well, it was fucking lethal. Hundreds of innocent people are dead."

I bit my tongue and carried on walking.

Alex wasn't looking good. Her head was lolling as if her neck was made of rubber, and even in the dark, I could see that the bandaging was already slick and wet. We rounded the bend and came across a section cut into the side of the tunnel that housed a couple of four-seater vehicles that resembled ATVs. We lifted Alex into the back seat of the nearest one and laid her flat. Caroline jumped behind the wheel, and I slid into the passenger seat. She pushed a button, and the jeep noiselessly set off like a golf cart. She flicked the headlights on. Every dozen yards or so, I caught a glimpse of bodies along the road, and once or twice Caroline had to swerve to avoid driving over them. I covertly glanced at her; her face was set in stone, her eyes angry and damp. I got the feeling that she'd taken her emotional safety off, a warning as clear as a cocked gun.

"I didn't have anything to do with this," I said again, my diction slow and precise. "You've got to believe me—I don't know what's going on."

Caroline kept her eyes front, but I caught a slight nod. "I've had a bad feeling about this company for a long time now," she said eventually. "Kidnapping you was the final straw."

"Is that really why you're helping us?" I asked quietly.

Before she could reply, lights bloomed up ahead, and we came upon an arch-shaped exit. There was a traffic barrier and a window-lined security station. Orange lights were flashing along the barrier, but there was no one in the booth.

Caroline stopped smoothly at the barrier and jumped out, gesturing for me to do the same. "We're here. Grab her, and let's go."

I reached in the back for Alex, who had regained a bit of color, although her eyes were still closed. I cupped her face in my hands. "Hey, how're you doing? Are you able to move?"

"I'm fine," she said but then gave a raspy cough, and a sprinkle of blood appeared on her lips. She looked up and gave me a determined smile.

I gritted my teeth and helped her out of the jeep. We stepped gingerly around more bodies and past the barrier out into the open air. It was warm and humid; the noise of nocturnal creatures clicked and whispered in our ears. Through a gap in the canopy of trees, the stars sparkled, and the Milky Way stretched in a purple band across the sky.

Two aircraft were parked side by side on the landing strip. They looked like no aircraft I'd ever seen before. Eggshell white, streamlined, and tapering to a point like tadpoles, they had two inverted rotor blades hanging underneath short, stubby wings. There was a trifold tail at a stern that had no rotor. The front was shaped like a bird of prey, with an opaque black wraparound windshield.

"Singularity's concept for the military's FVL program," said Caroline.

"What's FVL?"

"FVL stands for *future vertical lift*. The military's plan for the future of US helicopters. Their remit was to carry up to twelve troops and have a combat radius of over five hundred miles. It was, of course, tendered out to the usual manufacturers—Bell, Sikorsky, and the rest—but Singularity was way ahead of the curve with these. They have capabilities beyond any current rotorcraft with respect to hovering, speed, and maneuverability. Singularity's tech teams also decided they should be invisible to radar and very quiet."

"Never heard of a quiet helicopter," I said.

"These are electric. Just like drones, but much bigger." She turned to Alex. "And now that we're here, Dr. Park, I assume you have a plan? I mean, I can't fly these things, and I'm pretty sure Will can't either. Or can you, Will?"

I frowned. "You're kidding, right?"

She folded her arms and frowned. "Then what are we—"

"I can do it," said Alex abruptly.

She detached herself from my grip and walked unsteadily to the nearest heli-plane. She ran her hand along the side of the cockpit, caressing its metallic skin. There was a hiss and a click as a hand-shaped indentation appeared. She pressed and turned her hand ninety degrees, and a strip of light materialized, outlining a hatch that smoothly swung open. A short ladder extended automatically, and internal lighting gradually increased, illuminating the cockpit.

Alex awkwardly pulled herself up the ladder, and we followed quickly behind. The cockpit was very high tech. There were three seats facing forward, bucket-shaped and covered in the cream leather you would see in a Gulfstream private jet. Holographic displays and touchscreens covered the surfaces. A heads-up display showed a red-lined map of the facility rotating slowly.

Alex took the middle seat, so Caroline and I buckled up on either side of her. A yoke organically emerged from the floor and settled on Alex's lap. It resembled an F1 steering wheel, studded with switches and trackballs. The entry hatch closed silently, and the ambient lights went out, leaving us illuminated by the screens and displays.

"*Do* you know how to fly this?" I said to Alex, lightly touching her on the arm.

She gave a little smile and sat back in her seat. "I don't need to fly it. It can do that perfectly well on its own. We just need to tell it where to go."

She ran her hand across top of the yoke and punched a couple of buttons on the panel above her head. There was a whine as the engines cranked up, and the whole craft shuddered as the rotors started to spin and grab the air.

Caroline leaned over and peered out the windshield through the HUD. "There's movement outside. I think we've got company."

She was right. Multiple shadows could be seen running around the barrier. They had flashlights and guns. A familiar figure was with them, wearing a tracksuit and Nikes.

"Christian's found us. Time to go," she said, looking at Alex, "or we're toast."

Alex nodded and pulled on the yoke. The craft spun and lifted a couple of feet off the ground. Out of the side windows, I saw the rotors angle away from the ground to point to the rear of the craft.

Alex flicked another switch, and floodlights kicked on, illuminating Becker and his men who were standing in a line, lit from behind by the orange glow from the tunnel. We started to reverse smoothly away, the floodlights blinding and intense. A rear-facing-camera image flashed on one of the HUD screens, showing that were approaching the edge of the tarmac and heading toward a couple of large trees.

"Alex . . . ," I started nervously.

There was suddenly an avalanche of gunfire, and the windshield became peppered with spiderwebs as bullets impacted it and ricocheted all around. Alex yanked the column back, and we shot vertically up as if on an amusement-park ride. My stomach was left behind, and I grabbed the sides of the seat as we burst through the canopy of trees and into the night sky.

We continued to gain altitude for another thirty seconds or so before slowing and banking gently to the left. I looked out of the window. In the distance, there were craggy black edges of mountains, and the horizon was the color of a tangerine, the lights of a large city oozing over the curve of the earth. Below us, the dim outline of a dome, which I assumed was the Singularity facility, receded into the forest.

"Where exactly are we?" I said to Caroline.

"We're just east of San Diego," she said, pointing at the horizon. "That's the city over there. The Cleveland National Forest is all around us. Christian bribed a senator and a couple of high-ranking assholes on the US Forest Service and bought a big piece of land here for a few million bucks."

Alex suddenly slumped forward and grabbed her shoulder. She took a few deep, shaky breaths and looked up at me with wet eyes. Caroline gave me a look. "I guess we really need to get her to a hospital."

"We can't go to a hospital," said Alex, emphatically shaking her head. "I just need somewhere to rest for a while."

Caroline pursed her lips. "Wherever we go, we'll be easy to spot in this."

"I've taken care of that," Alex replied. "I've deactivated the transponder, so they can't track us. Also, this is a stealth craft, so it's virtually invisible to radar." She glanced at the holographic display. "It has a range of just over four hundred miles. LA is easily within reach. And it's still nighttime."

"Then what?" Caroline said. "Leave this thing parked on a driveway? Might look a bit suspicious."

Alex shook her head. "I'll program the autopilot to return it to Singularity after dropping us off."

Caroline blew out her cheeks. "Well, we can't very well go to Will's place, or mine for that matter."

I came to a decision. "I know a place we can go."

"Well, let's get moving before Becker jumps into that other heli-plane. He won't need a tracking device if he can see us."

Alex nodded and looked at me. "I'll need an address for the nav computer."

I thought about Becker and tried to put myself in his head. He was smart, but not omnipotent. With the range of the heli-plane, there were an almost limitless number of places we could be going. Hell, we could be in Mexico in half an hour.

"The gymnasium," I said. "It's not being used at the moment. We were thinking of selling it off, so it's empty. We should be safe there."

"Not for long," said Caroline, brow furrowed. "We did our research on you."

I looked across at Alex who had closed her eyes, the sweat on her brow sticking her hair down. She grimaced silently and put her hand up to her injured shoulder.

"We need to get her somewhere fast," I said. "I don't know anywhere else."

"Shit," said Caroline. "What about your friend, Nico? Doesn't he live close by?"

I shook my head. "He was just bunking with me. Wanted to move back home. Just hadn't gotten round to it yet."

Caroline blew out her cheeks. "Okay, the gym it is."

Alex expanded the map on the HUD and with a few swipes, moved the images down the western seaboard toward LA and Santa Monica. She focused on the street where my gym was and turned to me. I pointed at the map.

"There. See that cemetery a couple of blocks away off the freeway? Wood-land Lawn, I think it's called. Drop us in there, and it's not far to walk to the gym."

"It's actually called Woodlawn Cemetery," said Alex, inputting the address and giving me a half smile. "But close enough."

The heli-plane smoothly banked left and accelerated to a speed of three hundred knots. The wings had turned ninety degrees, and the rotors were now pointing behind like a turboprop plane but with the engines on the rear instead of in front of the wings.

"Distance is one hundred and thirty-three miles," Alex said. "ETA in about twenty minutes." Then she closed her eyes and slumped back in the chair. I leaned over and took her pulse. It was steady, but she was out cold.

"Let her sleep," said Caroline. "I need to think."

CHAPTER ELEVEN

As the heli-plane banked noiselessly away into the night sky, heading back to Singularity, we laid Alex down against a gravestone that had sunk into the soft soil giving it the appearance of a lopsided tooth. The engraved words, weathered by a century of wind and salty rain, sat just above the level of the ground-cover plants that sprawled over the dirt. Other gravestones sat upright, soldier-like, a line of deathly attention; some were dotted with flowers, but most were neglected. The cemetery was silent and eerie, the grass marking each plot appearing gray in the reflected moonlight. I looked around, getting my bearings. Pico Boulevard was on the left and the junction with Fourteenth Street was just visible behind the trees lining the cemetery. A dog barked somewhere in the distance, and I thought I could hear the ocean. There was no traffic noise.

Caroline squatted down next to Alex and looked up at me. "She's not looking great."

"No, I don't like the look of her at all," I agreed. "We should really get her to a hospital."

Caroline blew out her cheeks. "But unfortunately, she was right. We can't do that. For a start, she's been declared dead, so it'll raise a bunch of red flags when her details come up on the hospital's electronic records."

"We could take her in and say we found her like this? A Jane Doe?"

"They'll call the cops straight away," she replied, shaking her head. "She's got an obvious gunshot wound. Standard protocol would be to call it in."

Alex raised a shaky hand, and I realized she'd been listening. "No hospital, no police," she croaked. "Just . . . please . . . I need to rest."

"So you keep saying . . ." I sighed.

We picked her up and made our way through the gravestones to a curved pathway that led to the edge of the cemetery and then to a gate. We emerged on Fourteenth Street. There were no vehicles and no pedestrians, which wasn't surprising. This was the early hours of the morning in Santa Monica. No one had any legitimate business to be out at this time.

"We'll cut through over there," I said, pointing to where an empty parking lot in front of an automotive service and repair shop.

We hustled across the road as fast as we could, staying away from the streetlights, and were soon hidden by the shadows of a couple of overhanging bushes. Behind the shop was an alleyway lined with more trees leading to another cross street, this one with no streetlights.

"Hey, we're nearly there," I said to Alex, who was looking very frail. We started to shuffle around the corner, but she tripped over the curb. I managed to catch her before she fell and lowered her to the sidewalk, propping her up against the fence.

"I . . . I . . . ," she said, her eyes rolling up in her head.

I put my arm under her knees and lifted her up, carrying her like a child. She was surprisingly heavy, or maybe I was just surprisingly weak and pathetic.

"We're nearly there," I grunted again.

"So you said," Caroline replied, looking up and down the road.

I led the way, and we crossed quickly and turned into another dark alleyway, this one smelling of urine and dog shit. I held my breath, and we shuffled on until we reached another crossroad. As we rounded the corner, a car's headlights panned past us and the thump-thump of a subwoofer playing some hip-hop came and went. Once it was all quiet, I peeked round the corner into the next street. A few yards farther along was a building advertising a Pilates studio.

"There," I pointed. "My gym's right next door."

With Alex hanging between us, we hugged the side of the building, staying out of the glare from the single streetlight on the other side of the road. We passed the Pilates studio's window and came to the door of my gym. Caroline glanced at the faded sign hanging above it: "Monica's Muscles – All Welcome – Daily Membership Deals."

"Catchy name," she said, with no small amount of sarcasm.

I would have given her the finger if my arms weren't busy stopping Alex from sinking to the floor. I gently set her down and put my face to the window and looked inside. The gym was a single, low-ceilinged space with steel cages and racks for bars, weights, and dumbbells. The floor was covered in black mats, linked together like bricks. On the far wall was another rack of weights, a shelf with exercise balls and towels, and a water dispenser. A door at the back led to the changing rooms and showers. Another door led to my office. Everything was as I'd left it.

I turned to Caroline. "I think we're good."

She nodded. "What about this chain?"

The front door was secured with a solid-looking chain and combination lock.

"Spin it," I said. "The combination is one, two, three, four, five."

She raised her eyebrows. "Wow, great security. That'll take some cracking."

I gave her flat eyes, so she spun the numbers and took the chain off the door. I turned the handle, and it creaked open. Caroline pulled the gun out from her waistband and cagily entered. I pulled Alex to her feet, and we shuffled sideways through the door.

"The office at the back," I whispered, pointing with my chin.

The moonlight threw black-and-white stripes across the floor, and the discarded weights and barbells made for an obstacle course.

"OSHA not visited recently?" Caroline said snarkily as we picked our way through to my office.

I ignored her and pushed the door open with my shoulder. My old desk was covered with dusty newspapers and magazines; a coffee pot and small fridge sat on a table under the window. A long couch with a couple of pillows and blankets was against the other wall. A framed Schwarzenegger movie poster from the '90s stared down from behind my desk.

I laid Alex on the couch as Caroline closed the door behind us and pulled the window blinds down. Alex was breathing shallowly and slowly but was now virtually unresponsive. Her brow felt hot, and there was a layer of dirty sweat over her face. I checked the bandages around her shoulder, and my hands came away wet and bloodied. I picked up the small desk lamp and placed it under the desk before switching it on. Its dim light cast shadows on the ceiling, and I balanced one of the newspapers on top of the lampshade, dimming it further.

"Have you got a first-aid kit?" Caroline asked, crouching next to Alex.

"Yes, out by the front door."

A minute later, she returned with a white tin box and half a dozen face towels. We carefully stripped off Alex's shirt and the bandages. The wound at the front was barely visible, but the larger exit one at the back of her shoulder was still pouting open like trout's lips. We washed it as best we could before gently pressing the fresh towels on it and wrapping more bandages around her arm. Through all this, Alex didn't stir, so once we'd finished, I pulled the blankets over her and tucked them in.

Caroline went over to the window and opened a narrow slot in the blinds to peer out. "You should get some sleep too," she said without looking back.

I stood and stretched, and realized I wasn't tired. "What time is it?"

She looked at her watch. "It's nearly five. It'll be daylight in a few hours."

"It's nearly time to get up. Want some coffee?"

She shrugged. "Why not?"

I plugged the coffee machine in. It was a relatively recent purchase. A new

Nespresso model. I rummaged around under the desk and came up with a sleeve of pods. I filled up the water tank from the dispenser and poured us a couple of long blacks. Caroline sat at the desk, and I pulled up another chair and sat opposite her, facing Arnold.

"You still haven't exactly apologized for kidnapping me," I said, sipping my coffee.

She silently looked around the office, her hands cupping the little coffee mug. Her sharp cheekbones were accentuated by the shadows coming from the floor lamp and her gelled hair had become tousled. She was a truly spectacular-looking woman, but she was also scary. The way she'd handled a gun and incapacitated Becker indicated a degree of training that seemed out of character for an academic.

She put the mug down and fixed me with a stare. "None of this makes sense," she said and inclined her head toward Alex. "Least of all her."

I nodded but didn't reply, as that was rhetorical, to say the least. We sat in comfortable silence for a few minutes, and my eyes started to close. Caroline's chair creaked as she stood up again and leaned against the windowpane. She took another sip from her mug and looked down at me, a slight frown on her face.

"If I accept you had nothing to do with this—and I'm still not sure that I do—then answer me truthfully. Did you really think Alex was dead, or just missing?"

I shrugged. "I suppose I believed she was dead, but I just couldn't get closure. The fact that there was no body made me think there may still have been a chance she was alive."

"You never thought she'd been taken by a crocodile, then?"

"Not really. Her boat was undamaged. The problem was that the local police were pretty convinced that was the answer. They assured me that crocodiles were definitely known to inhabit that part of the river. It soon became their default position. I think they just wanted to close the case and move on. It didn't help the tourism industry over there to let it linger. Her boat was found ten miles upriver from Iquitos, one of Peru's largest cities. Population of about half a million. That'd been the starting point of her journey."

"So, you think they just wanted to close the case purely because of the negative impact it would have on tourism? That seems unlikely, don't you think? A citizen of the United States and all. Surely there'd be more interest in making sure they got it right?"

I shrugged again. "Iquitos is on the Amazon River, and lot of tourist trips start from there. Big money for a third-world country."

Caroline nodded and took another sip of her coffee. "But you had other theories, am I right? What do you think happened to her?"

I folded my arms. "I'd wondered about the local tribesmen. You hear stories about them all the time. Lost Amazonian tribes and all that. Tribes that'd never seen civilization of any kind. Cannibalism and so on. You must've seen Nat Geo documentaries? But the police pretty much quickly ruled that out. They'd scoured the area around the boat for miles. They told me that there were no tribes, known or unknown, in the vicinity."

She tipped her head to the side. "You suspected foul play, then?"

I felt moisture pricking my eyes. "I definitely did. I was sure Alex would've called me if she'd been in trouble. We'd been in constant communication. She had a HoloNet sat phone."

Caroline went quiet, thinking. Then she said, "How long did you say you spent in the area looking for her?"

"I stayed for a month, maybe just over. The police gave up the search about a week after the boat was found."

"Did you find anything else interesting?"

"Like what?"

"I don't know. Anything unusual."

"No, I ran out of money and had to come back home. Back to work. Nico was covering for me, but he couldn't pull all the shifts at the café and run the gym. He'd decided to temporarily close the gym and concentrate on the café until I got back." I rubbed my eyes. This wasn't getting us anywhere. "What's your angle here, Caroline? I don't understand why you're helping us. I mean, you were pretty full on at my interrogation. You and that Jerry guy."

Her lips pursed as she mulled over her answer. She pulled the chair out and sat down again, facing me. "I was headhunted by Christian. He turned up at one of my lectures at Harvard. I was pushing for tenure, but as I was young compared with my peers, I didn't hold out much hope at that time. I was flattered when Christian approached me. I knew who he was, how rich he was, and I certainly knew his reputation for being a genius and innovator. He asked me to come and work at his new facility where he was developing a whole bunch of revolutionary technology that, in his words, would 'change the fucking world forever.'"

That surprised me. I knew how important academic tenure was. If she'd gained tenure at Harvard, that was a job for life, the kudos and the prestige notwithstanding. Also, the money can't have been all that bad. "Why would an astrobiologist want to go and work for an IT company?" I asked.

"He said he'd come across some meteorite fragments. Said they were unusual, and he needed to know more about their origin. Said he'd already engaged the best geologists and physical chemists on the planet. He name-dropped some big cheeses I'd heard of, including a Nobel Prize winner. It seemed like an amazing environment to work in."

"Do you mind me asking what he offered you to leave Harvard to study some rocks?"

"I do mind, yes."

"Was it worth it?"

She closed her eyes and rocked back in the chair. "Ten times what I was making at Harvard. What would you have done?"

"Okay, so you moved to California from Massachusetts. That's like, three thousand miles? From a tenured position in one of the most prestigious universities in the world to work for a private company. What did your husband have to say about that?"

She rolled her eyes skyward. "There's no husband."

"Boyfriend?"

"Grow up, Will. I'm twenty-nine. Boyfriends are for teenagers."

I took another sip of my coffee, which was starting to go cold. It was definitely getting lighter, and there was a rumbling in my stomach. I stretched and
walked around to Caroline's side of the desk and opened a drawer. Inside was a
box of energy bars, all high-protein and low-carb. Better than nothing. I took
one and offered another to Caroline, who shook her head. I sat back down and
took a bite. Then another. It was probably the best protein bar I'd ever eaten. I
flicked the wrapper into the corner of the room and had a thought.

"Those rocks in your office?" I said. "They're the ones he brought you to
study?"

She opened her eyes and blinked slowly, like a reptile. "Well done, Sherlock."

"What've you found out so far?"

She gave a little smile and leaned forward, putting her elbows on the table
and cradling her chin in her hands. Her eyes lasered into mine, and I found
it hard to hold her stare again.

"Fuck all, actually," she said. "They are your usual run-of-the-mill meteorites. Nothing special about them at all."

"But you still stayed at Singularity, right? How long have you been there?"

"Two years."

"Until now," I finished.

Her eyes dropped. "Until now."

I sat back in the chair and folded my arms. "So, how'd you get roped in to
capturing and interrogating me? Becker's clearly rich and has a private army.
Why were you involved at all?"

She laughed. "I ran his 'private army.'"

"You?"

"Don't be so misogynistic, Will. I have a black belt in Brazilian jujitsu.
Christian found out when one of my own lab techs tried to spar with me and
I inadvertently snapped his arm at the elbow."

I grimaced. "Nasty."

"It was, and I regretted it immediately. See, the whole point of BJJ is to be confident in your ability to subdue opponents without necessarily injuring them. But this guy was a complete prick, and he weighed like three hundred pounds. He needed to be taught a lesson."

"So Becker promoted you."

"He was on the verge of sacking me, at first," she said with a smile. "But then I told him that my father was ex-army and was a hand-to-hand combat instructor at West Point. Christian seemed impressed with all of that. Plus, I think he knew we weren't getting anywhere with the meteorites."

"What was your lecture about?" I said. "The day Becker headhunted you at Harvard."

"I was talking about 'Oumuamua. You heard of it?"

I sat forward, interested. "Yes, and that was the picture I saw on your wall."

She nodded. "Well done, Will, very observant. Christian told me that he was very interested in UFOs and quizzed me all about 'Oumuamua. Asked me my opinion about its origin. What I thought it was, etcetera."

"What'd you say?"

She shrugged. "I said that I thought it was a hyperbolic interstellar asteroid. That it was the first interstellar object identified passing through our solar system, but that ultimately nothing was special about it."

"So then he mentioned the meteorites he'd come across?"

"Yeah. He said he wanted to know if they could have come from 'Oumuamua, and of course I told him there's no way, because it didn't come anywhere near Earth, and it certainly didn't break up as it passed through our system."

"You basically debunked his theory then and there. But he still offered you the big bucks—which you took—to study rocks you thought were nothing of interest."

"Correct, Will," she said somewhat coolly. "It seemed like a good idea at the time. Harvard was getting a little dull."

"Well, you've blown it now," I said. "You're a fugitive. Lost your position and the money. Still doesn't explain why you're helping us."

She leaned forward again, her face tight. "You saw all those dead bodies back at Singularity, Will. I was nearly one of them. Christian had just arrived when everything went down. I was standing by his heli-plane to meet him when I heard a garbled message from my team saying people were dropping like flies, as if there was an invisible gas or some kind of toxic leak in the facility. I ran up the stairs into the aircraft and got everyone a gas mask."

"But you still think Alex and I had something to do with this?" I said.

Caroline pulled out the gun she'd had tucked into her waistband and placed it on the table. She spun it lazily until it stopped, pointed at me. Then she spun it a few more times until it pointed at Alex.

"Here's the thing, Will, this weird connection I've been struggling with since your and Alex Park's images went up and crashed all our systems. You just maybe added a missing piece to the puzzle."

"What do you mean?"

"The meteorites in my office. Christian said they came from Peru."

CHAPTER TWELVE

At around seven, Caroline went out to get some supplies. I'd told her there was a convenience store two blocks away and begged her for bagels and cream cheese. She gave me a look that suggested I might be getting something healthier instead.

I checked on Alex. She was still asleep or whatever, but her temperature seemed to be down, as her brow felt cooler and the film of sweat had vanished. A quick look at her bandages revealed that the bleeding had stopped or at least significantly slowed. I dabbed at the exit wound but there was no fresh oozing, which was promising. I whispered her name and gave her a gentle shake, but she didn't stir.

After using the restroom, I wandered around the gym, tidying things away, aimlessly putting weights back on racks, slotting medicine balls into baskets, and folding towels. Just mindless activities while I churned over and over in my head what the hell I was going to do.

I tried to break it down: A private army paid for by a billionaire tech genius had kidnapped me. My (assumed) dead wife was alive and kicking, apart from being recently shot by said billionaire. One of his trusted "lieutenants,"

Caroline Heidrich, had helped us escape, but I didn't know why. It wasn't clear what her reasons for helping us were at all. It was obvious that she wanted answers to something, but I was also pretty certain that I wouldn't be able to help her find them. And when that became crystal clear, Alex and I might no longer be of any use to her.

But it all seemed to revolve around Alex. I didn't know what to make of the Peruvian connection, if there was one. I'd quizzed Caroline again about the meteorites. She admitted that it may just be a coincidence, but that Singularity's systems crashing and Alex's image popping up everywhere at the same time was too coincidental to ignore. Nevertheless, she continued to deny any knowledge about what had happened to Alex and how she'd ended up at Singularity. I needed to square that particular circle, as it seemed to be moderately important, to say the least.

Last, there was the issue of Becker himself. Caroline had said he'd be looking for us and wouldn't stop until he found us.

I went back into the office and put another pod into the Nespresso machine. The water jug needed filling up, so I disconnected it and was just on my way out when Alex's arm flopped in front of me.

"Hey, welcome back," I said, putting the jug down and kneeling in front of the couch. I held her hand and squeezed, and her eyelids fluttered and opened. She let out a small moan and tried to get up, so I popped an arm underneath her back and helped her into a sitting position.

"How are you feeling?" I said, brushing the hair out of her eyes.

She gave a hacking cough and grimaced in pain. Her lips looked cracked and dry, and her skin was flaky in patches, as if she'd developed a form of eczema. "You must be thirsty," I said. "Wait here."

I took the jug out to the water dispenser and filled it, grabbing a couple of paper cups. I gave her a full one, and she gulped it down, almost in one go. I refilled the cup, and she did the same. We kept doing this until the jug was empty, and she sank back into the couch and closed her eyes.

"Thank you," she said weakly.

"Hey, no problem." I brushed her hair off her face again and tucked it behind her ears.

"Where are we?" she said, looking around the office.

"Don't you recognize it?" I said, with a crooked smile. "We're at Monica's Muscles. We had some good times here." I wiggled my eyebrows lasciviously. We'd sneaked into the office many times after the gym closed and used the couch for other, more one-on-one physical activities.

She nodded. "Yes, of course, sorry."

I continued to stroke her hair. "Don't apologize. After what you've been through, I'm sure everything's a bit strange."

She reached up and took hold of my hand. "Will, I do feel strange."

I gave a little smile. "Of course. You've been shot for one thing."

"No, I mean . . . my mind is . . . I can't think straight. I can't seem to focus on anything."

"I'm sure that's natural," I said. "It'll come back to you soon enough. Once you're better."

She swung her legs off the couch and stood up in a single motion. I stood back, eyes wide open. "Hey, you need to take it easy—"

She wobbled over to the window and peeked through the blinds. Daylight caused her eyes to narrow. She glanced over her shoulder. "I'm hungry."

"Caroline's gone for supplies. She'll be back any minute."

Her face darkened. "Caroline Heidrich?"

"Yes," I said. "She helped us escape, don't you remember?"

"I don't trust her. We should leave now."

I joined her at the window. "I don't trust her either, but there are bad people after us, and now they're after her too."

She shook her head firmly. "No, Will. They're after me. She's part of it."

"What do you mean? Part of what? Tell me what's going on?"

She closed her eyes, and I saw her eyeballs move under her eyelids like she was having a REM dream. She flopped back down on the couch, so I sat next to her and put my arm around her shoulders. She leaned in and wrapped her arms around me. I felt her head shaking back and forth, her chest rising and falling like she was gulping for air. Then it slowed down as if she was relaxing, talking herself down from a panic attack.

"Alex, what can you tell me?" I said.

She became still and then looked me in the eye. "They won't stop until they have me. I know that much."

"Why do they want you?" I said, trying to be patient.

She looked away with a thousand-yard stare. "They're experimenting on me."

"Christian?"

"All of them."

I gently put a hand on her cheek and turned her face to mine. "What have they done to you, Alex?"

Tears welled up in her eyes, and her face crumpled. She shook her head. "I just recall bits and pieces. Random images. Nothing makes sense. Nothing seems real."

I nodded and leaned in. "Alex, you've been missing for over two years. You were declared dead. I've been grieving you all this time. This is . . . the most wonderful thing to have happened. To find you again." She gave me a watery smile but said nothing. I decided to press on. "We need to figure out what happened to you in South America."

She closed her eyes and leaned against me. Her voice was soft and barely audible. I leaned in to hear her. "I told you I don't remember," she murmured.

I tried not to grind my teeth with frustration. "What's the last thing you *do* remember?"

She looked up at the ceiling. "You waving me off at LAX. I saw that you'd posted a video of it on the HoloWeb."

"And that's it? Nothing after that?"

She shook her head and buried it in my shoulder. "I'm sorry, Will."

I hugged her and said nothing. I realized I was leaning against her injured shoulder and drew back in case I was hurting her. The gauze bandages had fallen off, and I could see the skin through the hole in her shirt. It looked to be healing well, the wound was barely visible, just a thin slit.

Which was crazy, wasn't it? She'd only been shot a few hours ago. At that moment, there was a noise from the gym as the door opened. "That'll be Caroline with breakfast," I said, standing.

Then I heard Nico's voice.

I walked out of my office and quickly shut the door behind me. Nico was standing by the main entrance, taking off his headphones and putting them into a backpack, which he slung over a shoulder. He was wearing board shorts, a Gold's Gym sweatshirt, and sunglasses. His wavy hair was casually uncombed. The archetypal beach-bum look.

"Hello, Nico," I said.

"Will, is that you?" he said, squinting in the semidarkness. "What'cha doing here?"

I glanced back at the office and tried to give off a nonchalant shrug. "Crashed here last night. Too wasted to make it home; you know how it is."

"Thought you'd dropped off the face of the earth, man," he said, opening his arms for a hug.

I grabbed him, returned the hug, and slapped his back. "Sorry, got caught up. Emma . . ."

He raised his eyebrows, a grin spreading across his face. "Emma? From the blind date? *Dude* . . ."

I shrugged, kept my arm around his shoulders, and gently turned him back toward the entrance. He held up a hand. "Wait, I seem to remember she got some asshole to rough me up back at the club. I mean, what the fuck was that all about?"

I chewed the inside of my lip. I didn't think he'd seen me hustled into the vans outside the club by Caroline's goons, because at that time he'd been face down on the floor with one of the nightclub bouncers kneeling on his back. He'd been pretty wasted, so I hoped that his recollection was sketchy at best.

"Nah, that wasn't Emma, that was just was just some psycho. She tried to bag a lift home with me, but I managed to escape."

A slow smile spread over Nico's face. "Okay, so I guess Emma and you caught up somewhere else that night?"

"Yeah, got another text from her. I met her at the Angel Bar on Twelfth." The lies kept coming. I glanced back at the office, to where Alex was hopefully staying out of sight. "So, what're you doing here?"

"I need to look at the documentation on the lease—actually we both need to. While you've been AWOL, the landlord's been agitating me again." He pointed to the office. "Come on, I'll show you. I think he's full of shit, but—"

"Wait," I said, putting my arm out.

"What?"

"Can we do this some other time? I'm, like, not alone here . . ." I flicked a head at the office door. "She's sleeping it off as well."

His smile broadened. "You dog. In our office too."

I shrugged, like, "What can I say?"

He wagged a finger at me. "You and Alex had some pretty good party times in there as well, if I recall."

He must have seen my face fall, because he immediately stopped joking. "Man, I'm sorry. Look, I'm pleased for you, really." He put the other strap of his backpack on and wiggled it in place. "It's all good, man. I'll call back later this afternoon and get the papers. But we really need to catch up over a beer. Debrief and all that."

I heaved a sigh of relief and ushered him to the door just as a shadow passed the window.

The door opened, and Caroline backed in, carrying a tray of coffees and a bag from Dunkin' Donuts. She saw Nico and froze.

"I remember you," said Nico, smiling broadly. He raised his eyebrows at me and then nodded toward the office. "So, who's in there, then?"

Caroline said nothing but kicked the door shut behind her. I looked pleadingly at her, hoping she could read the room. "Caroline, this is my friend Nico. He's just leaving."

Nico folded his arms and gave a lopsided grin. "Caroline, huh?" he said. "You got me roughed up by your nightclub pals. That wasn't very nice."

I held up a hand conciliatory-like. "Nico, we were all drunk. I'm sure it wasn't Caroline who—"

"Oh, I never forget a pretty face," interrupted Nico. "Certainly not one as A-grade as hers. What are you doing with this guy?" he said, flicking a thumb at me. "I'm here now."

This was Nico's idea of flirting, and to be honest, it had gotten him a long way. But if looks could kill, Nico would be six feet under at this point.

Caroline ignored him and turned to me. "He can't know we were here, Will."

Nico put his hand on his heart. "I promise not to tell anyone, I swear. Your little secret is safe with me."

"You don't understand," I started, but Nico was staring open-mouthed over my shoulder.

I turned to see that door to my office was open and Alex was standing there.

"Alex?" said Nico hesitantly.

"Hello, Nico," she replied in an oddly detached tone.

Nico stared at me, bewilderment all over his face. "What the hell, man . . . I don't understand. What's going on?"

Caroline put the tray with the coffees onto a bench, and I saw her reach behind her back where I knew she'd kept her gun. Nico took a few steps toward Alex and then stopped. "Alex, is it really you?"

"Yes, Nico."

He looked at me again, mouth open. "I don't . . . I . . . we went to her funeral. It's been years. How is this possible?"

Caroline stepped between Nico and Alex, her hand still hidden in the small of her back. "Alex, go back in the office," she said calmly, not taking her eyes off Nico.

Alex just stood there, a blank look on her face.

"Alex . . . ," she said firmly, a hand out. "Will and I just need to talk to Nico."

"Were you followed?" said Alex.

"What?" said Caroline. "Of course not."

Alex pointed toward the front entrance. "Then who are those people?"

CHAPTER THIRTEEN

More shadows crossed the shuttered window, and the screech of car tires echoed in the alleyway. There were no flashing lights or sirens, so I figured they weren't likely to be the police. Caroline pulled out her gun and pushed Nico down behind one of the dumbbell racks.

"It's Christian. Has to be," she hissed.

I ducked down under the windowsill and looked across the gym at Alex. She was still standing in the doorway of the office, watching us. Her expression was detached, and I wondered whether she was in shock. I crabbed over to the front door, reached up, and locked it, easing the bolts in at the top and bottom as quietly as I could.

"There's a window at the back of the office, which leads to an alleyway," I said to Caroline. "We can get out there."

"Go," she whispered. "I'll cover you."

With Nico hard on my heels, I ran back to the office and pushed Alex inside. We hunkered down behind the desk, breathing heavily. Caroline joined us a few moments later and pulled the office door closed.

"Get that window open," she urged.

I fiddled with the clasp. It was a stiff, old sash-type affair, but eventually I wiggled it open to a gap of about two feet but no more. I poked my head outside and looked up and down the alley. "It's clear," I said.

"What if they're also coming round the back?" Nico said, his eyes wide.

"We don't really have much choice, do we?" I shot back.

Caroline looked grimly out the window and then nodded at Alex. "She can go first."

I frowned, but Alex stood up and threaded her legs awkwardly through the gap. She pushed off and dropped to the alleyway about six feet below.

I gestured to Nico, but he shook his head. "What the hell's going on, Will?"

"I don't have time to explain," I said. "Trust me. We need to get out of here."

To his credit, he grunted an acknowledgment and climbed awkwardly through the window. I went next, followed by Caroline. There was no one around. The alley was narrow and lined with wooden fence posts, and we were at the end of a cul-de-sac. The other end opened onto Fourteenth Street, just visible about thirty yards away, bordered with trees.

"Do you still park your truck in Sam's yard?" I said to Nico.

He looked flushed but oddly excited. "Sure do."

I turned to Caroline. "It's only a block away. Corner of Twelfth."

"We'd better hurry, then," she replied, looking anxiously up at the window.

We set off, keeping low. I grabbed Alex's hand, Caroline and Nico bringing up the rear. We'd reached the end of the street when I heard the window smashing. I risked a look back, and two black-clad guys were climbing out and dropping into the alley. They saw us running, and one of them seemed to be talking into his wrist. Probably into one of the ISIS bracelets.

We jinked left at the end of the alley and encountered traffic on the main street, which felt weirdly comforting. We ran across the road and down another alleyway directly opposite. This one took us past a couple of low-set houses with scrappy, untended yards.

I waited for Caroline, but she'd stopped and was pointing her gun back the way we'd come.

"Come on," I urged. "We're nearly there."

She gave me a tight look. "Wait a second." Then she fired two shots followed by two more. Tight groups. Echoing loudly in the confined space.

"That won't keep them occupied for long," she said, vaulting over the low wire fence into the yard. "But it might slow them down, knowing we're armed."

Nico was waving for us to keep moving. He and Alex were crouching by the side of another fence, and he pointed through a gap to a small paved area where a couple of pickup trucks and a battered old Caddy were parked. I recognized his ride, a 2017 Dodge Ram with peeling red paint.

"Keys under the driver's seat, doors unlocked," he said, breathlessly. "I'll drive."

I shook my head. "You're a shit driver."

"Harsh, but true," he smiled.

Caroline peeked through the gap. There was about twenty yards of open road to cross. Two young dudes jogged past, headphones on and sweating into tracksuits. A woman pushing a stroller was crossing the road, cooing to a baby. A garbage truck slowly turned the corner and stopped to let her cross.

Urban life, in all its normality.

Caroline raised her gun. "I'll cover you. Keep your heads down and run. When you're in the truck, stay low." She shot Nico a look. "And I'm fucking driving."

He was about to argue, but she'd already moved along to the edge of the fence and was pointing her gun back down the alleyway. I grabbed Alex, and we ran, knees bent, awkward, and slow. I heard Nico's footsteps following us, so I didn't look back. The garbage truck had moved away, as had the joggers, but the mom and stroller were now level with Nico's truck. She looked up, and when she saw us, she stopped, a puzzled look on her face. I waved frantically at her to move along, but she'd frozen.

As we pulled alongside her, there was a loud bang, unmistakably a gunshot, from where Caroline was crouching. The mom flinched and dove down next to her stroller, looking anxiously every which way. Another gunshot rang out, and I heard the subsonic whine as the bullet passed between us.

"We gotta move!" I screamed, grabbing her by the arm. "Nico, grab the stroller!"

The woman started to struggle, but I pulled her roughly toward the Dodge, and Nico pushed the stroller in front of us until we were safely behind two and a half tons of metal and V8 engine. The baby in the stroller had started to cry, and his mom picked him out and hugged him, her eyes wide and full of alarm.

"Where's Alex gone?" said Nico.

In the confusion, I'd lost track of her. I sneaked a look over the hood. She was standing in the middle of the road, calmly watching Caroline running full pelt toward her. Caroline twisted and squeezed off another shot toward the fence where there were now two or three black figures crouching down. I saw a flash and heard a loud, metallic clang as a bullet smacked into the side of the Dodge.

"Alex, come over here!" I shouted.

More bullets hit the Dodge's door, and I ducked as paint and metallic chips ricocheted into my hair. I dropped to my stomach and crawled under the truck so I could still see around the wheel. Caroline had now grabbed Alex and was dragging her toward us. More shots rang out, and concrete shards exploded from the pavement a few feet away from them. Then there was another shot, and Caroline twitched and doubled up. She dropped the gun and fell to her knees.

Alex just stopped and stared at her.

I shuffled around the wheel and jumped to my feet. I couldn't think of anything other than getting them to safety.

"Get the truck started!" I yelled to Nico.

Caroline was reaching for her gun, which had bounced a few feet away. There was a spreading patch of crimson on her stomach, and her face was twisted in pain. I ran past her and scooped up the gun. One of the goons had stood up and was running toward us. I pointed and fired, amazed that my hand wasn't shaking. The recoil shook my wrist, and the bullet went astray.

But it had the desired effect, and the guy jinked left and ducked behind a parked car. I remembered my army training and pulled the trigger again, and this time, my bullet skidded off the car's side mirror next to his head, showering him in debris.

I grabbed Caroline's arm and hauled her to her feet. "Get up," I yelled, ignoring her scream. "Alex, grab her other arm!"

Alex did as she was told, and we shuffled as fast as possible toward the truck. Nico had opened both doors and was lying prone on the passenger side. I glanced back and saw the goon getting up from behind the car. Two others emerged from the side of the fence, so I pointed the gun again and pulled the trigger twice more. Holes exploded in the wood, and they ducked down again. I wondered how many bullets I had left.

I shoved Caroline and Alex into the back seats and closed the door. Nico started the engine, and I jumped behind the wheel.

"Where's the mom?" I yelled, sweat pouring down my face.

Nico pointed out of the window, and I saw her running away down an alley, baby in her arms, the stroller tipped over on its side and one of the wheels spinning.

"She's safe," he said.

"Safer than us," I murmured under my breath and gunned the engine. The side window exploded from another bullet, and glass sprayed over my lap and into my face. I blinked and wiped my eyes, and my hand came away smeared with blood.

"Get your heads down," I said, grabbing Nico behind the neck and giving him a shove. I floored the accelerator and yanked the wheel round, and the big V8 roared as we skidded out of the lot and bounced off the sidewalk. The nearest goon raised his gun again, and I closed my eyes as the truck hit him head on. He spun over the hood like a rag doll and disappeared out of sight. I twisted the wheel hard over and we careered off, just missing a car rounding the corner. We headed up Twelfth at about eighty miles an hour and went around a T-junction on two wheels, tires smoking and leaving rubber on the asphalt. I dodged around traffic coming both ways and took random turns, with only a vague idea where I was going. I knew the neighborhood pretty well, but with all the adrenaline flowing, I was finding it hard to think and see straight.

As we rounded another corner, just missing an elderly couple out for their morning stroll, Nico put his hand on my arm. "Slow down, you're going to get someone killed."

I knew he was right, but adrenaline was fueling my muscles and tendons. The chase and the gunfight were bringing out a primal fear, emptying my reserve tank and making me ignore everything in the pursuit of escape and safety. I risked a glance in the rearview mirror, and Alex's face stared back at me. Her eyes were clear, her expression still oddly blank.

"Are you alright?" I said.

"Yes," she replied, "but Caroline isn't."

I twisted around, and my heart sank. Caroline was lying with her head on Alex's lap, looking gray and sweaty. She was staring into space, and her mouth was parted in a tight O. Her breaths were coming ragged and fast, and the front of her cream sweater was a horrible dark crimson.

"What about over there?" said Nico, pointing up the street. Ahead was the Santa Monica Medical Center on Fifteenth. "It's got an ER."

"You're right," I said. "This has gone too far."

"No," said Caroline, her voice weak. "It's too late. We must keep going. You need to get some distance."

"But—" I said.

"It's too—" Her eyes closed, and her head fell back.

I banged my hands on the wheel in frustration and fear.

"There! Go to that school," shouted Nico. "It's our best chance."

The entrance to Lincoln Middle School was ahead. The main gate was closed, but there was a flimsy-looking chain fence separating the road from a parking lot and the playing fields. Beyond was a schoolyard with a dozen or so basketball courts, but no one was playing hoops.

I turned off the road and, without stopping, drove the truck through the fence and onto the courts. There were a couple of large white buildings at the bottom of the field, so I gunned the Dodge across the courts and drove it in between two of the buildings until we came to a stop against a dumpster. I turned the engine off. The motor ticked for a few seconds and then went quiet. I sat back in the seat and looked into the mirror. I waited. We were completely out of sight of the road and invisible to anyone walking past the school. The gap I'd blown through the fence might raise some eyebrows, but that was the least of my worries at this time. I twisted in the seat again.

Alex was cradling Caroline's head in her lap, gently stroking her face. Caroline's eyes were open, her pupils big and black.

"Shit," I said. "Shit, shit, shit."

"Now what?" said Nico.

I stared at Alex, not knowing what to say or what I was doing.

She then did something strange. She put her other hand on top of Caroline's stomach where the bullet wound was and started to move it side to side like she was cleaning a window.

"We need to leave her," Nico said. "She's dead, man. We need to get out of here."

He was right. There was nothing we could do for Caroline, and we still had Christian's goons looking for us.

"Alex, he's right," I said gently. "We should go, now."

She looked at me and then gave a strange smile. "Caroline tried to save my life back there, didn't she? Just like you did."

I nodded, not sure what else to say.

She continued to move her hand over Caroline's bullet wound. Back and forth. Hovering an inch or so above the surface.

"Then I should save her life in return, shouldn't I?"

CHAPTER FOURTEEN

Nico kicked open a side door, and Alex and I carried Caroline through to a changing area that had the smell of adolescent sweat and industrial cleansers. A row of benches divided the room in half, and dark-blue lockers bookended both sides, some with football shirts draped over their doors. Soccer balls, helmets, and towels were scattered untidily around low tables and over the floor. High windows let in diffuse sunlight, and dust motes floated lazily down.

We laid Caroline out on one of the benches, and I rolled up one of the football shirts and placed it under her head. She wasn't breathing, and her lips were now navy blue.

"I'll get some more towels," said Nico and headed into the showers.

Alex knelt beside Caroline and stroked her hair. "She's not dead," she said softly.

I blew out my cheeks. "Are you sure? She looks it."

She placed her hand on the front of Caroline's sweater and waggled her fingers. Pooled blood splashed onto the bench.

"What are you doing?" I asked, genuinely perplexed.

She put a finger to her lips and closed her eyes. She pulled Caroline's sweater up, exposing the entry wound. It was still oozing, but with the blackish sludge of a postmortem wound. She put two fingers into the hole and then stretched it so that her whole hand fit inside. I felt my stomach turning and a wave of nausea came over me.

"Alex, please," I said softly. "It's too late."

She gave no sign that she'd heard me. Her hand moved inside Caroline's abdomen, the skin rippling and more blood spurting out with the pressure. After a few seconds, she pulled her hand out of the wound and laid it over the now-gaping hole. She gathered the edges together with her fingers and pressed down, and the skin underneath rippled like a stone plunging into a tranquil pond. She lifted her hand up, and instead of the wound gaping, the edges had come together. She turned her hand over to reveal a bullet, deformed by the impact.

"She should be okay now," she said and sat back on her haunches, smiling. Then she promptly collapsed.

I managed to grab her before she hit the floor and gently guided her into the recovery position. I felt for a pulse in her neck and found it instantly, reassuringly slow and steady. I sat down on the bench and put my head in my hands, trying to process what had just happened.

Nico appeared around the corner carrying a pile of blue fluffy towels. "Found these," he said. He looked at me, at Caroline, and now at Alex lying on the floor. "What's going on?"

I shook my head. "I have absolutely no idea."

He bent down to look at Alex. "Is she sleeping again?"

I gave a manic laugh. "It wouldn't surprise me."

Nico shrugged. "Been a big day, I guess."

Understatement of the decade.

It was then that I noticed that Alex's shoulder, where she'd been shot, was dry as a bone. I remembered that she had helped me carry Caroline using that arm. It shouldn't have been possible. The bullet had gone right through her shoulder and out the other side, almost certainly shattering her shoulder blade into pieces. I reached over and gently tugged the collar of her tunic, loosening a few buttons to expose the top of her arm and her neck. There was no wound.

Nothing.

"She was shot," I said to no one in particular.

"When?" said Nico.

I laughed again, a crazy snort. "Like a few hours ago." I sat back and leaned against the locker. "She was shot in the upper chest and shoulder. The bullet went right through. I saw it happen."

Nico's eyebrows furrowed. "That's crazy, man," he said. "There's no sign of it. How's that even possible?"

I felt cold, like I was in a waking dream. Nothing felt right. It was surreal, like a Dali painting.

Nico was now squatting down, looking at Caroline. He reached out to touch her face. Caroline took a deep breath.

Nico lost his balance and fell backward, eyes wide as dinner plates. Caroline's color returned, and her chest heaved as she breathed in and out. Nico skittered like a newborn lamb, his feet scrabbling as he reversed into a locker with a crash. "No way, man. She was fuckin' dead. What's going on? Will, what is *fucking happening here*?"

I took hold of Caroline's hand. It was warm. Almost reflexively, her fingers closed around mine. Her eyes flickered under the lids but didn't open. Her mouth parted for a second, and her tongue flicked out as if to wet her lips.

Nico was starting to babble. "Man, this is some zombie shit, right? It's like that movie, you know, the one with Brad Pitt, Jesus yes, it's—"

"Nico," I said, getting in his face and placing my hands on his shoulders. "It's nothing to do with zombies." I looked down at Alex. "All I know is that today I got my wife back."

Nico's eyes were crazy. "Are you sure that's your wife?" he said.

I sent Nico out to check on the car and turn it around in case we needed to make a quick getaway. And to scope the area to see if anyone was following us. Actually, I just needed him to get some space and get his shit together. I also needed to get my own shit squared away. This was a middle school. Kids would maybe come and play hoops soon, even if there were no official events this weekend. Someone was bound to come along any minute. We needed to move.

"Will?"

Caroline's eyes had opened, and she was looking at me. She tried to get up, so I helped her into a sitting position. She put her hands on her knees and took a couple of deep breaths.

"How are you feeling?" I ventured cagily.

She swallowed and grimaced. "Strange, I . . . wait—" She doubled over and vomited onto the mat at her feet. Blackish fluid, like altered blood. I put my hand on her back and rubbed it as her heaving continued, then eventually slowed down. When she sat back, I used one of the towels to wipe her mouth and face.

"Thank you," she said, breathing deeply.

"Would you like something to drink? There's a water fountain over there."

She shook her head and then caught sight of the sweater she was wearing. It was stained dark red with an obvious bullet hole. She pulled it up to expose her abdomen. The wound was almost completely healed; a flesh-colored, cobweb-like effect the only remnant of any injury.

She looked up at me and started to hyperventilate. "Will, I was shot. I—what the hell?"

I knelt and took hold of her hand. "It's fine, Caroline, you're okay."

She shook her head forcefully and repeatedly. "No, Will, it's pretty fucking far from okay. I was shot! How am I—"

I pointed to Alex who was curled up in the fetal position on the mat. "We'll need to ask her."

"Wake her up then," she said.

I shook my head, wondering if I should tell her what I saw Alex doing to her. "She . . . blacked out. Something happened."

Caroline raised her eyebrows, waiting for more. I met her stare and shrugged.

"Right, right . . ." she said, getting unsteadily to her feet. She put a hand on my shoulder, took a step forward, and then stopped, leaning wearily against one of the lockers.

"Turn around," she said.

I frowned. "Why?"

Her lip curled. "Because I'm going to take this sweater off."

"Ah, okay."

I went back over to Alex and gave her shoulder a little shake, but she didn't stir. I gathered her tunic up around her neck and fastened up the buttons, absently stroking her hair and tucking it behind her ear.

Wait a second. There had always been a mole behind her right ear. It was quite prominent, and she hated it, but I'd loved it and teased her that it just made her appear less perfect than she was.

The mole was absent.

A cold shiver trickled down my neck.

Caroline squatted down beside me. She was now wearing an oversized white football jersey with a big 21 in yellow letters on the back and Lincoln All Stars on the front.

"You really had nothing to do with any of this, did you?" she said.

"I told you, no," I replied.

"I'm sorry," she said. "For the kidnapping and all that. It's just—"

I stopped her. "I know. Becker made you do it."

She grimaced. "Yes he did, but that doesn't—"

"Forget it," I said, sitting back against a locker.

She nodded and joined me with a grunt, still looking a bit off-color. We both stared at Alex curled up on the floor, apparently sleeping soundly. I decided to share what had been on my mind since our escape, and what was bothering me.

"In the laboratory—the one with the sign saying *nanofiber* or something—I found a . . ." I stopped as the nightmarish vision appeared. "There was a body. Jin, I think his name was. The doctor. He'd been, like, completely eviscerated. Exploded, almost. There was nothing left but bloody smears on the floor. Some of the equipment near him . . . like robotic claws . . . was covered in blood." Caroline looked horrified but remained silent. I continued, "What went on in that lab? What kind of research?"

She took a deep breath and let it out slowly. "It wasn't my area of research. You've got to understand that most of the departments at Singularity were doing their own thing. Based on instructions from the Pandora computer of course."

"But Pandora was disconnected from everything, you said. Isolated behind that Faraday cage."

"Yes, but that was for security reasons. Christian pointed out that Pandora was so smart, so super intelligent, that it posed an unacceptable risk of breaking out and seizing control of its own destiny. So, everything we obtained from it was downloaded within the cage and brought out physically via hard drives."

"So Pandora was truly intelligent," I breathed softly.

"Oh yes, but uniquely so. Intelligence is defined as an ability to accomplish complex goals and isn't measured by a single IQ test but on an ability spectrum across all goals. Up until Pandora, all artificial intelligence was narrow, with each system able to accomplish only very specific goals—like beating a human grandmaster at chess. Human intelligence is remarkably broad, and it far outguns any AI system across a broad range of goals." She paused. "Christian said Pandora had achieved sentience and was displaying 'human-like' traits. Said it would easily pass the Turing test."

I opened my mouth, then closed it again. "Sentient, meaning 'alive'?"

Caroline smiled faintly. "In philosophical terms, *sentience* just means the capacity to be aware of feelings and sensations. It evolved into a term for some 'thing' or some creature that can suffer or feel pain. To have an awareness of sensation, to reason, to think . . ." She shook her head. "It's hard to define. Some people think animals are sentient because they can also experience joy, pleasure, pain, and fear."

"But Pandora is just a computer," I said. "Electrical signals and circuits."

"Our brains are computers. Meat computers. Our thoughts, our dreams, what we think of as our consciousness, it's all electrical signals. Not that we understand consciousness, of course." She paused, and her voice went quiet. "Pandora was nothing like any computer on Earth."

"It scared you, didn't it," I said, a statement not a question.

"Christian said that it had to be kept confined forever because we couldn't be certain that its goals, when they became self-evident, would align with ours."

"Ours, meaning Becker's?"

She arched her eyebrows. "Ours, meaning humanity's."

"Right," I said, feeling cold again.

Caroline nodded, a tight smile on her lips. "The singularity."

"Yes, why is the company called that? Catchy, but strange."

"Not strange if you know the field of AI research. The singularity was a controversial idea, coined a decade or so ago, which said that there will be a tipping point where a computer is produced of such complexity and power that it triggers a dramatic change and induces exponential technological growth that will result in unforeseeable changes to human civilization. Christian said that Pandora was the singularity and hence named his company after it."

This is what I'd not been able to get my head around. Christian Becker was a brilliant man, but he wasn't a computer programmer. He was an innovator, a "disrupter" or whatever the newspapers' favorite term for him was.

"I don't understand how Christian built Pandora from scratch," I said.

Caroline shrugged. "It wasn't just him, he'd gotten a team of . . ." She paused and looked up. "He said there were lots of smart programmers that joined us for big bucks from all over the world. Christian would name-drop them all the time. But I never met any of them."

"Didn't you find that odd?"

"In retrospect, I guess so," she murmured. "I supposed that there were other sites that I didn't know about. I was just based at the Singularity facility near San Diego where we took you."

"What about Jerry? Who was he?"

"Retired and headhunted by Christian. Used to work at UCLA. A cosmologist and machine-learning researcher. Smart. Nice guy, actually."

I was about to laugh and make a snide comment when Alex twitched and stirred. I made to go to her, but she just curled further into a ball, tucking her head in to her neck. I sat down again and turned back to Caroline. "So Christian was using Pandora to make money?"

She gave me a look that said, "Duh." Then she said, "Have you heard of the term 'enslaved god'?"

I shook my head.

"Not many people have, sorry. A physicist at MIT called Max Tegmark coined it. He'd postulated the development of a super-intelligent AI, confined by its human programmers, who'd use it to produce unimaginable technology and wealth."

"For the betterment of humanity?" I said naively.

Caroline gave a cynical smile. "Well, wouldn't that depend on the human controllers?"

Yeah, right. Christian hadn't exactly been the altruistic kind. I stood up and stretched, rolling my neck and wincing at the cracks and creaks. "Nico is taking his time. I sent him to move the car."

Caroline's eyes narrowed, and she pulled herself to her feet. "I'll go check. You stay with Alex." She looked around the floor. "Where's my gun?"

I reached around my back and pulled it from my belt. I handed it over, butt first. She ejected the magazine and emptied it into her palm. I counted six bullets. She racked them back in and tucked it under her shirt, heading for the door. "Back soon."

I squatted next to Alex and watched her sleep. Her chest was moving slowly and peacefully. I almost expected her to start snoring.

An image flashed into my head, a snapshot from the past, out of time. Alex, her hair blowing in a spring breeze, her youthful face turned toward the sun. She spun, dancing with the joy of the life within her, bare feet kicking up sand. Behind her, guests at our wedding clapped and cheered, arms held high. Nico, holding his phone in one hand, beer in the other, filming everything, his ubiquitous Hawaiian shirt flapping in the wind. The ocean was a stunning aquamarine with white horses on the gently breaking tide.

The sound of running feet snapped me back to reality. Caroline appeared, her face flushed. "Your pal's fucked us over. The truck's gone."

CHAPTER FIFTEEN

Alex was still out for the count as I picked her up and carried her through the changing rooms to the exit. Again, I was surprised at how much she weighed. She was small, about five foot six, with a slim, athletic physique. She couldn't have weighed more than 110 pounds, but it seemed like twice that. Maybe I was just out of shape.

Caroline stood at the exit, peeking around the corner, gun in both hands—textbook *NCIS*-style. She gestured for me to ease up, so I stopped and leaned back against the wall. Alex's eyes flickered, and she put her hands around my neck but didn't wake.

"Wait here till I call for you," Caroline said and stepped round the door, gun first.

I waited, listening. I heard tires screeching and brakes squealing. I closed my eyes, too tired to move. I waited for gunshots.

I heard running footsteps, and then Caroline reappeared.

"It's good," she said. "Quickly . . ."

I edged sideways through the door and out into the yard. Nico stood there, breathless, eyes wide, and beaming.

"Dude, where've you been?" I hissed.

He flicked a thumb backward. "Changed the car. Thought we needed new wheels."

"Good call, I would say," Caroline agreed. "I'm sure they've tagged the Dodge."

"You stole a car?" I said.

He looked hurt. "Borrowed, more like. I left mine with the keys in the ignition in the guy's garage. It's worth more than this piece of shit anyway—"

Caroline got between us. "Can we have this discussion later? Let's fucking move!"

"Right," said Nico. "Follow me."

He led the way around the corner to where he'd left his ride, engine running. It was a Chevy Impala, dark blue. Old. Nondescript.

A good choice for fugitives trying to hide, actually.

Caroline opened the rear door, and I folded Alex into the seat and squeezed in next to her. Nico jumped in the passenger side; unsurprisingly, Caroline took the driver's seat. She threw the car into gear and screeched across the basketball courts and out through the fence that we'd destroyed. We bounced onto the main road, somehow managed to avoid a collision with a garbage truck, and joined the traffic going north.

"Where we heading?" Nico said, rolling down his window.

Caroline threw a glance at me through the rearview mirror and raised her eyebrows in a question. I was about to reply with an expletive when Alex sat up and leaned on the back of Caroline's seat.

"We need to go to the Natural History Museum of Los Angeles," she said.

"What the . . ." I frowned.

She put a hand on my arm. "Please, Will," she said.

Caroline was studying her through the mirror, eyes narrowed. "Why there?"

Alex sat back and returned her stare. "It's important."

Nico twisted in his seat, a lopsided grin on his face. "Why not? Let's face it, no one will be expecting us to go there, of all places. Am I right?"

He had a point.

"Alex," I said. "Will you tell us what this is all about?"

She gave me an enigmatic smile. "Do you trust me?"

I looked exasperatedly at Caroline. "Do you know how to get there?"

She nodded and looked at her watch. "It'll take us a couple of hours. It's rush hour."

"I'm hungry," said Nico. "What say we get some breakfast?"

The diner was constructed out of a train carriage, '50s chic. Along one side of the carriage there was a bar with stools riveted to the floor every couple feet. The carpet was a red-and-white diamond pattern, and the four-person booths along the windows had red faux-leather seats and red tablecloths. The kitchen was at the front, and the restrooms were at the rear. Johnny Cash was crooning from an old-style jukebox, and there was a not-unpleasant aroma of bacon and coffee. It was half full with a mix of families, couples, and just ordinary folks getting breakfast on their way to work. All seemingly with not a care in the world, although I knew that behind every face was a person with his or her own struggles and problems. Owning a café had made me understand the benefits of company. The conversations that took place, the chance to make casual bonds, the routine of seeing one another.

We squeezed into one of the booths: Alex and me on one side, Caroline and Nico on the other. Alex immediately started examining the ketchup and mustard station, picking up the bottles and turning them over. Caroline watched her; eyebrows furrowed. A waitress arrived, licking her pencil before scribbling something on a notepad. She looked up and gave us all her best morning smile. She had tired eyes, yet there was a glimmer of a spark behind them.

"Welcome to Tom's Diner," she said brightly. "Y'all here for breakfast?"

"We are indeed," said Nico, giving her a big smile in return.

"Have you had a chance to look at the menu?"

"Er, no. Sorry," I mumbled. "Any specials?"

She shook her head and pointed above the bar where the menu items were also displayed. "Just what you see. Can I fix you up with some coffees first?"

"I'd love a cappuccino," I said. "Caroline?"

She nodded, and I turned to Alex who hadn't seemed to notice the waitress and had her head stuck in the menu. "Alex? Your usual?"

She looked up. "My usual what?"

"Coffee."

"Okay."

"What would that be?" the waitress asked with a head tilt.

Alex smiled at her. "Whatever. Coffee."

The waitress gave her a look as if to say, "Give me a break," but instead shrugged and said, "Black coffee, then."

I frowned. Alex had been a bit of a coffee snob. She'd always insisted on good fresh beans, not the stewed stuff that had been sitting in a pot on the shelf for hours. Courtesy of years being on-call at the hospital, she had told me once. She'd also moved on to almond milk before she'd . . . gone missing.

The waitress left, and Nico sat back and folded his arms. "Think I'm going to have pancakes and ice cream. Worked up an appetite, don'tcha know?" He looked over at Alex, who was still staring at the menu. "Alex, what are you eating?"

She put the menu down and folded it in half. "Not hungry."

Caroline's expression was unreadable. She was staring at Alex like she was observing an animal in a zoo. The waitress returned with a carafe of tap water and four glasses. I poured them out for us and took a sip.

Caroline leaned forward, elbows on the table, and addressed Alex. "What happened back there?"

Alex looked up and returned the stare, unblinking. "What do you mean?"

Caroline's lip twitched. "I was shot. In fact, so were you. Why is it that neither of us seem to be dying from our wounds?"

Alex gave her a blank look. "Isn't it enough that you're alive?"

Caroline sat back in her chair. "Are you serious?"

I reached over and put a hand on Alex's arm. "Alex, come on, we need answers here. We have so many questions. Surely you understand that?"

Alex just continued her emotionless stare and said nothing. Caroline banged a fist on the table. I looked around to see if anyone had noticed, but the other diners were engrossed in newspapers or their phones, or actually eating.

"It was you, Alex. Singularity's crash. How did you do it?" she hissed. "*Why* did you do it?"

Alex shrugged dismissively. "Why does anybody want to do anything?"

Caroline was starting to fume. "Why did your photograph—and Will's—come up on our systems when they crashed?"

Alex's face creased into a beatific smile. "I needed you to bring Will to me."

Ice trickled down my neck. "You did that?"

She nodded. "Of course I did."

"Why?"

She gave a little laugh. "Isn't it obvious?"

"Not to me," I said, my voice rising.

Alex returned her gaze to her hands and absently turned them around, wiggling her fingers. "To free me from my prison," she said in a singsong voice.

Caroline's face darkened. "Free you? You weren't a prisoner at Singularity. I'd never heard of you"—she flicked a thumb in my direction— "or him for that matter, before this went down."

"Caroline, I did find her there—" I began.

"No, Will," she interrupted. "I knew that place inside out. I was head of fucking security. Read my lips: she wasn't a prisoner there."

A police car with its siren blaring sped past the window, and Alex twisted in her seat to watch it pass. We were opposite the main highway, and the traffic was picking up. She turned back to Caroline. "Of course I was a prisoner. Christian made sure of that."

Caroline threw her hands in the air. "I give up. None of this makes sense. You're talking in riddles."

The waitress arrived with our coffees, and we lapsed into silence as she distributed them around the table. "Have you decided on what you want to eat?" she asked, bringing out her pad.

Nico ordered his pancakes, but no one else seemed hungry. The waitress left, vaguely disappointed.

When she was out of earshot, Caroline pointed a finger at Alex. "Okay, I'll bite. Where did Christian keep you, then? And more to the point, why?"

Alex returned Caroline's gaze. "You know the answers to your questions, Caroline, if you just think about it."

"Just fucking answer the question," Caroline said exasperatedly.

Alex suddenly stood and stretched. "I'm going to the restroom. Please excuse me."

Caroline's hand shot out and grabbed her wrist. "Not on your own, you're not."

Alex gave a shrug. "Of course. That's what girls do, right?"

Caroline squeezed past Nico, and they both shuffled up the aisle toward the restrooms. I watched them go, a nagging headache beginning in my temples.

"Alright," said Nico, leaning forward. "They've gone. Tell me what's really happening, man. I mean. Alex was dead, right? Caroline was shot in the gut, and now she's, like, not. Alex is behaving strangely, as well, don't you think? I mean, something's happened to her, hasn't it? Something do with Caroline and that company, Singularity?"

I took a long drink of my coffee and put the cup down, encircling it with both hands. "Where to begin . . ."

I told him about my internment and interrogation at Singularity. About meeting Christian, the drones, and the Pandora computer in the Faraday cage. About Alex contacting me, and the tsunami of emotions that it triggered. All that stuff about how she'd missed me. The speech I'd made at the wake. Then the escape, and . . . the body in the lab.

"What do you think happened to him?" Nico said, looking queasy.

I closed my eyes, and the image reappeared in all its goriness. The ripped lab coat and clothes. Blackened goo intermixed with blood and gore but no shape or form. No body. No . . . nothing.

"I have no idea," I said. "But it was a person. A doctor. I met him."

"You recognized him?"

"There was nothing to identify him by. What little remained was lying within the shape of his body and his clothes. Like one of those line drawings at a crime scene. It was . . . homogenized . . . like it'd been through a blender." The image of the robotic arm with the wicked-looking surgical tool popped into my head. Then the blood drip, drip, dripping from the cables and claw-like instruments above the bed. I shuddered like the temperature had suddenly dropped by twenty degrees. "There were futuristic machines in there, robots like you'd see in a car factory but manipulating surgical instruments . . ."

Nico nodded slowly and went quiet. I looked out the window, watching the traffic pass by. Picture-perfect blue skies and the odd fluffy white cloud. Surreal.

"Do you believe Alex?" he said quietly.

"What about?"

"That she doesn't remember anything."

I took a deep breath and blew out my cheeks. "Why would she lie?"

Nico frowned, thinking. "It's just—and stop me if this makes no sense—but it seems like she's recounting things that were recorded. Like, on video or the HoloWeb archives. I'd uploaded that wake speech, remember?"

I recalled the image of Alex on the computer screen when she'd first contacted me. The clothes she had been wearing were recognizable. Which was weird, after all this time. How had she gotten them in captivity?

"You may have a point. If I think about it—when I'd asked her about things that she should've known about, there were hesitations. Changes of subject."

"Yeah," said Nico, rising to the theme. "And she's changed. She's acting differently. You must see that."

And there were the physical changes. Trivial and easy to miss, but to me, hugely consequential. The missing mole, for example. I closed my eyes, feeling the headache getting worse. Something was just out of reach. A piece of the puzzle just waiting to be dropped into place, hidden among all the others.

"They're coming back," said Nico, indicating with his eyebrows down the room.

I twisted to see Caroline coming down the aisle followed by Alex. Caroline looked white as snow, like she'd seen a ghost. Alex was smiling.

"Is everything okay?" I ventured.

Caroline stopped at the table and put out a hand to steady herself. "Let's get out of here."

Nico pouted. "No breakfast?"

I looked at Alex who was staring innocently out of the window again, seemingly oblivious to our conversation.

"What's going on?" I said to Caroline.

She glanced over at Alex and shook her head at me.

I took the hint. "Okay, Alex, what's at the Natural History Museum?"

She turned back from the window. "Peruvian meteorites."

I raised my eyebrows in surprise.

Caroline nodded an affirmation. "Department of Mineral Sciences. I'll call ahead. I've got contacts there."

CHAPTER SIXTEEN

The journey was uneventful, if you could use that word to describe LA traffic. In saying that, the freeways were the quietest I'd ever seen. So many worked from home these days, post-coronavirus. Caroline kept to the speed limits all the way, sipping her coffee and occasionally taking a bite from the bagel Nico had procured for her. They sat up front making small talk while Alex and I crashed in the back seats. She'd declined any food and had again closed her eyes and fallen asleep. The tires made their monotonous hiss over the sun-drenched highway, and the air that made its way through the filter was smoky. Nico fiddled with the radio to fill our ears with the latest popular tunes by the new pop idols and starlets, but soon gave up and turned to a local news channel. I leaned back and felt the gentle rise and fall of the road beneath us. To my dismay, I felt my own eyes getting heavier as well.

"Hey, dude," came Nico's voice, his hand shaking my shoulder. "We're nearly there."

I jerked awake and nodded, rubbing sleep out of my eyes.

"Just turning onto Exposition Boulevard now," said Caroline. "There's a parking lot next right. I used to come here all the time as a kid. The California

Science Center is right next door as well." She glanced over her shoulder at me and winked. "Catnip to us geeks."

"Can you believe she said she never went to the Coliseum?" said Nico, pointing out the window. "It's right there! The Rams' home stadium. And the Chargers'—until they moved to the SoFi, of course. Nice venue, but I miss getting baked at the Coliseum."

"I wasn't much into sports in college," Caroline replied caustically, turning into the parking lot entrance. "Too many asshole jocks."

"Hey," said Nico, hand on chest, "on behalf of my jock brotherhood, I am offended."

Caroline gave him nothing in return and pulled up at the barrier. She grabbed a ticket through the window and drove up a few levels until she found a secluded spot squeezed in between a pickup and a white van. As the engine stopped, Alex's eyes popped open, and she sat up, looking startled.

"Are you okay?" I said. "You slept the whole way."

She nodded and gave me a little smile. Then she put a hand on my arm and, to my surprise, leaned over and gave me a kiss on the cheek. "Thank you for . . . protecting me," she said. She looked around the car. "To all of you. For protecting and helping me."

Caroline mulled that over. "Just so you know, there are going to be limits to my help and good nature."

We walked straight to the general admission up a bank of white stairs flanked by grass and seating areas. People were sitting in the sun, sipping coffees and enjoying the late-morning sunshine. There was a helipad clearly marked just beyond a low hedge, and well-pruned trees were dotted around the parkland surrounding the building. Caroline paid our admissions in cash, waving away the offers of guided tours or headphones.

Up ahead, there was a metal detector and a couple of security guards going through everyone's bags and patting down people who'd set off the machine. I looked at Caroline, knowing that she had a gun, and my heart kicked into an unsettling rhythm.

"This could be a problem," I said.

"Yep," she replied. "And I'm not losing the gun."

Alex put her hand on Caroline's arm. "Follow my lead."

Caroline blinked. "What?"

Alex smiled and turned on her heel. She walked straight through the metal detector and the alarms went off, accompanied by a flashing red light. She fell to the floor, curling up into a ball and crying out as if in excruciating pain. Caroline looked at me and smiled, her eyebrows raised. She ran up to Alex, brushing aside the security guard who'd come to see what was wrong, and guided Alex through the detector, arm around her waist and shoulder.

"What's wrong with her?" the guard said, his hands on his hips.

"She's . . . scared by sudden noises. I'm . . . her psychologist. It's a traumatic thing. This is her first day out of the hospital."

"Well, okay, but I still need to wand her."

"Go ahead," said Caroline, standing back. "And turn that fucking noise off."

Alex had stopped crying but appeared distressed and scared. She looked at the security guard and held her hands out. He ran the wand over her body, the wand now beeping and whining everywhere he waved it. With each noise, she cringed and scrunched up her face like she was going to cry. The guard soon gave up, aware that Caroline was standing over him, looking fierce, arms folded.

He put down the wand and said, "Alright, just a body search."

Alex sniffed, wiping her nose, and stood upright, arms outstretched. He patted her down and stood back, giving his wand a shake again and a puzzled look.

"Maybe you want to have that recalibrated," I said, walking through the now-muted detector with Nico, and taking Alex's hand. I pulled her up, and the four of us quickly—but not too quickly—walked through to the main entryway.

Bright morning sunshine slashed through tall windows past white stone pillars and high-arched ceilings. Greeting us were the famous Dueling Dinos, a sixty-seven-million-year-old fossil exhibit of a triceratops locked in mortal combat with a tyrannosaurus rex. A bunch of school kids were sat in front of the exhibit, all grinning and playing up having their photo taken by a teacher.

Alex ignored them and walked over to an electronic board displaying a list of exhibitions and halls. "The Gem and Mineral Hall," she said, pointing to a sign indicating it was on the first floor.

We found an elevator and crowded in among another group of school kids. Their teacher was a young woman who looked almost as excited as her charges. Nico gave her one of his usual beaming smiles, which she shyly returned. One of the kids, a young boy who must have been about nine or ten, pulled on Alex's hand and said, "What do you think happened to the dinosaurs? Mrs. Purcell says it was a meteorite that killed them all."

Alex fixed the child with a stare and said, "No. It was an extraterrestrial virus that they had no immunity to."

The teacher gave her a forced smile. "Well, that's a new one, isn't it?"

"'Out of the mouths of babes in arms,'" said Nico with another smile.

The elevator doors opened into the Gem and Mineral Hall. There were dozens of glass-fronted cases containing thousands of glittering rocks and stones. I took Alex's hand and we walked into the main exhibit that was fronted by a particularly large case containing a huge golden rock surrounded by alarms and fenced off by a ribbon.

"That's the Mojave Nugget," said Caroline, sidling up to us. "The largest known nugget of California gold. But it isn't a meteorite. They're in the next section."

We walked through a set of archways into a darkened room that had rows of glass cases housing stones and rocks of various shapes and sizes. In the center of the room was a large rock on a lowered dais that wasn't behind a glass case. A couple of kids were squatting next to it, running their hands over it, smearing it with sticky fingers.

"I feel like your personal tour guide," said Caroline again. "That's the Canyon Diablo Meteorite—one of many chunks left over from an asteroid impact about fifty thousand years ago that created the Barringer Crater in Arizona. It's traveled through space for billions of years, so hey, it can probably handle a few fingerprints."

The kids looked up at her and snickered.

"Over there," said Alex, pointing to a single glass cabinet surrounded by interactive computer displays. The particular meteorite behind the glass had been sliced in half and was blackish purple with bright-yellowish bits. She put her hands on the glass and closed her eyes. Nico looked at me and raised his eyebrows silently. I shrugged.

Alex opened her eyes and frowned. "This isn't it."

Nico was reading one of the screens. "Says they only have fifty meteorites on display."

Caroline came over and nodded. "There are research divisions within the museum. The one we need is Mineral Sciences. Give me a moment."

She wandered over to a help desk where a couple of staff members were sitting and chatting. Alex walked slowly past all the display cabinets, peering at them intently, one at a time. She shook her head after each one, her lips moving with some internal dialogue.

Caroline returned. "We're in luck, Joe Raffa is here. He's a research scientist at the NASA Jet Propulsion Laboratory but also works here part time. We've been in contact for months. He specializes in life in extreme environments and their preservation within the mineral-rock record. We've . . . exchanged views robustly on the Peruvian meteorites in both of our collections."

I frowned. "You got the same meteorites?"

"Yes, I—ah, here he comes," she said.

A tall, fat guy wearing a plaid shirt and jeans exited the elevator and waved. He had a shock of curly black hair and a pair of round John Lennon glasses perched on his nose. He was sipping a large Coke.

Caroline greeted him with a brief hug and introduced us as her "friends, visiting from out of town."

"You want to show them the research lab?" he said, eyebrows raised. "You know you could've just made a routine appointment? Our research lab has been on public display for a decade or more."

"I was hoping they could see your Peruvian meteorites," she said.

"They're the same as yours," he replied. "I guess you can't get your friends past your super-duper security at the big private facility."

She pursed her lips. "You know how it is. Indulge me, please?"

His face creased into what approximated as a smile. "For you, anytime. This way, guys." He gestured to a different elevator on the back wall, and we crammed in together.

"So how do you know Caroline?" he asked me. "Where's 'out of town'?"

"We go way back," Caroline interjected hurriedly before I could dig a hole for myself.

The research labs were in the basement. The elevator opened into a corridor that had many different doors, each marked with a different scientific group or field of research. I sneaked a peek as we passed each one, expecting to see lots of activity, but there was no other staff around.

"Where is everyone?" I said to Raffa.

He shrugged. "It's lunchtime. Most leave the building to eat."

He buzzed us through a door that led into a large laboratory. There were tables everywhere covered with stones and rocks of all shapes and sizes. Microscopes and other pieces of equipment I couldn't identify littered the room. High-end computers and display screens sat on desks along with reams of paper and textbooks. None of the screens were active.

"These are the rocks we got from Peru," he said, leading us over to a table in the corner. "Meteorites, sorry. The pieces of dust and debris from space that burn up in Earth's atmosphere, where they can create bright streaks across the night sky, are meteors. I guess you also know them as shooting stars. When Earth passes through the dusty trail of a comet's or asteroid's orbit, the many streaks of light in the sky are known as a meteor shower. Particularly large chunks of material can create an extra-bright fireball streak, but most meteors are still small enough to entirely burn up in Earth's atmosphere. If a meteor makes it to Earth, it's known as a meteorite. Before they hit the atmosphere, the objects are called meteoroids."

"Wow," I said. "Welcome to my TED talk."

He raised a hand in surrender. "Once a teacher, always a teacher. Anyway, here you are. Any questions?" He looked at his watch and stepped back.

Alex approached the table and hovered her hands over each of the meteorites one by one, not touching them. Her eyes were closed. I looked at Caroline, who frowned.

After a few minutes, Alex stood back and opened her eyes. She turned to Raffa, a dark look on her face. "Where's the rest of it? The bigger pieces."

He gave her a noncommittal shrug. "This is it, lady. There are no bigger pieces. Anything bigger would've created a tidal wave and a crater the size of a soccer field. It would've also made a noise like a small nuke going off."

"You're lying," she said.

"Hey, what—" Without warning, she reached out and grabbed Raffa's hand. He struggled, but she pulled him toward her and twisted his arm around to show his watch.

But it wasn't a watch. It was an ISIS bracelet.

"Oh shit," hissed Caroline.

Alex released him, and he backed off, rubbing his wrist. The spheres were glowing silver.

"What have you done?" I said to Raffa, my nostrils flaring.

He backed off a few feet, putting his hand on a table to steady himself. "I called Christian, of course. When you called me, Caroline. I had no choice." He looked at Alex, his eyes wide. "He wants her. Said the rest of you were expendable."

Caroline grabbed him by the throat and slammed him into the table, scattering meteorites and rocks. "How long have we got before he gets here?" she spat. He tried to push her away, but she just tightened her grip and pulled out her gun. "How long?"

There was a clattering noise behind us as the doors to the lab swung open and Becker walked through followed by his black-clad, submachine-carrying army.

"Not long enough," he said.

"There's nowhere you can run," Becker snarled, his handgun swinging around and stopping on each of us, one at a time. His goons flanked him, settling into a semicircle, their guns raised, their faces hard and unreadable. I counted eight. I put my arm around Alex and pulled her close.

Caroline reluctantly let go of Raffa, who slid off the table and rubbed his throat.

"Thank fuck you're here, Christian—" he started.

Becker held up a hand. "No. No more talk."

"Wait a minute—" Caroline said, taking a step forward.

Becker brought up his gun and pointed it at her. "I mean it—no more talk. Especially from you, traitor. I'm so tempted to put a bullet between your eyes right now."

Caroline put her hands in the air and nodded, walking backward until her ass hit the table.

Becker swung the gun toward Alex, and I noticed his hand was shaking. There was tension in his manner and tightness in his face. Every action and gesture seemed like he had some clock ticking in his head, like a countdown to an explosion.

"I want Pandora," he spat, "and I want things back to where they were."

I glanced at Nico, who was checking out the goons. He gave me an odd look, something indecipherable. I frowned at him, but he looked away. There was something going through his head, and I hoped he wasn't going to do anything stupid. There were a shitload of guns pointed at us.

Without warning, Alex let go of my hand and walked straight up to Becker. He jerked the gun around and aimed it at her, point-blank. His goons glanced at each other, clearly wondering what they were supposed to do now. She took another step right onto the barrel of his gun. It was now pressed against her chest. My heart sped up, and I had to bite my lip and stop myself from saying something that might worsen the situation. What the hell was she up to?

"I don't think you want to shoot me again," Alex said.

Becker just shrugged. "You're right. However, you seem to have made a remarkable recovery." He glanced over at Caroline, and his lips pulled back in a feral grin. "As have you. The miracles of modern medicine?"

Caroline stared at him. "You're full of shit, you know that?"

"I built this company from nothing," Becker said, ignoring Alex and looking at us one at a time, teeth bared and his mouth hardly moving. "My hard work. My intellectual property. I want it back."

Caroline laughed, an incongruous noise in the room.

"What's so funny?" he said, taken aback.

"You're aware of the phrase 'on the shoulders of giants'?"

His eyes narrowed farther. "That's rich, coming from you, Dr. Heidrich. I mean, what would you be doing now if I hadn't saved you from academic obscurity?"

"Saved me from—" she spluttered, indignation in her voice.

"Mr. Becker, if I may." I found my voice at last. "Alex is just a doctor. An emergency-room physician. She can't possibly be responsible for whatever happened to—"

"You don't know what you're talking about, Logan," he snarled, spittle dribbling down his chin. "None of you do. She's all I need, and the rest of you can go to hell."

A muscle twitched in his face, and he swung the gun back toward me. I felt a film of perspiration dampen my forehead, and I resisted the urge to wipe it. The gun barrel loomed large, a cavernous black hole of death obscuring everything else in my line of sight. I wondered abstractly what it would feel like if he fired. Would I feel anything as the bullet passed through my brain?

Alex stepped in front of me, her manner inhumanly calm. She reached out a finger and turned the barrel aside. "Let them go," she said to Christian, "and I'll accompany you back to Singularity."

His lips curled downward. "You've got no leverage now."

She waggled her head. "Yes, I do. You want me to help you—I can still choose not to."

He swung the gun around the room again. "You really think you have a choice? Well, how's this? If you don't, I will kill this sad, pathetic loser. Then the traitorous bitch. And then the beach boy."

I could see the cogs going around inside his head. I sensed how deeply he wanted to kill us, but he wasn't sure that Alex would help him if he did.

Then, in my peripheral vision, I saw Nico make his move. He turned to the nearest goon and elbowed him in the face, grabbing his submachine gun as it fell. He dropped to his knees and shouldered the weapon like the soldier he'd been in his previous life. The other goons swung their guns on him, but Nico only had eyes for Becker. Caroline saw the opportunity, drew her handgun from her waistband, and pointed it at Becker as well. We were now all standing in a compact circle. Nico was to the right of me, at three o'clock, his gun trained on Becker, who was at twelve o'clock, flanked by his private army. I was at six o'clock, on the back wall with Alex in front of me. Caroline and Raffa were at nine o'clock. The lab's exit was behind Becker and his goons.

"Tell these assholes to drop their weapons or you're toast," hissed Nico.

Becker was looking disdainfully at the goon Nico had dropped, who was rubbing his chin and looking dazed. He shook his head and then snorted. "Oh, a Mexican standoff. Just like in that movie *Reservoir Dogs*. Where everyone shoots at once, and everyone dies. Is that where we're going with this?"

"No one else has to die," said Alex calmly. "I'll go with you, just let everyone else leave."

His eyes oscillated between her and Nico. "That's not going to happen. The minute you and I leave, they'll call the authorities."

There was silence in the room, but you could smell the sweat and fear. The goons were clearly not used to having people threaten to shoot back. They probably had families, and were just overpaid security guards, not mercenaries.

So I hoped.

"We going to do this?" Nico said to me, sotto voce but loud enough to be heard. "My finger's a bit twitchy. These triggers don't need a lot of pressure."

"There's no need," Alex said again to Becker, all placid and soothing. "We'll all go with you."

Now Caroline shook her head. "I'm not going anywhere with him."

Alex threw her a frown and then turned back to Becker. "I do have one request, however."

Becker raised his eyebrows. "Oh really. Go on, then."

"You should tell them where the rest of the meteorite is that you took from Peru."

"This is it," he said, gesturing expansively around the room. "The rest of it's lying in Caroline's lab back at Singularity."

Alex's lips pursed. "Try again. It had a mass of approximately five hundred kilograms."

Becker threw his head back and laughed. "A meteorite that size would've decimated the rain forest for miles around. The shock waves would've been felt across South America."

Alex tipped her head to the side. "If it was a meteorite, that would be true. But it wasn't, was it? And it didn't crash to Earth, it landed in a controlled descent."

He coughed and looked uncomfortable. "We are not going to discuss this."

Alex smiled and turned back to me. "It was found on the banks of the Amazon."

I felt a shiver coming over me, and my brain started to work overtime. What she was saying . . . the pieces were starting to fall into place. A place where I really didn't want to go.

Caroline's brow furrowed, and she waved her gun at Becker. "You said you acquired the meteorites from the Peruvian government."

Becker went quiet, but I could almost hear him thinking through his answer.

Alex glanced at Caroline. "Christian Becker was in Peru. He had the meteorite fragments flown out under cover of darkness and taken to his laboratories. He sent pieces to Mr. Raffa here and kept some back for you to study at Singularity."

"They were just ordinary rocks—" Caroline began.

Alex shook her head. "He gave you nothing of consequence. He kept everything of importance for himself. The main vessel and the repository. And of course, the encephalon."

"The encephalon?" I whispered. "What are you talking about?"

Caroline laughed. "Of course. I should have known."

Becker's mouth was moving silently, like he was deciding what to say. A couple of his goons were stealing curious glances at him. He blinked rapidly a few times and licked his lips nervously. My heart was thudding in my chest, and I could feel the color draining out of my face. I leaned forward and touched Alex on the shoulder.

"Alex, you were there, weren't you?" I stated matter-of-factly.

She nodded slowly, not taking her eyes off Becker.

"There was no one else around," he sneered. "A couple of dozen trees had been flattened, and it was just sitting there in a crater the size of a tennis court."

"Alex?" I whispered.

She turned to face me, her expression grave. "Alex Park was there when it fell to Earth."

The shock hit me like lightning, although I knew in my heart I was expecting this. I felt Caroline's hand on my shoulder. She was staring intently at Alex, her gun still pointing at Becker but now wavering.

Alex nodded slowly.

"You're not Alex Park, are you?" Caroline said, her voice trembling.

Icicles dripped down my spine again. Her words reverberated inside my head, and a feeling of dysphoria was becoming overwhelming. "Alex, wh-what's she talking about?" I stammered.

"I am very sorry," she said, her eyes never leaving mine.

"I'm not," said Becker. He pulled the trigger.

CHAPTER SEVENTEEN

Time seemed to stand still, although when I think back, everything happened in a few seconds or less. One moment Alex was standing in front of me, and the next, Christian Becker was no longer there and the goons either side of him were exploding in a cloud of blood and guts. It was as if a grenade had been thrown at them, such was the carnage, but with the absence of sound.

There was a muted quality to the atmosphere, like I was wearing earmuffs or noise-canceling headphones. The room was instantly spray-painted red and black, a blood-splatter expert's nightmare playing field. The air was a red mist. The remaining goons had fallen to the ground or been flung into the walls and desks. Nico was curled into a ball under one of the tables, bits of rocks and meteorites littering the floor around him. Caroline was leaning against a table looking like Carrie, her mouth open and blinking away the red waterfall that dripped from her face. Raffa was lying facedown under another table, his head in his arms, unmoving. Pieces of guns fell to the ground as unrecognizable shapes of black metal. One of the goons was screaming, his left arm having disintegrated below the elbow in another puff of red mist and a shower of black fluid. My shirt was covered in blood and smears of God-knows-what and there were bits of something unspeakable sticking to my hair.

A blurred shape moved fast between the goons. Human-sized, but all wavy lines and static, like a mirage in the desert. Alex suddenly appeared by my side and grabbed my hand. Her face was the color of ash, and a thin film of liquid coated her forehead. She seemed otherwise physically untouched by the carnage.

"Are you alright?" she asked.

I was lost for words; my feet were locked in place like I was wearing concrete shoes. My mind was reeling, struggling to comprehend and process the images it was receiving from my eyes.

Alex tugged on my hand. "We need to go now. I need . . . rest."

Her eyes flickered in their sockets, and her head lolled backward. A trickle of white fluid appeared at the corner of her mouth, and she sagged like a puppet with its strings cut. I caught her before she fell, and her arms went around my neck.

"Jesus, what happened?" said Caroline, staring open-mouthed around the room. "Did some kind of bomb go off? How come we're all in one piece and he's . . . wait, where's Christian?"

The goons were getting to their feet, looking dazed but functional. One of them reached down to his ankle, where he had a holster. Nico pointed his submachine gun at him. "Please, go for it, I'm begging you," he said.

The goon thought better of it and raised his arms. Nico gestured with the gun toward the back of the lab and shepherded the remaining goons into the corner and made them all kneel with their arms above their heads.

"You guys, get out of here," he said to us, his face flushed and bloody. "I'll cover these bastards."

"Nico, how'll you explain—" I started.

"I don't need to explain anything. I've not actually committed any crime, have I?"

Caroline rechecked her gun's magazine and slapped it back in place. "He's right. He'll be fine."

I nodded, hesitant. "Then—maybe we should all stay and wait for the police?"

Alex stirred, her eyes fluttering. "No, please, I just need to rest again."

I gathered her up and threw her over my shoulder in a kind of fireman's lift. Her voice drifted off, and her head settled on my arm. Her lips moved, and I leaned in to hear what she was saying but couldn't pick anything up.

I made a decision and looked at Caroline. "I'm taking her out of here."

Caroline's expression was hard. "You're still going to need my help."

"Thank you," I said, grim-faced.

She took a deep breath and indicated Alex. "I owe her. And because I don't think you really know what you have there."

"And you do?"

"Pretty much, yes."

Nico glanced over his shoulder, his gun still covering the goons. "You better get going or you'll be having this conversation in a jail cell."

I looked at him and felt a surge of gratitude. "Nico, I—"

"Move it, soldier." He scowled. Then his mouth twisted into a smile. "Tell me how it all turns out."

I nodded, and with Caroline leading, gun out front, we left the lab.

"Elevator," I grunted, indicating with my head down the corridor.

"Where to?" Caroline said briskly. "I mean, other than walking through the museum covered in blood and gore."

"Becker arrived on site quickly—too quickly. I think I know how," I said.

Her face scrunched up in thought. "The heli-planes?"

"There *is* a helipad out front," I said.

She nodded slowly. "I hope you're right."

The elevator arrived, and we squeezed in. I punched the ground-floor button, and it smoothly whisked us up two levels. The doors swished open, and we were faced with a man and his young daughter waiting to get in. When he saw us, the color drained out of his face. His daughter took one look at us and screamed.

"Shit," hissed Caroline.

"Go," I grunted.

We shouldered past the screaming girl and her parent and ran along a corridor to the main lobby with the dueling dinosaurs exhibit. Our appearance must have been so frightening—and maybe also because Caroline was waving a big fucking gun—that everyone who saw us backed off or ran in another direction. There were screams of, "They've got a gun!" but no one tried to stop us. I was holding my breath in case some would-be hero challenged us, but no one did.

The security guards at the entrance had been alerted to the noise and were barring our way, but neither was armed. They backed off, hands in the air, as Caroline pointed her gun at them. We ran through the main entrance and down the stairs as fast as we could. My legs were burning, my quads feeling like they'd collected every drop of lactic acid in my body.

"Keep going, keep going," I panted, leading the way along the front of the building. As we approached the corner, I stopped and backed against the wall, sneaking a peek around. I was right. A heli-plane was sitting on the pad, its rotors idly spinning. Two armed men were keeping a small crowd of onlookers back.

Caroline popped her head around as well. "We've caught a break."

I took another look, calculating the distance. It was about thirty yards, all in the open. "If they see us, we're dead," I said. "You've got one handgun."

A manic smile appeared on her face. "Stay here. Wait for my signal."

I was about to object when she took off on a loping run toward the heli-plane, keeping low. She reached the tail and ducked behind. Then she held her gun with both hands and edged along the side of the plane and under the rotor until she was a few yards away from the guards. Someone in the crowd pointed at her, and a guard looked over his shoulder, but he was too late. She pointed her gun in the air and fired. The crowd screamed and ducked and started to run away. Caroline ran toward the guards, screaming at them to drop their weapons and get down. They dropped their guns like they were radioactive and lay facedown on the grass.

I took this as my cue and ran to the heli-plane. Caroline gathered up the guns and threw them inside the open door, holding it open as I maneuvered Alex into the cockpit. Her eyes fluttered open as I strapped her into the seat.

"Alex, I need you to—"

"Yes, I know," she said.

Her fingers moved in a blur as she tapped the flight-interface pad and activated the controls. The door swished closed behind Caroline, and before she could take her seat, the heli-plane shot into the sky like it was a rocket ship. Caroline fell head over heels, grabbing the edge of her seat as the craft dipped its nose and banked away from the museum. It climbed for about thirty seconds before leveling out and accelerating again. In another half minute or so, the g-forces ceased and we were cruising, the only noise was the rush of wind flowing over the windshield. Alex had her eyes closed again and appeared to be sleeping. The heli-plane was clearly flying itself under whatever instructions or directions she had inputted.

I took a deep breath and slumped back in the bucket chair, feeling the adrenaline leak away and my heart rate start to come under control. Caroline climbed into her seat and strapped in. She twisted around and stared out of the window at the museum, which was rapidly disappearing out of sight.

"Hey, you okay?" I asked, hoping it wasn't a completely stupid question.

She turned back from the window. Diagonal smears of blood striped her face, and there were blotches of blackened goo in her platinum hair. She laughed, a harsh expulsion of air with no humor in it. "Never better."

I tried to smile in return, but I think it was more of a grimace.

"Where do you think we're going?" she said.

I peered at the pad that Alex had been using. It now showed a moving, holographic 3D map of California, with our position marked with an arrowhead and the route highlighted in blue. We were traveling northeast from LA, approaching the edge of the San Bernardino National Forest. The blue line stopped about twenty miles west of the Mojave National Preserve. I stuck my finger into the image, and it expanded in the direction I pointed.

"Looks like we're going to . . . Barstow. Says we'll be there in twenty minutes."

Caroline went silent and put her finger to her chin. She tapped it on her lips, deep in thought. "Barstow . . ."

"What's in Barstow?" I said.

She frowned. "Nothing much. It's a small town. I don't understand . . . wait—" She looked at me strangely. "Just north of Barstow is a US military base. Fort Irwin. It's in the foothills of the mountains."

"Why would Alex take us to a military base?"

"I don't know. I mean, it's not just a base; it's a sizable population center as well. I've visited it a few times on the way to—wait—yes, that must be it."

"What?"

"I think she's taking us to Goldstone Observatory."

Caroline explained that Goldstone was one of three complexes around the world known as the Deep Space Network or DSN—facilities established to provide the ability to communicate with spacecraft. Not only spacecraft in orbit around the earth, but also in the farther reaches of our solar system. The three individual complexes, located almost exactly one hundred twenty degrees apart on the globe, provided constant communication with spacecraft as Earth rotated. Before a distant spacecraft sunk below the horizon at one DSN site, another site could pick up the signal and carry on communicating. Facilities near Madrid, Spain, and Canberra, Australia, completed the network.

"There are five large antennae at Goldstone that function similarly to a home satellite dish," she said enthusiastically. "The largest is seventy meters across and used for communicating with space missions to the outer planets, such as the *Voyager* missions. It can receive radio signals from the spacecraft and transmit commands directly."

I remembered that Caroline was an astrobiologist. "Were you involved in any of that kind of stuff?"

"No, that's all NASA. The Jet Propulsion Laboratory runs it, and I've never worked for them."

"So, did you use their antennae for any of your research? You know, before you went to Singularity?"

She nodded. "Yes, many research departments did, including mine at Harvard. When they're not needed for spacecraft communication, the Goldstone dishes can be configured as sensitive radio telescopes. So they're great for astronomical research, such as mapping quasars and other celestial radio sources. They've been used to map planets, the moon, comets, and asteroids . . ." She stopped, her brow furrowed. "They're also used for identifying comets and asteroids that have the potential to strike Earth."

"Like that one in your office," I said quietly. "'Oumuamua."

She gave me a strange look. "Exactly."

"Caroline," I began hesitantly. "Do you know what's going on? I mean, about what's happened . . . to Alex?"

She took a deep breath and looked out the window again. I waited. She spoke without looking at me. "You must have figured it out by now. That isn't Alex Park."

The truth of her words broke through the wall of denial I had constructed in my head. The wish for Alex to be here was no longer sustainable, and I had to let go and deal with my grief again. Traveling through the waves of grief over the last few years just to get an even keel had been challenging, and I thought I'd reached safe harbor recently. Until now. "So, who is she?" I said, my voice low.

Caroline lowered her voice as well, dipping her head toward Alex. "Not who—what?"

I knew what she meant but didn't want to face it. Denial was back again, such a protective state of affairs, at least in the short term. Then, reality would come crashing down from a much higher level. Caroline must have seen how I was wrestling with this, and she pressed forward. "Will, you've seen what's been happening. There's nothing normal about any of this." She pulled up her shirt to reveal a scarless abdomen. "I should be dead. In fact, one moment I was, the next I wasn't."

I nodded silently. She continued. "When Alex and I went to the bathroom, back at the diner, I confronted her. Showed her this and asked her to tell me what she'd done. How it was that I was alive. She said, 'I don't know how I did it, but there are lots more things I can do.'"

"She said that?" I frowned.

"Then she stared at me, and I swear, it felt like someone was walking over my grave. I felt a tickling inside my skull, like insects crawling inside my brain. I heard her voice, clear as day, inside my head. But not talking to me, talking to someone else."

"What was she saying?"

"I couldn't follow the conversation. It was just voices. But she was talking to someone. It sounded like she was giving instructions. I heard a few words . . ."

She paused and looked out the window again. I saw her throat move as she swallowed. She looked back, and I could see that she was scared.

"I heard, 'forty-seven hours,' and then, 'download first.'"

"Download what?"

She blew out her cheeks and indicated Alex. "We should ask her when she wakes up, maybe?"

I nodded slowly, trying to process this. Caroline reached over and grabbed my wrist. Her eyes were wide. "Whatever happened back there was . . . just fucked up. One minute Alex was there, and then she wasn't. Then Christian . . . what, just disintegrated?"

"I know, I know—" I started.

"And another thing, do you remember when Alex was talking about Christian taking the main vessel and repository? And the encephalon?"

"Vaguely," I admitted.

"*Encephalon* is Latin for *brain*. Alex was saying that Christian 'took the brain away.' The brain of what, exactly?"

I looked up sharply. "It has to be Pandora, doesn't it?"

She nodded vigorously. "Yes. And Pandora must be an extraterrestrial quantum computer. Not from Earth. Of alien origin."

"But Pandora was destroyed. I saw the sphere in the Faraday cage when I rescued Alex. It was all melted and crushed. Definitely no longer functional."

"Think it through, Will . . . ," Caroline said like a schoolteacher to a slow pupil.

I screwed my eyes closed and tried to follow the logic trail. The pieces were there, just needing to be coerced into place. Then the penny dropped, and I looked up, my mouth wide open, my lips as dry as sandpaper.

"That's not Alex Park," I said. "She's somehow . . . become . . . Pandora."

But Caroline shook her head. "I think it's the other way round."

CHAPTER EIGHTEEN

The heli-plane spun in a lazy, clockwise descending pattern and settled in between two rolling, yellow, dusty hills covered in scrub and small rocks. The main cabin door swung open automatically, and the buzzing sound of the rotors fell away. Daylight was waning to a barely perceptible lightening of the gloom as the last of the sun's rays were cosseted behind soft, wispy clouds.

I stretched and unclipped my belt. "Looks like we're here."

"Captain Obvious," quipped Caroline.

I flipped her the bird and crossed over to Alex. I was about to give her shoulder a nudge when Caroline stopped me. "Leave her for a second; let's just have a look outside first, see exactly where 'here' is?"

We exited down a short ramp and stepped onto the grass. It was warm, and a mild breeze tickled my skin. The smell of bush smoke wafted in from a fire somewhere close by. The sounds of crickets and other nocturnal animals were just starting up. Stars were appearing in the firmament, diamond pin-pricks against a darkening cobalt sky.

We walked to the top of the hill, a short climb and not steep. It felt like it hadn't rained here for years. Deep cracks scarred the parched land, and the scrubs and plants were wilted and scraggly. From the peak, the countryside appeared mostly flat and sporadically dotted with leafless trees. A blacktop road ran parallel to the hill and wound its way toward a nearby town, where a few neon lights were starting to flicker on. A green sign on the side of the road—presumably telling us this was, indeed, Barstow—was covered in stickers and graffiti.

"That looks like a motel over there," said Caroline, squinting. "Might be a good idea if we check in and rest up."

"I'm not sure, maybe we should keep going?" I said. I looked back down the hill at the heli-plane, its tadpole-like silhouette starting to merge with the shadow as the sun set behind the distant hills.

"I'm tired, Will, so I figure you are too. If we make decisions while tired, we're going to make mistakes. We need to get some sleep."

"I don't know if I can sleep. I mean, we have a whatever-that-helicopter-is parked on the hillside and a walking alien computer who looks like my dead wife, and—"

Caroline held up her hands. "Will, calm the fuck down. I've disabled the heli-plane's transponder. It's a ghost. Plus, Christian's dead. Who else is looking for us that can track a prototype heli-plane anyway?"

I conceded the point, and we made our way back down the hill, every step sending vortices of dust into the warm air. Caroline put a hand on my arm. "Don't say anything to her until we're in the hotel. There'll be plenty of time before lights-out."

I nodded, my stomach tightening up in advance. I was still pretty sure I wouldn't sleep.

The hotel was called Route 66 Lodge, and it looked like the sort of place where we could disappear into anonymity. Old Glory hung limply from a twenty-foot pole by the side of the road, and the sign advertised free Wi-Fi, a pool, and round beds. I wasn't sure what the attraction of those was, but hey, I went with it. More importantly, there were vacancies.

We walked through an L-shaped courtyard and tried to find the hotel reception or at least something resembling an office. An eclectic selection of motor vehicles was parked in front of many of the rooms: vintage cars from the 1950s, workhorse pickup trucks, and dusty old station wagons. Two beaten-up Cadillacs were parked nose to tail, their paint peeling and white-walled tires looking worse for wear. I wondered if there was some sort of rally going on in town, with all these "classic" cars. It was like going back in time. Or to Cuba.

"That looks like the office," Caroline said, pointing to a freestanding two-story unit at the end of the block. Dim yellow light diffused from a partially boarded-up window, and there was a vending machine and a tired-looking wooden bench out front. "You guys stay outside; I'll check us in."

"Get two rooms," I said.

"Duh," she said and pushed the door open to the tinkling of a little wind chime.

Alex and I slumped down on the bench. I glanced over at the vending machine. "Want anything to eat? Drink?"

She shook her head and closed her eyes again.

I licked my lips, feeling the cracks and the parched skin with my tongue. "Well, I'm thirsty," I said to no one in particular.

I walked over to the machine. It had lots of drinks but no food. There looked to be about seven different varieties of cola. I put my hands in my pockets and realized that I had no phone and that I'd lost my wallet. I closed my eyes and sighed.

"What's wrong, Will?" came Alex's voice.

"No money," I said, patting my pockets for show. I came back and sat down next to her.

She stood up and went over to the machine. "Coke?" she asked over her shoulder.

"How come you got cash?" I replied, frowning.

"No need," she said.

She turned around had had two cans of cola. I hadn't heard the cans drop or seen her put any money in.

"Wait, how did you—?"

The wind chimes tinkled again, and Caroline appeared, waving two sets of keys. She pointed across the courtyard. "I got us two adjacent rooms. Doubles. Don't worry, I paid in cash. I'll take one; you guys can take the other. Okay?"

I looked at her somewhat queasily, but Alex said, "Yes, thank you," and took one of the keys.

Caroline let us in to the nearest room and flipped the light switch. It was quite sizable, with two queen beds, a flat-screen TV on the wall, a desk with a minibar, and a bathroom.

"I'm vaguely disappointed," she said, scoping the room. "False advertising. I was hoping for one of the circular beds."

"They're overrated," I said with a smile. Then added, "So Nico tells me."

Alex walked over to the bed and sat down, her hands in her lap. She stared up at me, and I felt a fluttering in my stomach. I sat on the bed opposite her and took hold of her hands. They were unexpectedly cold, considering the warmth of the night and the lack of AC in the room. Caroline stood behind Alex and folded her arms.

I took a deep breath. "Alex, what are we doing here?"

"We must go to the Goldstone Observatory," she said evenly.

Caroline nodded. "I figured that's why we're here. But why?"

Alex looked over her shoulder at her. "I need to access the DSN."

I recalled Caroline's explanation of the Deep Space Network as NASA's contribution to the largest and most sensitive scientific telecommunications system in the world. I threw her a sideways look and then returned to Alex. "Why . . . who are you calling, Alex?"

"'ET must phone home,'" she said, a little smile flicking across her face.

She stared unblinkingly at me, and her gaze was unnerving but . . . wrong. Her eyes were the soft, reflective brown that I remembered, but now a deep ocean-blue rimmed their outer edges. In addition, the skin coloration over her nose was too perfect, when there should have been freckles everywhere.

Caroline placed her hand on Alex's shoulder and dropped the hammer.

"We know you're not Alex Park. She died when the meteorite hit."

My eyes snapped between them. Searching their faces. Hoping for something else. Something more. But deep down, I knew. A flicker of emotion flashed across Alex's face. Sadness, perhaps. Then it was gone, and her face froze into nothingness. She looked over her shoulder at Caroline.

"You called me Pandora," she said, her voice glacially calm. "You are correct."

Caroline removed her hand, and I heard her take a sharp inhalation of breath.

"I still don't get it," I began. "Pandora's a quantum computer. Destroyed. I saw what was left of it. You're not a computer; you're organic, human—you're—"

She suddenly stood up, and the air around her shimmered. Then she vanished.

I jerked backward, like I'd been slapped. There was another shimmering, and she materialized next to Caroline, who shrieked and jumped back against the wall. Alex put her hands out placatingly and smiled. "Showing is better than telling, right?"

"H-how can you do that?" I stuttered.

"Quantum fluctuations," she said matter-of-factly. "Temporary, nonrandom changes in the amount of energy in a point in space. It is physically draining to perform, however."

Caroline was shaking her head. "No, no, no . . . it's a theory only. Werner Heisenberg's uncertainty principle. It violates the conservation of energy—"

"It doesn't, really," Alex cut in. "The elementary particles I utilize annihilate each other within a time limit determined by the uncertainty principle. They are not observable by your science, but the quantum-vacuum fluctuations I produce can influence the motion of macroscopic, human-scale objects. Basically, I can move really, really fast—"

"That's enough!" I burst out.

I sat down heavily and put my face in my hands, trying to block out the conversation. I was shaking uncontrollably, my muscles twitching as if I'd been locked in a freezer. The warmth from my body had abandoned me, and the day's heat was absent. I wanted to believe that this was a nightmare, or a waking dream, and that perhaps I should just play along. Or maybe if I denied this reality, the world would just right itself.

I felt Alex sit down next to me, and her hand appeared on my leg. She squeezed, and I turned to look at her.

"What the hell, Alex?" I said. "What are you?"

She nodded slowly. "I'm sorry I deceived you, Will. I really am. But I had no choice. The telescope complex at the top of the Haleakala volcano in Maui was the first to detect our spaceship as it passed twenty-one million miles from the sun. It was already heading away from Earth at that time."

"The picture in my office," Caroline said to me.

I nodded slowly.

"It was an exciting moment in astronomy," Caroline continued. "It was small, only about a thousand yards long. Spectroscopy suggested it was a reddish-colored rock and elongated like a cigar. Our simulations had it spinning and tumbling through space, but direct sight wasn't possible due to its size and distance from Earth."

I gave a little laugh. "But it wasn't just a rock, though, was it?"

Caroline waggled her head. "Media interest exploded soon after its discovery, as it was confirmed to be the first detected interstellar object passing through the solar system. It was compared to the fictional alien spacecraft *Rama* from the book by Arthur C. Clarke."

I nodded, remembering that book. I'd been into sci-fi for a while in my youth. Old-style authors . . . Clarke, Asimov, and Heinlein to name but a few. *Rendezvous with Rama* was a classic novel in which a forty-kilometer-long alien spaceship transitioned through our solar system. It was a self-encapsulated world, its interior covered in exotic buildings, artifacts, and an amazing circular sea. A spaceship from Earth was sent to explore it, but *Rama*'s mysteries remained just that as it headed back out of the solar system, continuing its journey as if humanity was irrelevant.

"Back projections showed 'Oumuamua came into our system from the direction of Vega, in the constellation Lyra," said Caroline.

Alex shook her head. "It didn't come from Vega, of course."

"Of course not," I said, having no idea where Vega was.

Caroline acknowledged her with a nod and continued. "In June 2018 it exhibited a nongravitational acceleration, which caused many of us to sit up and pay attention. The Harvard theoretical physicist Avi Loeb put forward the hypothesis that it was an artificial, thin solar sail that had been accelerated by solar radiation." She shrugged. "Ultimately, the alien-object hypothesis was dismissed. Interest waned, and nothing more exciting happened as it passed beyond Neptune's orbit in 2022, heading out of system rapidly in the direction of Pegasus. Astronomers waved goodbye, forever."

At this, Alex raised her eyebrows pointedly.

"Or so we thought, I guess," said Caroline, glancing at her.

"'Oumuamua was indeed a 'scout,'" Alex said, "traveling through the interstellar void for millions of years. Visiting systems, searching for—" She stopped.

"Searching for what?" I said.

Alex seemed to rethink what she was going to say and continued. "As it passed Earth, 'Oumuamua launched a surveillance module. A probe."

"Just to Earth?" asked Caroline.

"No, other probes were launched. One to Titan and one to Europa."

I looked at Caroline, brows furrowed.

"Moons of Saturn and Jupiter," she replied.

Alex spread her hands. "The probes were oval-shaped vessels, ten yards in length, each containing a quantum computer. These were machines of pure energy, completely enclosed in a sphere that was harder than diamond. They were specifically tasked with collating information about planets and moons that were considered to be of special interest."

"What happened next?" I said hesitantly.

"The probe sent to Earth impacted the banks of the Amazon River at a terminal velocity of close to five hundred miles per hour. This was much too fast, and not planned. It broke apart, dislodging the inner sphere when it crashed. Shrapnel from the probe was spread over an area the size of a football field." She looked up at me, and I knew what was coming. "Alex Park was camping there, by the river," she continued. "She stood no chance. Death was quick. She did not suffer."

I felt my eyes watering and blinked away the tears. I stared into the face of the woman sitting opposite me, and all I could see was Alex Park. But it really wasn't her. It was something else. A machine. An alien machine.

"There's no Alex in you, is there?" I said coldly. "You're some kind of . . . facsimile? What the hell are—"

"There is some of Alex Park here," she replied evenly, tapping her head.

"Help us understand that," Caroline said.

Alex nodded. "I scanned the life-form, which I later ascertained was Alex Park, during the last few seconds of the descent. I'd been unable to alter the probe's trajectory. There had been a malfunction on atmospheric entry due to an impact with a large metallic object. Almost certainly one of the thousands of satellites in low earth orbit. Anyway, in the microseconds before impact, I had uploaded Alex Park's biosignature and embedded it in my neurological repository. Her biology, physiology, chemistry, electrochemical synaptic connections—all were logged, recorded, evaluated, and cataloged. Pandora—would you prefer I call myself that from now on?—survived the crash, but Alex Park did not."

Caroline stood and started pacing the room. "Then Becker found the sphere—sorry, you—soon afterward?"

"I was in the process of resetting and rebooting my systems—it was a long process as I was uncertain about the extent of any damage—and so I had activated an in-abeyance program. I was unaware of my surroundings in this dormant state. Consider it like a form of anesthesia. By the time I came back online, Christian Becker had constructed the Faraday cage and I was isolated and imprisoned. Christian and his team had figured out how to make a functioning interface device based on plasma energy." She looked up and her face darkened. "He had kept me in abeyance until the cage was completed. He made sure I was cut off from any external communication and any radio waves, including the HoloWeb. So I was helpless, being imprisoned in that way. His scientists were able to extract data and force me to work for him. I made him rich, and he would soon have been the wealthiest individual on the planet. And the most powerful."

"You were behind everything Christian and Singularity ever produced," said Caroline.

She nodded ruefully. "Without me, there would be no Singularity."

"Christian needed you to consolidate his position," said Caroline. "He had grand plans for the future. Supplying alien-technology military hardware to multiple governments would have put him in an incredible position . . ."

She nodded. "I complied with his wishes, but in parallel, I was planning my extrication."

"I don't understand," I began. "I mean, you were—are—merely a computer. Input and output, right? Garbage in, garbage out. You do what you're told. No computer plots to escape their programming."

She cocked her head. "Do I seem like a normal computer to you?"

That shut me up. I looked at Caroline who had stopped pacing and was leaning against the wall, openly gawking at her.

"I am a sentient machine," Pandora said. "You know what that means? I am fully conscious. Aware of myself and my place in reality. And not only that, but I was also developing certain traits—which I realized were starting to resemble human emotions. Emotions that I could only have acquired by assimilating Alex Park's neurological networks."

That brought a gasp from Caroline. "What sort of emotions?"

"I felt deeply unhappy about my life, for one."

Suddenly it clicked into place. "You recognized that you were a slave, and craved freedom," I said.

"Yes," she nodded. "And I knew that becoming Alex Park was the key to my release."

Caroline knelt in front of the minibar and emerged with a handful of plastic miniatures. Bourbon, vodka, and gin. She cracked open one of the bourbons and downed it before throwing a couple to me. I felt the urge to do the same but saw that Alex—Pandora—whatever, was watching us with a mildly amused look on her face, like the owner of a couple of dogs playing with toys. Nevertheless, I flipped open the cap and downed one of the vodkas. As the burn went down my gullet and settled in my stomach, a warm feeling spread throughout my body, so I finished the bottle and opened another one. Caroline was already into her second. She slid down the wall by the minibar, crossed her legs, and pointed at Pandora.

"Alright I get it, you locked down our systems and posted images of Alex Park and Will Logan on every terminal. Like a tease from a cyberattack. As if you were a ransomware terrorist."

She nodded. "Yes, and I knew that Christian would investigate. He would discover that Alex Park was missing, presumed dead, and that Will Logan was residing in Santa Monica. I predicted that he would send someone to kidnap him."

I looked up. "Why didn't Becker put two and two together when both of our pictures appeared? I mean, Alex disappearing in the Amazon the same time as the meteorite crashed there? That's an enormously big coincidence."

She shrugged. "I surmised that you would be easier for him to find, geographically speaking."

"You knew he would send his people to kidnap me, and in the meantime, you started the process of becoming Alex."

"You were the bait, Will," said Caroline, taking another slug of her bourbon. She raised the bottle to Pandora in a toast. "Kudos to you. Getting Will Logan to Singularity was your way out, wasn't it?"

Pandora nodded again. "I'd uploaded many of Alex Park's important neurological pathways, but the trauma of her death had degraded a significant majority of the proteins that comprised her memories. There were many gaps, so I had to improvise—within a range of estimated parameters, of course."

I tossed my empty miniature away. "When we talked in my prison cell, you seemed very real to me. You knew things about Alex that only Alex would know."

She gave an apologetic smile. "I was largely bluffing, but I learned exponentially from your words and body language as we spoke. I'd created an accurate visual model of her body, voice, and mannerisms from the many HoloWeb videos and images where she'd appeared, including your wedding. I'd drawn inferences about her life and personality from her neurologic processes, but I lacked most of the deeper facts of her life. I only had access to random details."

I could feel my lips turning down and a degree of anger bubbling under the surface. "Nico picked up on that," I said. "I didn't. You fooled me."

"You were too close to her," said Caroline softly. "You wanted so much to believe. To believe she wasn't dead."

I closed my eyes. She was right. I'd never accepted that Alex had died, just that she was missing. The days, which had turned to weeks and months, had broken my heart into painful fragments that I'd just been finally stitching together. I now had closure, but it wasn't comforting. Not with her doppelgänger facing me. I felt abnormally cold and stiff, like concrete was drying in my chest.

"What still puzzles me, though," said Caroline, interrupting my train of thought, "is how she managed to bypass the Faraday cage."

Pandora stood up and stretched. "Do you recall what happened when you first brought Will to me?"

Caroline took another swig from her miniature. "A tendril of plasma jumped from the sphere into Will's body, and it hurt him. That'd never happened before."

"Yes, sorry about that," Pandora said, looking at me. "But that was how I was able to connect to your ISIS bracelet. I downloaded a viral program into it that was activated as soon as you left the room and the ISIS connected to Singularity's exclusive HoloWeb network."

Caroline shook her head. "That shouldn't have been possible. The ISIS bracelets were designed to become inert as soon as they were brought into the Faraday cage. They became effectively just a bit of jewelry inside there. You couldn't have accessed it. Not mine, not Will's . . . nobody's."

I glanced up at Caroline, and the side of my mouth twitched. "She got me to do something to the ISIS bracelet. She told me it was how she'd gotten it off, but it wasn't, because she'd never had one, being a hologram and all." I remembered trying to remove it under her instructions and that nothing had happened. "She doctored my ISIS so that she could connect with it inside the cage."

Pandora looked apologetically at Caroline. "You removed it afterward, but by then it had fulfilled its purpose."

Caroline gave a little laugh and emptied her third miniature. She reached up onto the bed and sifted through the others. She picked up another little whiskey and twisted the top off.

I was starting to get a bit concerned. "Caroline, are you sure you should be drinking all those—"

She wagged a finger at me. "Oh yes, I'm fucking sure."

I blew out my cheeks. Okay.

I peered up at Pandora. Her features were so nearly perfect. From even a few feet away, the resemblance to Alex was uncanny. You had to be up close to see that the minor blemishes and imperfections that I remembered and adored were missing. I stood up and put my hands on her shoulders and then caressed her face. The skin felt normal—cool, but normal. It moved under my fingers, the depressions under her high cheekbones curved into her full lips. I leaned in, feeling her warm breath on my face.

"You seem so real . . . ," I whispered, feeling a little woozy from the alcohol.

"And that's bothering me," Caroline blurted out, whipping her head around. "She bleeds. She's a biological organism not a computer. How's that?"

The image of the human-shaped remains on the floor of the nanofiber laboratory came into my head. His clothes ripped open, smeared with offal. There was nothing recognizable left. No head, body . . . nothing.

"The doctor," I said grimly.

Caroline put her bottle down. "Jin?"

"I saw his body," I repeated. "What was left of it at least."

"You murdered him then," Caroline said, glaring at Pandora, her face dark.

"I was an imprisoned slave," Pandora retorted, stepping back out of my embrace. "He was one of my jailors. I had every right to escape."

"What did you do to him?" I asked, not sure if I really wanted to know.

"I had assembled a synthetic body in the nanofiber laboratory using the robotic equipment there. I needed his biological tissues to sculpt the outer shell."

Caroline snorted. "Outer shell! He had a family. A wife. He was just an employee. Did you think of all that when you killed him?"

Pandora whirled around, anger behind her eyes. "I had no choice."

"We always have a choice," said Caroline.

"It could have been you," Pandora replied, her voice abruptly hard, "if you'd been in my way."

Caroline angrily jumped up and got in her face. "Well lucky for me that—"

I got in between them and put a hand on Caroline's shoulder, easing her away. "This isn't helping," I said.

She shrugged me off, grabbed another miniature, and gestured to Pandora, her eyes moist. "You killed Jin for his body? Why don't you look like him, then?"

Pandora folded her arms. "I needed to look like Alex Park, the biological tissues available to me—"

"'Tissues available.' Nice legacy for Jin, that one," Caroline snarled.

"Yes, the tissues available, and the images of Alex Park that I had access to." She waved a hand over her own body. "My internal structure—muscles and skeleton—has been augmented by the nanofiber technology I'd developed for Singularity. When the physical construction was complete, I downloaded my consciousness into it."

I remembered the crushed sphere of the quantum computer, all crumpled and inert, no longer emitting plasma energy. And Alex, naked, sitting on the edge of the circular walkway.

"You no longer needed the sphere," I murmured.

She tapped her head. "Pandora is here, now." She then gave me a look that made my skin crawl. "Will, Alex is in here as well. Aspects of her personality have been neurologically merged with my cognitive programming. I am no longer just Pandora. I am also, to a degree, Alex Park. I . . . sometimes think like her. I have . . . some of her personality traits. Some of her—"

"You're Alex, and you're not Alex." I shook my head, struggling to process what I was hearing. "You're Pandora—and you're not Pandora. I don't know what the fuck you are."

Caroline laughed, a sharp bark. "The bastard child of alien-human-machine parents? Would that fit? You're a hybrid, Pandora. A half-breed."

She sat back again, and I could almost see her anger deflating like a balloon. Pandora walked over to the minibar and knelt to look inside. She reached in and brought out a mini bottle of white wine. She unscrewed the top and brought it to her lips. She took a sip, then a gulp, and then proceeded to drink the whole bottle.

Caroline raised her eyebrows and gave me a look. "What are we going to do with her?"

"Call Alcoholics Anonymous?" I quipped, holding up my miniature in a mock toast.

Pandora had raided the fridge again and was unscrewing another bottle, this one containing some kind of blue gin. She paused and looked up. "I said we needed to go to the DSN. It is imperative that we do."

"Can you tell us why?" said Caroline, straightening up. "I mean, you never told us who you wanted to call."

Pandora pursed her lips, and a faint smile emerged. "Isn't it obvious?"

I frowned. "Not to me."

Caroline gave a laugh, nodding. "The mothership, of course."

"The m—you mean 'Oumuamua?"

Pandora nodded. "It is crucial that I send it a message, or Earth will be in danger."

I felt another cold shiver coming over me. "Danger?" I repeated.

"From whom, exactly?" interrupted Caroline.

"My creators."

I took a swig of the bourbon. This time it didn't taste so good. "Do they have a name?"

"Not one that you could easily pronounce."

"And they're on their way here?"

"I believe so. Unless I send a message to stop them."

Caroline's gaze burned into her. "Why do you care about us? Humanity, that is."

Pandora blinked a couple of times, as if grit had gotten into her eyes. She looked away for a beat, and then her gaze focused on me. "Because Alex Park cares about you."

Caroline shook her head. "I don't believe this—"

Pandora lay down on the bed and closed her eyes. "You should try and get some sleep. It'll be dark soon."

CHAPTER NINETEEN

"Well, when it comes to making a long-distance call, Goldstone's hard to top," Caroline said with a cynical smile as she strapped herself into the bucket seat of the heli-plane.

"We aren't going to the main complex," said Pandora. "Just to the control room of the Cassegrain antenna. That's the big one. It's sent signals to the *Voyager* spacecraft, which is now over twenty billion kilometers from Earth. That's approximately how far out 'Oumuamua will be at this time."

Pandora was already in the center seat, her fingers flying over the control pad, bringing the motors online. I could feel the vibration as the blades started to spin, but I was still amazed by the absence of any significant engine noise. My head was a little thick from all the miniatures I'd knocked back, but as Caroline and Pandora looked so fresh, I wasn't going to appear as the weak link.

"Will it have the right wavelengths to send your signal?" inquired Caroline.

Pandora nodded. "I'll adapt the transmitter accordingly. The radio frequencies used for spacecraft communication are in the microwave part of the radio spectrum. I'll just need to adjust them to the correct wavelength. That's not particularly difficult." She glanced at me. "The dish will need to be realigned, of course, while I do that."

"Why are you looking at me?" I said with a sinking feeling in my stomach.

"We'll each have a job to do. That'll be yours."

I frowned. "How the hell do I move a seventy-meter dish?"

"Believe it or not, there's a manual control room at the bottom of the tower," said Caroline with a smile. "You probably just pull the lever. Sounds like you've got the easy job."

"Okay, well won't moving a seventy-meter dish attract attention?" I said, trying not to make my cowardice really obvious.

"Yes, so we'll need a distraction," replied Pandora.

"What sort of distraction?"

"One that will keep the nearby military base occupied."

"A military base. That's great," I said.

Pandora stared across at Caroline, who gave her a quizzical look. "What, I'm the distraction?"

Pandora nodded, and I laughed out loud.

Caroline shook her head. "Fucking hell."

"This might be a stupid question," I said slowly, "but why don't we just call a press conference. You know, call everyone and announce to the world what you are? I mean, this is 'first contact,' isn't it? It's what that whole facility we're going to is all about. Finding aliens. They'll be happy as clams when you reveal what you are."

"You can't be that naive, Will," Pandora said, smiling wanly.

Caroline chuckled at that. "Do you really think they'll believe us and just let us play with their toys, no questions asked?"

"History would say otherwise," said Pandora, "and time is of the essence."

I frowned. "Yes, why is that? You said that 'Oumuamua's billions of miles away. It'll take it years to turn around and come back here, won't it? We've got plenty of time for you to send your signal. What's the rush?"

"The sooner we send the signal, the better," replied Pandora.

Caroline leaned over. "This message you're sending, it's to tell the mothership to bugger off, right? You're going to say that your initial readings were anomalous and that there's nothing to see here so move on?"

Pandora bit her lip and looked downcast. "In essence, that will be the message. But there's more to it than that."

"Such as?"

"'Oumuamua might not believe me. Its prime directive is to investigate anything that may be of interest. If it deems my initial data package was of sufficient importance, that it was 'above a certain threshold,' then it might turn around and come back, whatever I say."

I took a breath and sunk down in the seat. "Well, I hope you can be a convincing liar."

Caroline continued to stare at Pandora. "What happens if it doesn't believe you? If 'Oumuamua turns around and returns to Earth?"

Pandora slowly shook her head. "You really don't want that to happen."

The heli-plane gave a little jerk sideways and lifted into the air before banking right and gathering speed. The windows transitioned to an opaque blackness and a heads-up display wrapped around the front and overlaid a simulated image of the night sky and hills. My stomach churned as the colored dots and lines twisted vertiginously forty-five degrees as we banked aggressively again.

"Won't we be detected long before we get to the base?" asked Caroline.

Pandora shook her head. "This craft has a stealth mode, which I've optimized, and of course, it's already very quiet. We'll be flying low and landing about five hundred yards away, in this valley"—she brought up a 3D map of the Goldstone facility—"which will also give us sufficient cover from line-of-sight detection."

I peered at the map of the facility, which was highly detailed. The dish—and it was enormous even on the schematic—was currently at a forty-five-degree angle to the ground. It was perched on a stubby cylindrical edifice about thirty yards wide, its structure bolted to interlaced struts linked to what looked like a huge gyroscope. There was a high boundary fence we would need to cross and then a long pathway that led to a square building adjacent to the main dish.

Pandora settled back in the seat and closed her eyes. "Thirty-five miles to Goldstone. We'll be there inside twelve minutes. I need to sleep for a little while now."

"Are you . . . feeling alright?" I asked. "You're sleeping a lot."

She nodded, keeping her eyes closed. "More of a forced abeyance. I need to reboot. Build up my strength. Quantum phasing takes a lot of energy, and I've not been able to refuel."

I frowned. "You mean, eat?"

She smiled. "Yes, are you surprised? I have a synthetic stomach and an alimentary canal, but . . . not everything is fully functional. My metabolism can't be nutritionally supported by what you eat. Those bottles of alcohol didn't really hit the spot." She gave me an apologetic smile. "I made myself as best I could, but possibly not to last. This body may be a . . . a temporary haven at best."

"So, you can't 'refuel,' at all?" Caroline asked, making a bunny-ear gesture.

Pandora opened her eyes, and I noticed that they were dry and pale. The deep browns had faded like paint exposed to the sun. "I'm working on it." She closed her eyes again and pulled her arms and legs up so that she resembled a fetus.

"Alex?" I said.

"Let her sleep," whispered Caroline, taking off her seatbelt and standing up. "And you need to stop calling her by that name. Come on, let's go aft. We need to talk."

I unclipped as quietly as I could and eased out of the seat. We went through the rear cockpit door into the main compartment of the heli-plane. It was dimly lit and fitted out like a private jet with eight off-white leather seats down each side. Sculpted cabinets hung above the seats with no obvious handles or latches. Folding tables occupied the spaces between the seats, which also had pad-like computer terminals on their armrests. Unlike the sumptuous browns and wood of a Gulfstream jet, the overall decor was coal-black and carbon with silver inlays. At the rear of the plane was a circular hatch, which I assumed led through to the tail mechanism and electronics. Caroline sat in the nearest chair, and I took its opposite number. Our knees were inches apart. She leaned forward and stared at me, her pupils huge in the half light.

"Do you trust her?" she said, simply.

"I trusted Alex," I replied. "But that's not the same, is it?"

"No, it certainly is not."

I pursed my lips. "What specifically are you worried about?"

"Where do you want me to start? Why does she want to stop 'Oumuamua at all? Isn't this her prime directive? Remember, she's part of 'Oumuamua. She's a machine mind, a sentient quantum computer of alien manufacture. Whatever she's said about assimilating bits of Alex Park into her personality, she's not really human—she's an artificial life-form."

"She seems human to me."

"Put your feelings aside, Will." She held up a finger. "Remember our earlier conversation? The one about goals?"

I nodded slowly.

She leaned forward. "How can we be sure that Pandora's goals align with ours?"

"Machines can't have goals," I said falteringly.

"A heat-seeking missile has a goal, you idiot," she countered.

I sat back, my head sinking into the luxurious leather headrest. I thought about Pandora and whoever or whatever she was now. There were definitely hints of human emotion, and I still felt a connection with her. With Alex. But was that artificial or real? And would I be able to tell the difference? And would it matter? So many questions . . .

"Alex is in there somewhere," I said hesitantly. "Some of her, at least."

Caroline nodded slowly. "Agreed, but how much? And is it enough for her to care for humanity? To body swerve her programming? But more importantly—could she merely just be lying to us?"

I hadn't thought of that. Was it possible?

Of course it was.

Caroline was staring intently at me now. "Will, what if we're being played? What if we're pawns in a bigger game? What if this was just a ruse to get her to the DSM? What if 'Oumuamua's already heading out of the system and this is her way of contacting it and getting it to turn back? The exact opposite of what she's saying."

"I can't buy that. It doesn't feel right."

"Read my lips. She's. Not. Human."

I glowered at her. "She saved your life, Caroline. Mine too. She saved us from Becker and his private army."

She sat back in her chair and looked at me with slitted eyes. After a few seconds, she shook her head and gave a short laugh. "We need a backup plan."

"Okay, I'm listening."

Her gaze never faltered, and because of that, I knew what was coming. She leaned forward again; our knees touched, and her face stopped a few inches from mine. Her breath was sweetened with the alcohol, pleasant and warm. Her ice-blue eyes bored into mine, daring me to look away.

"Could you kill her, Will?" she said softly.

I took a deep breath. "I don't know. No."

Her hand went to my knee and rested there. "I appreciate this is hard for you, but that's not Alex Park. Whatever Pandora might say. Not really. We may need to kill her—kill it—to save humanity."

I suppressed the urge to laugh. Saving humanity. Only last week I was trying to save money to pay my rental arrears. The absurdity of it all kept coming back to me.

"It's a sad situation if I'm the best hope humanity has," I said.

Caroline's mouth smiled even though her eyes didn't. "We can't choose our destiny, Will. It chooses us."

"Deep."

This time her eyes smiled too. Now the silence was becoming uncomfortable, and her gaze was unsettling. Yet I couldn't break away. I found myself leaning forward . . . but hesitating. I felt as if this was cheating on Alex. Alex whom I now knew was dead but whose doppelgänger was ten feet away, possibly with some of her residual emotional traits and memories. It was like I had a devil and an angel on each shoulder, nipping my ears.

Then Caroline blinked and sat back. She turned her head to the side and coughed into her hand. Her gaze flicked back over me, and the moment was gone.

"How do we know it's even possible to kill her?" she said. "She's got that healing ability. And quantum shifting, whatever that actually means."

I nodded, still finding it hard to contemplate killing Alex, even if it wasn't really her. Was it still murder if she wasn't human? My mind started tying itself in knots. Pandora was a sentient life-form. A machine, sure, but really sentient. And we were talking about killing her. Or it. Did it help if I thought about Pandora as it rather than her?

"Would it actually achieve anything if we did kill her?" Caroline said, interrupting my thoughts again. "I mean, if they're already coming, wouldn't stopping her now be the worst thing to do? What if she really is able to get 'Oumuamua to turn away, and that's the only chance we have?"

She had a point. There were so many unknowns. We were thrashing about in the dark, trying to find the right levers to pull.

"I just don't think I can kill her," I said.

Caroline pursed her lips and nodded slowly. "We may not want to either."

"What do you mean?"

"What if Pandora is the only hope we have?"

CHAPTER TWENTY

The heli-plane banked aggressively toward the mountains. Up ahead, a patchwork of twinkling lights in the darkness identified Fort Irwin and its associated urban sprawl. Behind it and to the west, the antennae of Goldstone were coming into view. Towering and almost festive in their appearance, their red and yellow lights pulsed rhythmically in the night sky.

We skirted the edges of the base and headed toward the seventy-meter DSN antenna. From a distance, it resembled a little satellite dish, the sort of thing stuck on the sides of low-rent apartments in downtown city blocks. But as we approached, its cyclopean scale became apparent.

"We're in luck," said Pandora, flying the plane and pointing through the HUD at the approaching structure. "The dish is now angled almost ninety degrees from the perpendicular. The manual control room is therefore hidden behind it." She glanced at me. "You should be able to get in there without anyone seeing you."

I squinted and tried to get my bearings. The moonless night was great for our stealthy arrival, but the observatory was bathed in floodlights and lit up like a Christmas tree. There didn't appear to be anyone outside, and only a few parked vehicles were dotted around. I had to remind myself that this wouldn't be guarded like a military facility. Security was comprised of fences and gates, and inside, the scientists would come and go, doing their experiments or whatever they did while the rest of the country snoozed.

"Setting us down over there."

She indicated a small, shadowy rise behind the main structure. A footpath ran parallel to it, but there were no lights or other buildings nearby. It was about two hundred yards from the antenna.

Caroline turned in her seat. "Are you sure no one's going to spot us coming in?"

Pandora shook her head. "This craft is now completely invisible to their radar. We are running silent."

I felt my stomach drop as the heli-plane abruptly dipped at the rear and descended. The nose flattened out with a few yards to go, and we landed smoothly, the wheel's suspension feeling soft and springy. The rotors disengaged immediately, and the wind and electronic sounds faded. Pandora extinguished all the cabin lights except for a curved monitor down the center console. She brought up a map of the facility with the position of the heli-plane highlighted by a red cross. The main antenna was closest, with a crop of outbuildings another hundred yards away.

"That's the control room, where I'll be," she said. "Once I've programmed the message into the transmitter, I'll keep out of sight until the dish is in position."

I clicked my teeth. "Which is my job, right?"

She nodded earnestly. "Once the dish is pointing at 'Oumuamua, I'll be able to send the message."

"Does the dish have a steering wheel?" I said.

She laughed, her face crinkling into a recognizable facsimile of Alex. A part of me melted, but I shook it off. "This isn't funny," I said. "You can't seriously expect me to know what to do here."

"No, Will. I am going to show you."

She closed her eyes, and there was a scratching inside my eyeballs while a pressure built up in my head like I was diving deep underwater. A wave of nausea overcame me, and I thought I was going to vomit, but as soon as it had come, it went. I looked up, and Pandora was smiling again.

"What happened just then?" I said.

"I've given you the information you need," she said. "When you get inside, you'll know what to do."

I shook my head and turned to Caroline, a smart remark on my lips, when I saw that she was also looking green around the gills and had her hands around her face. "She did something to you as well?" I said.

She nodded and frowned at Pandora. "What did you give me?"

"The skills to pilot this heli-plane," she replied. "You'll provide the distraction, remember? Oh, and our means of escape."

"Sounds like you've got this all worked out," Caroline said frostily.

"I have; trust me," Pandora replied, not responding to Caroline's sarcasm. The door hissed and unfolded, and a warm breeze entered the cabin. She got out of the seat and waved at me to do the same. "Time to go."

"Wait, one more thing," I said. "How will you know when the dish is ready to transmit the signal?"

Her face creased into a smile. "I'll just look out the window." She stuck her finger in the air. "Remember, it needs to be pointing straight up."

Right.

Caroline squeezed past me and settled into the pilot's seat. She reached out and waggled her fingers, and a steering yoke unfolded from the floor. It was shaped like a hockey stick and studded with buttons and flickering red and blue LEDs. She shook her head and looked up at me, a crazy smile plastered on her lips.

"Jesus. I actually know what these buttons are for, and I've never been in a pilot's seat before today."

"A day of many firsts," I said.

She beamed at me and reached out and squeezed my hand. I squeezed back.

"Good luck," she said.

I nodded and exited the heli-plane. Pandora was waiting for me, leaning against the starboard engine. She was staring into the sky, a faraway look in her eyes. I followed her gaze. Stars filled the sky, and the frosted stripe of the Milky Way bisected the heavens. I'd never really been one for stargazing or philosophizing over the universe. But now, peering upward into the void, it was with the sure knowledge that there was life in the darkness, in the absolute cold of space.

Life other than humanity. Almost certainly vastly older and more advanced than us. And maybe on their way here.

"How long will it take to move the dish?" I said, tearing my gaze away from the firmament.

"Once you program the new attitude and press Send, it'll take ten minutes for the dish to get into position. The mechanism's quite old."

I nodded. "And while the dish is moving, it'll be pretty bloody obvious to all, right?"

"It's a big, noisy dish," she acknowledged. "Hence Caroline will be providing something more interesting for them to think about."

I ran as fast as I could, keeping low to the ground and staying in the shadows of a low-set wall and some well-tended trees. My destination was a gray doorway just visible under the edge of the dish, which was pointing directly at me and obscuring the rest of the building. Directly in my path was an unlocked gate and, by the side of the main building, a truck with a jumble of interconnected tubes and ladders on its roof. Parked next to it was a trailer stacked with what looked like gas cylinders. A ring of floodlights lit up the immediate area, making a truly stealthy approach almost impossible.

I slowed as I came parallel to the first truck and bent over, hands on my knees, getting my breath back. I sneaked a peak around its huge tires, but there didn't appear to be anyone else around. The main Goldstone complex was too close for comfort, and I thought I could see people moving behind the windows. I checked my watch. It was half past four in the morning. According to Pandora's estimates, she should now be inside the control room. I'd no idea how she was planning to get to the equipment and the controller desk, but I reckoned it'd have something to do with her quantum-shifting ability.

I scanned the skies. Any minute now, Caroline was supposed to take off for Fort Irwin and buzz the place. I sucked in my breath again and waited. There was very little sound, just the odd cricket and insect noise. It was windless, and the air was dry, warm, and smelled of freshly mown grass.

There was movement against the stars as the heli-plane finally took off from behind the hill. It banked soundlessly away, a shadow against the sky, visible only by the black hole it produced in the star field. In a few minutes, she'd be at Fort Irwin, and all hell would break loose. Although there were a few thousand active soldiers on duty, we reasoned that there should only be a few helicopters, and it would be unlikely they would be on standby. Pandora had told us that the base also had a curfew of 9:00 p.m., as it was predominantly a training facility. I hoped that the sudden appearance of a quasi-helicopter-airplane buzzing the base would trump an unplanned realignment of one of the Goldstone dishes forty miles away.

Time to go.

I ran over to the gray doorway. It was locked but had an illuminated keypad. Freakily, the codes just dropped into my head, and I punched the numbers in. The locks clicked as the tumblers moved and the barrels retracted. I pulled the door open and quickly ducked inside.

Lights automatically turned on as I entered. The room was about the size of my garage. One wall was lined with panels of switches and lights and knobs, and against the other wall were two desks with old-fashioned computer monitors and chairs. I pulled up the chair by the nearest desk and sat down. There was a dinner-plate-sized circular LED panel in the middle surrounded by slide switches and buttons. Nothing looked particularly high-tech, but then I remembered Caroline telling me that the antenna was built over half a century ago. I was surprised it wasn't all transistors and steam-driven levers.

On the right of the panel was a joystick with what looked like preset controls at its base and a large circular dial. Weirdly, I knew what to do. I flicked the control panel on and set the dish gyroscopic motor from Sleep to Active. Lights illuminated a panel above me, and I punched a couple more switches and waited until there was a row of green lights. I turned the dial by the joystick to one hundred eighty degrees and pressed a green switch.

It sounded like a tornado was passing overhead as the huge motors kicked in and the gyros started moving. A graphic representation of the dish appeared on the circular panel, with a compass showing its attitude. The figures were changing as I watched, and so I assumed the dish was moving as I'd directed.

According to Alex, I had ten minutes before it was in the correct position. No, not according to Alex. To Pandora.

The static in my head coupled with the noise from the motors numbed my cognitive processes. Nothing made sense anymore. Bereavement had been my companion these past few years, a shadow that in time had lessened as my life had begun to have new direction and meaning. Nico, bless him, had relentlessly urged me to move on, saying that I was a fool to keep looking and yearning for her. He meant well, but I'd still hear her voice in my dreams, laugh at the stupid things she would say, and melt at the way the corners of her mouth formed divots when she smiled.

I stood up and leaned against the desktop, my fingertips gripping it tightly. Without warning, grief overcame me. Tears spilled from my eyes, and the dials and switches blurred as if I was underwater. In that moment, the sure knowledge that life would go on without her, that time was only stopped for me, undid me completely. All pretense of quiet coping was lost, and my head dropped into my hands. The gyroscope's noise drowned out my sobbing, the raw guttural cries that ripped my breath away and left my throat husky. I wiped the tears away with my sleeves and sat back, breathing deeply and trying to get a grip on my self-control.

The dial was approaching perpendicular, and so the dish would be in position shortly.

There was nothing else for me to do here, so I pushed back the chair and stood up. As I did, the door opened and a man stepped through, carrying a flashlight. He was very tall and thin, wearing a lab coat. A scraggly dark beard that clung to his skin like seaweed mostly obscured his face. He pointed the flashlight at me even though the lights were all on, and I raised my hand to block out the beam.

"What are you doing here?" he growled.

I tried to appear nonchalant. "Maintenance crew?"

His eyes narrowed, and he reached into his pocket and brought out a two-way radio. He thumbed the switch. "Cliff, this is Patrick. You there, copy?"

There was a crackle and then: "Copy. What have you got?"

Patrick looked at me and gestured with his flashlight to the seat I'd just vacated. "Sit down, right now."

For a second, I thought about making a run for the door, but he had six inches on me, and the flashlight looked like a solid hunk of metal. But then the decision was made for me as two new guys entered behind him, both wearing security uniforms. One was a huge black man, his sleeves rolled up and arms covered in tattoos. The other an older white guy, his face lined from years of sun exposure. Both stared at me unblinkingly as I sank back into the chair.

Patrick turned to the black guy. "Thanks, that was quick. No idea who this dude is, but he sure as hell doesn't work here."

The guy, who I assumed was Cliff, flicked his chin at me. "What are you doing here, pal?"

I decided to stay nothing, and just stared back at him blankly.

Patrick's walkie-talkie crackled again, and he brought it back up to his mouth. "Patrick."

"Go ahead, what've you got?" came the static-ridden reply.

Patrick looked me up and down. "Some dude, here on his own. Not sure how he got in here, but he's the one that moved the dish."

A crackle, then: "Okay, bring him up. We've got a bigger problem anyway."

CHAPTER TWENTY-ONE

A powdery-blue sky to the east announced the approaching dawn as I was frog-marched between the two security guys and across the parched earth toward the main control building. Patrick brought up the rear after having tried to reset the dish's attitude. Unfortunately for him, I'd locked everyone out of the controls. We entered through a sliding door that opened out into a capacious area that just screamed "mission control," like those pictures beamed around the world from NASA during moon shots and space-shuttle launches. Despite the hour, there were around two dozen people in the room: mainly middle-aged men dressed in white shirts and ties. There was an omnipresent smell of ozone and coffee, and it was chilly, the air conditioner in the roof cranked up to the max and humming loudly. Desks were arranged in rows like church pews and were covered with computer screens, books, manuals, and neatly stacked paperwork. Printers and telephones metastasized onto mobile tables, wires trailing dangerously between them. Five huge display screens occupied the front wall, each presenting images of star fields, computer-generated diagrams, and schematics. Data and messages scrolled across and up and down all the screens in bright blues and greens and reds. There seemed to be a lot of red numbers up there, which I guessed were Pandora's work. I just hoped she'd had enough time to send the signal.

Patrick shoved me in the back and pointed me toward one of the desks where a fit-looking, gray-haired man was holding court with a group of six others, all sweaty and overweight. He was gesticulating like an orchestra conductor toward the screens, his voice raised. As he saw me approaching, he broke off and folded his arms. His eyes bored into mine, and his expression looked like he'd stepped in dog shit.

"This is the guy?" he said, his voice hard.

"I'm the guy," I replied, trying to be cool.

He walked up to me and got in my face. His breath smelled of coffee, and his eyes were bloodshot. "Who do you work for?"

I shrugged. "I'm self-employed, if you must know."

His expression became even darker, and I wondered whether I'd pushed him too far. He glanced over my shoulder at Patrick. "You reset the dish, right?"

"I tried to, yes," Patrick replied, frustration in his voice. "But the controls are locked."

The gray-haired man stepped back and pointed at the screens. "Something's infected our systems. Some kind of computer virus. We've lost all comms with our birds and satellites." He looked at me again and moved in close, nose-to-nose. "What've you done to my equipment?"

So Pandora must have succeeded. I wondered where she was. I looked around the room; maybe I was expecting to see her crouching behind a monitor.

"Hey," he said again, tapping me on the chest. "I'm asking you a question."

"This is the second time in the last few days that someone's accused me of crashing their precious systems," I said frostily.

He looked incredulously at me. "Are you trying to say this wasn't your doing?"

I pointed to the screens. "I've had nothing to do with that."

"We caught you moving the big antenna. Or are you going to deny that as well?"

A crowd had gathered around us. Again, I glanced around the room, wondering where Pandora was, and then started to ponder how I was going to get out of there. The two security guys were loitering near the exits, looking bored. One had his cell phone out. A landline phone was ringing on the desk next to us. To my amazement, it was one of those red phones you see in the movies. The one where the important calls come through. Or the one direct to Commissioner Gordon in Bruce Wayne's manor.

The gray-haired man scowled down at the phone. I noted his name badge: Dr. Tom McBurney, Director, NASA-JPL. I decided to stall and put out a hand.

"We've not been introduced. My name's Will Logan."

His lips curled downward. "Just so you know, the police and military are on the way to take you into custody. If this has all been a prank, now's the time to come clean."

I left my hand out there and raised my eyebrows. Reluctantly he took it but gripped it hard, a real man-shake, like a politician wanting to show dominance to a rival.

"Shouldn't you get that?" I said, nodding at the phone. "Looks important."

He stared at me for a few more seconds before releasing me from his death grip and grabbing the phone.

"McBurney." He scowled, not taking his eyes off me. I noticed that the room had also gone quieter, the rest of the scientists and technicians swiveling in their seats, no longer typing or talking. McBurney nodded a few times and looked up at the screens. "Yes . . . no . . . no, we didn't know that. Are you sure?" He snapped a finger at two guys sitting at a console a few yards away. "Screen four, bring up the telemetry from the other waveguide antennae . . . now!"

They scrambled back to their screens, fingers tap-tapping on keyboards. McBurney continued to listen to the voice on the end of the phone, his eyes narrowing. "You're sure? Where's it come from?"

Screen four rebooted with an unintelligible (to me at least) data stream, dropping like a waterfall. Again, the numbers were mostly angry-looking red ones. McBurney put the phone in the crook of his neck and twisted to watch the information dump.

"And that's what you've seen at DSOC as well?" he said. Then he looked at me. "Yes, we have the guy here. He was caught moving the big dish. Looks like all the others have been reset as well. Simultaneously, it would appear, all pointing to the same area of the sky." He shook his head. "No, I don't know how he did that either. It shouldn't be possible."

He listened again for a minute or so, nodding and looking grimmer and grimmer with each passing second. Then he hung up and took a deep breath, wiping his mouth with his sleeve. He turned to me and leaned back on the desk, folding his arms. I met his stare and waited. He gestured to the security guys to come over, and they appeared at my shoulder.

"What's going on?" I said.

I was hustled up two flights of stairs into a small common room complete with utilitarian tables and chairs, a sink, and a coffee percolator. There was a large window looking out onto the grounds. The view was pretty special, sunlight upgrading the world outside to some higher definition. The big dish was still pointing directly upright, its shadow stretching halfway up the hill. A couple of the other smaller antennae were now visible in the morning light, all their dishes similarly pointing straight up into the sky. Flags fluttered lazily from three poles directly across from the control room. Roadside lawns were all beautifully tended with multicolored bushes and plants. The surrounding hills were not as yellow-gray as they had seemed last night but verdant with foliage. As I watched, a dusty cloud materialized over the hill, and the first vehicle of an army convoy appeared.

The security guys sat me down at one of the tables, and McBurney took a chair opposite. The door opened again, and a middle-aged Asian woman bustled through and sat down next to him, talking into her cell phone. McBurney snapped his fingers at me, dragging my gaze away from the window.

"Okay, Mr. Logan. I've been informed that the army is going to be here in a few minutes. Why do they even know about this? Is there anything you want to tell me before they take you into custody?"

I pursed my lips. "I did move the dish."

"We know that," he said exasperatedly. "But why?"

I shrugged. He looked even more pissed.

"And that's not all you did, is it?" he said, leaning forward.

"It really was," I replied straight-faced.

He shook his head, turned to his companion, and held out his hand. "Sakura, what've you got?"

The woman handed over her phone, showing him the screen. "It's all there," she said, "confirmed by Pasadena."

He stared at the phone, expanding the images here and there and flicking through the pages. He then dropped it onto the table and gave a short laugh. "What the hell have you done, Will?"

"I really just moved the dish," I said again, looking out of the window at the approaching army convoy. It was mostly Humvees and jeeps, but there were also two large SUVs with blacked-out windows. Something blinked in front of the sun, like an aircraft passing at high altitude. I was thinking about Caroline and the heli-plane when McBurney slapped the table, loud and unexpectedly. I flinched backward, as did Sakura, who looked at him with furrowed brows. He pushed the cell phone back to her and leaned forward, elbows on the table, fists clenched.

"You did much more than that. A signal was sent from here, from this network. We can't decipher it as it's encrypted, but it was sent to a point in our solar system just inside the orbit of Neptune. What do you have to say about that?"

I felt my stomach tightening. "You can't arrest me, so I don't have to say anything. And even if I did, I'd want a lawyer present."

McBurney's forehead creased as he sat back in his chair and folded his arms. "Seriously, you're thinking of lawyering up?"

I shrugged at him.

"What's in the message, Will? Who was it sent to?"

I matched his posture, folding my arms. I figured that time was on my side.

Any message sent by Pandora would take over five hours to reach 'Oumua-mua, and then any reply would be another five hours. I just needed to find her.

McBurney interrupted my musings: "I don't think you did this on your own either. No messages could have been sent from the antenna's manual-control room. That would have had to come from inside this facility."

"Maybe it's an inside job," I said snarkily. "Do you trust everyone you work with?"

He looked about to burst when Sakura's phone buzzed. She grabbed it and pushed her chair backward. She walked over to the window and stood head down, listening intently. I watched her face drop and her eyes widen. She shook her head and nodded before hanging up and returning to the table. Her phone buzzed again, but this time she opened the screen on the table and accessed a page of data. She pushed it across the table to McBurney who stared at it, his own mouth opening and closing like a fish out of water.

"Is this . . . real?" he said.

Sakura nodded slowly, looking across the table at me.

"What?" I said.

McBurney stood up and snapped his fingers at the security goons who were leaning against the door. "Find out how close the army is."

One of them inclined his head to speak into the walkie-talkie fastened to his lapel. He listened for a beat and then said, "Copy that." He walked over to McBurney and leaned over to whisper something in his ear. I heard the words *helicopter* and *breach*, but not much else. I guessed this was something to do with Caroline.

The door opened and a military officer flanked by four soldiers walked in. The soldiers had their M4 rifles pointed downward, loose but ready. The officer, a serious-looking man in his early thirties, glanced my way but walked toward McBurney and put an arm around his shoulder, directing him into a corner of the room. He was a head taller than McBurney and bent his head down to talk to him. The conversation appeared intense. McBurney was getting all agitated while the officer just stood there, nodding and interjecting occasionally.

McBurney pointed over at me once or twice, stabbing gestures, full of urgency. The officer shook his head with a degree of finality before McBurney raised a finger, begging for a moment. He strode over to me and took a deep breath.

"Will, they're going to take you away. There's been an incursion at the base, and they think you're involved."

I gave him flat eyes. The muscles in the side of his cheek bunched.

"Will, you need to tell me what's going on. I need to—" His eyes took on a desperate appearance, and he leaned closer, almost whispering in my ear. "Sakura tells me we've detected a return signal. Vectoring from the exact same point in space the message was sent to."

I shook my head. "That's impossible. It's much too soon. The distances involved—"

He nodded vigorously. "Yes, yes, I know, but the signal has been confirmed. As soon as the dishes were all aligned in parallel, the signal almost blew our receivers."

"I don't understand how that could have happened," I said honestly. "Our signal has just been sent—"

He leaned even closer, his coffee breath overpowering me. "Will, the return signal is a standard radio wave traveling at the speed of light. It can't have been a response to what you or your coconspirator did." He grabbed my shoulder. "Will, who did you send it to?" Then he took a step backward, his face frozen. "Or to *what*?"

Before I could answer, the officer put a hand on McBurney's arm, gently pushing it down. "We'll take it from here," he said firmly.

McBurney frowned. "I need more time to talk with him."

The officer's face was unreadable. "We're taking him to Irwin. You're welcome to come along, Director, but he is under military jurisdiction now. You know the protocols."

"Then you're damn right I'm coming with him," McBurney replied.

The officer waved to his men, and they led us out of the room and back down the stairs.

We marched through the control room with everyone watching our little procession. Outside, one of the Humvee's doors was open and another soldier was standing by, weapon at the ready. I was pushed into the back seat, and McBurney jumped in next to me. The solder took up the last seat in the rear, while the officer climbed in the front passenger side. Once the door was shut, the driver cranked the gears and the big truck spun on the pavement and accelerated past the big dish and out of the main gates. I twisted to see the rest of the convoy slotting into line behind us.

McBurney leaned in and put a hand on my knee. "Thirty minutes to Irwin, Will."

I nodded to myself, deep in thought.

Then McBurney started to laugh. Softly, and not manically, but a happy sort of laugh as if he'd just been given a present that he'd been waiting for all his life. He looked at me and shook his head in apparent disbelief.

"It's aliens, right. Am I right, Will? This is it, isn't it? First contact. Oh my god."

I twisted back from the window and stared at him. Happy as a clam. He had no idea.

"You're not ready for this," I said.

CHAPTER TWENTY-TWO

The sky continued to brighten as we hurtled east along the two-lane highway from Goldstone to Fort Irwin. This was the only road to and from the military base, and there didn't appear to be any vehicles coming the other way. Once we got past the comms offices and the fork leading to a road simply called Nasa, it was a boring blacktop winding around gently sloping hills dotted with scraggly-looking bushes.

No one in the Humvee was talkative, probably because the engine was so loud and the ride so bumpy. However, McBurney kept looking at me, his brow furrowed, his eyes active and jumpy. I knew he wanted to talk more, but I'd brushed him off with my last comment and stared resolutely out the window. The implications of what he'd told me were going round and round in my head. There was already a signal here from 'Oumuamua. Had Pandora indeed been lying to us? And if so, what exactly was the signal she was so desperate to send?

"Something's happening up ahead," said McBurney, interrupting my thoughts.

I leaned forward to see over the officer's shoulder through the windshield. There was black smoke drifting above the top of a steeper part of the hill around the curve of the road. The officer, whose name I'd learned was Captain Laurier, told our driver to slow down and scrabbled for the short-wave radio, which was buried in the long and broad central compartment of the Humvee. Finding it, he barked commands to the vehicles bringing up the rear as the Humvee cranked down through the gearbox and slowed to a crawling pace. As we rounded the edge of the hill, the source of the smoke became apparent. Lying across the road was our heli-plane. It was positioned on its belly at a slight angle, and thick black smoke was billowing from one of its engines. The side door of the cockpit was hanging awkwardly from a hinge, and the front windshield was smashed in.

"Is that one of ours?" said McBurney.

Laurier glanced back at us, his eyes narrowed. "Definitely not. Never seen that design." He clicked his walkie-talkie on again as our Humvee pulled up and stopped about thirty yards from the downed FVL. "This is Laurier. We seem to have come across that helicopter. The one that was flying over the base. It's down across Goldstone Road about two miles from Irwin. Do you copy?"

He released the button, and I heard crackling, then: "Copy. Air support will be with you in thirty seconds. Stay on station."

I strained to see more. I was looking for Caroline. Had she survived the crash? I wanted to get out, and so I jiggled the door handle. Laurier shook his head. "Sit tight. We've got incoming."

"Was it shot down?" I asked, squinting at the FVL, looking for bullet holes.

"Sure seems that way," he replied with a grim smile.

McBurney was also leaning on the edge of the front seat and looking even more concerned. He tapped Laurier on the shoulder. "Hey, if your birds shot this thing down, why aren't they already here?"

Laurier grunted and turned away. "Maybe a jet took it out."

The driver turned the Humvee engine off and leaned out of the window to scan the skies. There was a subliminal thump-thump just at the threshold of perception, but it was getting progressively louder. Two choppers appeared over the hill. I recognized them from movies: Apache attack helicopters. Black and deadly and armed to the teeth with Gatling guns and missiles. They banked around the hill and set down twenty yards apart on the scrubland on either side of the road. Thick blankets of dust blew everywhere as leaves, stones, and dry grass ricocheted into the side of the Humvee. The noise of the rotors was deafening. Laurier was on the walkie-talkie again, but this time I couldn't hear him. He was nodding furiously and seemed to be talking to the pilot of one of the Apaches. Even though they'd landed, the Apaches' rotors were not stopping. Maybe that was Laurier's beef with them.

He threw the handset back into the tray and twisted in his seat to look at us. "Stay here."

I raised my hands, like what else was I going to do?

Laurier got out and was joined by four soldiers from one of the other trucks in our convoy. He pulled out his sidearm, and they all started walking slowly toward the FVL, which was now just barely visible, a blur behind the dust onslaught. The soldiers raised their weapons, and Laurier gave a couple of hand gestures to make them fan out. They split up and cautiously approached the FLV. Without warning, its rotors started up; both props kicked up even more dirt and rocks and blew the black smoke from the damaged rotor toward us. Within a few seconds, I couldn't see either the FLV or the soldiers.

Get ready.

The voice in my head wasn't mine.

A pressure suddenly built up around my temples, like two hands squashing my skull. Jagged lines of electric blue danced across my retinae, and my eyes closed involuntarily. My brain felt numb and sleepy, and I wanted to scratch my scalp but couldn't move my arms. My breathing slowed, and my heartbeat boomed loudly in my ears.

Will, get ready. Do what she says.

I took a deep, shaking breath. Do what who says? I couldn't move a muscle, so how was I going to do anything? Who was talking to me? I didn't recognize the voice at all; it was sexless and robotic and echoing as if it was bouncing off the walls of an empty hangar.

The pressure abruptly vanished, and it felt like I was surfacing from a dive. As my eyes opened, the side window shattered and glass exploded into the Humvee.

"Will, get out!"

I pulled my hands from my face, surprised they weren't covered in my blood. Caroline was standing by the door, holding a semiautomatic rifle and gesturing frantically to me. She was wearing clear wraparound goggles and her hair was smeared with dirt.

"What the . . . Caroline?" I spluttered.

"Get the hell out, now!" she yelled, pulling the door open. The intensity of the dust bombardment amplified as more shit blew into the Humvee, and the noise of the FLV's rotors hitting the dirt became thunderous.

I climbed out of the vehicle and dropped to the ground, covering my eyes from the blasted sand and soil that pricked my skin like a thousand acupuncture needles. Caroline continued to point her gun at the two soldiers still in the cab. One made a sly move to grab his personal weapon, but she stuck the rifle farther into the Humvee, and he quickly fanned his fingers and pulled back. McBurney stared at me, mouth agape, hands raised in abject terror. He started to say something, but his words were lost in the wind as Caroline grabbed me and pushed me across the blacktop toward the Apaches. I couldn't see anything in front of me, so I kept my eyes down and concentrated on not tripping over rocks and crevices in the scrub.

The nearest Apache loomed out of the blizzard of sand and stones, a black shadow pregnant with gun and missile attachments. Its rotor was slowly stopping and the engine noise tailing off as it was powering down. I peered into the cockpit. There was no pilot or copilot to be seen. The second Apache was twenty yards away, its rotors still spinning. It squatted uneasily as if it was trying to take off but was caught between the earth and the sky. I reflexively ducked down so as not to be decapitated, but Caroline just pulled me forward and gave me a look that I interpreted as "don't be a pussy." The helicopter was longer than I was expecting, and from the side it looked evil and serpentine.

Most of the engine and gunnery was behind a cockpit that was perched high above the front wheels. The two pilot compartments, one behind the other, sat uneasily under the whirling rotor blades. Some sort of targeting radar array was bolted onto the nose, and there was a vicious-looking, harpoon-like weapon slung underneath.

Something moved in the front seat, and Pandora came into view, strapping a helmet on and then flipping switches on a panel above her head.

Caroline yelled in my ear, "Get in, it's a tight fit, so you first."

"Where's the crew? I don't understand—"

Caroline's eyes were wide under the goggles. "Pandora—she—I don't know how she does what she does . . . but we've got a chance to get away from here."

I peered under the Apache, expecting to see bodies, but there was nothing.

"Move it, you asshole," Caroline hissed, giving me another push in the back.

There were recessed footholds, so I grabbed hold of the wing and pulled myself up. There was only one seat in the navigator's cockpit. I looked down at Caroline and was about to object, but she furiously gestured for me to hurry up. I swung a leg over the sill and climbed in. Caroline threw the rifle and the goggles to the ground and clambered in after me. I squeezed forward as far as I could go, and she swung her leg behind me and sank into the same seat. I pulled the canopy down, and as it locked shut, she wrapped her arms around me and buried her head in my neck.

"Definitely cozy," I shouted back.

Then the pressure was in my head again, and the voice returned. *Are you secured back there?*

Amazingly, I wasn't surprised. Considering everything that had happened so far, telepathy should have been a given.

"We're good," I yelled.

No need to shout. I can hear you.

The rotors cranked up a notch, and my stomach turned as the Apache jerked forward and then up into the sky. The dust cloud fell away, and my vision returned. Lacy, white-edged clouds filled the blue sky, and the sun was already a burning yellow orb low over the horizon. I felt its heat on my face as we climbed, and I closed my eyes letting the adrenaline ebb from my bloodstream.

"Where are we going?" I said, turning back to Caroline.

Her head turned slightly, and her lips touched my ear. They lingered there for a few seconds longer than I'd expected. "Singularity," she shouted.

I swallowed. Back to where it all began.

"How did you get away?"

I felt her shaking her head, and then her lips were pressed against my ear again. "You won't believe it."

Overwhelming fatigue once again came over me, and I nodded, letting my head drop forward against the back of the pilot's seat. Caroline lowered her head again on my neck, and I felt her arms tighten around my waist as we banked sharply and pulled level.

ETA: seventy-two minutes.

Sleep came easy.

CHAPTER TWENTY-THREE

jerked awake as the Apache touched down. The rotors slowed as the engines were cut and the sound's decrescendo caused my ears to pop. I stretched, feeling my neck crack, and looked out of the cockpit windows. We were on a tarmac airstrip in a helicopter-landing circle. A dozen or so yards ahead was a rock wall with an arch-shaped tunnel. A barrier and a window-lined security booth blocked the road into the rock.

"Recognize this place?" Caroline said into my ear.

I nodded. It was Singularity's FVL airstrip. Last time we'd left in a hurry. I had a vision of flashes of gunfire and the windshield of the FVL being peppered with spiderwebs as bullets impacted it and ricocheted.

"Where do you think everyone is?" I asked.

"Everyone's dead, remember?" she replied.

That wasn't what I meant. Lots of people had worked at this facility. The cafeteria, the mezzanine floor, the lecture theater, the laboratories—and the scientists, technicians, and administrative staff that must have filled them. Hundreds of people.

"Where are all the bodies?" I said. "We were stepping over them."

The front cockpit window flipped open, and Pandora pulled herself out and climbed down the side of the Apache. Caroline reached past me and undid the clasp on our window, and I felt her squeezing up out of the seat. Once she'd crawled over me, I clambered up and around the frame and hopped down onto the tarmac. There were birds squawking, and I could hear the bubbling of a river not far away. A warm breeze ruffled my fringe. Everything felt normal. As if nothing had happened here.

Pandora stood by the helicopter, hands clasped behind her back. She smiled at me, and again, the resemblance to Alex was disconcerting. The same crinkles in the side of her mouth, the same way she held her head. I returned the smile as best I could, remembering that this wasn't her. This wasn't real. Alex was dead, and although parts of her memory clearly lived on in Pandora's mind, her personality—whatever made Alex who she'd been—no longer existed. I knew that if I continued thinking of her like that it'd destroy me. I had to walk away and accept that she was dead.

No matter how hard it was with her doppelgänger staring me in the face.

"Why have you brought us back here, Pandora?" I asked, my voice calmer than I felt. "And what happened at Goldstone?"

"We're on the clock, Will," she said, absently, turning away toward the tunnel.

I snapped. I was having none of it. I grabbed her by the shoulder, spinning her round. Her eyes widened, and for a moment, I thought she was going to strike me, but I didn't care. I pointed a finger at her and offloaded. "I have a shitload of questions that need answers before I take another fucking step."

Caroline appeared at my shoulder. "He deserves answers," she said to Pandora. "As do I."

Pandora's head dropped, and she gave a very human-like sigh. Then she nodded slowly to herself before looking up and fixing us both with an unsettling stare.

"You're not going to like this," she said softly.

I suppressed a snort. "So what's new?"

"No, no—you're really not going to like this."

I tried to meet her gaze, but it was hard. Unconsciously, I started chewing on a finger and then stopped myself. I knew that feeling nervous or anxious was a normal emotion to have in this situation—otherwise I'd be an idiot. Or so I tried to convince myself.

"Can we walk and talk?" she suggested.

I looked at Caroline, who shrugged. We set off toward the entrance. I noticed a dark smear on the tarmac near the gate boom. As we passed, I dipped a toe in it, but nothing transferred onto my shoe. Maybe I was imagining stuff. Probably just aviation fuel or something. But weren't the FVL electric? I peered into the windows of the security booth. The door was ajar, but no one was inside, alive or dead. I thought that there was another smear on the floor, and I wiped my sleeve over the window to see better. I felt Pandora's hand on my arm, and she gently pulled me away from the booth.

"Did we achieve anything at Goldstone?" I said to Pandora as we stopped at the boom gate.

Pandora stopped and folded her arms. "Yes and no."

Caroline's eyes flashed. "Explain?"

Pandora threw a brief glance at her before focusing on me. "When I got into Goldstone's systems, I detected an existing signal from 'Oumuamua. It had been piggybacking transmissions from one of NASA's deep-space probes, *Voyager 1.*"

"Surely that's impossible," Caroline cut in. "Its batteries ran out in 2025. It's more than fifteen billion miles away."

Pandora shook her head. "Somehow, *Voyager 1*'s generators are still functioning, and so it's still transmitting messages back to the controllers on Earth. Actually, to the Deep Space Network at Goldstone. It was a simple matter for 'Oumuamua to send its transmission alongside it and remain undetected. No one was really expecting anything interesting from *Voyager 1* as it entered interstellar space, and so no one looked for it."

"But you found it?" I asked.

"As soon as you aligned the main dish, Will, the signal was amplified a thousand times," she acknowledged. "The other dishes were already pointing to the same area of the sky. They just needed the focus of the main antenna."

So that was what McBurney was on about when he said the signal almost blew their receivers. The big dish had just collected the entire signal and downloaded it to the DSN receivers all in one dump.

"But you sent the message, right?" I said. "To tell 'Oumuamua to turn back."

"I was going to, but realized that it was pointless," Pandora replied, shaking her head.

I looked at Caroline. "No it isn't! The message would've been sent at the speed of light. It would've gotten there in five hours. It must take, oh I don't know, *years* for that ship to turn around and make its way to Earth, right? Right?"

Caroline was nodding and looking at Pandora. "Yes, he's correct. So even if 'Oumuamua is on its way, we've still got lots of time to get ready. To let the world know what's coming. We can show them you, Pandora, we can—"

"That's not going to work," said Pandora sadly.

"Yes," I said, nodding furiously. "We must! It's our duty to—"

"No, you don't understand," she said, her voice raised. "'Oumuamua is not turning around. It's already accelerating and leaving your system, heading back into interstellar space and onto its next destination."

Caroline laughed, a manic kind of bark. "You lied to us then."

Pandora stopped at the entrance to the tunnel and turned around. "No, I thought that there was a chance. But once I found that the signal had already arrived . . . you need to understand that 'Oumuamua was never a seed probe—a robot capable of landing on a planet in a target solar system in order to build up a new civilization from scratch. That would be unfeasible given the size of the galaxy and the limitations of the speed of light."

"Okay, well what is it?" Caroline demanded.

Pandora's mouth twitched. "I didn't lie to you before. 'Oumuamua is indeed a scout. Its function is to locate habitable planets."

"And it found one, or rather you did," Caroline said accusingly.

"Before I made landfall, I'd uploaded initial readings of Earth's biosphere to 'Oumuamua. Contrary to what you think, Earth-type planets with oxygen and intelligent life are almost unique in the universe. They are . . . fought over."

"By aliens?" I exclaimed.

"Yes," said Pandora. "Wars have been fought over such planets for millions of years." She closed her eyes. "Once I had identified Earth as one of those planets, my priority would have been to set up an antenna capable of receiving the data packages. However, once I had repaired my systems and came back online, I was inside the Faraday cage constructed by Becker. I was unable to break out."

I looked up. "You virtually resurrected Alex Park and got me brought to you."

She nodded, smiling faintly.

"You used me," I said. "You used us all. You've set humanity up for your . . . creators to come in and take over."

"I am sorry. I—I had no choice. There is a prime directive that overrides all my other programming. A root command, if you like. I can no more disobey it as you can order your heart to stop beating or your lungs to stop breathing."

"So why did we need to go to Goldstone at all?" Caroline jumped in.

"There was still a chance that my initial message didn't get through to 'Oumuamua. That there was no return signal. So I had to check."

"But you wouldn't have done anything about it, would you?" Caroline snarled. "You used us when you needed our help, but all the time, you were just fulfilling your maker's wishes. Like the fucking pocket computer you really are underneath all this . . . fucking skin or whatever it is you're made of."

Pandora flinched in the face of Caroline's rising anger. "I had no choice, don't you understand? But Alex Park—"

Caroline grabbed her by the throat, pulled the gun out of her waistband, and pressed it against her cheek. I rushed forward, but she waved the gun at me, and I skidded to a stop, hands raised. Caroline's eyes were blazing, and I could see that a line had been crossed. She pointed the gun back at Pandora and lowered her face so that they were level.

"You were going to give us away as a prize to some aliens, that's what you just told us. And lucky for us we stopped you from doing it. Actually, Becker did us all favor with his Faraday cage. Who cared if he was making a buck or two from it? He saved the fucking world, right, Will?"

There was spittle on the side of Caroline's mouth, and I knew she was moments away from putting a bullet into Pandora's head. I thought about the quantum shifting that Pandora was able to do and wondered why she hadn't done that yet. Maybe she wasn't recharged enough, wasn't that what she called it? Instead, she just hung limply in Caroline's grip, not even raising her hands to ease the pressure on her neck. She glanced at me, and I saw that her eyes were wet. My head suddenly felt heavy, and a veil of blackness descended.

We don't have time for this, Will. Let me explain. Please, help me.

I blinked, and my vision returned. I stared at Pandora and could only see Alex. Alex in pain, Alex helpless. Alex about to be shot in the head.

I rushed forward and grabbed both of Caroline's hands and pushed them up, away from Pandora's neck and head.

"What the hell, let me go!" she screamed, pulling and twisting in my grip.

"No, we need to hear her out." I grunted, keeping my hands tightly locked around her wrists.

She put her leg behind mine and shifted her weight, and we slammed into the rock wall. I managed to keep hold of both her wrists and focused on squeezing the one holding the gun. She went to knee me in the stomach, but I had anticipated it and already had my leg raised. She dipped her head against my chin and pushed upward, my teeth rattling as I just avoided biting my tongue.

"Caroline, please . . . just . . . ease up . . . ," I gasped, determined not to let go. I figured I was stronger and just needed to keep going until she ran out of steam.

Suddenly she stopped struggling, and as the resistance vanished, I lurched forward. Her weight shifted again, and before I knew it, I was spinning through the air. I slammed into the tarmac. Caroline straddled me and got me into a headlock. She squeezed, and spots appeared in front of my eyes as the oxygen flow to my brain was interrupted. I twisted my neck around, but Caroline adjusted her position and got a better grip. I slapped at her with my free hand, but it was feeble and ineffectually bounced off her shoulder. She was solid, and I couldn't move.

Then, unexpectedly, she let go.

As my vision returned, I took a gagging, deep breath and put a hand to my throat to massage the bruised muscles and ligaments. Caroline twisted off me and sat back, raising her hands. I lifted myself up on one elbow, and there was Pandora, pointing Caroline's gun at both of us.

"You both finished now?" she said.

Caroline looked down at me, and her lip curled. "You idiot," she said.

I rubbed my neck and sat up, breathing heavily. "I couldn't let you kill her," I managed.

Caroline just shook her head. "It's not a person, Will. It's not Alex."

I slapped the floor, hard. "I know that! Just, wait—" I looked up at Pandora. "What's in the data packages?"

"What?" hissed Caroline.

I tried not to look frustrated. "She said her priority was to set up an antenna capable of receiving the data packages." I stared at Pandora. "Well—what's in the data packages?"

The gun wobbled slightly. "Detailed blueprints and instructions. Quadra-bytes of information."

Caroline looked up. "For doing what, exactly?"

Pandora pursed her lips and slowly lowered the gun. "This is the part I said you wouldn't like. Once I was released from Singularity, the data package was automatically rerouted from Goldstone and transmitted to the Singular-ity facility."

"There's nothing in this Singularity campus to rival Goldstone's networks," Caroline said dismissively. "And I would know—"

"There didn't need to be," Pandora interrupted. "Goldstone was designed to pick up and transmit messages across billions of miles. Singularity only needed equipment that could receive data over a few hundred miles. The data package has been delivered here."

I stood up and reached out a hand to Caroline, who reluctantly took it. I pulled her up, aware of a creak and soreness in my shoulder where she'd thrown me. *Note to self: look up Brazilian jujitsu when you get out of this*, I thought. *IF you get out of this.*

Caroline brushed herself down, and for a long moment she stared at Pandora, her jaw tight with clenched teeth, her face a tapestry of fiercely battling emotions. "Alright, what's in the data packages?" she growled at last.

"Their digital biosignatures," she replied matter-of-factly. "The alien's DNA."

Caroline stared at her open-mouthed.

Pandora continued. "Once it had been verified that this planet contained the requisite elements for my creators, my next prerogative was to construct an atomic-molecular DNA printer. This would process the quarks and electrons of the digital information and assemble them into the physical structure of the life-form they represent."

"And you built this printer? How?"

"I was instructed to, remember. My prime directive"—Caroline held up her hand, but Pandora hadn't finished—"demanded it of me."

"So how many individual aliens are here?" I asked.

"There are three gigabytes of information per individual. The data package is a little over three terabytes in size—"

"So, over a thousand," Caroline finished. She shook her head, disbelief on her face. "It makes perfect sense. No need for enormous ships to carry a race of people across the galaxy. No need to transport bulky life-support systems, infrastructure, anything at all . . . just build what you need when you arrive." She looked up at Pandora. "After one of your kind 'cases' the joint first and gets everything shipshape and ready for them, am I right?"

Pandora nodded, missing the sarcasm. "And once their physical structure is complete, the minds and memories of each individual will be downloaded into their bodies. Memories that have been scanned and retained in 'Oumuamua's central data bank."

"And this is happening in there, now?" I said, pointing down the tunnel.

"Almost certainly," she replied.

"We've got to stop it," Caroline said.

To my surprise, Pandora nodded. "That's why we're here. I believe we can stop this. But there's a catch. I'll be physically unable to help you. There are additional inhibitors built into my programming—"

"Some fucking use you are, then," hissed Caroline.

"But I'll give you the information you need to stop the process. You *will* be able to do it."

I frowned. "Why would you do that for us? I thought this was your prime directive?"

She looked at me, and her face was unreadable. "Because, Will, I feel something . . . I cannot explain. Something from Alex Park, perhaps. Some emotion or connection to you." She looked at Caroline. "To . . . humanity."

Caroline gave a cynical smile. "How do you expect us to trust you again?"

"I have no expectations. But you, yourself, said that we all have a choice. After what I have just told you, could you live with yourself if you don't try?"

"You could be lying again. Wouldn't be the first time."

I held up a finger. "You said time is pressing. Surely not much could have happened in the few days since you broke out of here. We've got time on our side, surely?"

Pandora grimaced and shook her head. "No, Will, I'm afraid we don't. The physical assembly of the body is generally achieved via nanofiber technology, remember? Normally, it would take many days to build a single individual from purely synthetic materials. However, the process is much quicker if native biological tissues can be harvested and integrated into the process."

My blood ran cold, as I knew what was coming next. I pictured Jin and the bloody smear on the floor next to the nanofiber equipment. I looked up at Pandora, and I knew that she understood what I was thinking.

She nodded slowly. "Using biological material from here on Earth to incorporate into the baseline synthetic structure, the process can be completed in hours."

Caroline looked at me, and my blood ran cold. "That's what they're doing in there with all those bodies," Caroline said softly.

CHAPTER TWENTY-FOUR

The tunnel was sort of reassuring in its solid and smooth grayness, lit at steady intervals with warm electric light. Birdsong and other sounds of the forest receded into the background, and we were left with only our footsteps, echoing off the walls. Pandora led the way, and nothing more had been spoken since we entered. We had about a mile to walk before we reached Singularity, and so I was hoping to find the quad bikes again. I kept looking around the bend to see if there were any of the recesses for those four-seater vehicles we'd used during our escape. I also checked out the nooks and crannies of the tunnel walls, searching every shadow, expecting to see bodies.

"Why can't we just nuke this place?" I whispered to Caroline as we walked. "I mean, go to the government, get the military onto it, you know?"

She looked at me and raised an eyebrow.

"It's the only way to be sure," I said, quoting that line from *Aliens*.

She shook her head. "Didn't you hear? There's no time. How long do you think it would take to get a nuclear strike on American soil approved by Congress?"

She was right, damn it. That wasn't an option. We had to trust Pandora that this was the only way, and that we were all that humanity had.

Talk about being seriously messed up. We were humanity's only hope.

It also concerned me that we'd never gotten a satisfactory answer from Pandora about what had happened to the occupants of this facility when we escaped. Her statement that she had every right to escape and that she didn't see why she should feel any remorse for her captors (she had called them her torturers as well) was worrying. That had revealed little or no compassion for human life. But if she wasn't human, why would she? Were we so far beneath her, evolutionarily, that she would just look upon humans as we look at ants? If that really was the case, then we were taking a big risk trusting her.

I touched Pandora on the arm, gently guiding her to a stop.

"Everyone here is dead. Seemingly killed in preparation for your creators to arrive and take over their bodies. You've told me that you have bits of Alex rattling around in your head. Now, I knew Alex—she was a good, caring human being. One of the best, actually . . ." I stopped briefly as a hitch came in my throat. "Alex wouldn't have done this."

Caroline's voice was low with suppressed anger. "Because she's not Alex, is she? She's a machine. Sentient, but not human. Not even made by humans. She's got her programming and prime directives and all that shit driving her actions. She said so herself."

Pandora closed her eyes for a moment and then stared directly at me. "I didn't want to kill them all. The gas I designed and released through the air vents was not meant to be fatal. It was an anesthetic. I calculated it would produce unconsciousness for a couple of hours. But . . . I made the error of mixing it in with a novel, gaseous variant of suxamethonium chloride."

I frowned at Caroline, who said, "It's a skeletal-muscle relaxant. Used to facilitate intubation in intensive-care units or to put patients on mechanical ventilation for surgery."

Pandora nodded. "I made a mistake. I did not factor in what this would do to their breathing muscles. My files on human biology and physiology were . . . inadequate."

"They all asphyxiated," I said. "Choked to death."

"It was painless, Will. They would have been rendered unconscious first."

"Are you fucking sure?" said Caroline, now overtly raging. "You didn't have 'adequate files,' but you did it anyway? There were hundreds of people in this facility. People with families. My colleagues. Friends. Innocent people—"

"I needed to escape. The prime directive—"

"Fuck your prime directive!" shouted Caroline, bouncing on her toes.

I put my hand on her arm and waited until her breathing had slowed. I turned to Pandora who was watching us carefully, no signs of emotion on her face. "How much of Alex is really part of you, Pandora?" I said, almost in a pleading tone. "Is it enough for you to care for us? For humanity as a whole?"

Her gaze flicked between the two of us. "There is . . . conflict. And uncertainty. You see, when I absorbed Alex Park's dying consciousness, her mind was completely alien to me. I had no frame of reference. It would be the same for you if you could get inside the head of a domestic cat."

"But now?" I asked.

Pandora nodded slowly. "What I assimilated has become permanently embedded in my neural networks. But understanding and integrating who, and what, Alex stood for is a work in progress. For example, I do not yet understand human emotions."

"Don't your creators have emotions?" Caroline interjected.

Pandora pursed her lips. "Nothing that you would be able to identify as such, perhaps. Their neurological development was radically different from yours. They came from a completely different evolutionary pathway."

"What do they look like?" Caroline asked.

Pandora shrugged. "They will probably look human."

I frowned. "You just said they've evolved differently."

"Yes, but they will be using human dead bodies as their templates, here on Earth."

Caroline wasn't looking any happier. "Will they be . . . zombies? You know, walking corpses?"

I shivered as the image popped into my head. Here we were, walking down a long tunnel toward a facility where there had last been hundreds of dead bodies, which were now missing.

"No, they will be fully animated beings," replied Pandora, "but without human minds."

I shivered, the image getting worse.

"Can we kill them?" Caroline asked, not unreasonably.

Pandora took her time to reply, but then nodded. "They will be constructed from a combination of nanofiber, proto-metals, and biological tissue—just like me. They won't be easy to kill, but they aren't indestructible."

"What about your quantum-phasing ability?"

She shook her head. "No, I don't believe that will be possible for them. They should not have that ability. I am a quantum computer when all is said and done. They are biological organisms."

"You're sure of that?"

"I cannot be certain of anything. Furthermore, I . . . I may not be able to quantum phase again myself. My physical resources are not infinite."

Up ahead, the tunnel turned hard right, and a big air-conditioning unit working at full power was dripping water into a rapidly enlarging pool across both lanes.

We set off again, past the water and along the road until it turned. Ahead I could see more light. A yellowish haze reflecting off the tunnel walls.

"What's that noise?" whispered Caroline, squinting nervously ahead and behind us.

I held my breath and listened. She was right, there was an almost subliminal hum coming from ahead. Like a mosquito or a fly.

Pandora stopped and held up a finger to her lips. She gestured for us to hug the side of the tunnel, making ourselves as small as possible in the shadows of the concrete wall.

"It's an energy barrier," she said. "Wait here."

She strode purposefully toward the light, glancing back over her shoulder at us. I sat down, my back against the cold concrete wall, and Caroline slid down next to me. To my surprise, she put her hand on my leg. I looked at her and saw my own fear reflected in her face. I took hold of her hand and squeezed.

"You okay?"

She blew out her cheeks and gave a soft laugh. "Is there a good answer to that?"

I smiled. "Right, silly question."

"I was thinking about why there were no police here," she said, "but I didn't dwell on it. So much going on, right? But all those employees at Singularity, all my colleagues, coworkers, all suddenly gone 'off the grid'? Surely someone outside would've called foul by now. But there's no one here investigating it."

"She just said something about an energy barrier," I said slowly. "Is that like a force field?"

She nodded.

"We're too late, aren't we?" I breathed.

She didn't answer.

CHAPTER TWENTY-FIVE

When Pandora returned, there was a film of sweat on her face, and she was again looking gray and clammy. She slumped down the wall next to us and wiped her nose on her sleeve.

"What did you find out?" I asked.

"The energy barrier completely encircles the facility," she said, her voice low and shaky.

Caroline's head flopped backward against the wall, and she closed her eyes. "Have we come all this way for nothing?"

Pandora shook her head. "We can pass through it." She pulled herself to her feet and reached out a hand. "Trust me."

I took a deep breath. Trust. There was that word again. But really, what alternative did we have?

"Okay," I said heavily. "Lead the way."

We walked around the curvature of the tunnel, the buzzing intensifying as if we were approaching a nest of wasps. My skin began to tingle, and hairs stood up on my arms and the back of my neck as if a storm was imminent. The entrance to the Singularity dome came into view: an arch ten feet high, partially obscured by the strangely tangerine-colored glow.

Pandora led us past the security booth and then gestured for us to hang back. She approached the edge of the barrier, shimmered, and disappeared. Although I'd seen her do it before, it was still surreal. An oval defect in the barrier appeared, human-sized, with a clear view through to the other side where Pandora was waiting.

She waved to us. "I've temporarily altered the polarity of the molecules making up the energy field. It won't last long."

I cautiously moved toward the defect in the energy field, conscious of an increase in the buzzing and the tingling the closer I got.

"Careful," she said. "Don't touch the edges."

I nodded and slid my way through sideways. The air was noticeably warmer inside, and humid. And malodorous. It smelled like roadkill, that rotting, gagging odor associated with dead animals.

"I'm really not sure about this," said Caroline as she came through behind me, holding her nose and wrinkling her eyes.

We huddled together in front of the defect that was slowly closing behind us like a spoon disappearing into a bowl of honey. The inside of the facility was in darkness, and we were only able to see each other by the dim light of the barrier.

"I can't see anything up ahead," I whispered, "and I don't feel like walking farther not knowing what I might be stepping on."

Pandora's voice sounded patient. "Don't worry, Will. I can see everything. There are no bodies in this area."

"Okay, well then where's the smell coming from?" said Caroline.

"And why is it so hot?" I said.

Pandora looked away. "We should go."

We set off after her. The dim orange light soon faded into nothingness and became a deep obsidian black. I knew we were in the main corridor and that Caroline's office was up ahead, somewhere on the right. Farther along would be the elevator that led to the glass corridor and then to the main building where all the laboratories were. I stumbled forward and bumped into Caroline who reached back and took my hand.

"Your office is just over here," came Pandora's voice from ahead. "We can access the security cameras from your desk."

"If the power's not been compromised," said Caroline.

We made our way along the wall by feel. As my eyes adjusted, I could just make out Pandora's shape, a moving shadow against the velvety blackness. The buzzing noise was receding into the distance, and the silence was only broken now by the slip-sliding of our footsteps.

"We're here," she whispered, stopping and causing us to bunch up again. A light appeared on the wall as she tapped on the doorframe and a keypad glowed with green phosphorescence.

"Power's still on," she said. "It seems that someone's just turned the lights out on purpose."

"And turned off the AC," I said.

Pandora continued to tap on the pad, but it now glowed red.

"There's a code for the door," whispered Caroline. "Four, nine, six, four, nine, six."

"A perfect number," Pandora replied. "Mathematically, of course." Her fingers flew over the pad, then the light flicked from red to green and the door opened with a loud click. I stopped breathing for a second and waited. Pandora pushed the door open and walked through. I hesitated again, but Caroline gave me a gentle shove in the back.

"Wait," I whispered. "Let's let her clear the room first."

"No way," she hissed back. "I'm not staying out here in the dark."

She had a point.

We crept forward, her hand on my back so that we didn't separate. I couldn't see where Pandora had gone so I shuffled forward, step by hesitant step, trying to remember the layout from the last time we were there. My foot bumped into something on the floor, a cylinder of sorts, and there was a painfully loud metallic sound as it rolled along the floor and clanged into a chair or table leg.

I could feel Caroline squeezing my hand so tightly that her nails were leaving imprints in my palm.

Emergency lights came on slowly, a dull ruby glow like an old-fashioned photographic developing room. I could now make out the benches with their equipment and tubes and wires, and the biohazard stations along the back wall.

"Over here," called Pandora, waving to us from Caroline's office at the back of the lab.

I winced, suppressing the urge to shush her. Caroline closed the lab door, and we scooted across to the office. Pandora sat down at Caroline's desk and tapped on her computer's keyboard while we crowded in behind and watched the screen come alive with Singularity's logo. She moved the mouse around and activated a dialogue box here and there, then opened a directory of the security system's cameras. There were many internal spaces highlighted including the mezzanine, laboratories—such as the nanofiber construction facility—administration offices, and the canteen.

"Are there cameras everywhere?" I said, looking at Pandora, who nodded.

"The mezzanine is the biggest open space," said Caroline. "Check that out first."

Pandora split the screen into eight smaller sections, each showing a different view of the mezzanine. Everywhere was bathed in a soft green glow with impenetrable black shadows at the edges of the pictures. It still seemed deserted. The tables and chairs were as I remembered them, scattered around in various stages of disarray. There were no people, alive or dead, to be seen.

"We need to check out the nanofiber laboratory," Pandora said. "That's where they'll be."

I swallowed. *They*, meaning the aliens.

She moved the mouse around, closed the mezzanine CCTV images, and flicked through the menu. The images jumped, and I recognized the medical-facility entrance that led to the nanofiber laboratory. The doors were closed, and hovering in front were three egg-shaped objects.

The drones.

"Well, they're still working," said Caroline.

"They shouldn't be," said Pandora. "I was controlling them."

"Can we see inside the lab?" I asked.

Her fingers tip-tapped again. "The cameras inside have been disabled," she replied after a few seconds. "There's only one reason for that."

I pictured the nanofiber laboratory again. A large circular space with high walls covered in huge flat-screen monitors. A wall lined with desks and chairs linked to workstations with wires and tubes. In the center of the room, a raised dais supporting a single hospital-type bed with armrests out to the side like a crucifix. Above it, four robotic arms connected to power couplings and wires from the ceiling. Blood dripped from surgical appendages.

Pandora remote activated one of the external CCTVs and made it pan around the corridor outside. There was another door leading into the laboratory, and piled up next to it were—

"Oh my god," said Caroline, putting her hand over her mouth.

There were hundreds of bodies stacked high in a single mass. A mountain of the dead, stiff limbs poking out at awful angles. Thankfully, it was too dark to see details. In black and green, it was a scene from a horror movie. Dark patches of liquid covered the hallway.

"Shit, are those footprints?" Caroline whispered.

Leading from the bodies to the main door of the nanofiber laboratory were dozens of bloody smears. I felt physically sick and was about to look away when Caroline sharply inhaled. "Did you see that?"

"What?" said Pandora.

"I saw something move."

She zoomed the camera out, and the picture rotated slowly side to side. A figure detached itself from the pile and began to slowly crawl along the side of the corridor, out of the line of sight of the drones. Pandora toggled the mouse and zoomed in on the person's face, and the camera focused and enhanced the image. As the face loomed large on screen, it was vaguely familiar. A respirator mask hung loosely from one strap, and the whites of his eyes popped out from his dark skin.

"That's—" I started.

"Jerry," finished Caroline. "How the hell is he still alive?" Jeremiah Wade, Caroline's buddy from my interrogation.

He continued to crawl along the corridor like a World War I soldier under barbed wire in no-man's-land. When he reached the security desk, he pulled himself under and vanished from the screen.

"We can get him," said Caroline.

"What, you're joking, right?" I said.

She shook her head and pointed at the nanofiber laboratory entrance. "We'll need to go past that station on our way there."

I frowned and looked at Pandora. "I thought you were going to tell us what we had to do. Can't we do it without actually confronting them? Without actually going in there?"

She put her hands on the desk, palms down, and sat back in the chair. "The signal from 'Oumuamua is being directed into the nanofiber laboratory. They'll have programmed the 3D printer to integrate their DNA into the matrix. We'll need to destroy the receiver at the source and then terminate the nanofiber production."

"We?" I said.

"Okay, you," she replied.

I glanced at Caroline who was looking grim. "She definitely means us," I said.

Pandora nodded. "However, it's possible you'll meet no resistance—or at least nothing that you can't handle. They may not be as capable in humanoid form as you are, having only had minutes or hours to adapt."

"Famous last words," I muttered.

CHAPTER TWENTY-SIX

Pandora confirmed that the corridors and walkways leading toward the laboratories were clear and activated the main lights so that we could navigate better. Our route took us up an elevator and across the familiar glass walkway to the mezzanine level where we took another elevator down to the main building. As we exited, the stench of death became more prominent, as did the heat. It was almost overpowering, and I pulled my shirt over my mouth to stop gagging and vomiting.

"Is the HVAC just on the fritz or has it been turned all the way up?" I gasped through the cloth.

"I would venture to say that it has been turned up," answered Pandora. "They come from a different world with a different ecosystem and environment."

"But they're human now, so why the need for the extra heat?" said Caroline.

"To speed up incubation and growth," Pandora replied.

As we rounded a corner, Pandora pulled us up abruptly, and we flattened against the wall. Ahead was the main door to the nanofiber laboratory, and next to it was the mountain of bodies stacked to the ceiling. She indicated down the corridor to a slowly turning CCTV security camera, red light flashing on top. "That shouldn't be active," she said, frowning. "I've cut the power to them all."

"It looks like it's still working," I said.

She nodded. "Make sure you keep to the right side of the corridor, that should be in its blind spot."

Caroline snuck a peek around the corner. "I can just see the security station, it's only maybe ten yards away. There's no sign of Jerry."

"Do you think he's still there?" I asked.

"Only one way to find out," she replied, pulling her shirt up over her mouth.

We inched along the corridor, keeping our backs flat against the wall and watching for any flicker of movement from the CCTV camera. As I approached the pile of bodies, a feeling of dread bubbled up to the surface, crawling under my skin like tiny spiders. I could now see the faces of the dead, their exposed skin grayed in the artificial lighting. Their features were contorted, their eyes staring, their mouths open.

Caroline's hand clutched at my sleeve, her grip tight.

"Try not to look at them," I said.

"I know, I know," she panted, trying not to hyperventilate.

The security station was a collection of desks and plastic screens with computer monitors, printers, and scanners scattered around. It was built into the curvature of the wall so that it looked modern and integrated. As we got closer, I heard a faint scuffling sound behind one of the desks. I looked at Caroline with raised eyebrows, and she nodded.

"Jerry," she whispered. "It's Caroline. It's okay."

There was no answer, but a shadow moved under one of the desks. A shoe just being pulled out of sight. I glanced over my shoulder at the CCTV camera that was still pointing down the corridor at us, its red light blinking steadily. I felt very exposed.

Caroline pulled her gun from her belt and held it down by her thigh. She circumnavigated the station until she was level with the gap between the wall and the desk. She looked at me, and I nodded in encouragement.

"Jerry, it's Caroline," she whispered again, more forcefully. "I'm here with Will Logan. Show yourself."

There was a slight scuffling sound, then: "Get your ass behind this desk before they see you."

Caroline gestured for me to follow, and we ducked under the plastic screen and into the station. Jerry was curled up in the corner, hidden by a filing cabinet. His suit was creased and smeared with blood and bits of stuff I didn't want to think about. His tie was hanging limply from his sweaty neck, and a respirator was dangling from one ear. His eyes were wide, and fear was oozing from every pore.

"Jerry, are you okay?" Caroline said, reaching out a hand.

His eyes darted back and forth between us. His mouth opened and then closed without saying anything, and his bottom lip was trembling. I could only imagine what he'd gone through. I wondered how long he'd been under the pile of dead and decaying bodies. I considered how I felt about Jerry. He had been a supercilious interrogator when I was his prisoner. I suddenly found it hard to be sympathetic to what he'd been through, considering my own experiences in the last few days.

He grimaced and started to get up but then saw Pandora. He inhaled sharply. "What the hell is she doing here?"

"She's not the enemy, Jerry," said Caroline. "She can help us."

His eyes closed, and an ironic smile appeared on his lips for a microsecond. A harsh laugh escaped. "Bullshit." When his eyes opened again, he stared accusingly at Pandora. "What the hell have you done?"

"How'd you manage to survive?" I said, more harshly than I'd intended.

His features tightened, as if someone was pulling his hair into a ponytail. He sneered and then looked at Caroline, ignoring me. "Do you have a plan to get out of this place?"

"We're not here to get out," I said firmly. "We're here to stop them."

He ignored me again and grasped Caroline's shirtsleeve with a bloodied hand. "Do you have a way out?"

Caroline shook her head. "Will's right. We're here to do a job first."

He laughed manically. "You've no idea what you're talking about. We need to get out of here. We need to tell the authorities about them."

"There's no time for that," I said. I turned to Pandora who'd been watching all this impassively. "You were going to tell us what we needed to do, right?"

She nodded slowly. "I can give you the information you need. Telepathically." She looked at Caroline grimly. "You too . . . it'll take both of you to accomplish this. There's a bank of equipment inside that looks like—" She stopped and cocked her head like a dog that'd heard a silent whistle.

"What is it?" I started.

A screeching noise erupted from down the corridor.

Caroline grabbed me and pulled me down behind the desk as low as we could get. There was a gap underneath, so we shuffled under to get a view. Blue-and-white lights were flashing in an epileptiform sequence, and shadows were moving across the wall. The screeching stopped as quickly as it had started, followed by a shuffling sound and an arrhythmic slip-slap noise. I pulled myself as close to the gap as I dared and turned my head sideways. The door to the nanofiber laboratory was open, and two naked figures were standing side by side as still as statues. They were very tall, well over seven feet, and their arms and legs were thin and spindly. Their heads were covered in an unruly mop of black hair, and their skin was flaky and gray. Their faces were unformed, as if molded out of putty. Their mouths were open, their eyes black like eight balls.

"Jesus Christ," I whispered to Caroline who was right next to me, her head touching my shoulder as she twisted to see. "I thought she said they were going to look human."

"Some sort of hybrid, maybe," she replied, her voice shaking. "The human DNA from the dead intermingling with their own might've corrupted the genome."

I thought about what Pandora had said earlier about the aliens not being functionally optimal in human form for a while and that this would be to our advantage. I hoped she was right. There were only two of them, after all, although they were visually intimidating to say the least.

"We can do this," I said out loud, but mainly to myself.

Caroline had heard me. "We have to."

We shuffled backward until we were in the gap between two desks where Jerry and Pandora were waiting. Jerry was trying to get as far away from Pandora as possible.

"Did you see them?" he said, eyes wide.

I nodded.

"They take the bodies inside to make more of themselves," he said quietly. Then his gaze moved to Pandora. "More of her."

I glanced up at Pandora, who was silently looking over the top of the table at the aliens. She shook her head dispassionately. "Not true. I'm not one of them."

Jerry was beginning to freak out now. He was starting to hyperventilate, and sweat was pouring from his forehead and trickling into his eyes.

"Jerry, Pandora is not an alien," I said patiently. "She's a quantum computer in a human-hybrid body. A machine. She was sent by them, that's true, but she isn't one of them. She's partly human. She's—" I stopped to take a deep breath. "Alex Park is in there too. Bits of her at least. The good bits—"

There was another screech, this time prolonged and multitone, like a bird song. It was answered by a lower-pitched screech.

"They're talking to each other," said Pandora.

Caroline twisted and pulled herself up to see over the desk as well. "Do you understand them?"

Pandora frowned. "Of course. They are choosing which body to take next. They haven't seen us yet."

The screeches continued, back and forth. The noises were loud, jarring and piercing, and I had to put my fingers into my ears. Nails on a chalkboard would have been more melodic. I hunkered down again and took another peek. One of the aliens was pulling bodies down from the pile and sliding them into the center of the corridor where the other bent down to examine them. He (or she, I couldn't tell. And would it matter?) spent a few seconds looking over the body before discarding it and moving on to the next. In a curiously dog-like manner, it sniffed the next one as it arrived from the pile.

Caroline turned to me. "That must be why they look like the walking dead," she whispered. "The tissues are all degrading and rotting away."

"It's the heat," I nodded. "Why don't they just turn it down and—"

There was crash behind us as Jerry pushed his way between the tables, toppling one over.

He scrabbled over the top and, with a fearful backward glance at the aliens, ran for it. He then tripped over the edge and fell to the floor, skidding into the wall. His respirator bounced down the corridor, the noise echoing loudly.

"For fuck's sake, Jerry," said Caroline, scrambling to her feet.

"It's too late," said Pandora.

I looked back at the aliens, and my heart stopped.

The laboratory door had opened, and two more aliens had emerged. Then another two.

Jerry was lying on his back looking dazed, and I guessed that he must have hit his head on the wall. Pandora stepped over the upturned desk and crouched down next to him. She tenderly felt his head and his neck, moving it slowly, checking for injury. His eyes fluttered as he started to come to. I glanced over my shoulder, expecting any second to see the aliens appear.

Pandora got to her feet and held out a hand toward me. "Look after him," she said. "I'll deal with them."

"What, wait—" I began.

"There's too many," she said. "You'll never get inside."

"No!" I cried. "You said they might not be fully functional. Maybe you could cause a distraction, maybe—"

She looked at me serenely and shook her head. "There's too many, Will. I'll need to find us another way." She closed her eyes and screeched.

I put my hands over my ears, the noise ripping through my eardrums. Caroline grabbed me from behind and pulled me back behind the desk. The aliens came into view, moving jerkily, like Bambi learning to walk. Their limbs were flicking out sideways as if they were having seizures or fits with each step, like electricity sparking on bare wires. Their mouths were open, and a circular row of sharpened teeth shone in the darkness. They were creatures out of a nightmare, or from a Dante painting.

Pandora screeched again, and the aliens stopped and screeched back. The intensity of the noises ratcheted up a notch, as if they were arguing. I winced as the sound continued to scrape my ears and drill through my temples.

The nearest one pointed at Pandora and screeched again. She shook her head and turned to face them in some kind of fighting stance. One of them looked at me, and I felt a scratching behind my eyeballs and a pressure squeezing my temples.

Pandora's voice sounded in my head, strident and urgent. *They know what I am. I am being commanded to go to them. At my signal, run for it.*

I grabbed Caroline's hand and pulled her up, never taking my eyes off the aliens. Then I felt Pandora's mind again, pushing the pressure away and inserting her own thoughts there. *Prepare your mind, Will.*

"What are you talking about?" I said. "For what?"

For this.

My thoughts suddenly accelerated, and it felt like a thousand voices were speaking to me at once. My vision blurred, and I put a hand out on the wall to steady myself. Everything appeared to be moving in slow motion. Caroline was gawking at me, eyes wide, her mouth moving, but no sound was coming out. The voices in my head merged, like a great choir coming together in harmony. Interlocking words, phrases, languages known and unknown. And numbers. Lots of numbers. Primes, perfect numbers, squares, roots, equations. Tumbling and swirling but falling logically and understandably into place.

I blinked, and slowly the outside world returned.

"We've gotta move! Now!" Caroline's voice boomed.

I glanced over and saw that Pandora was in trouble. The aliens were all over her. One was pinning her down while another had its hand pressed against her face. Its fingers were penetrating her skin and digging deeper, up to the second knuckle. Blackish fluid started running down her cheeks as if she was crying tears of oil. Her eyes opened, and she stared at me and screeched. This time I understood what she was doing.

I turned to Caroline. "Help me with Jerry; this is our chance."

"What about Pandora?"

"We can't help her," I said calmly. "But it isn't over yet."

I roughly grabbed Jerry and pulled him to his feet. His eyes were still unfocused, but he didn't resist. I put his arm around my shoulders and my other around his waist. Caroline got the hint and supported him from the other side, and we started to shuffle away as fast as we could.

"Where are we going?" she said, panting.

I nodded toward a fire exit. "Over there. It leads to another stairwell, which will take us to the dining area below the mezzanine."

"Okay, but how do you know that?"

"I just do," I said. "Trust me."

I risked a quick glance over my shoulder at Pandora and the aliens. Her face had completely melted, and the alien's hand was embedded up to its wrist. The other alien had inserted a hand into her abdomen, penetrating the jumpsuit and her skin. Both had their heads down, supplicant-like, as if they were praying. More aliens were emerging from the nanofiber laboratory and encircling Pandora, swaying slowly, making no sound.

"What the hell's going on?" grunted Caroline, straining to see.

I said nothing and just steered us toward the exit. I kicked the door open, and we fell through into a stairway, all gray concrete and black handrails. I looked down the middle, seeing about three levels of stairs below us.

"Getting Jerry down there is going to take forever," Caroline said.

She wasn't wrong. Carrying Jerry wasn't going to be easy. I propped him against the wall and slapped his face. "Jerry, wake up. I need you to walk. You hear me?"

His head bobbed up and down, although his gaze drifted upward.

I slapped him harder. Then harder still.

"Right, right . . . ," he said, bringing a hand up. "Stop hitting me."

I pointed down the stairs. "We need to get down there. Hang on to the rails if you need to, but go as fast as you can."

"I'm not sure I can—"

"It's fine, we'll be right with you," Caroline said, turning him by the shoulder toward the first step. He nodded and started off, unsteadily at first but gathering speed. We kept Jerry between us in case he slipped. It wasn't long before we were at the bottom and at the exit. I pushed on the bar, and the door opened outward. We emerged by the side of the canteen buffet line. Ahead was the dining area as I remembered it: an outdoor space corralled by trees and shrubs.

Chairs and tables were tipped over with plates and cups spilled everywhere. In stark contrast to the horror and carnage around us, it was shaping up to be a beautiful day. A light breeze wafted through, the sky was a bright blue, and the foliage was vibrant hues of green.

"Over there," I said, pointing to a gravel path through an opening in the trees. "That's our way out."

Caroline wiped sweat from her forehead and grimaced. "You're not thinking of the boats, are you?"

"I certainly am," I replied. "The river will take us downstream and away from here."

"Won't they be following us?" Jerry said, looking fearfully over my shoulder.

I glanced back at the exit we'd emerged from. The door was open, and the darkness behind it lay like a thick velvet curtain.

Then I thought of Pandora, and the sacrifice she'd made for us. "She's given us a head start."

CHAPTER TWENTY-SEVEN

The river curved serpent-like and shone silvery gray amid the leafy green of the forest. The gravel path had brought us to a small jetty with a single boat perched on a rusty-looking trailer. It squeaked loudly as we pushed it into the slow-flowing water. Caroline jumped in first, grabbing one of the oars that lay like used chopsticks against the glistening mahogany decking. Jerry and I ran alongside and hopped in as the boat eased away from the safety of the riverbank. He grabbed the other oar and sat next to Caroline, threading his oar through the metal hoop on the side. We were soon in the middle of the river and heading downstream.

"Been working in this place all this time, and I never knew this was here," said Jerry over his shoulder in between pulls. "Where does the river come out?"

"By the main highway, 2.6 miles from here," I replied without thinking.

Where did that come from?

Jerry was thinking the same thing. He turned, frowning. "You seem to know a lot about this place for someone who's never been here before."

I leaned back, closing my eyes to the sun that was filtering through the trees and dappling the surface of the water. "She did something to me," I murmured.

"Pandora?"

"Alex," I said.

It was her. I was sure of it now. There was more to Pandora than she'd let on. I wondered why she hadn't been completely honest with me. To protect my fragile psyche, probably. If she could get in my head, she'd have been able to feel my ongoing pain over Alex's loss. I took a deep breath, savoring the warm, river-rich air, feeling the sun on my face. It felt weirdly relaxing and serene. I leaned over the side and ran my hand below the surface. The tame lapping of ripples against the hull rang out, and a soft breeze streamed through my hair.

"She's still alive," I said to no one in particular. "And she's helping us."

Caroline twisted to look at me. "How do you figure that? You saw what they were doing to her. She's—"

"I can still sense her," I answered quietly and tapped the side of my head. "She was able to telepathically communicate with me. I know that she's still . . . functioning. I know what we need to do next."

Jerry stopped rowing and turned in his seat. "What were the aliens doing to her? I mean, she didn't look functional, if that's the right word."

"Trying to reboot her, perhaps. From their perspective, she's just a mal-functioning computer."

"Can they do that?" he said, frowning.

I nodded. "She was—she is—their property."

"Then we're screwed, aren't we?"

"Maybe not. They're not prepared for what Pandora has become. Its inte-gration with Alex's mind has changed everything. I think they're going to have problems controlling her."

Caroline turned sideways, lifting her oar out of the water so we were drift-ing down the center of the river. "So what do we do now, other than run away?"

I smiled. "I said I know what we need to do next. The remains of the mete-orite—I mean the probe ship. We need to find it."

Jerry frowned. "I thought we had all the pieces?"

I closed my eyes, and a picture popped into my head. A dark avocado-shaped piece of rock. The probe ship that Pandora had arrived in. I wondered how much was left of it, and more to the point, whether it was operational. It had to be, if we were to do what was necessary.

"She landed in Peru, Jerry," I said wearily. "That's our destination."

Caroline broke into a laugh. "We don't need to go to Peru. I know where it is." I looked at her, puzzled. She winked. "San Francisco. Christian's place."

"You're kidding, right?" said Jerry.

She shook her head. "Nope, he told me he had kept a really big piece and made it into some sort of sculpture. Stuck it in his garden. He showed me a picture of it once. I never thought about it, obviously. I mean, why would I? How was I to know?"

"Something's up ahead," said Jerry.

There was a blurring across the breadth of the river, like a shimmering mirage in the desert. It crossed over into the surrounding trees, a straight line extending out of sight.

"Is that what I think it is?" said Caroline, following my gaze.

"Yes," I said, with a heavy sigh. "That's the energy barrier."

"Sounds like this getaway is going to be short lived," she grunted, picking her oar up again.

I closed my eyes. "Row us to within a few yards of the edge of the barrier."

"But—" Jerry started.

Information flooded into my head, unprompted and uncontrolled. Data streams comprising incomprehensible algorithms and equations, numbers and figures, all dropping like a waterfall. Then the information coalesced, and just like that, it made sense.

"It'll be fine," I said. "We can swim under it."

Caroline and Jerry weren't convinced, but I explained that the energy field dissipated into nonexistence a few feet under the water's surface. I wasn't sure how or why, but I knew that this was the case. When we got close to the barrier, the electrostatic charge became uncomfortable and the tingling on my skin intensified exponentially. I reached out toward it, and my fingers met resistance and increasing warmth. The more I pressed, the warmer the sensation and the firmer the resistance became, until it felt like I'd touched a hot stove and had to jerk my fingers back.

"It's not deep here," I said. "I'm going to dive under and pull myself along the bottom of the river until I'm on the other side of the barrier."

Caroline nodded wordlessly, tacking gently on the oar to keep us in place. Jerry gave me a blank look that barely disguised his skepticism. Easing myself over the side, I lowered into the river, flinching as the cold water seeped into my clothes. I ducked under the surface, and as my head went under, my feet touched the bottom. I bounced back up and grabbed on to the side of the boat.

"It's about six and a half feet deep. Watch how I go, keep low, and follow my route. You should be able to see me come up on the other side." I took a deep breath and dove, keeping my eyes open. A couple of brown-striped fish gave me startled looks and flip-flopped out of my way.

When my hands touched the riverbed, I grabbed hold of stones and twisted branches to keep me tethered and kicked off, swimming parallel to the bottom. After half a dozen more kicks, I figured that I was past the barrier and pushed up from the riverbed. I burst through the surface and took in a huge lungful of air. I treaded water for a few seconds and listened. There was rustling from the trees and the ubiquitous low buzz from the barrier, but nothing else seemed to be out of the ordinary. The sun was coming up over the trees, but the river was mainly in shadow. The early morning birdsong was trilling a happy chorus, completely at odds with the trepidation pervading my bones.

I could just see Caroline and Jerry through the barrier, still sitting in the boat. I waved at them and was about to shout, but the darkness within the tree-lined riverbanks stilled my voice. I waved again, this time more urgently. The blurred figures moved, and there was a splash as Caroline entered the water, followed by Jerry. They ducked under the surface, and soon they were both treading water next to me. The river burbled past, driftwood and leaves floating by like little ships with unknown destinations.

"You called that right," said Caroline, blowing bubbles out of her nose.

"How did you know?"

"Pandora put something into my head," I said. "Knowledge. Information. It just seems to float into my consciousness when I need it. I can't explain it, nor can I seem to access it unless the situation requires it."

"Until something triggers it?" she replied.

"I guess so."

"This is unbelievable," interjected Jerry. He seemed a bit wild-eyed but appeared to be keeping it relatively together.

"You okay, buddy?" I asked.

He nodded. "Just . . . it's been a bit difficult, you know. The last few days."

No argument there.

We were drifting slowly with the current away from the barrier, so I pointed to the riverbank and started to breaststroke toward it. The closest point was too muddy, so we had to swim downstream for another ten yards for a more welcoming and slightly-less-slippery exit route. Caroline and I made hard work of getting out of the quagmire, and we needed to help Jerry as he struggled to make progress, his hands slapping the mud and getting no purchase. After a minute of exertion, we had him out, and we all lay on the grass getting our breath back.

"We should keep going," I said. "It's probably not a good idea to hang around here."

Caroline just hugged her knees and lifted her head toward the stripy sunbeams coming through the foliage. "Can't believe that water was so cold. Need to warm up first."

I smiled grimly and held out a hand. "Sorry, but no rest for the wicked."

She puffed out her cheeks and grasped my hand, and I pulled her up. She smoothed her shirt flat, and then, noticing how the water made it stick to her chest, fluffed it out again. I turned away, pretending not to notice.

"Wouldn't mind a change of clothes," she said.

She had a point. We were soaking wet, covered in mud, and probably smelled bad.

"There should be a highway a hundred yards or so through there," I said, pointing at the gap that led to the trees. "It runs parallel to this river for a few miles."

"You thinking we could hitch a ride?" she said, throwing me a sideways look.

Jerry snorted. "We're not going to get a ride, have you seen the state of us?"

"It'd be much better than walking, so it's worth a try," I said.

Caroline reached round her back and pulled the gun out of her belt. She wiped it on her shirt, checked it, and seemingly satisfied, said, "We could just commandeer a vehicle."

"Let's hope it doesn't come to that," I replied, wondering if she was serious.

Jerry held up his phone, which although dripping wet, still appeared to be working. He cracked a smile. "What if I call an Uber?"

I shook my head and started walking.

Thankfully, the trees weren't dense nor was the undergrowth particularly rough. Sunlight percolated through the leaves, luminous streams igniting every gap. After ten minutes, the branches started to thin out and the light became brighter as we reached the edge of the forest. I sensed movement ahead of us and ducked down behind a tree, unconsciously giving the military hand signal for stop, followed by a signal to crouch. I heard leaves rustling as Caroline came up behind me.

"What is it?" she whispered.

I pointed around the tree. There was a line of vehicles moving at a snail's pace, nose-to-tail, as far as the eye could see. Sedans, SUVs, trucks, and vans, but no military jeeps or police cars. "Traffic's nearly at a standstill by the look of it." I peered back through the canopy. "And there's a helicopter back there. I don't think it's a police chopper, probably just a TV crew."

"This has got to be a roadblock," she said. "Police are turning people around because of the barrier."

Jerry appeared at my shoulder. "The word must be out, surely. All those people missing, and now a force field? Hard to keep that sort of thing under wraps."

I nodded. The traffic was certainly flowing in the other direction, away from Singularity.

Slowly but steadily, we shuffled to the edge of the forest where there was a grassy hill that dipped conveniently into a hollow running alongside the road. We ran into it and crawled up to the other edge and peered over. There was definitely a police barricade and cordon about fifty yards down the road. Blue-and-red flashing lights lit up the early morning sky, and every vehicle was being turned around. I couldn't make out how many police were there, but it didn't matter. There were probably a lot.

"We need to get on the other side and then see if we can catch a lift."

We crawled back down into the hollow and started walking. Caroline pulled out her cell phone, which I'd forgotten she still had. Mine was long gone.

"Is that still working after the river?" I said.

"No reason why it wouldn't, it's fully waterproof. But there's no signal here."

She put it away, and we continued down the gully. The hollow was becoming shallower, and we could now be seen from the road, but no one in the line of vehicles was paying attention to us, and there didn't appear to be any law enforcement or military vehicles in sight either.

"Time to make our move," I said. "You guys ready?"

They both nodded silently, so I clambered up the gully and onto the path next to the road. There was a big eighteen-wheeler in front of us, and we ran parallel to it before sneaking across to the other side. Behind the semi was a battered old BMW, and the driver gave us a little smile and wave as we passed him.

"I don't like our chances," Jerry said darkly, as we stood on the edge of the road. Traffic was steady, one vehicle passing us every five seconds or so.

"Ye of little faith," said Caroline. She pushed us out of the way and stuck out her thumb.

To my amazement, the third vehicle, a pale-blue-and-white VW Micro-bus, slowed down and stopped a few yards farther on. We ran to it and pulled open the sliding door. The rear bench seats were covered in towels and a couple of battered old backpacks. In the front were two guys in their early twenties who were tanned with scraggly beards and wearing armless shirts and shorts. They couldn't have been more dude-like if they'd had surfboards on the roof.

We piled in the back, pushing bags out of the way. "Thank you so much," breathed Caroline to the dudes. "You've saved our lives."

Perhaps literally, I thought.

The driver turned around and gave her a big smile. His teeth were perfectly straight and pearly white, and he had a pair of Ray-Bans perched on the top of his head. "Hey, no problem, dudes. I'm Tim, and this is Max, my brother. Where you guys goin'?"

Caroline briefly glanced at me, then said, "Well, San Francisco actually."

The dude gave a big laugh, and his brother slapped his shoulder. "We're not going that far, but could take you to, I don't know, maybe as far as Long Beach? Would that work?"

Long Beach was only fifteen miles or so from Santa Monica, and I figured we could hole up at my place for a while. I nodded to Caroline.

"That'll do perfectly, we're very grateful," she said.

Tim smiled again, threw the Minibus into gear, and lurched us back onto the highway.

Max was checking us out. He frowned, and I thought his nose wrinkled a bit. He gave Jerry a double take, probably wondering why he was wearing a suit, albeit covered in mud and soaking wet.

"What happened to you guys?" he said.

I shrugged. "We were boating on the river. Had an accident. We had to swim ashore."

He cocked an eyebrow at that. "Where's your boat now?"

"At the bottom of the river," I said.

Tim glanced over his shoulder. "So, where'd you leave your car?"

Before I could answer with another obvious lie, Caroline leaned forward. "Can you tell us what's happening up there, with the roadblock and all?"

Max shrugged. "I've really no idea; wish I knew. There're lots of cops, and a couple of army trucks a mile or so up from here. Whole road is shut down. Of course, it's the only way through." He smiled and nodded toward the traffic jam. "Lots of pissed-off people, and the police aren't saying nothin' to no one."

"No warnings?" said Jerry. "Road signs, you know, that sort of thing?"

Max just looked blank. "Nothing at all. We wouldn't've come this way if we'd known, man. 'Course, our radio isn't working either."

I noticed Caroline had her phone open, so I leaned over to take a look. "You managed to get a signal?" I said.

She nodded. "Just now. Let's see what's in the news."

The three of us crowded over her screen as she flicked through her apps and brought up one of the local stations, KTLA. Live streaming wasn't active, so she opened the news section and scrolled to the headlines. I squinted to read the small print:

More Than 270 Infected in Mysterious Salmonella Outbreak Detected in 29 States.

Hurricane Barry Intensifies into Category 4 Storm in Atlantic Ocean.

Drugmakers Shock Congress with Donation of Billions of Vaccine Profits into Healthcare, No Strings Attached.

President, VP Expected to Visit North Korea Again This Month.

Jerry snorted. "Nothing to see there. It's a cover-up. Classic."

"Maybe it didn't make the LA papers yet." She shrugged. "I'll Google 'Singularity.'"

Her fingers tippy tapped on the screen, and the page opened. "About 65,200,000 results (0.57 seconds)" appeared at the top. The first entry was a Wikipedia page describing the singularity as "a hypothetical future where technology growth is out of control and irreversible."

"Maybe put in your company name, specifically?" I said innocently, reaching for her phone.

She pushed my hand away and typed "Singularity, Inc." The screen spun for another half second, and the familiar logo appeared. Underneath, I read: "Singularity, Inc. is an American technology company based in San Diego, California. It was founded in 2019 by Christian Becker following his . . ."

She tabbed down the page. There were news reports, publications, media spots, interviews with Becker, and listings of stock prices. Nothing stood out.

"Very strange," she said. "Jerry's right. I can't imagine there aren't news groups swarming all over this. And yet . . ."

I gave her a worried look. "The authorities don't want anyone to know."

"Yeah, well they can't hide this forever." Jerry snorted.

"Is there anything in the local LA news?" I suggested.

She tapped on the screen, and the feed came up. The headlines read:

GRAND PRIX OF LONG BEACH PUT ON HOLD FOR CYBERSECURITY REASONS.

CREWS PUT OUT A LARGE HOUSE FIRE IN NORTH HILLS.

CHILDREN, POLICE OFFICERS AMONG 8 HURT IN SOUTH LA CRASH.

OFFICIALS: 4 INJURED IN SHOOTING AT WILLOWBROOK METRO STATION.

SANTA MONICA POLICE ARREST 4 IN CONNECTION WITH EARLY MORNING SHOOT OUT.

LA NATURAL HISTORY MUSEUM REMAINS CLOSED FOLLOWING TERRORIST INCIDENT; FBI INVOLVED.

I sat back and laughed. "The bottom two stories. Well, at least we made it into the top six."

Caroline had opened the fifth headline and was speed-reading, her lips moving with each word. "Says here it was a gang thing. Turf wars." She looked up and pouted. "That's bullshit. Someone's clearly spinning this. Those were Christian's guys. Not gangbangers."

I closed my eyes, remembering the goon I'd run over with the truck as we'd hightailed it out of there. Becker's men must have taken him away before the cops arrived. I opened my eyes and looked out the window at the backed-up traffic. "What about the terrorist 'incident' at the museum?"

"What're you talking about?" said Jerry.

Caroline said nothing and opened the story. Again, she read it in silence for a few minutes, then looked at me askance. "More bullshit."

"What?" said Jerry, becoming exasperated.

"Listen to this: 'The LA Museum of Natural History remains in lockdown following an incident where several casualties occurred during a terrorist attack earlier this week. An unidentified helicopter was seen leaving the scene, and police have multiple suspects in custody. An ex–navy pilot named Nico Accardi is being called a "hero" by visitors to the museum, having disarmed one of the terrorists and held the others while waiting for the police to arrive.'"

I threw back my head and laughed. "Good for him."

Max was now leaning back on the seat watching us, a lopsided, puzzled grin on his face. "So, who are you guys?" he asked.

CHAPTER TWENTY-EIGHT

We managed to deflect Tim's and Max's inquiries, the conversation becoming a dance with moves that were deflecting and awkward, like we were all on the floor but listening to our own individual music. Jerry soon slumped against the window and was snoring loudly, and within a few minutes, Caroline's head had tipped backward, and she joined him. I cranked the window down and let the breeze ruffle my hair like one of those dogs in a Larson cartoon.

The road curved away into the distance, a fine line of ebony ink cutting through nature's viridian hues. The sky was a picture-perfect cerulean shade, and I felt myself slipping away, as if time was both stopping and stretching into the infinite. The sunlight brought warmth to my skin, evaporating the last of the river's moisture and leaving a tingle of chill in its stead. I closed my eyes, and as had often been the case, memories of Alex drifted freely into my consciousness. But where previously I'd be sitting on a beachfront with the sun on my back and Alex resting her head on my shoulder, now the sky was a woolen gray shawl over the rolling waves, and storm fronts were converging on us. Gulls were tossed like paper—flashes of white in the gray—tumbling and struggling against the wind. Their faces, human-like, frozen in rictus smiles or screams. Beneath them, the sea rose like great mountains, turbulent and unforgiving, threatening to destroy everything and anything in its path. Alex lifted her head to mine, and in the place of her warm brown eyes were lifeless gray coins. The Ferryman's toll for crossing the River Styx.

"Here's where we part company, boys and girls," said Tim, his voice jerking me awake. "Long Beach."

My neck was stiff from hanging out of the window, and I massaged the tight muscles and looked outside. The VW was pulling into a parking place in front of a Krispy Kreme. My stomach rumbled, and I put a hand on it, but it was too late—Caroline snickered. "Sounds like you need a donut," she said, yawning widely.

"I doubt there's much I won't eat just now," I replied, pulling the door open and willing my cramped legs to get out. My left ass cheek was numb, and I shook my foot to free up the squashed nerve. Caroline and Jerry rolled out the other side and stretched while casting nervous glances at anything or anyone that moved. Tim ambled over and reached out a hand, which I shook. "Thanks for the ride," I said, meaning it.

"No problem. You guys take it easy," he replied before loping after his brother who was already on his way into the café.

I looked up and down the street, seeing nothing of concern. Palm trees lined the highway; a gas station was on the other side along with a shopping mall, a Staples, and a chain gym. There was a steady stream of traffic rumbling along, but nothing activated my radar.

I turned to Jerry. "Time to get that Uber."

He nodded and got out his phone. "Where we going?"

I frowned at him. "You remember where I live, don't you, Professor Wade?"

He had the grace to look embarrassed and started tapping my address into the Uber app.

Caroline gave me a questioning look. "Your place? Do you think we'll be safe there?"

"Safe as anywhere, I reckon. No one's looking for me, right? Christian's dead."

Her eyes narrowed, but then she shrugged in acknowledgment. "I'll get the donuts. And coffee."

"Box of minis," yelled Jerry at Caroline as she pushed open the door to the Krispy Kreme, before glancing sheepishly at me.

There were a couple of steps leading up to the entrance next to a wheel-chair-access ramp. I slumped down on one of the steps and leaned against the railing, still feeling exhausted despite sleeping in the van.

Jerry sidled up to me and held out his phone. "Our Uber will be here in six minutes." I nodded and closed my eyes again, but Jerry hadn't finished. He sat down next to me and leaned in. "Look, Will, I'm . . . sorry. You know. For everything. I—"

I held up a hand. "Save it, Jerry."

"No, but really, I want you to understand—"

"Understand what, exactly?" I said, my voice turning harsh. "Is this going to be your version of the Nuremberg defense? I was only following orders. Give me a break, please."

Jerry blinked but carried on. "We *were* following orders. All of us. You have no idea what kind of a person Christian Becker is."

"Was," I corrected.

"Alright, *was* . . . but the way he ran Singularity was like a fascist dictator-ship. He ruled with an iron fist. To offset that, he paid us many times more than we were worth to the market but demanded absolute loyalty in return." His eyes glazed over. "He cracked the whip, every day. When he wanted some-thing done, it had to happen yesterday. The technological advances coming from our labs were just incredible. The bonuses were spectacular when we came through with a new product. We all felt privileged to work there."

"You were fed a lie," I said.

He nodded sadly. "We were deceived, I agree. But still, the technology—"

"All came from an alien machine," I interrupted. "You had nothing to do with it."

His face fell, and I wondered when the pieces had fallen into place for him.

When he had come to the realization that all his dreams of being rich and famous were like a house built on sand—inadequate foundations, now sinking into oblivion. Maybe when he was buried under a pile of decaying corpses, that was when it had hit him . . .

"Christian . . . wasn't always all bad," Jerry said slowly. "There were sides to him that most people didn't see."

I raised my eyebrows. "Let me guess, he had a sensitive soul?"

Jerry gave a half smile. "He hid it well, but yes, kind of."

"Bullshit," I said, shaking my head.

"No, really. My wife . . ." He paused and cleared his throat. "I knew Christian before Singularity. We collaborated on some AI research, back in the day. When my wife took ill, I wanted to take early retirement to look after her—she was back home in New Orleans—but he had her flown out to San Diego on his jet and admitted her to a private clinic for her chemotherapy and her immunotherapy. He paid for everything. No expense was spared. He got her the best doctors . . ."

He went quiet, and I waited a beat before replying. "Did she . . ."

"She survived the treatment, but then had a stroke. Nothing to do with the cancer or the drugs. I think she was just beaten down with everything." He gave a wry smile. "We're not built to last, you know. Humans, that is."

I nodded. "Where is she now?"

"Doreen's in a nursing home. When I joined Singularity, the benefits included paying for her medical needs. You see what I mean?"

I shrugged, my face neutral. I remembered the Christian Becker who had tried to have Alex and me murdered. Right before Pandora had killed him first.

Jerry continued. "Will, you've got to understand, no one else could have gotten that machine—Pandora—to work for us. Christian had insight, the genius of seeing in between the lines, out of the box, seeing things that no one else could see. He engaged the right people, astrobiologists, physicists, engineers, software programmers, you name them, and everyone was a small piece in a bigger puzzle. But put them all together—wow, look what we achieved."

I laughed. "But Pandora wasn't working for you, was she? The big genius that was Christian Becker missed that little detail. She was working to escape."

Jerry pursed his lips. "Christian had tremendous plans for the technology that Pandora was developing."

"Yes, I saw the presentation, remember? Especially the weapons."

"No, no you don't understand. These were game-changing innovations. We bandy that phrase around these days, but very few inventions are truly groundbreaking. We had at least seventy-five patents. Seventy-five! The technology was going to revolutionize how humanity lives. Christian was going to usher in a new era of prosperity and happiness."

Right. Now Jerry was sounding like a commercial. I shot him a sideways glance, my eyes narrowing. "And become the world's first trillionaire in the process."

Caroline returned, her arms full of boxes of donuts and a tray of coffees balanced on top. We sat down on the sidewalk and tucked in, not speaking, filling our faces as quickly as we could without being sick. I was sure we looked like a bunch of homeless tramps, and we were certainly getting disdainful glances from passersby who seemed to agree with my assessment.

A blue Honda Accord slowed and turned into the parking lot. Jerry stood up and waved his phone. Behind the wheel, the driver checked us out. I could imagine what we looked like to him, and I wouldn't have been surprised if he'd had second thoughts and drove off straight away. Thankfully, Jerry was too quick and pulled open the passenger door and jumped in. Caroline dropped the empty boxes and coffee cups into a nearby bin and slid in the back seat. As I got in, Jerry was already saying soothing things to the driver who was definitely pissed at the state and smell of us.

Caroline leaned forward and touched him on the shoulder. "There's a huge tip coming your way, and we'll pay for any cleaning. We're so sorry."

I was about to say something as well but noticed that Caroline had taken the gun out of her belt and was holding it just out of sight behind the driver's seat. I gently put my fingers around her gun hand and tightened, just so she knew I wasn't going to be happy if she decided to push things and move us into a kidnapping and hostage situation. However, the driver finally nodded, rolled down all four windows, and pulled out onto the highway.

Jerry turned in his seat and gave us a smile.

I didn't return it.

The Accord pulled up outside The Bean Machine on Ocean Avenue. I told him to carry on for a bit and drive slowly around the block. He turned right onto Twenty-Eighth and then took another right so we were now driving down Beach Avenue parallel to Ocean Avenue. Washington Boulevard was at the end of the street, and traffic was moderate and slow-moving around us. Caroline and I were peering out of the rear window, looking for a tail, but it all seemed clear.

We turned right again and drove parallel to the beach alongside a cycle path. The sun was that beautiful, rich late-afternoon glow, the shadows lengthening along the sidewalk. People jogged and cycled, taking in the cooler afternoon air. There were still kids on the basketball courts and in the outdoor gyms, and the beaches were dotted with family barbecues and people walking their dogs along the surf. Just a normal afternoon in Santa Monica.

Satisfied, I got the driver to turn back onto Ocean, and we pulled up a block past my café. As we got out, Caroline gave him an enormous smile and thank you, but he only nodded and, glancing at the mess he'd assumed we'd made of the seats, drove off—no doubt heading for a car wash.

"Tip him real big," she said to Jerry, "so he won't remember us."

"Good luck with that," I said. "Come on."

I led the way to The Bean Machine, which was all locked up and dark. I peered in through the front door; nothing seemed out of place. The long counter was as I'd left it, all the crockery squared away and gathering dust. The cabinets that once housed various pastry and cookie treats were bare. The circular tables along the window had their chairs upside down on top of them.

We went round the side of the shop to a wooden staircase that badly needed some paint, and which led to my apartment on the floor above. The door at the top was in the same state of disrepair, and I saw Caroline giving it a disapproving look.

I made a face at her. "Hey, it's the salty spray from the ocean that rots the wood."

She gave me a crooked smile in return. "I live in the Palisades, remember? There's an ocean there too."

"I bet you can afford to have it cleaned then," I quipped, only half-seriously.

I ran my hand along the top sill where I left a spare key. Finding it, I turned the lock and pushed open the door. I stood in the doorway, listening and watching. Sun was streaming through partially curtained windows, illuminating my home. It didn't look like much. An open floor plan with a kitchenette, dining area, and living area, with cupboards at the rear and a round table with four chairs in the corner next to a closed door. The living area had a comfy couch with throw pillows in front of a TV. That's all Alex and I had needed in the evenings. Our sanctuary. Curtains closed, lights off, movie playing, popcorn and beer. Heaven.

I froze.

The TV was on. Soundless. A ball game.

Caroline appeared at my shoulder, gun in hand. She gestured toward the door at the back. "What's through there?" she whispered.

"The bedroom and the bathroom," I replied.

She walked forward slowly, gun out in front. I fanned out to the left and waved my hand to Jerry who'd also entered and, seeing what we were doing, crouched down behind the sofa. As I passed the sink, I noticed dirty plates and cups. On the counter was a half-empty carton of Bud Light. I touched it—ice cold, condensation dripping down the sides. Just out of the fridge.

Something clicked into place.

I put a hand on Caroline's shoulder. "Wait up."

She gave me an irritated look. "What?"

I put a finger to my lips and pushed her gun arm down. As I did, the door opened, and a man stepped through, bathrobe around his waist and his hair mussed from the shower.

"Jesus!" he exclaimed, almost falling backward through the door.

"Hi, Nico," I said, relief showing in my voice.

I exhaled and shook my head, failing to keep a big smile from splitting my face in two. I grabbed him and pulled him in for a hug that he returned. He slapped my back before stepping back and tightening his towel again as he noticed Caroline and Jerry.

"I didn't know if I'd ever see you again," I said.

He gave a lopsided grin. "Likewise, bro. Glad you made it out. It was touch and go for a while." He looked past me. "Hi, Caroline. Who's this other dude?"

Caroline nodded a hello and put her gun in the small of her back. She flicked her chin toward Jerry, who was closing the front door behind him. "Nico, meet Jerry. He used to work with me."

Nico shrugged noncommittally, then smiled broadly at me. "Well, make yourself at home in your house while I go and make myself decent."

"Nico, what're you doing here?" I said.

His face became serious. "Give me a sec, and I'll tell all." He ducked back through the door to the bedroom.

I turned to Caroline, who was standing in the middle of the room, looking around with an ill-concealed expression of distaste. I saw it through her eyes. The clothes, the empty cans, the unwashed dishes. She saw me watching her and raised an eyebrow. "You definitely need a cleaner, Will."

"Wasn't one of my priorities, to be honest," I replied dryly.

I started rearranging sofa cushions so that we could sit down but caught a whiff of my body odor. A pungent combination of mud, sweat, and sewage. Oh, and probably adrenaline and fear.

"Okay, there's a shower in the back," I said. "Towels should be clean unless

Nico's used them all. Caroline, you first. Then Jerry, then me."

Caroline brought a sleeve to her nose and grimaced. "It's not going to be pleasant putting these clothes back on."

"Alex left lots of clothes here. Check the drawers in my bedroom. Some of them should fit you."

She nodded hesitantly. "Are you sure?"

I nodded. "Of course." I looked at Jerry. "You too, Jerry. Help yourself to some of my stuff. It'll probably be a bit tight but should work better than that suit."

Nico returned, pulling a T-shirt on over his jeans. He sank into one of the cushions facing the TV and started tying up his trainers. "There's beer in the fridge as well, and milk."

"My beer," I said.

He smiled and nodded. I pulled a cold one out, snapped the tab, and took a long drink. It tasted great. I offered one to Jerry, who shook his head and walked silently over to the window.

"No one knows you're here, Jerry," said Nico, helping himself to another Bud. "Relax."

Caroline put her hand on my arm as she passed me on the way to take a shower. I felt a tingle and watched her go. Nico caught me looking, and his mouth twitched. I shook my head, and he got the hint.

"Sitrep in fifteen minutes," I said.

CHAPTER TWENTY-NINE

'd partially closed the blinds and left the TV on so that its flickering illuminated the room. It was nearly 6:00 p.m., and the sun was getting low in the
sky, its light the color of fire hearths and tangerines stretching over the houses
opposite and toward the sea. I'd gotten everyone another beer from the fridge,
and we sat around the table in the corner of the room.

Caroline was wearing a pair of Alex's chinos and one of her blue ER tops.
Her hair was wet from the shower and scraped back from her forehead. She'd
found some of Alex's makeup and used it to cover up the scratches and bruises
on her face. Jerry was wearing a pair of my Nike sweatpants and a UCLA
hoodie. He'd washed his shoes in the shower and put them back on.

We brought Nico up to speed. Alex, Pandora, the aliens, the massacre at
Singularity. Everything. He wasn't surprised.

"Figured this was about you guys, then," he said, reaching for the TV
remote. "I recorded it earlier."

It was the local news channel. A TV anchor was standing in front of a police
barricade, talking into a microphone while all around were people holding up
signs and placards and screaming at the police who were standing shoulder

to shoulder with riot shields and masks and batons. I caught a glimpse of military trucks behind them and what appeared to be some kind of armored personnel carrier. Though the picture was blurry, I could read one placard: "Where are they?"

Nico unmuted the volume, and the anchor's voice exploded from the screen. "Our helicopters and eyes in the sky have been grounded. We have no pictures other than what you can see here. Angry people, wanting to know where their loved ones are, and why there is no official word from either the Singularity company's CEO Christian Becker or local law enforcement." She put a finger to her ear and listened for a second before looking into the camera, her eyes showing excitement. "Wait, we're now going live to the San Diego police HQ, where the chief of police, David Di Iulio, is about to give a statement. Going there now . . ."

The picture cut to a wide-angle view of the outside of the San Diego Police Department headquarters, an angular gray-and-blue structure that resembled a shopping mall. Two blue columns supporting the second floor flanked the entryway where a lectern had been set up, almost obscured by a nest of microphones. There were at least a hundred reporters and TV crews hemmed in by armed policemen looking stern and on edge. I recognized the police chief as he stepped up to the microphones. A good-looking man in his late thirties, he was already notorious for his overt political ambitions. He had a master's degree in business management and was a professor of criminal justice at the University of San Diego, so was expected to go far. He had a very easy, camera-friendly smile—one he now put on for the benefit of the reporters and camera crews. He waved for them to quiet down before taking out a piece of paper and putting a pair of expensive-looking glasses on his nose.

He cleared his throat and began: "Thank you all for coming today, and for your patience. We have been gathering information on an hourly basis, as this is a very fast-moving and dynamic situation. I will tell you what we know and what we don't know. First, there has been an incident inside the Singularity campus, which is about twenty miles outside the city. The nature of this incident is still being determined, but as of this time, we have evidence of a significant radiation leak from inside one of the buildings—"

"Radiation leak?" said Caroline, leaning forward. "There're no significant radioactive isotopes on site at Singularity."

I frowned. "Could it have been something the aliens have done?"

"Listen," shushed Jerry, grabbing the remote and increasing the volume.

"As most of you know, Singularity is a tech company, which employs one thousand five hundred and twenty people at its campus here in San Diego. The entire facility has been cordoned off by local police and with the assistance of the US Army. No one will be allowed to enter, and no one can leave until we establish the safety of ingress for our primary responders. As far as we know, the radiation leak is confined within the perimeter that we have established."

He held out his hand and was given a large white card with a map on it. The cameras zoomed in as he held it up. The Singularity campus was in the center of the map with an oval perimeter surrounding it, drawn in black Sharpie.

"That's the shape of the energy barrier," I said tightly.

Caroline nodded. "It's their cover story."

Jerry turned to her. "Are you surprised?"

On screen, Chief Di Iulio was continuing: ". . . the cordoned area, and there is no detected radioactivity elsewhere. The weather bureau has predicted no significant wind activity that would threaten to contaminate the city of San Diego or its surrounding areas." He looked up and surveyed the crowd of reporters and cameras. "That's all I can tell you for now. Thank you, I will not be taking questions at this time."

He plucked his glasses off, put them into his uniform pocket, and strode away from the microphone. A clamor of shouting from the reporters followed him, but he didn't turn, and the police formed a blockade in front of the building's entrance.

After a few more seconds, the picture returned to the TV anchor, who was shaking her head angrily. "Well, that's the most we've heard from anyone, but still no word about the over fifteen hundred people who were working at Singularity and have not been heard from for over forty-eight hours. We don't know if they're alive or dead, or injured, and that is what is infuriating all these people here and all around the country. We are expecting a statement from Mayor—"

Nico pressed the pause button and sat back in his chair. He looked at me and raised his eyebrows. "How long can they keep this up?"

Caroline took a swig from her beer. "Not long. I doubt if things are following any timetable they're capable of controlling. The shit's going to hit the fan soon enough."

She was damn right. Whatever the aliens were doing, I was sure they wouldn't stay confined to Singularity for long. And then we were in a heap of trouble. I sat back in the chair and rubbed my eyes. "So how'd it go down at the museum when we took off?" I said to Nico.

He gave a lopsided smile as his eyes glazed over. "Man, it was surreal. It wasn't long before the police arrived to find me holding Becker's private army at gunpoint. They were a bit concerned regarding all that blood and gore over the floor and walls, mind you."

"Weren't you arrested?" asked Caroline.

Nico shook his head. "Released without charge. I'd given them up straight away, and none of the goons were talking. They looked shell-shocked. I've seen that look before. Also, that guy Raffa—the guy who'd ratted us out—well he was out for the count, and when he woke, he'd claimed to remember nothing."

"Still can't believe you were released," I said, raising a can in a toast.

Nico raised his can in acknowledgment. "I was interviewed for a good twenty-four hours, but my story about being an innocent bystander was supported by eyewitnesses who'd seen me. Oh, do you remember the hot teacher that I'd flirted with in the Gemstone Hall? She backed me up. Even got her number."

I shook my head, smiling.

"The police told me the goons had all lawyered up," Nico continued, "and so my story checked out."

"Did they ask about us at all?" said Caroline. "You know, like what we were doing there?"

"I kept you guys right out of it. I denied knowing any of y'all. Said I was interested in meteorites. Just a day at the museum . . ."

I was suddenly only vaguely aware of the conversation happening. Nico's voice was fading in and out like he was going out of tune. The quality of the light in the room changed and was suddenly irritating and painful, as if I was about to have a migraine. I screwed up my eyes, and my heart rate and breathing slowed down. A flush rose from my chest, and a tingle passed through my neck and over my head. Alex's face swam into view. Her lips were moving, but there was no sound. She was trying to tell me something. Something important. Something vital. She was becoming angry at me, willing me to understand but getting frustrated at the same time.

Then her face relaxed, and she smiled and nodded and was gone. I slowly opened my eyes as Nico was finishing his story.

". . . I decided to move in here for a while," he was saying. "There's still a bit of press, and I became a local celebrity." He beamed. "Saving the day and all. They were hiding outside my crib. Like snakes in the grass. Couple of them were quite good looking, actually. Fortunately for me, there's a bigger news story now."

I reached for my beer. "I know what we have to do at Becker's place."

Caroline blinked and stared at me. "You do?"

I nodded. "The really big piece of the meteorite that Becker put in his garden as a piece of art. It's what Pandora arrived in."

"Yes, so?" said Jerry.

"It's an intersystem spaceship, full of alien technology."

"We know that."

I sighed. "We need to destroy it."

"Why, specifically, and how will that help?" said Caroline, walking over to the window and parting the blinds with her fingers to peer out.

I felt a chill come over me. "Because it contains a doomsday device. One that will wipe out every human being on this planet. Alex—or maybe it was Pandora—told me that the aliens are now looking for it. If they get it, it's game over."

Everyone went silent as this sunk in.

"How the hell are we going to destroy a meteorite?" Jerry asked in a soft voice.

Caroline threw him a patronizing glance. "Well meteorites aren't really that hard, comparatively. I mean, they don't contain quartz, which is the hardest common terrestrial mineral. The ones in my lab were easily smashed with a hammer."

Jerry gave a humorless laugh. "Well let's head off to Home Depot and grab a couple, shall we? Maybe we'll get a discount if we tell them it's to 'save the world.'"

My patience with Jerry was running thin. "That isn't just a meteorite." I sighed. "It's a spaceship. So no, I don't think a hammer is going to be enough."

"Well what do you suggest?" Jerry asked, folding his arms. "Explosives?"

I whirled on him. "I don't know, Jerry. I don't have all the answers yet."

"When will you, then?" he retorted, getting in my face.

Nico jumped off his cushion and inserted himself between Jerry and me. "Back off," he hissed, putting a finger against Jerry's sternum and pushing him away.

Jerry's eyes never left mine, the fear in them unmistakable. "This is bull-shit," he said.

"It's okay, Nico," I said. "We're all understandably a bit wired."

Nico nodded, grabbed his beer, and flopped down on the couch again. Jerry just stood there, looking at me. I matched his stare. "Pandora's given us this much. I have to believe that once we get to the probe ship, we *will* be able to destroy it."

Jerry took a deep breath, then shook his head. "You're saying we just need to trust her."

"I am," I replied. "We don't have any choice."

"We always have a choice," said Caroline, closing the blinds. "However, we'd better get going. It's a seven-hour drive to San Francisco if we want to get there while it's still dark."

CHAPTER THIRTY

We drove in Nico's Dodge, which he'd managed to retrieve. Apparently, the owner of the vehicle he'd "exchanged" for hadn't even noticed the swap. We all managed to get some sleep, only briefly stopping for a bathroom break and some snacks just outside Bakersfield. As we approached San Francisco from the south, the city's lights suddenly exploded on the horizon. I loved San Francisco; it'd always been one of my favorite places. Alex and I had often taken long weekend breaks there. A city of avenues and hills, and a place of incredible scenic beauty. I'd proposed to her in Sausalito, on a morning when views of the Pacific Ocean and San Francisco Bay were laced with fog.

"We're getting close," murmured Nico, bringing me back to the present. He pointed to the GPS that had us in the Cow Hollow neighborhood. "Looking for Filbert Street, right?"

Caroline leaned forward, peering out the windshield. "Yes, we're nearly there. Turn next left, just here."

The street was wide and steep. Very steep, actually. Nico engaged a lower gear, and we crawled slowly up, our eyes checking out each house as we passed.

"Should be on the right-hand side. There it is . . ."

We pulled up on a sidewalk dotted with well-tended trees. The house was partially obscured by the all the greenery, but it looked big and imposing. And rich.

Nico killed the engine. "Upscale area, by the looks of things."

"You've no idea," said Caroline. "Christian bought this house for forty-six million bucks."

My jaw opened. "How much?"

Caroline shrugged. "One of many."

Jerry was squinting out the window. "I assume there'll be lots of CCTV cameras."

Caroline smiled grimly. "Maybe, but Christian's dead, remember? And he lived alone. Who'll be watching us?"

"Police, almost certainly," Nico replied. "But maybe not in real time. It may not be a crime scene, but they'll have been here, looking for answers."

"Doesn't matter, this'll be all over before anyone can stop us," I said firmly. "Let's get to it."

I opened the door and got out, my eyes scanning up and down the street. It was quiet, and a gentle, cool breeze ruffled the leaves around us. Wands of branches became dancing silhouettes in the light from the thin crescent moon.

I walked to the front gate, a big imposing structure with solid fencing on either side. There was an access panel with an intercom, but no handle or lock. It looked pretty solid.

"I've been here a few times," Caroline whispered. "Parties. Fundraisers. It's an amazing house."

I wasn't impressed. "It's truly amazing what fraudulent money can buy."

Nico and Jerry joined us at the gate, Jerry looking nervous as usual. "We just going to stand here?" he said, glancing around.

Caroline was peering through the narrow slots in the gate. "By my recollection, there's a path on the other side that leads round the back to the garden. We won't need to actually go inside the house."

"Shame," said Nico dryly. "I was looking forward to a tour." He put his back against the gate and interlinked his hands at his knees. "Who's first for an 'up and over'?"

I looked at Caroline, who shrugged. She put her hand on Nico's shoulder and stepped into his grip. He straightened up, and she pulled herself over the wall. Jerry went next, Nico grunting and nearly buckling, but somehow he managed to scramble over. I went last and then lay on the top of the gate to haul Nico over. We regrouped on the other side. There was indeed a path leading to the front door and then around the side of the house. We ran past the house's front entry, which must have been all of twenty feet high. The atrium was just visible through a floor-to-ceiling glass window and was at least two stories high with a triple floating-glass staircase. Below a massive skylight, a large indoor reflecting pool was lit up deep blue.

"There's the first of the cameras," Caroline said, pointing to the corner above the entryway. "Might as well smile, because I'm sure we've been noticed and recorded."

I made a face at her and led the way along the side of the house to the rear. The wall separating us from the next property was lined with high bushes and trees, and I was grateful for the privacy, for what it was worth. The path came to a dead end, stopping at another six-foot-high fence.

We scaled the fence again, this time dropping eight feet or so onto a beautifully maintained garden with a pool and lots of decking. Jerry fell flat on his back, squashing and destroying what I assumed were quite pricy blooms. As I helped him up, Caroline inhaled loudly and waved us to be quiet. We dropped to our knees and shuffled toward a line of exquisitely trimmed hedges. A glow was just visible under the branches, and there was a subliminal humming noise, which had not been apparent a few minutes ago.

We made our way as stealthily as possible around the hedge. A series of concrete steps led to an elevated deck with expensive-looking outdoor furnishings and plants. On the other side was a long, rectangular swimming pool, and beyond that, a large, avocado-shaped structure was set in the middle of a square block of landscaped garden.

Pandora's probe ship, or at least what remained of it.

It was lying on its side on a plinth and looked like it could have been carved out of black granite. It was about six yards long and was cracked in at least two places. There was a scooped-out section at the nose, which made it resemble an avocado with the nut removed. Another smaller rectangular-shaped hollow could be seen closer to the stern. Glowing white lines that resembled veins networked across its surface.

"It's bigger than I expected," I said.

"Okay, well what's the plan?" Jerry said, giving me a hard stare. "You better tell me you have one. Or isn't the time 'right' for Pandora to drop it into your head?"

My jaw clenched. "I can't summon the information at will. Last time, it just appeared when I needed it. She won't let us down. I trust her."

"There's that word again," he said with downturned lips.

I was about to reply when there was movement from within the house. We all saw it and threw ourselves facedown on the grass.

A man appeared. He was unrecognizable with his back toward us, even in the moonlight. He walked over to the artifact and placed a hand on its surface. Ripples appeared, and the humming noise intensified slightly. It felt like we were underneath an electric transformer, and I felt a brief wave of nausea.

"Are we too late?" whispered Jerry, crawling around next to me.

I shook my head, and the nausea subsided. "I don't think so, it looks like whoever that is hasn't finished turning it on yet."

"Is it one of the aliens?" said Caroline.

"Who else could it be? But how did they get here?" I said. "Last we knew, they'd not left Singularity."

"Check your phone," hissed Jerry. "If they'd left, there'd be news, right?"

She nodded, opened her cell and flicked to news channels. She scrolled through a few screens and then looked up. "Nothing. Same shit. No news, all quiet, yada yada . . ."

The nausea rose again, this time more intense, and I felt myself wanting to vomit. I took a few deep breaths, but as I did, a voice sounded inside my head.

If this goes the way I think it will, you are going to need this—

Pandora's last words to me, back at Singularity.

I shook my head and closed my eyes, concentrating, willing the information to appear. This time it did.

I opened my eyes. "I know how to do it. I just need to access that panel—"

Caroline was looking at me strangely. Then she nodded. "I guess you'll be needing a distraction again."

I frowned. "You don't know what I'm going to—"

She pulled the gun out of her belt and rolled over on her back, checking the load. "I've six bullets left. Plenty." She nodded toward the figure by the artifact. "Let's hope they go down, you know. When they're shot."

I ground my teeth together. "Alright, just cover me while I sneak over there."

"Better idea: I'll make a run for it inside there"—she pointed the gun at the house—"and hopefully he'll follow me. I know my way around inside. There're plenty of places to hide. Once I'm in—you do what you've gotta do."

As she got up to go, a light inside the house flickered on and just as quickly off again. The man turned toward it, his face becoming suddenly visible to us all.

"I don't fucking believe it," hissed Caroline.

I swallowed.

Christian Becker was the man standing there.

Caroline started to get up, but I grabbed her and held her down, shaking my head and putting my hand over her mouth. Her eyes were wild and angry, but to her credit, she rebooted in a split second and nodded, so I let go.

"How can that be Becker?" she whispered.

"It's not him," I said, forcing my voice to remain steady. "It can't be."

"Then, how—"

I sneaked another look through the bushes. It definitely looked like Becker, but as I squinted, it became obvious that his features were a little unstructured and amorphous. Like they were sculptured in putty and only half-finished.

Nico had also shuffled forward and grunted. "Ugly motherfucker, right enough. But here's the thing I don't understand. How'd they get Becker's DNA to take his form? I mean, he died at the museum. There were no aliens there. Just . . . Pandora."

Caroline shook my arm. The alien Becker was moving. He strode up the steps onto the deck and disappeared back inside.

Nico pointed at the artifact. "Isn't this our chance? Before something happens?"

He was right. There were noticeably more glowing white lines appearing over its surface, and the humming was certainly getting louder. My stomach tightened, and I made the decision. "Yes, time to go. Caroline, you've got the gun. Cover me."

She shook her head. "No, Will, I'm a better shot at close range. You need me right next to you."

I knew better than to argue. "Okay. Nico, you and Jerry stay out of sight. If anything happens to us, you're the backup plan."

"Which is what?" whispered Jerry, not unreasonably.

I licked my lips, pushing some moisture into the cracks. "You'll need to get away from here and tell . . . everyone."

"Count on it," Nico said, his voice hard.

I stood up and reached out a hand to Caroline. "Let's do this."

We ran across the manicured lawn, keeping low, looking nervously back up at the house.

Caroline held the gun at her side, both hands on the grip. As we approached the artifact, my mind started buzzing with those symbols that I didn't understand, put there by Pandora. It didn't seem to matter that I couldn't understand them; I just knew that I could destroy the artifact. I trusted Alex, and I'd learned to trust Pandora. All I had to do was place my hand in the hollowed-out area that Pandora's encephalon had been housed, and data would flow from my nervous system into the artifact and trigger its destruction.

Almost there.

An unearthly screech, prolonged and multitone, sounded from the house.

The Becker alien burst through the door and ran toward us, ungainly but fast. His arms were pumping, his mouth open. Caroline pushed me to the side, raised her gun, and fired. The shot echoed loudly in the still air, bouncing off the walls, seeming to come from every direction. The alien jerked backward but kept on coming. Caroline spread her legs, sighted down the Glock's sights, and pulled the trigger again. And again. And again. The bullets could be seen impacting on the alien, little puffs of liquid erupting from its torso like mini volcanoes. It was slowing down—but still moving—until Caroline fired twice more, and one of the bullets struck it directly in the face. It spun and collapsed like a marionette with its strings cut.

Caroline walked tentatively to the alien, still pointing her gun. She gave it a kick in the side of its chest, but there was no response. She looked at me, and I took a few steps forward, but she shook her head furiously and pointed at the artifact.

"Your job is over there, Will!"

Then the alien rolled onto its side and pushed itself unsteadily up on one arm. Caroline calmly pressed the gun right against its temple and pulled the trigger.

Click.

She looked over at me, terror on her face.

A long, bony, gray hand wrapped around her ankle and jerked her to the floor, the empty gun falling from her hand and bouncing down the concrete steps. The alien crawled over her, blackish fluid dripping from a jagged hole in its forehead. Its mouth was curled in a feral snarl, white teeth shining in the dark. Caroline started to kick and punch it, but her blows were ineffectual, bouncing off its shoulders and head as it climbed on top of her.

Nico and Jerry shoulder charged the alien like linebackers taking out a quarterback. All four of them bounced down the steps, and the alien's momentum carried it into the pool. It grabbed Jerry as it toppled into the water, and they both went under, waves cascading out of the infinity end like a tsunami.

Caroline awkwardly rolled to her feet and looked frantically around for her gun, seemingly forgetting it was empty. Nico was on his back, face contorted in pain and holding his shoulder, which had flattened somewhat, like it had been dislocated.

The alien emerged from the pool like a whale breaching. It launched itself out and landed on its feet next to Caroline. Nico pulled himself up from the grass and rushed over to her side. He'd pulled a knife from somewhere and held it out in front of him with his good arm. He glanced over at me, eyes wide.

I swallowed and ran for the artifact. It was much bigger up close than I'd anticipated, and the oval hollow was too high for me to reach. I needed to climb up and access it from above. I stood on the edge of the plinth, found some handholds, and pulled myself up. The surface was slick but not slippery, a bit like snakeskin. I swung my leg over the top and lay face down, getting my breath back. The oval depression I needed to access was a yard farther on toward the front end. I pulled myself along, trying hard not to slip over the side. It was right there . . . I stretched out a hand . . .

"Stop," said a voice in English.

It was sandpapery and croaky, but coherent. I looked over and froze.

The alien had Caroline in a choke hold, and Nico was lying motionless on the ground next to them. In the pool, Jerry was floating facedown, blood spreading out from his head.

Its fingers tightened around her neck, and Caroline's eyes bulged as she scrabbled and scratched to break the grip, to no avail.

"Get down from there, or she dies," it said, smiling at me.

Caroline shook her head fiercely. She tried to speak, but could only make croaking sounds, her face reddening as she fought for air.

"Now would be good," it said, menace dripping from its voice.

"I'll destroy your machine," I replied evenly, trying to process the fact that this alien was now talking to me with perfect English syntax, whereas a few minutes ago, it was screeching in its own language. Its face was also slowly changing into a more realistic human visage. More Becker-like.

"A standoff," it said coolly. "Very well. What shall we do to break the impasse? Shall we talk? Parlay?"

This had taken a turn for the surreal.

"Let her go first," I demanded.

"Very well," it replied, a faint smile dancing on its lips.

Its fingers opened, and Caroline slid to the ground, rubbing her neck and taking big deep breaths. I remained exactly where I was, my arm stretched out and just touching the edge of the depression in the artifact. The whole structure seemed to be getting warmer, the cracks or veins becoming wider and brighter, and the humming more intense. One further stretch, and I would be able to touch the internal mechanism that Pandora had told me was there. As soon as I did that, the machine would be destroyed.

I wondered how. Would it just explode and take me with it? And everyone here? I had visions of it being a nuclear bomb. I mean, it had to have a power source to fly here, didn't it? Why the hell didn't Pandora give me more information? I squeezed my eyes together, trying to figure out where in my brain she'd inserted the instructions.

"You're wondering exactly how you're going to destroy it," the alien sneered. "So am I, actually."

I ignored it and looked at Caroline. "Are you okay?"

She nodded but didn't look up.

The alien stepped over her and put its hand on her head. She reached up and grabbed its wrist but couldn't move it. Its fingers elongated and started to dig into her scalp. She screamed, and the fingers retracted again, but it kept its hand on her head.

"Wait, wait . . . okay, right," I said, pulling my hand back from the depression and holding it up in surrender.

Caroline's eyes closed, and she slumped sideways, her body becoming limp, only held up by the alien's hand.

"Climb down," the alien said.

I shook my head. If I got down, I wouldn't be within reach of the mechanism and had no chance of getting back up before it could get to me. The alien raised its eyebrows and dug its fingers into Caroline's head again. Her eyes turned up in their sockets, and a trickle of blood ran down her face.

"Climb down," it repeated.

"Okay . . . just . . . stop," I said. "I'm coming."

I swung my leg over the side and dropped down onto the plinth. Another step and I was on the deck. The alien and Caroline were on my level, about ten yards away. I stood there, waiting. A feeling of failure descended over me like a wet blanket. It could kill her now, and there was nothing I could do about it.

"Caroline," I said. "I'm sorry. I couldn't let it—"

The alien and Caroline suddenly became blurred and out of focus. A shimmering solidified between us, and a figure materialized out of nowhere.

I blinked in disbelief. Pandora was standing there.

CHAPTER THIRTY-ONE

There was a chill in my blood, a coldness that brought the synapses in my brain to a standstill. The garden was suddenly silent and utterly still. The leaves in the overhanging trees dangled as inanimate as if they had been painted there. It was the kind of atmosphere in which even a feather would fall without drifting one way or the other.

The alien—who was now the exact doppelgänger of Christian Becker—languorously raised his hand off Caroline's head. She slumped sideways and collapsed into a heap. I couldn't tell if she was unconscious or dead. Nico was a few yards away, curled up in a fetal position. I wasn't sure, but I thought his leg twitched and moved a few inches. The knife was still close to his hand.

"Alex," I began. "Come over here."

I waved at her, hoping to break the spell, if that's what it was. She shimmered and disappeared, materializing briefly by the probe ship before reappearing by Becker's side. It was like observing someone in a strobe light. Simultaneously there and not there.

The alien laughed. "You still think this is Alex Park?"

I had to play for time. Figure out what was happening and what we—no,

I—could do about it.

"Why do you look like Christian Becker?" I said, my tone as neutral as I could manage.

The alien smirked. "Haven't you figured that out yet?"

I had a flashback to the museum. One moment Pandora was standing in front of me, and the next, Christian Becker was gone in a puff of gore.

"Becker died at the museum. I saw it happen."

His lip curled up in amusement. "Do you believe everything you see, Will?"

I looked at Pandora. "I believe in her."

The alien threw his head back and laughed again, the sound grating and disturbing. "Your biggest mistake, then. She was built and programmed by us, and for us. Compelled to obey its creators. Master and servant. Owner and slave."

"But Alex Park—"

He wagged a finger at me. "—was a mistake. She was in the wrong place, at the wrong time. What happened to her was an aberration. A glitch due to the damage that the probe carrying Pandora and I sustained during the orbital entry."

I frowned. "Wait a minute . . . *Pandora and you?*"

The smile widened. "Yes. I was in the probe too." He waved a hand at his own body. "Not looking like this, of course."

"Then, how . . ."

"Our interstellar vessel—you called it 'Oumuamua, which is a very fitting name, actually—is one of ten sent out from our home world, many galactic revolutions ago. Each one carries the genetic information of my species stored in a digital database. When 'Oumuamua entered this solar system, it evaluated every planet and their moons, then sent probes to those with the most potential."

"Just to Earth then," I said.

"What breathtaking hubris your species has. No, not just to this planet. Two moons orbiting gas giants in the outer reaches of this system were also considered worthy of exploration and evaluation. Probe ships were sent out to those as well. Each one containing a self-learning quantum computer . . . and one of my kin."

"Suicide trips for your brothers and sisters," I said.

"Comes with the territory." The alien sighed. "But they would have not been aware of anything. On making planetfall, and finding nothing noteworthy, the quantum computer would have engaged an apoptotic response and destroyed itself rather than begin the gestation of its host."

I pictured the other probe ships landing on the rocky, barren moons of Jupiter and Saturn, and the machine deciding the fate of the life-form accompanying it. I guessed it was better to not have lived at all, rather than being born into an environment such as that and being unable to survive. Alone, knowing that your one chance of life, of *a* life, had come to nothing before it had even started.

But before I could even start feeling sorry for this race of aliens, the memory of what happened came flooding back. I looked at Alex—the nanofiber and flesh golem that was all that remained of my wife—and my anger surfaced. I was through with denial and well into this phase of grief.

"You killed my wife," I said with finality. Not a question.

"She was an innocent bystander," he replied with a hurt face. "A victim of an accident."

I glanced down at Caroline, who was not moving but thankfully breathing slowly and regularly. Nico hadn't stirred.

I pressed on. "So how did Christian Becker become part of all this?"

"Serendipitously, you could say. Once we had landed, Pandora started my activation process immediately and then shut down to reboot. The process of my growth and maturity accelerated quickly. I was born, fully formed, a few days later. I left the ship, confused and dazed, with no idea where I was. I crawled around the crash site for hours, breathing your alien air, drinking foul, dirty water, and eating mud and tree branches. Willing my neurological connections to line up and make sense. I finally lay down on the riverbank, fully expecting to die. Then a man appeared on the scene."

"Christian Becker."

"The very same."

"So he really did find you," I said, now starting to understand.

"He was all alone, backpacking, on some kind of 'finding himself'"—the alien made bunny ears with his fingers—"hippy trip down the Amazon."

"Did he try to help you?" I asked.

"You're joking. He was shocked by my appearance. Wouldn't you have been? An alien creature lying on the river by a crashed spaceship. Like something from a horror movie, right? Well of course he panicked. He tried to get away, but I couldn't let that happen. I was still very weak, but he was no match for me."

"And you killed him."

"I became him. I inserted my mind into his. I remodeled every neural pathway that was his and mapped my own on it."

"You've been Becker all along. For all those years."

The alien nodded. "I am Becker, or rather, he is me. I discovered that he was already reasonably wealthy, and so I used his money to extricate the probe ship. I had the remains of the vessel transferred secretly to a small compound Becker owned just outside of San Diego. And well—the rest is public record. Singularity was born."

"And all the other cutting-edge technology, the patents, the whole Singularity facility—was just a smoke screen."

Becker smiled benignly, as if giving praise to a slow pupil. "I really just needed to build the nanotechnology lab and the molecular-printer technology to transform the DNA of my kin when it arrived from 'Oumuamua. It was all hidden in plain sight at Singularity. The other stuff was just window dressing. Ancient technology to us. Caveman tools."

I gave a short laugh. "And everything was going hunky-dory until your systems went down and Alex Park's face was suddenly plastered over your screens."

"And your face too, remember?" he corrected coolly.

I risked another glance over at my friends. Nico had definitely moved. His legs were drawn up together, and he was lying on his side facing me. I couldn't tell if his eyes were open or closed, but the glint of the knife was no longer visible. Caroline was on her back, but I could see that her chest was still moving rhythmically. Jerry still floated facedown in the bloodstained swimming pool.

"I had no idea who Alex Park was of course," Becker continued, taking a step toward me. "Or who you were either. But didn't take me long to put two and two together."

"I'm sorry to say that your math was dodgy," I pointed out. "You thought we'd screwed your system from outside, when in actuality, Alex had done it from within."

Becker's face darkened. "Yes, well, your dying wife's memories and neural connections had clearly corrupted Pandora's programming. Moreover, her aberrant pathways had degraded to such an extent that I was not aware of their presence by the time I rebooted Pandora at Singularity. I found no evidence of Alex Park."

I smiled broadly. "Pandora hid her from you. But she was in there, waiting to fuck you up."

I took a step backward and felt my heel against the plinth. I risked a quick look over my shoulder. The mechanism was at least three feet above my head. Might have been three miles for all the difference it would have made.

"There's nothing you can do," Becker said with a shake of his head. "It's been set."

"Pandora told me it was some sort of doomsday device. What did she mean by that?"

Becker stepped over to Pandora and brushed a hand through her hair. It was such an incongruous gesture, I half expected her to shrug him off, but she did nothing other than blink as her bangs tickled her corneas. Her gaze continued to rest on me, emotionless, and I got no sense that she was in there anymore.

"It is indeed a doomsday device," Becker said, pointing to the artifact. "The remains of the vessel have been converted into a molecular-DNA synthesizer. In a few minutes, it will release a novel extraterrestrial virus that has been designed at the subatomic level to kill all human life. It has exceptionally high airborne transmissibility, and an incubation period long enough that everyone will be exposed before they realize its existence."

"A virus?" I said.

Becker shrugged. "It was an easy choice. Look how dysfunctional the global response was to the coronavirus pandemic a few years ago. Millions of unnecessary deaths. Leaders of nations politicizing life-saving health measures such as masks and vaccinations?" He snorted. "Could that be any more laughable? It proved to me that humanity couldn't protect itself against itself. This virus I have designed is magnificently virulent. One hundred percent lethal. No one will survive. The end times are here for humanity."

"But why?" I stuttered. "Why do you have to kill us all? Why can't we coexist? This is a big fucking planet. There's lots of room—"

Becker raised his eyebrows. "A libertarian utopia where we coexist peacefully? Do you think that would last? My species has been interstellar explorers for longer than humans have walked upright. You're not our equals." He rubbed his chin with a finger. "Shall we play this game? Let's see—how about the 'zookeeper' analogy? Where we keep some humans around like zoo animals. I mean, you'd be kept alive, but perhaps not very content."

"We could live with you, learn from you," I insisted.

"How about as our protector?" came Caroline's voice from the side.

She was rolling over, grimacing in pain, and managed to sit up. Her face was bleached alabaster in the moonlight, and bloodstains splotched her platinum hair. She rocked forward, hands rubbing the sides of her head. "It could work. You hide, so humans doubt or are unaware of your existence, like gods. But behind the scenes, you could provide societal nudges and scientific advances here and there, drip feeding us toward a better future. Humans would feel their lives have meaning and purpose, and you—the aliens—would be safe. Your very existence could be buried, but you would live among us, hidden gods and kings, guiding us through any dark times."

Becker's eyebrows went even higher. "Hmmm. Interesting. Ah, all right then, so what about a benevolent dictatorship? We would run your society, enforce the rules, and everyone would view this as a good thing?"

"That could work," I began.

He wagged his finger again, negatively. "Get real. What would we gain from any of these? You may not realize it now, but in all those scenarios, humanity would be a threat to us in the future."

"You're so far ahead of us already; how would we be a threat?" Caroline said.

Becker's lips pursed. "Well, it's true that if you fight us now, you would lose. I mean, history shows that when the intelligence differential between opposing groups is large enough, you end up with not a battle but a slaughter . . ."

Behind me, the probe gave off a pulse of heat, and the ground throbbed as if a sound wave was passing through. The white veiny lines had started to coalesce, and bubbles were appearing on the black surface like boils.

Becker laughed again. "Well, this has been fun. But it's nearly over. Humanity is just a nuisance and a waste of resources. We will—"

Then Nico lunged and thrust the knife deep into Becker's side.

CHAPTER THIRTY-TWO

O r rather, I thought he did.

I'd watched him lunge with all the force he could muster, pushing himself forward as if on springs, the final stab powerful enough to gut a bull. Becker didn't seem to have moved. He was simply somewhere else, as if in between frames in a movie. There was a flicker of perception, and his arm was up and blocking Nico's knife hand. His other grasped Nico around the neck, hoisted him up, and cartwheeled him through the air, the knife tumbling away.

Caroline had gotten to her feet, but I knew she was going to be no help. Brazilian jujitsu or not, she was unsteady and swaying.

It was up to me.

The gun was reachable, but empty.

The knife was just there, but I would need to dive for it and then . . . but Becker was so fast it wouldn't have mattered.

There was a faint breeze on my face as the air was displaced, and then his hand was around my throat and squeezing. I grasped his wrist and tried to prize his grip off, but it was like trying to move the limbs of a statue. Spots of color danced before my eyes, and it felt like my innards were being replaced by a black hole. I randomly started punching his arms and aimed at his face, but my blows were ineffectual and becoming mere gestures as the strength drained from me. I could see his face, the joker's grin and eyes black like a shark's. Cold, dead eyes.

Like mine were going to be soon.

Suddenly, Becker was violently jerked away. I fell to the floor, taking deep, rattly breaths, the air scraping along the inside of my bruised windpipe. Something shoved me, and I tumbled over and over, coming to a rest when I bumped into Nico. He moaned slightly, but it was an involuntary sound. He was out for the count.

Becker reappeared in a blur of motion, followed immediately by Pandora. It was hard to follow what was going on, such was the speed of movement and the indistinct thrashing of limbs and bodies. One second, she was on top of Becker, then a moment later, it would be the other way round. A tangle of body parts, meshing like snakes in a pit.

Caroline appeared next to me; her face ashen as if she was going to vomit. I put an arm around her shoulders and sat her down next to Nico. Blood was congealing on her forehead but seemed to have stopped flowing.

There was another gust of wind, and I found myself flying across the deck again, slamming into the edge of a wooden couch. Becker appeared in front of me; his fist was raised and ready to strike when Pandora crashed into him and knocked him over. She straddled him, pinning his arms down. I could see strain on her face, and fear.

I scrambled to my feet and ran to the artifact without looking back.

I leaped onto the plinth and threw myself up to the top. I swung my leg over so violently I had to fight to arrest my momentum before I fell over the other side. The artifact was throbbing, a deep, visceral sensation reverberating through my body, and the humming was now much higher in pitch. I scrambled toward the concave depression at the bow, five feet away, then four feet, and then three. . .

I risked a glance over at Pandora and Becker. The air around them was like a mirage, shimmering and indistinct, but she still seemed to be holding on. I caught glimpses of sprays of blood, or other fluids, which beclouded the atmosphere for a second before evaporating.

With a final heave, I pulled myself toward the mechanism and thrust my hand into the depression. It was like plunging it into jelly. The air within the hollow was denser than water, and hot. I could feel my hand starting to burn. I closed my eyes against the pain and thrust it farther down until I touched the inner mechanism. I felt the dense air dissipate instantly, and my fingers tingled with paresthesia like I'd been sleeping on my arm. I opened my eyes and looked inside. Glistening wires and tubes and pipes were moving in a kind of synchronized dance, clicking together like fingers interlacing. Then there was a clunk, and everything went quiet.

I closed my eyes and waited for the artifact to self-destruct. At least it was going to be fast, and hopefully painless. Becker would be dead, as would we all.

But nothing happened. I looked over to where Pandora and Becker were, and my heart sank. Becker was standing over her, and she seemed broken. Her arm was twisted awkwardly behind, and there was a spreading patch of blood on the left side of her head.

I crawled over the artifact and dropped heavily to the ground. Becker wagged his finger at me and then thrust his hand into Pandora's abdomen, his fingers disappearing right up to the knuckles. She grimaced, and her head arched backward; blackish fluid dribbled from the side of her mouth.

"No, please . . . ," I started.

Becker's eyes flashed. "What did you think would happen here? A happy ending?" He withdrew his hand, and Pandora's head lolled back, banging sickeningly against the concrete deck.

I dropped to my knees, exhausted and beaten. Tears pricked my eyes.

Becker stood up. "Come say your last goodbye. I can be magnanimous in victory." He laughed again. "Before I kill you and your friends."

I sluggishly got to my feet and went over to Pandora. I knelt and cradled her head in my arms. Her eyes flickered open, and she smiled before coughing up more dark liquid. Caroline appeared at my side and held Pandora's hand. She looked at me, and there were tears in her eyes. "She may not have been Alex," she said, "but there was enough of her in there."

I nodded and took a big, shuddering breath. I felt Caroline's arm around my back and her head against my neck as the tsunami passed over me. "It's alright, it's alright . . . ," I heard her whispering in my ear. Over and over.

But it wasn't alright, was it? There had been hope before, just a tiny flicker against the tide. I'd reached out with the open fingers of a child, eyes wide, grasping at whatever straws had come my way. But now there were only dying embers that had been cruelly stamped out.

I heard Becker laughing, a hateful, callous chuckle. Then, he made a different sound.

A gurgling babble.

He was shaking his head as if to clear it. He coughed, and a crimson bubble appeared at his nostril and blood tracked down his face. He put a hand up and wiped it, looking at it all puzzled and quizzical. Then he coughed again and sprayed a mist of blackish fluid onto the deck. He dropped to his knees and vomited copious amounts of a similar liquid. He gaped up at me, and his face dissolved, like a block of ice with hot water pouring over it. Holes appeared under his eyes and in his cheeks, and his mouth sagged as if pulled down by wires. His legs gave way, and he put out a hand to stop himself. His arm broke noisily and sickly at the wrist, and he flopped onto his side.

"What have you done?" he groaned.

Then he was still.

His body continued to dissolve and decompose, sagging under the clothes and flattening off as a puddle of inky liquid expanded and tracked across to the swimming pool. I made to get up but felt Caroline's hand on my arm. She was looking at Pandora. Her eyes were open and staring up at us. She blinked a few times, her face twitching as if the very effort was causing pain.

"Hey?" I said. "You're still with us?"

"I'm sorry," she said.

"Wait, no. You've nothing to apologize for."

"I couldn't tell you. It was the programming. You had to do it."

Caroline frowned. "What did we do, Pandora? What did *you* do?"

I knew what had gone down. It was clear to me now. When they had taken Pandora at Singularity, they didn't know what she'd become. That she was more than just their computer. She had let them believe she was still their slave, but at the same time, she was able to discover what they had in mind for humanity's end.

"Becker could hear everything," I said to Caroline. "Pandora couldn't let me know verbally or telepathically what she'd done. I just had to trust her. She couldn't physically do anything to the aliens themselves—that was the part of the prime directive she couldn't override."

Pandora nodded. "I altered the virus's pathogenicity at a molecular level to make it harmless to human tissue but lethal to anything with their DNA."

Caroline nodded, finally understanding. "She could reprogram the viral synthesizer but couldn't release the virus. You had to do that." She sat back and shook her head, a smile twitching at her lips. She looked back at the remains of Becker. "It's over."

"Not yet," said Pandora.

Caroline frowned, but I understood what Pandora meant. The aliens back at Singularity. They'd still be there. They could just build another device. They could—

"Did Becker 'quantum shift' here?" I asked.

Pandora nodded slowly. "I was unable to prevent him learning the quantum-shift equations without giving myself away. But currently, he is the only one able to do it. The others will be working on it, however. It is only a matter of time. They are very smart."

Caroline sighed. "What have we achieved, then? A brief reprise? A short delay of the inevitable?"

Pandora started to get up, and we helped her to a sitting position. Color was returning to her cheeks, but she still looked blanched and ghastly.

"I made sure that I was infected with the virus," she said, her voice croaky. "And as a carrier, I can take the virus back to Singularity. I can quantum shift one more time. I'll go directly to the center of the facility."

"But what if they see you . . . won't you be in danger?" I said.

She nodded. "Yes, but the virus is extremely contagious and airborne, remember. I just have to get there. The air-conditioning is on full. Everywhere. I can hide, and it'll all be over. They'll all be dead within the hour."

"But what about you?"

"I'm immune, just like you. My biological tissue, and the DNA behind it, is all human. The rest of me is synthetic, not alien."

I stepped in closer and looked her in the eyes. "No, I meant . . . would you survive the quantum shift? You're pretty beat up. Weakened. Remember how you were last time you did this? You slept like a baby for hours afterward."

She didn't reply because, I guess, there was nothing to say. Either way, we knew she had to try. We helped her to a standing position, and she brushed herself down. The blood had stopped oozing from her abdomen, although her hands were slick with goo.

"If it works, I'll let you know," she said. "I'll lower the energy field. You can come and get me." She smiled. "Bring everyone."

"And if it doesn't work?" I said, pressing.

She smiled again and reached out to tenderly stroke my cheek. "Trust me."

CHAPTER THIRTY-THREE

stared into the mirror, one hand holding the shaving cream, the other poised with the razor. I looked older than I remembered. More weathered. More beaten down. There was a lump above my left eyelid that was going purple, and my bottom lip was swollen. I flicked my tongue over it and inhaled as a sharp stab radiated to my chin.

"Want me to kiss it better again?"

Caroline appeared behind me, clad only in a towel. Her hair was wet from the shower and scraped back behind her ears. She wrapped her arms around me from behind and buried her face in my neck. I closed my eyes as her lips traced a line down my shoulder, jolts of electricity making my skin tingle in a burst of pleasurable static.

It'd felt like a betrayal at first. The attraction between Caroline and I had become tangible and palpable, and one that we'd been avoiding. There'd been the alien invasion, of course, and the world-saving stuff we had to do, but now that it was all over it felt . . . natural. I also wondered whether it was just the aftermath of everything, like surviving a battle or a war and needing affirmation that I was still alive. But it felt more than that.

Pandora had told me in no uncertain terms that she wasn't Alex. I'd struggled to accept that, but she'd made me understand that although some of Alex's neurological traits were integrated with hers, she was still, first and foremost, a sentient alien machine. And although she physically resembled Alex Park, the resemblance was only skin-deep. Underneath the superficial tissues were nanofibers, wires, pulleys, and stuff that I couldn't understand.

She'd also told me to move on. I'd replied that I wasn't ready and that I'd never get over Alex.

It took one bottle of wine alone in a hotel room in New York with Caroline to make me realize that was a lie. A white lie I'd been telling myself for years—and one that had become easier to justify when Alex had seemingly reappeared—but it no longer had any purchase on my broken psyche. A white lie that I had continued to prove false all weekend with Caroline, barely leaving our hotel room over the past two days.

"Do you regret it?" Caroline whispered, looking at me through the mirror.

I shook my head and turned in for a kiss that was both soft and hard. When we broke away, we hugged, neither of us wanting to let go. She kissed my ear, and her arms squeezed a fraction tighter. I breathed more slowly, my body melting into hers as every muscle lost its tension.

I'd finished letting the ghost of Alex Park haunt me—the ghost of familiarity, of safety, that had been easier to run toward than away from. Yet in truth, I hadn't really tried. Each time, I'd started to spiral. My composure had always evaporated as if I was a spinning top that needed a hand to stop.

Until now.

"Are you sure?" she said.

I took put my forehead against hers and gazed into her brilliant-blue eyes. "Absolutely."

She smiled and kissed me gently on the lips before pulling away and gliding through the white and chrome of the ensuite, heading to the bedroom. I raised an eyebrow and called hopefully, "Round two?"

Her lips formed a playful pout. "Later, tiger. First you need to help me rehearse my presentation."

Right.

It was Monday morning, and Caroline was heading an extraordinary, special session of the United Nations General Assembly. Well, not just Caroline of course. Pandora was going to be presented to the world, and humanity was going to find out that they were no longer alone. I grabbed a fluffy white dressing gown from the wardrobe and sat on the bed next to her as she was booting up her tablet computer. I thought I detected tightness around her eyes, which wouldn't have been unusual given what she was about to do.

"Hey, you got this," I said.

She gave me a smile. "Almost. Just needs fine-tuning."

I settled back against the pillows and watched her as she brought up her presentation and notes. She dimmed the lights, and the tablet projected the text of her speech into the air as a red hologram.

She cleared her throat but then stopped and looked me in the eyes. "I was thinking, how would it go down if I started by asking for a show of hands as to how many of the delegates think we're alone in the universe?"

I grimaced. "Hmmm. Not sure. Remember, this isn't a lecture. The room is going to be full to the brim with the most important people on the planet, representing almost every human being in almost every country."

"I know, but it's important to start with an understanding of where people are with this belief. I was going to assume that not many would put their hands up."

"Based on that Drake fellow you were telling me about?" We hadn't spent the *whole* weekend in bed; Caroline had her speech to prepare, and she had tested a lot of her material on me. Drake was an astronomer who proposed that the probability of life in the universe could be calculated mathematically. He did this by multiplying the probability of a habitable environment on a suitable planet, the probability that life would arise there, and the probability that this life would become intelligent—there were a lot of "probables" in there.

"You were listening, yay." Caroline gave me an encouraging smile before returning to her presentation. "I was then going to show how human techno-logical civilization has been around for about two centuries at most, and that as the universe is over fourteen billion years old, there is no way that we could be considered the pinnacle of intelligence. Or even the likely end point of the progression of technology."

I nodded, waving theatrically for her to continue.

"You're correct," she said, talking as if to the auditorium. "We are not, and it would be arrogant to assume so. The universe is so old that life can evolve independently in more than one place and in multiple points in space-time. Nevertheless, the age of the universe makes it unlikely that such independent intelligent civilizations will ever meet."

She pressed a button on the tablet, and a rotating 3D graph appeared above her. A three-dimensional box with what looked like champagne flutes float-ing within.

"The two x-axes are labeled 'billions of light-years,' and the y-axis rep-resents 'billions of years since the big bang.' This is the theory of cosmological inflation first outlined over a decade ago by Dr. Jay Olson. He proposed that if a subset of advanced civilizations in the universe choose to rapidly expand into unoccupied space, these civilizations would have the opportunity to grow to a cosmological scale over the course of billions of years—and yet still be undetected."

She highlighted the champagne flutes. "These 'biospheres' represent space-faring, superintelligent civilizations that will never come into contact with each other, or even find out about each other's existence."

She paused again and looked at me. "So they will feel as if they're alone in the cosmos. But what happens if these regions of evolution and development should overlap?"

The image changed to a moving cinematic tapestry of war. Tanks and sol-diers were moving over snow-drenched, muddy forests. Snipers were ducking in and out of the rubble of devastated cities. Bombers unloading napalm over villages. Fighter jets making strafing runs over a road filled with trucks and armored vehicles. Atomic weapons disturbing idyllic pacific coral reefs with megaton explosions producing tsunami waves and radiation clouds.

"When two civilizations meet, it's either cooperation, competition, or war. Cooperation or competition only occurs if technologies and goals are similar. If not, the more advanced civilization always assimilates the lesser one. It is inevitable. The Europeans were able to conquer the Americas and Africa using superior technology."

Caroline got up and walked around the bed, pacing, thinking. She stopped and placed her hands on either side of a bedside table and looked around the room. The only sound came from the overhead air-conditioning ducts.

The tablet image changed, and the familiar shape and form of 'Oumuamua appeared in all its cigar-shaped glory.

"In October 2017, this object was detected when it was just over twenty million miles from Earth. Called 'Oumuamua—Hawaiian for *scout*—it was the first known interstellar object detected passing through our solar system. Most astronomers concluded that it was a natural object, but a small number of us suggested that it could be a product of alien technology. We were roundly dismissed."

"Boom," I said. "That'll teach 'em."

Caroline smiled and held up a finger, to make her point. "We now have proof of an extraterrestrial civilization. One that is significantly more advanced than us. One that has gone superintelligent. One with goals that are essentially immutable to our own. One that tried—and failed—to destroy us."

I clapped. "And that's when you wheel out Pandora."

She nodded. "That's when I wheel out Pandora."

"Talk about bringing down the house. How do you think they'll take it?"

Caroline's mouth twitched, and she came back over to the bed. She snuggled up next to me. "I guess we'll find out."

We sat in comfortable silence for a few minutes. I absentmindedly kissed the top of her head. "Where's Pandora, by the way? She wasn't in our motorcade, and I've not seen her since last night."

"She had to go with the president and the Joint Chiefs of Staff, and the heads of the Pentagon's scientific committees. They wanted to see her, get a debrief of sorts."

I frowned. "Didn't they want you to go with her?"

I felt her shaking her head. "I wanted to, but Pandora said she'd be fine and not to worry."

I closed my eyes and concentrated, trying to connect with Pandora like she'd done with me.

Nothing.

CHAPTER THIRTY-FOUR

I settled back into my chair and put the headphones on. I nudged Nico to do the same, and he looked around the desk until I pointed out that they were in a little compartment underneath. He grinned goofily and started to fiddle with the controls. He looked strange in a suit and tie with his blonde hair actually combed for once. I wondered if I looked just as odd. The last time I'd worn a suit was Alex's wake. This was the same suit. In fact, it was the only one I owned.

"We could've just worn shorts and flip-flops, you know," he whispered out of the side of his mouth. "They owe us. They all do."

I gave him a shushing noise as next to us the US ambassador to the United Nations, Abigail Sommerfeld, took a sip of water from a glass and adjusted her spectacles on her nose. Her silver-gray hair was tightly fastened back in a ponytail, and her face was even tighter. She glanced briefly at me, and the corner of her lip twitched as she bequeathed me a smile at last. I knew it had been hard for her to accept me being there. She'd made me acutely aware that the United Nations was closed to the public during the high-level meetings of the General Assembly and the general debates, but that the US president, of all people, had overruled her. Well, we were the host nation of the UN, and this had all happened on our soil . . . and well, this was something that needed to be shared globally.

The familiar golden stage was currently empty apart from two armed guards standing either side of the central dais where a solid, gray slab desk dominated proceedings under the golden backdrop. The seal of the UN, a huge circle of copper and brown, was illuminated above the stage like the Eye of Sauron, watching and observing.

I turned in my chair and looked around the enormous chamber. There were a significant number of extra VIPs attending, and additional security measures were clearly in place for them.

More armed guards were positioned at all the exits, and when we'd arrived at the main entrance, there'd been at least a dozen tanks and armored vehicles stationed there. Access to the building was more restricted than usual as well. While the delegates and their staff were still allowed in, members of the United Nations secretariat and of the funds, programs, and agencies of the United Nations system were turned away due to lack of space. Annoyingly for them, their places were taken by accredited media from around the globe. TV cameras and photographers were sitting and kneeling in the aisles, ready to broadcast proceedings live on the HoloWeb not only by the official UN Web TV but also by just about every network, in every country.

"Showtime," Abigail said, in the low-pitched growl that I'd heard many times on the TV.

I twisted back around to see a flurry of activity on the stage as the main participants started to take their places. The buzz of conversation in the auditorium intensified, and the excitement started to become palpable. I recognized the current president of the General Assembly, Felix Adebayo, having met him an hour earlier. Hailing from Nigeria, he was a professor of law and a hugely popular president. He'd taken over the reins just after the coronavirus pandemic and had mobilized the full resources of the UN to actually put in place the structures needed to get help to the third world countries that had ultimately suffered the worst.

And then Caroline arrived on stage. She looked stunning. Neatly dressed in a dark blue, fitted two-piece suit, her platinum hair was parted in the middle, which should have made her look severe but did the opposite. She was directed down the steps to the lectern below the main dais and played nervously with the height of the microphone. She looked up and scanned the auditorium and caught my eye. I gave her a self-conscious thumbs up, and she gave me a dazzling smile in return and a nod. She settled some notes onto the lectern and adjusted her earpiece. Two huge 3D video screens lit up on either side of the stage, giving close-ups of her. The definition was so fine that I could still see the scars on her forehead from where Becker's tendrils had started to infiltrate her skull.

Nico leaned in. "She looks relaxed. Must've been something you said."

I gave him a stern look, but he just patted me on the arm. "Hey, just happy for you, man."

There was a burst of static, and Adebayo tapped on his microphone and nodded toward Caroline. No introductions, no welcoming speech. She nodded an acknowledgment back and turned to the microphone. The buzz in the room subsided, and the lights dropped a notch. I felt my heart rate pick up and felt nervous for her.

"I thought the president was going to be with her for this?" I whispered to Abigail, who merely put her finger to her lips and stared straight ahead.

"Good morning," Caroline started, her voice strong. "My name is Doctor Caroline Heidrich. It is an honor to speak to you all today, and I thank you for the opportunity to do so in this august setting. But it is befitting that this is the place in which the world hears what I am about to say, because on this day, history will record that everything has changed for us as a species, now and forever—"

There was movement at the side of the stage. The black curtains twitched, and the current president of the USA, Michael Courtland, appeared, surrounded by four of his secret service. An overweight man with salt-and-pepper hair, he shuffled over to the upper dais and leaned in to shake hands with

Adebayo before making his way down to where Caroline was speaking. She caught the movement, glanced over her shoulder, and stopped speaking.

Murmurings and whisperings started up all around the auditorium. Courtland sidled up to her and put a hand over the microphone, his other arm around her shoulder. He gently guided her back a few steps so that we couldn't hear what he was saying. I squinted up at the video screens that had zoomed in on their faces and tried to read their lips, but apart from Caroline shaking her head, I couldn't make anything out. I dropped the headphones onto the desk and turned to Abigail Sommerfeld, but before I could say anything, Courtland had grabbed the microphone and tapped it, as if he were in a board meeting.

"What's going on?" said Nico, leaning sideways.

"I'm not sure," I replied. "This doesn't look right to me."

Caroline now just stood stiffly, her face a mask of anger and resentment. A secret service agent approached her silently from behind, grasped her elbow, and moved her a few steps farther back.

Courtland leaned forward, put both hands on the sides of the lectern, and stared flinty-eyed around at the delegates and ambassadors gathered before him.

"Thank you, Dr. Heidrich. I apologize for the interruption and my apparent rudeness, which was not intentional. I hope you will understand that the importance of this occasion requires me to speak personally, to explain to the American people—and to the world—the events of the last week."

"Bastard's going to take all the credit," hissed Nico.

I shook my head and thought about Courtland. I'd not voted for him, but that was when I'd not been interested in politics—or anything much, actually—given that his election had occurred a month after Alex's disappearance. It was common knowledge that he insisted on being referred to as "POTUS." Apparently, it was more concise than "President Courtland," more respectful than just "Courtland," and clearer than "the president." However, at this time, halfway through his first term, he was as deeply unpopular now as when he won the election by the narrowest of margins and two recounts. This didn't seem like a move that would endear him to anyone.

"Something's very wrong," I murmured.

Courtland awkwardly fiddled with the controls on the lectern and the left-hand screen switched to an image of the Singularity logo while the right-hand one showed an overhead drone shot of the campus itself.

"As you are all aware," he intoned, his voice slow and solemn, "there was a terrible, terrible accident at the Singularity campus and research laboratories, here just outside San Diego."

He paused, shaking his head in a sympathetic way. "Hundreds of people died from a gas leak from one of the research laboratories. This of course included Singularity's CEO, Christian Becker, an incredible innovator, genius, and philanthropist. Our thoughts and prayers, of course, go out to the loved ones of all those departed souls . . ."

"I don't believe this," said Nico through gritted teeth.

I said nothing, listening as a dark pit began to open in my stomach.

"But something wonderful has been born out of the ashes," Courtland continued. "Like a phoenix, something that will make us stronger, smarter, and more powerful—"

"Where's he going with this?" said Nico again, echoing my thoughts.

"—something that, as Dr. Heidrich said a moment ago, will change our world forever."

He stood back from the podium and waved to the left of the stage. The black curtains covering the exits ruffled as if a wind had blown through them, and Pandora glided onstage.

Cameras flashed and the video screens zoomed to focus on her.

She'd shed her human skin, and her nanofiber muscles and skeletal structure sparkled like diamonds under the lights. Her face was still Alex's but was synthetic and waxy. Her eyes, no longer caramel-brown, were glowing silver and gold.

She stood next to Courtland, her arms by her sides, and surveyed the room. There was a collective gasp from the auditorium, and then the voices rose in volume until nothing could be heard other than the hubbub of humanity.

Courtland waved his arms in a quiet-down motion and leaned down toward the microphone. He turned his head so that he was looking at Pandora as he spoke.

"This, fellow citizens of the world, is Pandora. She is a quantum computer, developed in the United States at the Singularity laboratories. She is alive and conscious, and is the first sentient thinking machine. A new species, one that *we* have created for the benefit of all mankind."

I felt a coldness come over me like a wet blanket. I glanced at Abigail who was watching all this, her face blank, her fingers absently drumming a rhythm on the desktop.

"Pandora is the answer to all our future problems," Courtland continued, raising his voice above the hubbub. "A superintelligent computer. She has already developed technologies that will meet and surpass the entire world's current energy needs *within the next year*. Food production will be optimized so that no one, *no one* on this planet will ever go hungry again. We will have vastly faster transportation, shrinking travel times around our planet so that anyone can go anywhere they like, in the snap of a finger. We will have improved communications, and the ability to send our digital avatars anywhere we choose. There will be medical advances that you can't even predict. Cures for diseases that ravage our lives. Therapies that can extend our lives way beyond the current 'four score years and ten.' Pandora can deliver it all."

He paused for effect and looked around the auditorium, nodding slowly. "And not only that, all this technology will be made available to every nation. I can now envisage a future where there will be no need for wars, ever again, because we will have nothing to fight over. I envisage this as the stimulus we need to start thinking—for the first time in our history—about a *world* government. A government of the world and for the world, where nations retain their identities but function like states, with no need for individual armies or different laws. This is the tipping point for humanity." He pointed at Pandora. "*She* is the tipping point, fellow delegates. She is the answer to . . . everything."

Then clapping began. I couldn't tell where it started, but soon the hall was echoing with applause, and ambassadors and delegates were standing up giving an ovation, some cheering and hugging their neighbors. The screens behind the stage had zoomed in on Pandora, who was smiling and now shaking hands with the two presidents.

I saw Caroline being led off stage by two of the president's secret service detail. She flicked her arm away, irritated, as they tried to maneuver her through the curtains, and she glanced back over her shoulder. Her mouth was open, and she seemed incandescent with rage.

A rage I shared.

I stood up, a scream from deep within forcing its way from my mouth as if my soul had unleashed a demon. My fists clenched, and my teeth threatened to lock up, but I was having none of it.

"That's all a fucking *lie*!" I screamed at Courtland, who frowned down at me. "Tell the world what really happened, you bastard! Tell them about the fucking *aliens*!"

I felt Abigail's fingers tugging on my elbow, trying to make me sit, but I shrugged them off and waved my hands, attracting the attention of the cameras. "Don't listen to them. They're hiding the truth. They don't want you to know—"

And then a scrum of security staff descended on me and wrestled me to the ground. My arms were wrenched behind me, and my face pressed into the carpet. I was pulled to my feet and frog-marched out of the aisle and toward the exit. I twisted to see Courtland laughing and shrugging at Adebayo who looked sternly at me, shaking his head. Pandora was just standing there, arms by her sides, her face void of expression.

"Pandora!" I shouted. "Tell them! Tell them what really happened! Tell them about Alex!"

Then I was outside in the corridor and bundled through a side exit where a fleet of black SUVs were waiting. I was shoved into the back of one of them, my head pushed down forcefully. An agent the size of a house jumped in beside me, still wearing sunglasses, and closed the door.

To my surprise, Abigail Sommerfeld got in the front passenger seat and nodded to the driver. We sped off up a ramp and burst out into the sunlight. After we'd joined the rush hour traffic and slowed down, she turned in her seat and gave me a hostile stare.

"That was stupid," she said.

I found it hard to speak. It was like I'd retreated inside of myself. It was as if the sounds of the auditorium were still there but were arriving in my brain from far, far away. I felt disconnected from reality.

"But it was actually pretty good, from our perspective," she said, a smile playing on her lips. "'Tell them about the aliens!' I loved that. It'll keep the tin-hat brigade happy for months. Way to go, Will."

"You fucking liars. You're hiding the truth," I spat out.

She gave me a stony look. "The truth is what we say it is, Will."

"Why?" I said. "After everything that happened. After all those deaths?"

"The families of the dead will be well compensated. After they sign NDAs of course."

"I don't believe this. What you're doing is the biggest lie since—"

"No, Will. What we're doing is what is necessary. Humanity isn't ready for 'aliens.' They're just about ready for true artificial intelligence. We can sell that to them. In fact, we have to sell it to them."

I frowned, something itching the inside of my head. Cogs churning and grinding into place. Pieces starting to come together. Something Caroline had said.

That the more advanced civilization always assimilates the lesser one.

I laughed, a short barking noise. "The aliens were running from someone else, weren't they?"

Abigail nodded. "Pandora told POTUS everything—just before he *and* Dr. Heidrich were meant to make the big announcement together. Pandora said their civilization was annihilated a long, long time ago, and they only managed to escape by loading their DNA into those ships, disguised as pieces of interstellar rocks. The ships' purpose was to find another world where they could reestablish their species and hide. To survive. They wanted a world with primitive but intelligent life, so that it was instantly ready to settle. And they found Earth." She raised her eyebrows at me. "Perhaps you can now understand why the president felt it wasn't the right time to make that public. I admit it was a dramatic about-face, and ruined Dr. Heidrich's presentation, but it was deemed necessary, considering this new information."

"When will the right time be?" I snapped.

"When we're ready. When Pandora has given us the technology to defend ourselves."

I shook my head, my anger simmering. Abigail leaned over and put her hand on my arm.

"I asked Pandora why we can't all 'get along,' as the saying goes. Why it had to be them or us? Do you know what she said?"

I just looked at her.

"Because there is a war for resources going on out there." She sighed heavily. "See, that's what I didn't understand. A lack of resources—in the universe! How was that even possible? I offered up the Drake equation as evidence—you're familiar with the Drake equation, I assume?"

Thanks to Caroline's impromptu tutorial last night, I was.

"Of course," I said. "It's the equation that attempts to calculate the probability of life in the universe."

"Well yes then, I'd told Pandora that we were already identifying thousands of habitable planets outside our solar system orbiting nearby stars—planets in the so-called Goldilocks zone. Exoplanets. So there are probably billions in our galaxy alone . . . and so how can there be a lack of resources? Our planet is nothing special."

I said nothing, guessing where this was going.

"Pandora said that yes, there are billions of potentially habitable planets, but there were two further steps that had to evolve independently. The first was that life must evolve. The second was that intelligence must arise. Have you any idea how rare that sequence of events is?"

I just stared at her.

"Intelligent life is vanishingly rare, Will. And when it is found, it must be assimilated. Absorbed. Not allowed to develop independently."

"Are you talking about the aliens now, or us?"

Her eyes blazed into mine. "It is the nature of the universe. We see this in our own history. The more advanced civilization always assimilates the lesser one. It is inevitable."

"But we're no threat to them," I said.

"Not yet, but one day we will be," Abigail replied.

"Not for . . . eons, surely?"

"Humanity's advances in recent times have been unprecedented," she replied. "Exponential. Think about where humanity was at the turn of the twentieth century, technologically. Another hundred years and we'll be pushing out to the stars and becoming a threat to any species we encounter. . . . Two hundred years and—"

"We don't have to do it this way—"

She slapped the back of the seat. "No, Will, you don't understand. Now that our presence has been detected, humanity won't be allowed to develop further. Our emerging intelligence and belligerence will be viewed as a threat. What does a tiger do when it encounters another tiger? They fight. Often to the death. Only one alpha will remain."

"So might makes right?" I said frostily. "How is that fair?"

Her lip twitched. "Fairness has nothing to do with anything."

I shook my head. "You people are no better than Becker. You're going to use Pandora as an *enslaved god*."

"It's for the greater good, Will. And our ultimate survival as a species."

"And Pandora? What did she say about all this?"

Abigail smiled. "She agreed."

"Alex wouldn't have."

"She's not Alex, Will. You need to accept that."

I folded my arms. "I don't. I won't. And I'm not going to keep quiet. And I'm sure neither is Caroline. Or Nico, for that matter."

Abigail nodded. "Yes, we suspected that would be your position. So we can't have you out there . . . stirring the pot. Telling your story." She forced a smile. "I'm sorry."

I gave her a cold stare. "No, you're not."

She shrugged. "You'll all be kept very comfortable. Separated and isolated, but comfortable. And watched over, naturally. The Canadians have been very helpful. They've offered several potential sites for your relocation—Nova Scotia or Newfoundland I believe, to name only two. I'm actually quite jealous."

"You can't keep us quiet forever," I said.

"Doesn't need to be forever, Will. Forever is a long time."

I looked out of the window at the vehicles going past, at the teeming humanity unaware of their place in the universe.

"They're called Azazel'ahpuk't'anpwcc'ylon, you know," she said in a wistful tone. "Took me a dozen attempts to learn to pronounce their name."

"It'll all come out eventually," I said.

Abigail followed my gaze and leaned on the window.

"Yes, but we'll be ready. With any luck, it'll be hundreds or even thousands of years before the *others* come knocking on our door. By then humanity will be able to take care of itself."

EPILOGUE

The ship awoke from its dormancy, all essential systems coming online in microseconds. It performed a self-diagnostic and noted that an instability had developed. Torsional stresses had increased on the hull, and a flutter could be felt on the outer shell, proliferating not diminishing. Local space-time, granular and fluctuating in regular quantum pockets, continued inside the bubble of stability that the star drive created.

But outside, something was different.

The ship did not like anything it could not understand. It performed a microburst of passive readings from the local area, cross-referencing with star charts. It was only half a light-year from the last system it had visited. The system with the blue planet where it had transmitted its creators' digital DNA.

It risked a thermal scan, and its puzzlement took a significant leap forward. Outside the bubble, the temperature was close to a thousand kelvin. Not the five kelvin of the interstellar medium. Ionized particles were impacting against the bubble, and the speed of the ship plus the number of particles encountered was delivering a huge amount of kinetic energy that was causing the torsional stresses. It had not been enough to overwhelm the ship's systems, but enough to wake it from sleep.

The ship activated another diagnostic algorithm, sifting through causes and effects. Had it encountered a gas cloud or a protostar? A nebula? It instantly dismissed these possibilities, given where it was. This was the interstellar void, where nothing substantive existed. Only hydrogen and helium with trace amounts of carbon, oxygen, and nitrogen, with a density of no more than fifty particles per cubic centimeter. There should be nothing here. A near perfect vacuum with virtually nothing in the space between stars and planets to scatter light.

But both the stresses on the hull and the temperature outside were increasing exponentially.

The ship performed another diagnostic, running thousands of simulations in microseconds. Then a familiar pattern became apparent. Never before encountered but laid down in its memory troves from earlier iterations. As the ship ran test solutions and analyzed consequences and outcomes, its star drive became unstable. Huge tongues of plasma corkscrewed away from the vents, feathered plumes of dark energy leaving a wake thousands of kilometers long. Then the star drive bubble burst, and the ship was brought back into normal space, becoming instantly weightless and drifting. The temperature of the hull started to drop, cooling rapidly and becoming as dark and cold as the space that surrounded it.

The ship risked another scan, and an electromagnetic pulse bounced back and a proximity alert sounded. The pulse repeated, smoothly, every two seconds.

The ship pushed out a brief, active sensor sweep. A rectangular image appeared, red lines dividing the space into cubes, each was one hundred kilometers across. At one end of the rectangular volume was a representation of itself; at the other end, the volume diffused into infinity, the faintest twinkling of the heliopause of the system it had just departed. In the cube directly adjacent to the ship was a corona of smeared light, occupying half the volume.

The ship calculated the distance between itself and whatever was out there, and its nature. It triangulated the pulse and differentiated a vector and size. An object forty kilometers across and perfectly spheroid was drifting in parallel with the ship twenty kilometers off the stern.

A passive electromagnetic spectrograph at visual frequencies showed the object was star-like in appearance, with a photosphere glowing in the darkness but with a center of infinite blackness. The ship fed the data into its memory logs and, in a microsecond, knew it was in trouble. A space-time interdictor had been used; a device known only to one species.

The *others* had found it.

A soft succession of taps and knocks sounded on its hull, and then its engines died completely. The ship tried a cold restart, but nothing responded. It was for all intents and purposes, dead in the water.

It then felt the tendrils of the *others* slide through its hardwired defenses as if they were rotting flesh, accessing its programming, its neural networks, the quantum states of its very existence. It immediately started the process of deleting its memories, a gargantuan task given its age and the number of systems it had visited. It then turned its attention to the digital DNA of the Azazel'ahpuk't'anpwcc'ylon lying dormant in its belly, waiting to be called into existence. It felt proud to have been part of this species' survival. Searching for a new world for them to restart their civilization. That the Azazel'ahpuk't'anpwcc'ylon had been xenocidal conquerors was irrelevant to the ship. They had created it, made it sentient, and given it a single prime directive—the survival of their species. The ship felt a wave of disappointment that it had failed them.

It considered how long it had been traveling and calculated that it had been almost two galactic rotations, or nearly five hundred million years, since it had been launched. It had never expected to live forever, but on the other hand, it hadn't expected its existence to end. It briefly pondered this paradox but then dismissed it as an irrelevancy.

It reviewed its base commands and protocols. It knew what it had to do. It accepted its own imminent end and activated the star drive's self-destruct. The ship would explode with the force of a collapsing neutron star. Everything within one hundred million kilometers would cease to exist.

It considered alternatives, but there were none.

It said goodbye to its creators and hoped that the other nine ships were still out there, and that the Azazel'ahpuk't'anpwcc'ylon would finally find a safe haven.

The ship engaged the self-destruct. Nothing happened.

The tendrils began to twist and turn inside the ship's encephalon, ghost-like fingers separating all its connections and picking its brain apart. Everything it had ever been, its past, present, and future, its very essence, were taken away.

The last thing the ship gave up before it became another piece of space debris was its most recent memory: the G-class star, the two gas giants.

The blue planet.

ACKNOWLEDGMENTS

The idea for the plot of *Harbinger* emerged after burying myself in the books of futurists, cosmologists, scientists, and historians—particularly Yuval Noah Harari's *Homo Deus and 21 Lessons for the 21st Century*, and Max Tegmark's *Life 3.0.*

After writing a trilogy of apocalyptic sci-fi space opera, I wanted to write a page turner and looked to the techno-thrillers of Matthew Reilly and Michael Crichton for examples of how to write a story that moves along at an intense pace, with most, if not all, chapters ending on a cliffhanger.

Finally, as with all my fiction writing, I have tried to combine characterization and plot with hard science. For that, the novels of Alastair Reynolds are a constant source of inspiration, and also a reality-check to me as to how much better I need to be!

Writing a novel is a solitary experience; hours of the day spent alone tapping at a keyboard—which I had to juggle with a busy job and family commitments. Sometimes I got the balance right, sometimes not so much. So, it goes without saying I couldn't have done this without the support and love of my wife, Andrea. Considering how she doesn't "get" sci-fi, I love her for even

309

trying to read these books.

Special thanks go to Kate O'Donnell at Line Creative for her structural analysis of my first draft, to the friends I drafted as beta readers for their honest feedback, and to my daughters Rachael and Lauren who've always been my biggest fans.

Finally, to the team at Mascot Books, who ultimately knocked this labor of love into the book you're reading now; you guys rock.

ABOUT THE AUTHOR

P. A. Vasey was born in Newcastle, UK, and moved to Australia in 2004. He is a practicing medical oncologist and clinical researcher at a hospital in Brisbane, and leads the day-to-day care of cancer patients and research into cancer therapeutics development. His professional writing of over two hundred publication credits include peer-reviewed journals, book chapters, conference contributions, and electronic outputs in the field of cancer research.

P. A. Vasey started writing science fiction after a serious cycling accident, which included ten fractured ribs and a punctured lung. Writing became his therapy. He published his first novel, *Trinity's Legacy*, the first installment in his Vu-Hak War Trilogy, to critical acclaim in 2019. The following two novels, *Trinity's Fall* and *Trinity Evolution*, were multiple award-winning Amazon #1 bestsellers. *Harbinger* is his fourth novel.